10667655

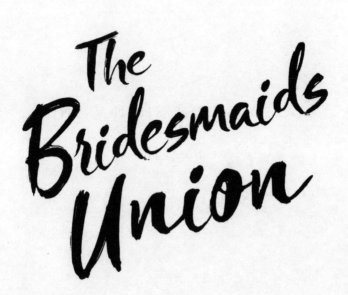

ALSO BY JONATHAN VATNER

*Carnegie Hill*

# The Bridesmaids Union

A Novel

## Jonathan Vatner

ST. MARTIN'S PRESS
NEW YORK

First published in the United States by St. Martin's Press, an imprint of St. Martin's Publishing Group

THE BRIDESMAIDS UNION. Copyright © 2022 by Jonathan Vatner. All rights reserved. Printed in the United States of America. For information, address St. Martin's Publishing Group, 120 Broadway, New York, NY 10271.

This book has been designed using resources from Freepik.com, GIPHY.com, KindPNG.com, OpenMoji.org, and PNGWing.com.

www.stmartins.com

Designed by Devan Norman

Library of Congress Cataloging-in-Publication Data

Names: Vatner, Jonathan, author.
Title: The bridesmaids union: a novel / Jonathan Vatner.
Description: First edition. | New York: St. Martin's Press, 2022.
Identifiers: LCCN 2022003290 | ISBN 9781250762399 (hardcover) |
    ISBN 9781250762405 (ebook)
Classification: LCC PS3622.A8825 B75 2022 | DDC 813/.6—dc23
LC record available at https://lccn.loc.gov/2022003290

Our books may be purchased in bulk for promotional, educational, or business use. Please contact your local bookseller or the Macmillan Corporate and Premium Sales Department at 1-800-221-7945, extension 5442, or by email at MacmillanSpecialMarkets@macmillan.com.

First Edition: 2022

10  9  8  7  6  5  4  3  2  1

For Morty

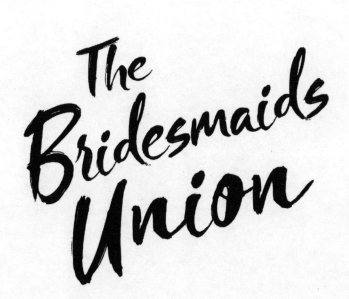

The Bridesmaids Union

# Chapter One

*I*ris arrived at Amber and JonJon's wedding venue, a genteel estate on the outskirts of Miami, an hour before her hair and makeup slot. She carried her seafoam bridesmaid dress and matching sandals, a box of tealights, and a fat envelope of programs, which she had individually tea-stained and bound with twine.

In the rose garden, a perfumed breeze enhanced every view like a gauzy Instagram filter. Peach climbing roses twisted around the wrought iron wedding arch, presiding over twin flanks of gleaming white folding chairs. The terraced lawn stepped gracefully toward the bay, spangled in the afternoon sun. Such breathtaking beauty pricked Iris in a tender place, as it reminded her of her own wedding, scrapped six years earlier. She tried not to think about Forrest on Amber's special day. Weddings were a kind of reunion for married couples, a pep rally for the rite and covenant of marriage, but they demanded a reckoning of single people, and it was impossible not to think back with regret.

In the courtyard, girded with slender fluted columns, event staff arranged banquet rounds in staggered rows. Iris stepped into the cloister and deposited the tealights next to the tablecloths wrapped in butcher paper and the trays of dishes and glassware stacked in modernist towers. She glanced around. Where were the centerpieces?

The event planner rushed toward her with panic in her eyes. "Iris, right? Maid of honor?"

Iris nodded.

"We have a problem. The florist went out of business—I just found out. We don't have centerpieces."

Iris stared at her in disbelief. The wedding started in three hours. "You must know another florist—maybe they can give us some premade arrangements?"

The event planner shook her head. "I called all my contacts—no one has that many flowers on hand."

A better event planner would have confirmed with all the vendors the week of the wedding, but this woman had come free with the venue. Anyway, there wasn't time for assigning blame. There wasn't time for a stray thought. Iris took a deep breath. She could handle this. "Have you told Amber?"

"I didn't want to disturb her unless it was absolutely necessary."

Iris looked around, thinking of centerpieces from past weddings. Not all of them had been floral. She'd seen candles floating in water and vases filled with lemons, stacks of books and explosions of ostrich feathers. None of those seemed right. Her gaze settled on the ocean, and she had an idea.

She texted the other bridesmaids and tore off three black garbage bags from a roll. Amber and Iris's mutual friend Sophia, who was getting married in September, appeared a minute later, and they picked their way down the rocky path to the beach. Into one bag they placed all the pretty stones they could find; into the second, unbroken shells. They filled the third with as much sand as they could carry. In the damp heat, the beached seaweed stank of dead fish. Iris was sodden with perspiration, and her hair reached maximum frizz.

Iris, Sophia, and the event planner used serving spoons to scoop sand onto the middle of the tables, then planted stones, shells, and tealights into the piles. Iris had purchased the candles to edge the courtyard as night fell, but this was more important.

The sand drifts could pass as centerpieces, and they didn't smell, but they looked more haphazard than Iris had anticipated. At the craft store the day before, she had seen dried starfish in neon hues; without a second thought, she and Sophia jumped into their rental car and cleaned out the shelves in a *Supermarket Sweep* frenzy. In the giddy dash toward the register, Iris tossed in sheets of silver netting with a maritime vibe and another box of tealights for the courtyard walkways.

The pop of color and texture elevated the sand into gorgeous, artistic centerpieces.

"This is boss," Sophia said. "Amber doesn't know how lucky she is to have you."

"She would have done the same thing for me," Iris said, flooded with relief and excitement. Amber was going to love them.

⌒

Once Iris was dressed, braided, and painted, she slipped into the bridal suite, where Amber perched on the edge of a rococo armchair, answering text messages as the makeup artist dabbed at her face. Her hair was done up like a chandelier, and her dress, a sheath of white silk lace, pooled at her feet. Four years living in Miami had darkened her skin and lightened her hair, and she looked radiant.

"Hey friend," Iris said, "how's your last hour of singlehood treating you?"

"My mom is giving me hell about the heat," Amber said without looking up. "She literally said that if my grams dies of heatstroke, the blood will be on my hands. As if I could control the *temperature*. And I'm starving. Everyone tells you not to skip breakfast, but I was afraid the food baby would show in the dress."

Iris found a tray of pretzel sticks in her purse—motherhood had transformed her into a mobile snack bar. To keep crumbs off the wedding dress, she snapped the sticks in half before placing them in Amber's mouth as if giving communion.

"I need to tell you something," Iris said. "Everything is fine, but there's been a change of plans with the centerpieces."

"Could you blend that a bit more?" Amber asked the makeup artist. "It's looking a little clowny."

"The florist no-showed," Iris continued, "so Sophia and I improvised new centerpieces with a beachy theme. I think you'll like them—I just didn't want you to be surprised."

"Shit!" Amber said, staring at her phone. "My dad thinks he's too good for the GPS, and now he's halfway to Palm Fucking Beach."

Iris was taken aback. This was not the Amber she knew. Real Amber would have kept calm while defusing every crisis with breezy dispatch. Real Amber would have eaten breakfast.

"Let me talk to him," Iris said, reaching for Amber's phone. "So it's OK about the centerpieces? Sand, not flowers?"

"Sure, whatever you think is best." Amber stared into the mirror. "Still way too pink. It looks like a rash."

Iris needed to let this go. Amber clearly was too overwhelmed to think about centerpieces. Maybe, when she saw them, she would realize what a huge feat Iris and Sophia had pulled off.

~⊙

On the flight home the next afternoon, Iris gazed out the window at the nubby carpet of clouds and the metallic sky. The wedding had been flaw-less, but—was it petty to dwell on this?—Amber hadn't acknowledged the replacement centerpieces. Those sandy mounds were pure inspiration, and it stung that Iris's whirlwind save had been ignored. Of course the wedding wasn't about her. She just couldn't help feeling erased.

At the farewell brunch that morning, she had joked that she should start a career as a centerpiece designer. Amber laughed politely and turned away.

Iris and Amber had been littermates, growing up on the same block in Tenafly, New Jersey. Amber had always been gracious and generous, considerate and composed. In high school, she went out of her way to ensure that no one felt left out, and she sent a thank-you note to Iris's parents every time they had her over for dinner. But as her wedding ap-proached, she became self-absorbed and demanding—and treated her bridesmaids like hired help. Iris wouldn't have believed it possible for a person to change so radically if she hadn't witnessed it more times than she could count. Weddings were a perfect storm of anxiety and scrutiny, and no bride was immune. Nor were the grooms, as Forrest had proven.

Iris turned to Sophia, watching a *Dance Moms* marathon on the screen in the seat back. "Random question, but did Amber say anything to you about our centerpieces?"

Sophia plucked out one earbud. "No. She didn't thank you?"

Iris shook her head.

"You must be pissed. That wedding would have sucked without you."

"I'm disappointed," Iris said. She didn't get angry the way most people did, popping off at the slightest insult. There was too much anger in the world and not enough understanding. "I mean, I could see she was stressed."

"She did yell at me for changing out of those heinous sandals when a strap broke."

The sandals had been Amber's gift to her bridesmaids. Iris wouldn't have called them heinous, though they were too costumey to wear again. As a gift, they had been a little misguided, a little perfunctory, a little dismissive of the labor her bridesmaids had put into the wedding. "Wow, yeah, they didn't seem very sturdy."

"Now I can't sell them," Sophia said.

"You can sell mine."

"That's really sweet of you." Sophia sounded so genuine that Iris snorted her water and started hacking.

But her joy was tinged with sadness. She'd formed close friendships when she was younger, but being a single parent made it impossible to sustain them. The other pre-K moms were all smiles at drop-off and pickup, but they never stuck around to chat, and her coworkers were a definite no. Her life was her terrible job, her wonderful son, and her difficult parents. She hadn't had a real conversation with either of her sisters in months.

⁓⊙

Spike, Iris's father, picked her up at Newark airport in his orange Corvette with her son in tow. As soon as she unlatched Mason from his car seat, he leaped into her arms and soaked up her kisses. In those perfect few seconds when they reunited, she felt the pain of their separation most sharply.

"Mason," Spike said in a singsong, "how much did you miss your mom?"

Mason wiggled out from Iris's embrace, stretched his arms wide, and shouted, "I missed you this much!"

"That's my man," Spike said, ruffling Mason's hair. It was sweet that they'd rehearsed a welcome.

"Well, I missed you *this* much," Iris said to Mason, extending her arms before wrapping them around him.

As she strapped Mason back into the car seat, she noticed a tablet next to it. "What's this?" she asked.

Mason replied, "Grandpa gave me a iPad!"

Spike was grinning. "Don't worry, I only downloaded games you already vetted."

"Wow, what a generous gift!" she exclaimed, modeling enthusiasm for her son. "Did you say thank you so, so much?" Mason would love it, and it would make travels easier, but she wished her father would have run it by her first. It felt like a power play for her son's loyalty.

"Thank you, Grandpa Spike!" Mason screeched.

"Inside Voice," Iris said.

"You're most welcome, Master Mason," Spike replied. "And you can use any voice you like with me. Real men shouldn't be afraid to speak up."

"Rawrll!" Mason shouted.

"That's the spirit!"

Iris tried to remain grateful that her father didn't mind shouting and not become frustrated that he was undermining her rules.

They headed north from the airport. "Your mother made lasagna," Spike said.

From experience, she heard his statement as an invitation. She wanted to spend more time with her parents, to repair the breach that the presidential election had caused—just not when she'd been craving a quiet night with Mason. She'd saved him a fat slice of wedding cake, their tradition when she went to weddings without him. "I hate to miss dinner, but I'm exhausted, and we have to get up early tomorrow."

"Mom made a vegetarian version just for you," Spike said, not looking at her. She bristled at the guilt trip coming on.

"Can we do it next weekend?"

"I didn't have to pick you up at the airport," Spike said. "I didn't have to buy Mason the iPad, either. A family isn't a buffet. You can't pick and choose the pieces that are convenient for you."

"OK, fine," she said, massaging her temples. Inside every request lurked a demand. Inside every suggestion, a threat. She was practically thirty, and whenever she asked for the slightest autonomy, her parents treated her like an ingrate. Which was doubly painful, because she craved closeness with them in a way that her friends seemed to have outgrown. "Is Jasmine home?" Iris couldn't decide whether she wanted the answer to be yes.

"She's out with her boyfriend tonight," Spike said.

"Boyfriend?" Surely their mother would have mentioned this development. Once the girls had graduated from college, Connie Hagarty saw her primary role as a cheerleader for marriage.

"Nobody tells me anything," Spike said, briefly taking his hands off the wheel to hold them up in surrender. "But apparently, Jazzy really likes this one. It doesn't hurt that he's got a buck or two." This was a variation of his favorite maxim, "It's just as easy to fall in love with a rich man as a poor one." He'd say it as a joke, and yet it wasn't one, not exactly.

"It's been a while since we've spoken," Iris admitted.

"You should call her. She's really taken life by the reins."

Iris looked out the window. She couldn't imagine calling her sister.

"You need to forgive her," Spike said with a tender glance at Iris. "'For if you forgive others their trespasses, your heavenly Father will also forgive you.'"

"Maybe you should preach to her," she said. "She hasn't called me, either."

"Your friends will come and go, but you'll always be sisters. Don't spurn that gift."

⤔

After a long but peaceable dinner at home, Spike dropped Iris and Mason off at her apartment in Yonkers, past Mason's bedtime. She dragged her luggage inside, then went to fetch Meatball, her escape artist of a cat, who had darted into the hallway. Pickles, Meatball's brother by another mother, sniffed the luggage. Her retired neighbor Marilyn had left a note on the dining table. *We mist u soooo much, Mommy!* she had written. *Antee Maralinn sez we was good kitteez.* She'd signed it with paw prints. Iris chuckled at Marilyn's LOLcat spelling.

She changed Mason into pajamas and tucked him into bed—it was too late to worry about brushing. His baby teeth were going to fall out anyway.

"Mommy?" Mason asked, his eyelids drooping. "Is it cake time?"

"It's too late for cake tonight, but tell you what. You can have a little with breakfast. Deal?" It was a small disappointment, forgoing this tradition, but after devoting her entire weekend to others, it made her want to cry.

"Deal," he said, already cradled by a dream.

Iris finished unpacking, poured a glass of box wine, and scrolled through Facebook on her phone. Amber had shared a photo of her and JonJon boarding the cruise ship for their honeymoon, their heads tilted together in connubial bliss. Iris didn't understand how everyone but her had found love. What was she doing wrong? She no longer blamed herself for Forrest's disappearance, but no one else had come along to take his place—and help raise his son. She needed to recommit to dating. Plenty of single moms found time for romance.

Sophia had already sent an email with the subject line "FINAL STRETCH!" It was a list of bridesmaid assignments for her September wedding. Would Iris mind "heading up the gift sitch?"—in other words, soliciting giveaways from local businesses, ordering custom favors, and stuffing all two hundred bags. In Iris's opinion, gift bags should be optional. No one went to a wedding for the swag. She had already volunteered to embellish the masquerade masks for the photo booth, and she wasn't even maid of honor; Sophia's sister was.

Exhaustion pulled Iris deeper into the sofa. She'd been in at least one wedding per year since she was twenty-four, and who knew who might walk down the aisle after Sophia? The twenty thousand dollars she'd spent on bridesmaiding had piled up so much credit card debt, she couldn't bear to think about it. As much as she loved weddings—the comforting formality, the beauty, the joy of the betrothed—being a bridesmaid was sucking her dry. Sure, she didn't have to accept every invitation, but it never seemed OK to turn them down.

She hit Reply and wrote, **Absolutely! So excited for your big day.**

She needed to vent. It didn't feel right to gossip about Amber and Sophia to any of their mutual friends, and she couldn't imagine breaking her silence with Jasmine to complain. And their older sister Rose . . . ! That was funny to consider.

As she stared at her phone, a thought occurred to her. An online community of bridesmaids might understand the frustration of saving your best friend's wedding without her acknowledging your work, of receiving gaudy sandals as a bridesmaid present, or of being asked to rustle up needless parting gifts. Iris googled "bridesmaid horror stories" and found an article recapping the most egregious situations from a subgroup on Reddit. According to one bridesmaid, the bride had demanded she lose ten pounds before the wedding. Another had handwritten all the table cards at the bride's request, only to discover at the wedding that the perfectionist bride had hired a professional to redo them all. A third caught the groom kissing the bride's mother. Reading these posts, Iris felt understood. She refilled her wineglass and navigated to the original Reddit page, created an anonymous account, and began to write.

> OK, so my best friend got married this weekend, and I was MOH. The florist in charge of the centerpieces no-showed, so my co-bridesmaid and I improvised new centerpieces in literally an hour—and that included ransacking a Michaels! Also, not to brag or anything (well, maybe to brag), I performed all of the following bridesmaidly duties: (a) fed the bride by hand to keep her from passing out, (b) got the caterer to set out snacks before the ceremony to proactively absorb alcohol and curb drunkenness, (c) distracted the bride's busybody in-laws before she walked down the aisle, (d) singlehandedly bustled the wedding dress, which involved lining up eighteen loops with buttons at the waist, and (e) executed a game of Twister to keep the dress clean when the bride had to

pee. That was some peak bridesmaid sh*t right there. I am all about helping within an inch of my life. But a little gratitude would have been nice. The bride is my BEST FRIEND, and she didn't thank me.

Iris attached a photo of one of the centerpieces and reread her post. She liked how she sounded, bolder and more honest than in real life. Like someone who could command an audience, who could speak truth to bad behavior. Like someone she would never be.

⌒

On the standing-room-only train into Manhattan the next morning, Iris checked her Reddit post. She didn't expect much; after all, she'd never garnered more than four likes from a tweet. To her giddy astonishment, the post had been upvoted more than six hundred times. She squealed, eliciting a raised eyebrow from a businesswoman doing a crossword on her phone. The flurry of comments vilified Amber and praised Iris for her compassion. She didn't want Amber to collect shade, but the chorus of disapproval felt restorative. The Reddit community acknowledged her humanity and dedication when her family and friends could not. They confirmed she was not crazy.

The validation gave her a much-needed boost at work. She was the assistant compliance officer in the Department of Compliance, Audit, and Training at New York City General Hospital (D-CAT for short—the hospital couldn't resist an acronym). When she told people she worked in a hospital, they imagined her in scrubs, racing through a crowded emergency room to deliver a bag of blood to a patient with a gunshot wound. In reality, she sat at a computer in a windowless, airless basement office that used to be a storage closet for medical records before they all went online. Her to-do list felt like an avalanche, because her boss, Assistant Vice President Jeremy McDonnell, spent his days surfing the internet. That day's project, apparently, was reliving the supermodel era by watching classic Victoria's Secret fashion shows, Cindy Crawford's Pepsi commercials, and George Michael's "Freedom! '90" video. When Iris admitted she'd never heard of Herb Ritts, Jeremy clicked through a slideshow of supermodels, some topless. She retreated to her cubicle, shellshocked.

Her friends were appalled at Jeremy's behavior. Once he had asked her if she'd ever date someone as old as he was. Once he told her his wife hadn't slept with him in more than a year. Once he "accidentally" showed her a pornographic picture when clicking through windows on his computer. She knew she should report him, but whom would she report him to? As the assistant vice president of Compliance, Audit, and Training, he was in charge of triaging harassment complaints. In that case, she was technically supposed to go to HR, but Barbara, her only female coworker, had warned her not to take that step lightly. Once you crossed that threshold, someone was going to get fired.

She opened the emails that seemed urgent: a meeting with the CPR (Committee for Policy Review) that needed to be rescheduled, some notifications from the PMS (project management system) about documents ready for her eye, and a password expiration notice from the ION (interoffice network).

At lunch, she checked her Reddit post again. It was already slipping in the feed. So she wrote another.

My second cousin got married last year. She had a nonexistent budget and couldn't afford a wedding cake, so I offered to bake cupcakes for dessert. She estimated two hundred guests. A few weeks before the wedding, I reached out to ask for an updated count and didn't get a reply—from her or the other bridesmaids—so I baked three hundred cupcakes, in case anyone wanted seconds. I spent literally hundreds of dollars on ingredients and tiered cupcake stands. I even rented a minivan to carry everything. As I was unloading cupcakes at the venue, I noticed that not a lot of chairs were set out for the ceremony. My aunt told me that they'd halved the guest list to save money. Thankfully, the cupcakes didn't go to waste—the venue had some to-go boxes, and people took them home—but the bride didn't apologize. And instead of a thank-you card, I received a terse email asking if I was planning on purchasing anything from the registry.

Immediately this post got a handful of upvotes. After biting her tongue with her friends, her parents, and her boss, it was healing to express herself and be listened to, even admired. Iris went back to work and powered through the rest of the day, not caring when Jeremy winked at her on the way to a meeting. Someday, she might write about him, too.

⚬

The next morning, she wrote a post about Sophia's gift bag demands and included a photo of the mask-embellishment operation taking over Iris's bedroom. This third post became so popular, Reddit's algorithm exposed it to numerous users who weren't looking for bridesmaid stories. Comments rolled in, some of them mean-spirited. She flinched at one blaming her for being friends with "this terrible human being"—meaning Sophia. Another shamed Iris for being stingy. Iris realized an open forum was not the place for commiseration after all. And if her friends looked at this page, they'd recognize themselves. But having tasted the support she starved for, she couldn't give it up.

She decided to start a secret group on Facebook. It would be airtight: no one could see the page without emailing her or being invited by a member. She would approve each applicant, and if anyone put down another member, she would kick them out. This wasn't about forbidding criticism; it was about preventing trolls from taking potshots. The privacy might encourage others to share their bridesmaiding war stories, too.

She added a comment to all three Reddit posts, explaining that she was starting a bridesmaids' support group and that anyone who wanted to commiserate in a private space could email her to join. She created an anonymous email account and a second Facebook profile. Facebook forced you to use your real name—or some approximation thereof: many of Iris's friends went by extremely loose nicknames that would thwart a Google search. Employing her middle name, Fay, Iris named herself Eye Fay. She used a close-up of her eyeball as her profile pic. Better safe than sorry, she thought.

She decided not to invite anyone she knew. Someone might tag her main account in a post about the group, so that Amber, Sophia, or another bride she wrote about might see it. This would be a community of strangers with a common plight.

Creating the group was easy; naming it was not. "Bridesmaids Support Group" sounded like work, and some might think it was group therapy. "Bridesmaid Stories" sounded dull. "Bridesmaid Horror Stories" was too negative. She googled "Facebook bridesmaid group names" but only found names for bridal parties, like "The I Do Crew." When she checked her email next, she'd gotten the weekly newsletter from the hospital employees' union. And it came to her.

---

**Eye Fay**

May 23, 2018, 10:09 P.M.

Welcome to the Bridesmaids Union! I created this page as a safe, private place to write about the indignities we gals have suffered in helping our female friends and family members walk down the aisle. I hope you'll each share your own bridesmaid stories, moments of inspiration and misery and hilarity. As an eight-time bridesmaid (soon to be nine), I have some serious tea to spill. I also think this group can be a great place for sharing ideas and advice for the many challenges a bridesmaid faces. And I hope everyone will cough up a pic of their worst bridesmaid dress—I know they're in your closets, next to your college cap and gown, your prom dress, and the wedding dress from your own canceled wedding. Or maybe that's just my closet 👻

Without further ado, please introduce yourselves! And tell us about your bridesmaid martyrdom.

Love,
Eye

 29                                    15 comments

**Arden Woodbine**

Thanks for starting this group! A new friend asked me to be a brides-maid. Her wedding is in January in Barbados, which would be per-fect, except the cost of the flight + hotel + transportation + meals + excursions + dress + jewelry + gift (her maid of honor is forcing all the bridesmaids to pitch in to buy her and her wife a sofa) adds up to $4,000. I told her nicely that I couldn't afford it, and she hasn't answered my texts in almost a month. Maybe she's just busy plan-ning the wedding?

⊙♥ 9

**Eye Fay**

I've so been there. That is a CHUNK of money, and though I'm sure it's going to be a beautiful wedding, we shouldn't go into debt be-cause we think we have to.

⊙ 2

**Verena Lightfoot**

Perhaps you could offer to celebrate her at your home, on your budget. If she is worthy of being your friend, she will surely take your offer seriously.

⊙ 3

**Eye Fay**

Thanks Verena Lightfoot for your wisdom! <3

⊙ 2

**Jaclyn Arias**

Here's my worst dress, babes! It was atrocious!

**Eye Fay**

Looks like the sewing machine went haywire!

**Jaclyn Arias**

TRUTH.

**Anna Banana**

Hey Bridesmaids Union! Get this: my friend fell in love with an $8,000 wedding dress, which blew her budget out of the water, so she started a GoFundMe page to raise money for it. She made a video of herself holding the dress and singing to it like it's a baby. One of our mutual friends asked if it was fine to donate to the wedding dress in lieu of a gift, and the bride insinuated that she wanted both. So far, three people put money toward it—she's raised $125 of $8,000. And now everyone is afraid to talk to her because we haven't helped her buy that dumb dress.

♡ 6

**Eye Fay**

😂

By the weekend, the Bridesmaids Union was forty members strong. Jaclyn Arias was from the Bronx, less than five miles from Iris's apartment. "Anna Banana" lived in Brooklyn. Arden Woodbine was from Wisconsin, Verena Lightfoot from California, and Madison Le Claire lived in Australia. That Iris shared no mutual friends with any of them was a relief, a testament to the size of the world.

Not since giving birth to Mason could Iris remember feeling so optimistic about her future.

# Chapter Two

**Eye Fay**

September 8, 2018, 1:42 A.M.

Greetings, fellow bridesmaids!!! I'm in Cabo for S's bachelorette party. It has been a DAY.

Last night wrapped up at three a.m. at a VIP table in a nightclub where we polished off an entire bottle of Grey Goose. The bill came to a thousand dollars, which—thank the Lord—S's sister (who is MOH) offered to shoulder. I could barely afford the resort. I've been leaving my cell phone off to save the ten bucks a day for the international calling plan.

We slept a grand total of four hours and ate breakfast by one of the three thousand pools on property, maintaining our buzz from the night before with a steady stream of Bloody Marys. S's roommate got up to pee; after ten minutes, S's sister checked on her. She wasn't in the nearest bathroom or her suite. Girl flew the coop. We called her cell like ten times—and realized it was in her handbag, sitting on her chair.

I offered to look for her myself, as I didn't want S's last vacation as an unmarried woman to grind to a halt. While everyone else worked on their tans, I checked every cabana, restaurant, and bar in the resort, which was the size of a small country. I made the mistake of wearing these sexy Cleopatra sandals I'd bought for the trip, and by the time I gave up, overheated and delirious, the blisters on each of my feet had united Power Rangers–style into a giant Megazord. When I hobbled back to the group after THREE HOURS of searching, everyone was at lunch, including the rogue bridesmaid, who had gone to her room to use the bathroom but got lost on the way. They'd called me and left a message, forgetting my phone was off.

I accept that all my looking accomplished zilch. I should have checked in before three hours went by. I didn't need everyone to rend their garments over how I'd suffered. But nobody, including S's roommate, acknowledged what I'd done. S herself barely seemed to notice I'd been gone. All she did was inform the group that the next round of drinks was on me.

Eye

 28                                              25 comments

**Jaclyn Arias**
I totally feel your pain. A simple thank you goes a long way.
👍 2

**Alex Oberlin**
You deserve a medal for what you went through! As a guy, the posts in this group have been a real eye-opener.

**Eye Fay**
Marry me!
😂 5

**Alex Oberlin**
Definitely! But my husband might be annoyed.
😮 3

⌇

Iris had to proofread the hospital's internet use policy and update the compliance microsite by "COB"—close of business, in Jeremy's parlance—but as soon as she opened the policy draft and encountered the subheading

"Reasonable Social Media Use," she remembered she hadn't checked Facebook that day to see whether her last post in the Bridesmaids Union, about Sophia's bachelorette party, had garnered any new comments. It hadn't, but she enjoyed scrolling proprietarily through the page. And two people had applied to the group that morning. In just three months, the Bridesmaids Union had attracted more than two hundred members, both through referrals from existing members and emails to the address she'd posted on Reddit. Out of an abundance of caution, she'd deleted the content of her Reddit posts about her friends' weddings but left in mentions of the Facebook group.

It was exciting to watch her internet baby grow, and validating to see that she wasn't the only one who'd been worn down by bridesmaiding. It was also a little scary, because as kind as she tried to be, the brides she wrote about would not like being exposed. She vetted each prospective member, ensuring no mutual friends, and she left out names and identifying information in her posts, but she was definitely taking a risk. She decided to limit the group to five hundred, and if any of her friends found out, she'd delete everything and apologize like hell. For now, the honesty, the camaraderie, and the validation were too wonderful to give up.

She minimized the browser window just as Jeremy stepped out of his office, a manila folder pinched between two fingers. He'd just gotten back from three weeks of sunbathing on Shelter Island—a vacation spot for wealthy New Yorkers who considered the Hamptons to be tawdry—and his skin was fuchsia. "Hey you," he said, leaning against her low cubicle wall. "Where are we on the internet use policy?"

"I'll have it to you by five o'clock," Iris said.

"Great. Great. I mean, if you don't get to it, that's also totally OK. This isn't some evil corporation. You can take all the time you need."

One upside of her job was that no one cared if she met her deadlines. But she cared. "It's no big deal."

"Great. Great," he said again. He looked back at his office door, paused, then cast his gaze toward the wall clock by the front door, making a pit stop, as he often did, at her cleavage, as if glancing at her body on the way toward another destination would confuse her into thinking she'd only imagined being mentally undressed. "So . . . what are you up to this weekend?" It was Tuesday.

Mason had just started kindergarten, and she would be attending the fifth birthday party of his new friend Rafael, held at one of those maximum-security jungle gyms where the parents could socialize while the kids wore themselves out in the ball pit. To Jeremy she said, "Cleaning, errands, that sort of thing," with a friendly lilt that still communicated her complete lack of interest in sleeping with him. In her last performance review, Jeremy had singled out her off-putting tone, the kind of criticism given to no man, ever. Maybe she would sound more congenial if she didn't have to ward off his advances, she didn't say.

"Well, Ms. Hagarty, if you get tired of cleaning, give me a shout. I'll buy you a drink. My wife is out of town until next Monday night. It'd be nice to kick back and not have this power hierarchy for once, just be two people looking to have a good time, you know? Oh, hey, would you reschedule that HIPAA appointment? I think I'm going to take the day off tomorrow. They say it's going to be the best beach day of the year."

She took a deep breath, letting some of her frustration dissipate—anger would do her no good. But she wished she could have a conversation with her boss that didn't involve being hit on. And finding a mutually available hour for the chief of medicine and the vice president of Human Resources was like waiting for a solar eclipse. He'd just had three weeks of beach days! "You know it could be months before we can meet with them, and we need to complete those trainings by the end of the year."

He shrugged. "Don't worry about it. That's my problem—and anyway, it'll be fine."

It might have been his neck on the line, but she was the one who had to shelve her to-do list to play email tennis with the two busiest administrative assistants at City General. The hospital's calendaring software was about as good as the paper one her parents got from the insurance broker at Christmastime, and at least that one came with pretty landscapes.

When he retreated to his office, she clicked through the flotilla of job listings in the promotions tab of her inbox. Now, as always, some openings looked interesting—a global skincare company needed a compliance assistant—but she doubted any of these jobs offered the hospital's combination of unreal health insurance and generous time off. Would a corporation let her stay home whenever Mason got sick or for every holiday his school was closed—which included Election Day, two presidents' birthdays, and celebrations for all three major Abrahamic religions? When it came down to it, she couldn't risk her son's well-being for the dream of the perfect job.

Besides, she wasn't certain she wanted to stay in the field. She'd trained to be a paralegal, thinking naïvely that she could help achieve justice for her clients, and after a string of jobs disabused her of that notion, ended up at City General in hopes of implementing practices that would prevent bad behavior and avoid fines and lawsuits. Unfortunately, all their office did was annoy employees with rules that no one followed. She wanted to work in criminal defense, helping victims of the justice system, but that would require a breathtaking drop in salary, and she was already drowning in bridesmaid debt. An attorney would make more money than a paralegal, but she would never emerge from the abyss of student loans.

She returned to the internet use policy. As usual, she'd exhaustively researched best practices and drafted the policy in elegant English, and Jeremy chopped it up into word salad. Following his never-ending sentences made her brain feel drawn and quartered. Some would have called him a genius, able to cram so much jargon into a two-page document that she couldn't make it through one paragraph without glazing over and having to start again. The hospital could have used these policies for sedation.

The gist was that employees were allowed to spend a reasonable amount of time online during the workday, as long as they didn't operate a business, implicate the hospital in their personal views, or write something discriminatory or offensive. Also, every keystroke made on a company computer could be tracked, so employees were advised not to write anything private. The one digestible sentence was, "If you don't want to see it on the front page of *The Times*, don't put it in an email."

She didn't post to Facebook at work, and she actually worked hard, unlike her colleagues. Chase, director of internal investigations, spent half the day posting photos with his Stepford family and selfies on hunting trips and defenses of Trump's most inhumane policies. Barbara, manager of institutional audit, frittered away her mornings reading online news. She wasn't loathsome, at least.

Iris's cell phone rang. She stared at the screen, confused. It had to be a butt dial. Why would Jasmine reach out on a random Tuesday after nine months of silence? And since when did her sister call instead of text? Maybe something terrible had happened.

"Jasmine?" she asked.

"Iris! What's up?"

"Not much," Iris said cautiously. "What's going on?"

"So, big news: I'm engaged!"

"Congratulations!" Iris said three times, since Jasmine was still squealing at her revelation. "Who's the lucky guy?" This must have been the boyfriend their father had mentioned after Amber's wedding.

"You are going to *love* him. His name is David, and he's successful and funny and such a good listener, and sooo cute, like a sexy koala bear. And he's a literal genius. He went to Harvard and founded this tech firm . . . he's basically Mark Zuckerberg but with amazing emotional intelligence. It's like he can read my *mind*, Iris."

"He sounds awesome," Iris said, adjusting to Jasmine's zero-to-sixty. Hadn't they been practically estranged a few minutes ago? Jasmine had the emotional consistency of a Facebook feed. Then again, Iris had been the one holding the grudge. "When do I get to meet this perfect man?"

"I guess at the engagement party? Mom and Dad are hosting it on the twenty-second. I've been begging them not to do it at home, but whatever. It's not like I'm the one who's getting married . . . oh, wait."

Having the engagement party at home seemed kind of nice, Iris thought. "How did he propose?"

"On my birthday, he took me to Buddakan—"

"Happy belated!" Iris interrupted. She'd privately acknowledged her sister's birthday as it passed but hadn't thought Jasmine would want to hear from her.

"Thanks, babe! David is super generous, and it is so refreshing to just order anything on the menu without looking at the prices. I had the most delicious lamb chops with, like, rosemary. When dessert comes, he gets down on one knee, and I'm like, 'What are you doing? Oh my God, you are *not*,' and he gives me the most beautiful ring. There's a photo of it on my Instagram."

Iris had never gotten into Instagram; the pictures she took never seemed pretty enough. "That sounds really romantic! I'll check it out."

"It's a princess cut, which the old dude at Orogio's said was not in style, but I was like, that's because it's timeless, and then David said, 'You are my Princess Jasmine.' It was so romantic, I almost died."

Jasmine had been one year old when *Aladdin* came out, and as a young girl, she pretended (or believed?) that Princess Jasmine was named after her. "I'm glad you didn't die."

Jasmine laughed hysterically.

"So you chose the ring?"

"Yeah, of course," Jasmine said. "David's taste level is not amazing."

Would Iris gain anything by pointing out that the "surprise" proposal wasn't a surprise if Jasmine had picked out the ring? "He still sounds like a catch."

"He absolutely is. Anyway, the wedding is May eighteenth. Mark your calendar."

"Of next year? So soon!"

"The venue had a cancellation—otherwise, we'd be waiting until 2020, and it seemed really conventional and boring to wait that long. I mean, I'm not going to be one of those brides who obsesses over every detail."

Iris knew a stone-cold lie when she heard one. "Where are you doing it?"

"It's called The Farm in the Willows, near Princeton, and oh my God, it's the most beautiful place you've ever seen. They have this super romantic barn and, like, a duck pond."

"I didn't realize barns were romantic."

"Jesus Christ, Iris, open up a wedding magazine. That's all anyone cares about right now. Barn weddings are huge."

"Are there going to be, like, cows and pigs?"

"No—I mean, probably—I mean, I don't know. Not in the wedding."

Iris restrained herself from laughing. The barn thing did sound sweet, though.

"And one more thing," Jasmine said.

"Yeah?" Iris felt suddenly anxious. Was Jasmine about to ask her to be maid of honor? Or had Iris eighty-sixed that possibility by taking distance?

"I wanted to invite you to a little get-together I'm hosting on Sunday afternoon at our new place."

"You moved in together?"

"Yeah, this summer, like, on the extreme DL. Mom and Dad didn't want anyone to know we're living in sin or whatever. BTW they think we're sleeping in separate bedrooms. *Please* don't shatter their delusion."

"Of course." Spike and Connie were lax about some religious precepts (e.g., temperance and forgiveness), but they went all in on forbidding pre-marital sex. "Where is it?"

"In Alpine. I'll text you the address."

"You live in Alpine? That's . . . wow!" The New Jersey town, adjacent to their hometown of Tenafly, was basically reserved for celebrities. Growing up, Iris had sensed its moneyed presence as a kind of taunt.

"Yeah, it's super nice. I do feel blessed."

"So is this a housewarming party? Or . . . ?"

"No, not that. It's kind of an experiment. Just wear something festive."

Iris wasn't sure she wanted to be part of her sister's experiment, especially since their relationship wasn't on firm footing. But she was curious to meet Jasmine's fiancé and see their new house. "Can I bring Mason?"

"Sorry, adults only. He wouldn't have fun anyway—we're going to get *so* drunk." She laughed. "So you'll come?"

Iris hadn't quite adjusted to this abrupt closing of their rift, but it was good news, right? Maybe it was David's influence.

"I would love to," Iris said.

After hanging up, Iris understood with a pang of disappointment that she was probably not going to be maid of honor, maybe not even a brides-maid. Jasmine would have gotten those assignments squared away first thing, especially if the wedding was in eight months. Maybe it would be a relief not to be in the wedding party for once—certainly a relief for her finances—though it hurt not to be invited. They were sisters! Wasn't their bond supposed to be stronger than a political disagreement?

# Chapter Three

**Erica Black**

September 10, 2018, 10:10 P.M.

Aaaahhhh! My younger sister just had a nightmare experience and I had to tell someone! She was in a hoedown-themed wedding, and the bride, her best friend, wanted everyone in the wedding party to play an instrument for the procession. My sister thought she was going to get a tambourine or something, but the bride assigned her the fiddle. She didn't know how to play the fiddle. The bride insisted that it was a really simple piece of music and that if my sister just gave it some effort, she'd pick it up. My sister had to pay for private lessons and did not improve. One of the groomsmen was a professional violinist, so my sister's instructor suggested she pluck the strings while he plays. The bride was vehemently against the idea and accused my sister of being selfish. At the wedding, she played better than anyone could have expected, which was still pretty bad. The bride was furious and hasn't spoken to her since.

👍😮😲 22                                                5 comments

**Anna Banana**
Wow. Just wow.
👍 2

**Eye Fay**

Was the wedding held in a barn? I hear those are in.

🌀 1

**Erica Black**

Haha it was. My sister said it was a lot of fun, outside of the fiddle incident.

🌀 1

Iris lived with her son in a two-bedroom apartment in downtown Yonkers, across the Hudson River from Alpine, so close that her weather app often thought she was there instead. An apartment in New York City would have been more convenient to the hospital, but here she paid only twelve hundred a month for a nice-enough place in walking distance of the commuter train. Through her living room window, she could see a slice of the river and the Palisades behind it, majestic cliffs that shone a coppery red in the morning and cast stark shadows as the sun set behind them. She had a beautiful son, two beautiful cats, and a beautiful view: sometimes she felt like the luckiest person in the world.

That night, after retrieving Mason from after-school daycare, dancing with him to Taylor Swift until they fell down panting, eating reheated roast chicken and potatoes, and giving him a bubble bath, they cuddled on the sofa and had device time. He took the iPad to work on his Mine-craft city while she picked up her phone for a research binge. Pickles and Meatball settled in around them and purred in stereo, Pickles staccato like an idling snowblower, Meatball steady like a diesel engine.

First, Iris googled "The Farm in the Willows" and found Jasmine's barn venue. The images looked dreamy: banquet tables set with chargers and crystal, string lights entwined around the rafters, and a giant square doorway framing a pond and a willow tree.

Next, she navigated to Jasmine's Instagram page in search of the engagement ring—and was impressed to see that her sister had more than nine thousand followers. Jasmine described herself as a "wellness guru | creative rebel | animal rights activist." All of this was news to Iris; she'd thought Jasmine worked in marketing. She clicked on her website, PawCouture.com, and was blitzed by photos of Elsa, her sweet-faced Morkipoo (a Maltese/ Yorkshire terrier/poodle mix, apparently), shod in sneakers, shearling boots, and a pair of kitten heels "for a night on the town." These booties cost anywhere from eighty to three hundred dollars. When Jasmine had mentioned her business at Easter dinner, Iris had assumed she was selling dog sweaters, not designer shoes.

The "about" page of the dog-bootie website featured a sun-dappled photo of Jasmine lifting Elsa, Simba-style, in a park. The text went on about how dangerous a sidewalk can be to a dog's paws, both when the summer sun scorches the pavement and in winter, when ignorant landlords and homeowners sprinkle rock salt on the sidewalks—and how high-quality "paw wear" can prevent damage. OK, but did a dog need a three-hundred-dollar set of fur-lined booties for protection? At least the fur was faux.

"She's pretty," Mason said, peering at Jasmine's photograph.

"You know that's Auntie Jasmine, right?" Iris hoped her tiff with Jasmine wasn't depriving her son of connection to his family.

"Yeah." He didn't seem certain. "She's pretty," he said again.

"You know, sweetie, what people look like on the outside doesn't matter as much as what they look like on the inside."

"Like their blood and guts?"

She kissed the crown of his head—he was so cute it was hard not to literally eat him. "Inner beauty is about a person's good qualities, like kindness toward people less fortunate than they are. You can't tell those things from a picture, but they're way more important than looks."

He considered this. "She has really good inner beauty."

Iris wasn't sure about that, but Jasmine's outer beauty was impossible to debate. She had glittering blue eyes and a fourteen-tooth smile. Iris's face was squarish, with a strong nose, thin lips, and limp brown hair immune to product: pretty, but not terribly feminine. And in contrast to Jasmine's hourglass figure, Iris's body had always been a straight line, and her proportions held steady as age and childbirth thickened her.

When they were teens, Iris had noticed boys staring at Jasmine but not her. Indoctrinated by the church youth group, Iris had once thanked

God for making her less beautiful than Jasmine because it made it easier to maintain her virginity—a blue-ribbon rationalization. Deep down, she resented her sister for hoarding the good genes.

In high school, Iris found kinship with the misfits who devoted their lives to bit parts in school plays, while Jasmine hung with the cool girls in her grade who took turns dating the quarterback. But Jasmine wasn't embarrassed by Iris, and they shared lollipops, outfits, and secrets. When Iris was in her mid-twenties, though, Jasmine stopped returning her calls. Iris figured she must have offended her in a moment of graceless self-congratulation when first engaged to Forrest, or with neglect when Mason was an infant and Iris had zero time and less energy.

Then came the 2016 election. Jasmine admitted that she hadn't voted: she didn't agree with Trump and she didn't trust Hillary. Iris could only see her sister's misgivings about Hillary as sexism, and her non-vote had been a shock and a betrayal. Their parents had voted for Trump—they *loved* the guy—but even if they'd hated him, they would have supported him. They were one-issue voters, pro-lifers to the death.

In those dark months after the election, when the world's days seemed numbered, Iris had been too hurt to call any of them. She did call Rose, her older sister who was a satellite engineer—a literal rocket scientist—on the Space Coast of Florida. Rose had opted out of their family, didn't play into their parents' loyalty games, and seemed happily and permanently single. As usual, the conversation was like trying to sail on a breezeless day. Rose waited for Iris to finish complaining, then reminded her with a sigh that New Jersey wasn't a battleground state, so their parents' votes hadn't counted. At least Rose had voted for Hillary.

Three months into Trump's presidency, Iris and Mason showed up at the Hagarty homestead for Easter dinner. She hadn't forgiven them but wasn't going to rob Mason of his family over politics. But whereas before, she'd felt a wary allegiance with Jasmine against their parents, post-election, she was alone in enemy territory. Jasmine pretended nothing was amiss.

Iris returned to Jasmine's Instagram page and scrolled through photos of her breakfast laid out in a precise grid, her cloudy iced latte sweating lusciously, Elsa in a slicker and rain boots, and countless selfies taken from the Paris Hilton angle: driving a boat in a bikini and a floppy hat, posing in a bikini in front of a waterfall, laughing in a bikini with her sunglasses slipping off her nose, floating on an inflatable swan . . . in a bikini. Iris remembered Jasmine being more modest than this. She did have an amazing body, though.

Jasmine had posted a picture of her engagement ring in a snap dated three weeks earlier. It looked expensive, the diamond comically large against a slim pavé band, like an overzealous boob job.

Iris was taken aback at her own judginess. She needed to dial down the envy. She was happy for her sister; why did she have to be catty? Maybe because Jasmine had been engaged for three weeks and had told all of her followers before mentioning it to her sister. Their parents had kept it from her, too.

Something was odd about the feed, and finally Iris put her finger on it: there was not one picture of David. Iris didn't post photos of Mason on social media to protect him, but who hid her fiancé? Now she was determined to find a picture of him. She didn't know his last name, but a Google search uncovered the wedding registry of Jasmine Hagarty and David Leiman—which was just a list of their favorite charities, including an animal rescue organization and a fund offering microloans to women in developing countries. No gifts? That didn't sound like Jasmine.

Mason was mesmerized by the blocky landscapes of his video game. Minecraft was too advanced for five-year-olds, but it was a way for Mason to bond with Marilyn's grandsons, who were seven and nine. Iris had researched it and allowed him a configuration that wouldn't give either of them nightmares: solo games in "creative" mode, which let him build worlds without encountering monsters or internet creeps. The way she'd set it up, the game looked almost educational.

She googled "David Leiman Harvard," but he didn't seem to have a social media presence except for a LinkedIn profile with no headshot. It said that from May 2018 to present, he was a "Freelance Techie and

Philanthropist"; before that, he'd owned a company called Life Harvest, and before that, he'd been a software engineer at Cisco in Silicon Valley. He had a bachelor's in computer science from Harvard. She googled "Life Harvest" and found, after references to a church, a video game, and a recipe blog, a 2018 news story from *Fast Company* announcing its sale to a firm called Deep Analytics for an undisclosed sum. Apparently, Life Harvest collected consumer data and sold it to the highest bidder. It sounded unsavory.

In the comments of the *Fast Company* article, someone had written, David is a common thief. He got kicked out of Harvard for stealing and made his 50 million doing the same. If there were any justice in this world, he'd be doing hard time.

*Fifty million?!* she thought, then realized she'd spoken it aloud. It figured that Jasmine would fall in love with a criminal. Why was the Venn diagram of the morally corrupt and the uber-wealthy an eclipse?

With a little more digging, she found a picture of him, taken at a charity gala for a children's hospital. At least he was generous, though maybe his donations were merely a tax write-off. He had sleepy brown eyes, jutting ears, dense stubble crowding his lips, and thinning curly black hair. He looked . . . normal.

"Who's that?" Mason asked, pointing to the picture of David.

"That's David. He's going to marry Auntie Jasmine."

"He has good inner beauty," Mason decided.

"I don't think he does," Iris said.

She googled a bit more, trying to confirm David's net worth, then chastised herself for being shallow and took a break on BuzzFeed, where she looked at "You Won't Believe What These Child Actors Look Like Now," "Sixty-One Reasons the Nineties Was the Best Decade Ever," "A Pancake Hack You Literally Cannot Live Without," and "Drop Everything to See These Pictures of Cuddling Polar Bears." A sponsored link sent her to images of actresses with bad plastic surgery, which clogged her screen with so many pop-up ads and virus alerts that she returned to the safety of Facebook, where Sophia had posted bachelorette party photos and Amber had shared an oldie but goodie: Chihuahua or blueberry muffin? Labradoodle or fried chicken? Shiba Inu or marshmallow? A banner ad brought Iris to a brand called Jasmine that sold wrinkle-free jumpsuits, possibly because she had searched for her sister; another ad, which she didn't click on, linked to an online course that promised to triple her net worth. The Life Harvest video game was trolling her, too: It looked dumb.

She'd burrowed too far down this clickhole, and she felt hollowed out. If she didn't waste so much time on the internet, letting it tug her around as her curiosities flickered past, who knew what she could accomplish? She might have a better job by now. Or a boyfriend.

She sighed. Jasmine, the youngest of the three, would be the first down the aisle, and Iris was heading into spinster territory. She wanted to be in love, to share her life with a man who loved her, and to raise Mason with a partner. But who had time to date?

Well, she had time now, at least to look. "Mason, sweetie, let's go to bed," she said.

He didn't respond.

"You need to turn your game off. It's past your bedtime."

His face glowed alien blue in the light of the screen.

"I'm going to take it on the count of three," she said. "One, two, three." She grabbed the tablet and pressed the Home button, and the game window was sucked away. The cats scattered.

"Give it back," he whined.

She slid out from underneath him as he began to thrash. "Don't," she said. "You had plenty of time to play. Now it's time for bed." Just once, she wished he would listen to reason. "If you don't get up now, you're going to lose video game privileges for tomorrow."

This time she counted to ten. He didn't stop.

"That's it. No game tomorrow."

"No!" He banged against the wall and screamed.

She took a deep breath, fighting her urge to scream back. "I'll be waiting in your bedroom," she said. "Brush your teeth first."

Moments later, she heard the faucet, and then he shuffled in, whimpering and apologetic, his feathery eyelashes speckled with tears like raindrops in a spiderweb. The miracle of motherhood (and the reason for humanity's continued existence, she believed) was that a moment of peace helped her forget his worst tantrums. As she tucked him in, he mumbled, "Will you check for monsters?"

She looked under the bed, where their winter clothes were stored, then his closet, an armageddon of toys. "No monsters here." She kissed his forehead, and—finally!—he fell asleep.

She got ready for bed, slid under the sheets, and opened up Bumble on her phone. Meatball waded onto her chest, settled down, and resumed his machinelike purr. Pickles colonized her pillow and licked the wax out of her ears with his spiky tongue. As the alpha kitty, Meatball always took the prime spot.

She didn't love dating apps, or maybe it was the people on the apps she didn't love. She'd been on two dates that year, and both had bombed. The first guy revealed halfway through their coffee date that he was married, and that his wife was "fine with it," as long as she didn't "know the particulars." The second, whose body odor reached across the table to embrace her, did not stop talking about blockchain from the moment they sat down to the moment the doors of her Metro-North train closed between them. When she got home, she put Mason to bed and took a silent bath in the dark.

In her years of bad dates, she'd become skilled at judging men based on their photos, age, and location, swiping left or right without a second's thought. She didn't veer from her dealbreakers: no one more than five years younger or fifteen years older than her, no guns or dead animals in the photos, no shirtless selfies, and most importantly, no couples looking for a third. If she couldn't decide, she passed on men who seemed unemployed, who were under five-three or over six-four, who didn't post a full-body shot, or who wrote cryptic or overlong profiles. Anyone who liked "old-fashioned romance" was probably sexist. Anyone who described himself as "easygoing," "laidback," or "chill" was probably a stoner; if he was all three, he probably wasn't big on affirmative consent. Sometimes she left-swiped motorcyclists and smokers and men who tried too hard to be clever. Maybe she would mindlessly discard her perfect match with her knee-jerk judgments; maybe she already had. But that fear was based on the myth that she could only find love with one person. If she could live happily with, say, a hundred different men in New York, and ninety of them would annoy her or have to be apologized for, she didn't mind waiting for the better ten.

That night, with her sister's wedding nipping at her heels, she swiped right on a few she would otherwise have rejected: a thirty-nine-year-old radiologist who wore a shirt in precisely none of his photos, a twenty-nine-year-old real estate broker in Brooklyn who described himself as a Libertarian Democrat, and a beautiful forty-eight-year-old photographer who was "looking for my muse."

To her disbelief, she matched with that last guy, Christof. He had a welcoming face with a broad smile and steel blue eyes, short brown hair and a stubbly beard. A tuft of fur was visible in the V of his hermetically fitting polo. He claimed his photos had been taken that year; if that was true, he looked fantastic for his age. Maybe he didn't feel like being witty in his profile. It could be nice for a change, a conversation that settled into a topic instead of dancing around the edges of everything.

Since she was on Bumble, as opposed to the rest of the dating apps clustered on page four of her home screen, she would have to make the first move: on this app, the woman had to message the man before they could start chatting.

I've never been anyone's muse

He replied a few seconds later.

Would you like to be mine?

Umm, maybe! What exactly does that entail?

Just being yourself.

I guess I'm disqualified. 😂

I don't believe that.

OK, you got me.

But she did have trouble being authentic on dates. She believed a man could love her for who she was; she just wasn't sure a man would fall in love with that self, unadorned.

A moment passed before his next message.

You have a beautiful smile.

Normally she would have unmatched someone so forward, but she let herself soak up the compliment.

Thanks. You're *very* handsome.

She rubbed Meatball's belly, and he stuck his legs in the air to give her better access.

Thank you. What are you looking for in a
lover?

It was an oddly phrased question, though no worse than most guys on these apps. One had asked her what flavor of ice cream she wanted him to lick off her body; another called her a cliché when she admitted she hated football.

I'm looking for someone who isn't
afraid of commitment and who doesn't
play games.

I don't want to feel like I'm auditioning
for his affections after we fall in love.

That describes me.

She waited a few seconds to see if he'd elaborate, then asked:

What are you looking for in a partner?

I'm attracted to intelligence and creativity.
I like to be challenged. But most of all, I'm
looking for honesty. I take people at their
word, and I've been burned too many times.
I need someone who will be careful with my
heart.

At this admission of vulnerability, her defenses fell away.

I want that, too. So much.

She looked again at Christof's photos. This guy was not going to re-main single for long.

Want to get coffee sometime?

I hope I'm not being too forward

Not at all. I like that you ask for what you want.

I would love to meet you.

She felt dizzy with excitement at being wanted by someone so hand-some.

Great! I work in the East 20s . . .
maybe lunchtime near there?

Weekday lunches were the only hours she had to herself, and this way, the date had a natural ending.

**Do you like tea? I know a great Japanese tearoom in Soho.**

She wasn't a tea person, but she wasn't doing this for the beverage.

As a reward for her initiative, she watched a ten-minute YouTube video of unlikely animal friendships: dog and raccoon, cat and duck, ostrich and giraffe. Then came a compilation of soldiers returning home to their ecstatic dogs. Then cats leaping in terror at the sight of cucumbers. When she finally shut her eyes, ghostly abstract images, residue of her screen time, echoed in her vision as fantasies with Christof played out in her mind. It took her another hour to fall asleep.

# Chapter Four

**Madison Le Claire**

September 14, 2018, 4:37 A.M.

A close childhood friend asked me to be a backup bridesmaid—in case one of the "real" bridesmaids dropped out. I was a little put off by the idea of going through the motions when I probably wouldn't be a bridesmaid after all, but I told her I would be happy to do it. I also explained that I couldn't attend the shower and bachelorette party because I live in Australia, and she lives in Connecticut. She was fine with it. She asked me to buy the bridesmaid dress and shoes, which I did, reluctantly.

Then she conscripted me for help in planning the wedding. I was to do "vendor research," calling around to different companies to get prices and examples of their past work. Because of the time difference, I stayed up an hour late every night for a month. I must have called a hundred vendors. She didn't use a single one—I guess I was the backup researcher, too.

The night before the wedding, my father had a heart attack and needed an emergency triple bypass. I was very lucky to have flown to Connecticut for the wedding, because I was able to be in the hospital with him. I felt bad for missing the wedding, but in my mind there was no question. I emailed the bride, not wanting to wake her with a phone call. I trusted she would understand.

In the morning, I got a frantic call from the bride, saying that one of the bridesmaids didn't show and I was urgently needed in the wedding party. I reiterated that I had to be there for my dad. She flipped out. She told me she'd never speak to me again if I didn't show up in thirty minutes. I hung up, and that was the end of our friendship.

 44                                                 7 comments

**Breanna Naglehopf**
You really went above and beyond, Madison Le Claire. I would have said no at "backup bridesmaid."
4

**Erica Black**
Is your father OK???
1

**Madison Le Claire**
Thanks for asking! He's doing much better.
9

**Alia Singh**
I don't understand why she'd be upset to have one less bridesmaid. I think there's something wrong with her.
2

**Madison Le Claire**
Even when we were kids, she knew she wanted three bridesmaids. She used to draw her wedding portraits, and there were always three.
4

**Madison Le Claire**
Maybe I'm proving your point :)
3

Iris didn't know thing one about architecture, but as she drove her mother's Buick up the winding driveway, through the wrought iron gate, and around the cul-de-sac to reach Jasmine and David's new home, she recognized it definitively as a McMansion. It was crammed with gables and shutters and bay windows and not one but two turrets, as if the happy couple would need to ward off intruders with snipers. Her annoyance was amplified by the knowledge, courtesy of Zillow, that David had paid nine million dollars for it.

A Prius and a CR-V were parked out front; Iris guessed that neither of these belonged to Jasmine and David. Indeed, she found a cream-colored Range Rover in an attached four-car garage. Of course Mr. Moneybags would own an exhibitionist car. Or was that Jasmine's? Maybe he drove a Porsche.

Iris caught herself. Her sister had found a nice guy who happened to have a lot of money. Why did she have to be so petty and jealous? If she was going to make peace with Jasmine, she had to start within herself.

"Be kind, Iris," she whispered. "Be kind."

The doorbell triggered a cascade of chimes. Jasmine texted her: **Door's open. We're in the back.**

Inside, Iris found herself in a three-story foyer wrapped in a grand staircase; a chandelier, dripping with crystal, hung above her head. Elsa the Morkipoo bounded in from another room to bark and hop and sniff Iris's feet. Iris scratched behind her ears, and the manic pup maneuvered away from her touch to lick her fingers.

Seeking out the sounds of laughter, Iris wandered through marble-floored hallways, Elsa scampering beside her. This house had so many rooms, Iris wouldn't have been surprised to find Colonel Mustard in the conservatory with a candlestick.

Jasmine and two other twentysomething women were lounging on a low-slung sectional in a sunken, wood-paneled den, lined with shelves mixing books and knickknacks: a globe, a Buddha, a bouquet of freesia in a vase made from a bottle of Veuve Clicquot. Jasmine's long chestnut hair gleamed in the light from the windows; a nose ring with a diamond stud made her look vaguely spiritual. The TV played *The Real Housewives of Atlanta* on mute.

"Oh my God, Iris!" Jasmine hopped up from the sofa, and they embraced.

She smelled like the kind of shampoo you'd buy in a spa, lavender and candy and unknowable minerals.

"You look amazing," Jasmine said, picking up Elsa.

"You look . . . better than amazing," Iris said.

"How are you? It's been forever."

"Good, really good. I mean, tired, always tired, but good." Iris didn't know why she had to add the tired part. Maybe because Jasmine looked like she'd just woken up from the best sleep of her life.

"I megadose vitamin B12, and it gives me so much energy," Jasmine said. "Do you supplement?"

"Sure," Iris said. "I mean, I take a Centrum most days."

"The over-the-counter stuff is actually worse for you than taking nothing. You need micronutrients sourced from organic plants. Don't worry, I've got you. I'll send you a discount code."

Iris undoubtedly could not afford Jasmine's organic vitamins, but she thanked her and introduced herself to Jasmine's friends.

Brittany, a petite redhead with a bob haircut and a raspy voice, was Jasmine's partner in the dog-shoe biz and a project manager for the publications department of a large consulting firm. She looked to be about nineteen but spoke with the authority of a CEO. Electra, a tall Black woman with a heart-shaped face and a permanently wry expression, had been Jasmine's roommate from a briefly leased apartment in New Brunswick, when she worked the front desk at the Hyatt.

"Can I see your ring?" Iris asked Jasmine.

Jasmine maneuvered Elsa into her right arm and held out her left hand.

"Oh my God, it's stunning," Iris whispered. In person, the diamond looked elegant and proportioned. She lost herself in the complexity of its sparkle.

"It's so weird, I have this amazing eye for jewelry. David says I should become a jewelry designer, but it's not a passion project for me, the way my paw wear line is."

"The dog shoes?"

"You know they're going to be in *Vogue*?" She said it with fatigued annoyance, a tone she used to prevent accusations of boasting. In the Hagarty household, braggarts had to recite a litany of Bible verses about the sin of pride.

"No—that's amazing!" Iris exclaimed.

"Yeah," Jasmine said, as Brittany nodded vigorously. "Kim Kardashian ordered a set of kitten heels for Sushi, so now you can't go two clicks on Insta without running into them."

Was Sushi the name of a dog? Did everyone know this?

Jasmine rolled her eyes. "*Vogue* played hard to get for, like, a year, and now they're *begging* for more photos."

"If only it didn't take so long for people to realize how amazing you are," Brittany said without irony.

"OK, enough about me," Jasmine said. "Let's get this party started." She withdrew three square envelopes from a drawer in the built-in entertainment center and arranged Iris, Brittany, and Electra around her. She didn't turn off the TV. "I bet you're all wondering why I invited you here."

"The anticipation is killing me," said Brittany, so unconvincingly that she must have known what was going on.

Jasmine handed out the stiff envelopes, personalized with her guests' names. Iris's had been written in a different shade of pink. "On your mark, get set, go!" Jasmine said, raising her arm as if signaling the start of a drag race.

Iris slid a finger under the flap and opened it cleanly. Inside was a pink limestone coaster that read, in cursive,

*I'm getting hitched!*
*Won't you be my b!#/h?*

Now she understood. This was an elaborate version of a "bridesmaid proposal," in which the bride invites her closest friends and family members to be bridesmaids. Wait . . . these were her bridesmaids? Where were her best friends?

Then a humiliating possibility occurred to her. It had seemed strange to be invited to a party just a few days in advance. What if the whole thing had been set for some time, and Iris had been the last to be invited? Had Iris been a backup bridesmaid? That would explain why Iris's envelope was personalized with a different marker. The more Iris turned this over in her mind, the truer it seemed. Iris, sister of the bride, was less important to Jasmine than these two women Iris had never met. And where did that leave Rose?

Brittany and Electra were laughing. Brittany took Jasmine's hands, thanking her, and Electra patted her on the back.

"Stop it, stop it, I want to do the ceremony," Jasmine said. "Brittany, will you be my bridesmaid?" She wasn't going to say "bitch," of course. Iris was the only one in her family who cussed.

"Hashtag definitely!" Brittany said, then gripped Jasmine in a fearsome hug.

"Electra, will you be my bridesmaid?"

"Let me think about that . . . *yes!*"

"Iris, will you be my bridesmaid?"

"Of course I will. I'll do anything you need." Iris embraced Jasmine. She tried to be grateful that she was invited without obsessing over the circumstances. Jasmine was allowed to choose any bridesmaids she wanted, and Iris hadn't exactly been a model sibling.

"Thanks, Iris. You're the bomb."

Jasmine snapped group selfies, flipped through them, and took more.

"Are you posting these on Instagram?" Iris asked Jasmine. If she'd known she was going to be seen by thousands, she would have spent a little longer on her makeup.

"No, these are just for us," Jasmine explained. "I'm posting really selectively right now—I want my wedding to be a special private thing for friends and family."

That was a relief. Iris was glad not to be on display.

⟡

After taking a YouTube mixology class in Jasmine's gymnasium-size kitchen, during which they drank their weight in cocktails, Jasmine addressed the group. "I'm super excited that you're all going to be my bridesmaids, but I haven't picked a maid of honor. The truth is, I love all three of you, and I just couldn't choose one bestie over another. So we're going to play a little game."

"Really?" Iris asked.

"Yes, really," Jasmine responded. "Is there a problem?"

"No, it's just . . . I don't think any of us would be offended if you just picked someone."

Jasmine's face fell. "But I planned this whole game for you. Don't you want to play?"

"I think it's a great idea," Brittany said, raising her glass. "May the best bitch win."

Iris gulped down the rest of her strawberry martini, sturdying herself for whatever emotional bloodshed would ensue.

They returned to the room with the wood paneling and the *Real Housewives* marathon silently unfolding, and collapsed onto the huge couch. Iris decided not to try. She wasn't going to stoop to Jasmine's ploy for affection, and if this was how she was selecting her maid of honor, Iris didn't want to endure whatever indignities her sister was going to inflict on the winner.

Jasmine took out a deck of pink notecards from the entertainment center. "Here are the rules," she said. "It's like *Jeopardy*. I came up with ten questions about myself that my maid of honor needs to know out of the gate. I'll read a question and call on the first person to raise her hand. Whoever gets it right gets the card. The girl with the most cards wins."

"Do we have to answer in the form of a question?" Electra asked.

"Girl, what nonsense are you spewing?"

"The rules of *Jeopardy*."

"I just told you the rules," Jasmine said. "Do you need me to repeat them?"

"No, I got it," Electra said with a suppressed grin. Iris exchanged a knowing look with her.

Jasmine read the first question. "I went on a weeklong meditation retreat last summer that changed my life. What was the name of the retreat center?"

A meditation retreat sounded more mature than the Jasmine Iris knew. Brittany edged out Electra in raising her hand. "Kripalu," she answered.

"Correct!" Jasmine said, handing her the card. "Question two: What was the name of my douchebag boss at the Hilton?"

Electra raised her hand. "Gemini Treadwell."

"Don't you mean Hyatt?" Iris asked.

Everyone stared at her. "No, the Hilton," Jasmine said. "I worked at the Hilton after the Hyatt."

"Right, now I remember," Iris lied.

"It's an honest mistake," Electra said. "She went through jobs like Pringles. There's a reason she's self-employed."

"OK, settle down, you," Jasmine said, swatting at Electra with her notecards. "Question three: What object did Elsa swallow that sent her to the doggie emergency room?"

"A ribbon from a cake box," Brittany answered, when Jasmine called on her.

"Correct! Next question: As you all know, I am a total foodie. What is my favorite dish?"

Brittany raised her hand first. "The protein avocado toast from Dr. Smood. Extra spicy."

"You go, Brittany!" Jasmine said. "You've got this on lock."

Iris was disappointed that she couldn't have guessed any of these. Sure, they'd barely talked in years, but it seemed Jasmine had saved nothing from her old life. As recently as five years ago, Jasmine's favorite foods had been the Parmesan-crusted chicken pasta from The Cheesecake Factory and Reese's Pieces Blizzards from Dairy Queen. Anyone who didn't love junk food as much as she did was "wasting their lives." When had Jasmine become a wellness guru? When had she become obsessed with Instagram? And when had she traded in her friends? It wasn't hard to imagine Jasmine ending things with Jillian and her other college suitemates, as they had made a game of being cruel, but had she also parted ways with her BFF from high school, Emily? And Kaitlyn from the church youth group, and Nikki and Farah, her teammates at the marketing firm, and

Samantha, her training partner for high school track? People changed, and old friends drifted away, but . . . all of them?

Being shut out of this game solidified Iris's fear all along, that she and Jasmine had become sisters in name only. But didn't it matter that she was the one person here who knew, if not the "real" Jasmine, then the historical one? She resented being cast aside for these new arrivals, whose relevance might expire as soon as Jasmine switched out the dog booties for protein shakes or bath salts or kids with cancer.

Question five was "What breed is my dog?" Electra's hand went up first, and she said, "Poodle?" which was one-third right as the genetics went but completely bonkers if you actually looked at the pup. Brittany would know, but Iris didn't give her a chance to say it. She shot her hand into the air and answered, "Morkipoo."

"Nice work, sis," Jasmine said, sounding both surprised and impressed as she handed Iris the card. "Actually, we did a DNA test, and she has like two percent corgi and bichon frise in her. She comes from a long line of swingers."

Iris laughed, imagining Elsa at a key party for dogs.

"Question six," Jasmine said. "How many Instagram followers do I have?"

Iris raised her hand, and Jasmine pointed at her. "Nine thousand."

"Nine thousand, one hundred and fifty-eight, but close enough." As Jasmine said this, she tapped her phone screen with her thumb. "Nine thousand one hundred and sixty!"

Iris rode a vicious thrill: she could win this.

Electra won the seventh point, about Jasmine's favorite beauty product (something called Unicorn Snot), and the eighth, about the first guy who proposed to Jasmine, a widower named Tucker who owned four gas stations in Hudson County. How had Iris missed a marriage proposal?

Jasmine held up the last two notecards, one in each hand. "Last two questions, ladies. Brittany and Electra are neck and neck with three, and Iris has two."

"Yep," Iris muttered. She had to get both right.

"Testy, testy," Jasmine said. "Question nine: Where did David propose to me?"

Iris knew this—Jasmine had told her! But all the bridesmaids raised their hands. Without waiting for Jasmine to call on someone, Iris blurted out, "Buddakan."

"My hand was up first," said Brittany.

"You ordered lamb chops," Iris said, unable to account for her desperation. "He got down on one knee. The ring is a princess cut with a pavé band." It was a gamble, but Iris had no choice.

"I don't think she should get the point," said Brittany.

"You remember all that?" Jasmine asked, her voice wobbly. She squeezed Iris's hand. "I love you so much."

"The feeling's mutual, Jazzy," Iris said, employing her sister's childhood nickname with proprietary emphasis.

"Oh, this is exciting!" Jasmine gripped the final card in both hands and kissed it. "The person who answers this correctly truly knows me best and earns the right to call herself maid of honor. What is my favorite drink?"

Iris raised her hand before Jasmine finished speaking. If she let Brittany answer, all was lost.

"Yes, sister of mine?" Jasmine asked.

It was probably one of the cocktails they'd just made, right? The lemon drop? She tried to remember if Jasmine had finished any of them.

Electra nodded toward the bookshelf containing the Veuve Clicquot vase. "Champagne," Iris answered breathlessly.

Jasmine's eyes lit up. "That's it! You're right! OMG you're going to be my maid of honor! It's what I wanted from the beginning!"

Iris squeezed Jasmine, feeling triumphant. She had reclaimed her rightful place beside her sister.

Electra winked—Iris could have kissed her. Only then, as Iris studiously avoided meeting Brittany's glare, did she feel dread seeping into her stomach. Had she just made an enemy?

"I'm feeling all the feels," Jasmine said, nuzzling into Iris's neck.

"Right back atcha," said Iris.

# Chapter Five

**Eye Fay**

September 16, 2018, 9:03 P.M.

Hey bridesmaids (and groomsmen, bridesmen, groomsmaids, friendly rubberneckers, and everyone else in our union!),

There have been DEVELOPMENTS.

1.  My sister is getting married!
2.  I'm her maid of honor!

Item number two might not seem quite as unlikely if you knew our relationship. We've barely spoken in years.

The whole MOH thing went down in the strangest way. She lined up her bridesmaids and made us compete, game-show style, for the job. So it's not like she chose me—she sort of made me choose her. In fact, it seems like I barely made the cut as a bridesmaid. But then she said she'd wanted me to be her MOH from the beginning. My head is spinning.

We're meeting tomorrow to talk about her expectations. I hope I can live up to them. Either way, I'll be reporting from the front lines.

XOXO

The One Bridesmaid to Rule Them All

 29                                            10 comments

**Arden Woodbine**

Congratulations! Based on what you wrote, it sounds like your sister was testing you. She wanted you to want to be her maid of honor. It seems kind of cowardly on her part, but I think she is legitimately happy that you're doing it.
👍 1

**Anna Banana**

She sounds like a real piece of work.
👍 1

**Alex Oberlin**

Friendly rubbernecker here 🙈
Pleeeez send us a pic of the bridesmaid dress.
😭 1

**Eye Fay**

Abso-effing-lutely—as soon as she picks it!
👍 1

**Madison Le Claire**

Congratulations! I hope her wedding gives you the chance to iron out your differences.
👍 1

**Eye Fay**

I'm not sure that's what weddings are good for . . .
💬 3

**Anna Banana**

(Microwaving popcorn . . . )
👍 1

ᦔ

When Iris had told Christof on Thursday night that she'd have tea with him on Monday, she hadn't predicted how quickly Monday would come. Now she was having second thoughts. First of all, his seriousness was beginning to feel like a dealbreaker. A man nineteen years her senior *and* who didn't banter? Her parents had warned her against dating artists: the successful ones were usually on permanent power trips, and the rest were broke and looking to blame someone for their misery. But then she flipped through his photos again and let the date stand. Even if he wasn't marriage material, she could use a mindless fling. It had been months since she'd had sex—with a diversity trainer at a compliance conference in Minneapolis—and her body yearned for a man's touch.

She was still weighing the pros and cons as she approached the café, and then it was too late to change her mind, because there stood Christof with his hands deep in the pockets of his faded jeans. The photos had been spot-on re: his handsomeness. In addition to the jeans, he wore a bohemian linen shirt with a Nehru collar and pristine leather mandals. He had a sturdy, powerful presence.

"You're even more beautiful in person," he said after a quick, firm hug. She found his slight German accent sexy.

"You too," she said. "I mean, I'm sure women tell you that all the time."

"Not really, no." He sounded sincere, but how was that possible? He gestured toward the café. "Shall we?"

Inside, high-backed blond-wood chairs were pulled up to concrete tables, surrounding a tiny koi pond set into the gray stone floor. They chose the table closest to the pond; Iris enjoyed watching the scaly orange fish surface and submerge. The oversized menu listed hundreds of teas, divided into a dozen categories that Iris recognized but couldn't have described: sencha, matcha, oolong. She looked up from the menu to see Christof smiling at her, and she felt a warm buzz. She couldn't remember the last time she'd been admired by someone other than Jeremy McDonnell.

"I'll have coffee," she said with a forced laugh. "Just kidding."

"What kind of tea do you like?"

"Green?"

The server, an elderly white man dressed in traditional Japanese garb, tonged hot towels into their hands. Iris never knew whether it was gauche to wipe your face with the towel. Christof wiped his hands and placed his towel on the bamboo stand between them. Iris followed suit.

To Iris's surprise, Christof ordered in what must have been fluent Japanese. The server bowed and walked away.

"They have a delicate genmaicha here that I think you'll love," he said.

"You speak Japanese?"

"I have Japanese cousins—I lived with them in Osaka for a year after college."

"What other languages do you speak?"

"German, Italian, and French, though my French could be stronger." Five languages! Some people might have offered a discomfited smile at this admission. Christof seemed at ease with his excellence.

"That's amazing," she said.

He smiled. "Thank you. So what do you do?"

"I work in compliance for New York City General Hospital."

"Compliance?"

She sighed. "It's boring."

"No, tell me. I want to know."

She took a deep breath. "OK, so there are tons of regulations that apply to workplaces and hospitals in particular, and large organizations have compliance departments to make sure the company is following those laws, because the goal, of course, is to be fined and sued as little as possible. We have a policy review committee that meets quarterly to decide what policies we need and to approve the policies that my department— well, that I write. On paper, my job is to research the law and draft policies, but honestly . . ." She stopped herself. She didn't want to complain about Jeremy to Christof, especially not on their first date. She could hear her mother warning her to remain cheerful.

"But honestly what?" he asked.

"But honestly, most of what I do is admin support. Scheduling meetings and sending emails and epic print jobs that require a master's in collating. I became a paralegal because I care about justice—about the little guy not getting trampled by the system—and I feel like a cog in a bureaucratic machine."

"You're a middle child, aren't you," he observed, sending a lightning bolt down her spine.

"And you're a psychic?"

"Middle children are often shortchanged by their family, and this instills a quest for justice."

She considered this. "My parents' favoritism is insane."

In high school, Jasmine had complained for months that all of her friends were laughing at her because she didn't have a five-hundred-dollar Coach bag. Spike and Connie bought it for her birthday, though they had never spent nearly as much on Rose or Iris. A few months later, Jasmine's friends decided the Coach bag was lame, and now she needed a twelve-hundred-dollar Gucci bag if anyone was going to take her seriously. Instead of giving her the "it's what's inside that counts" lecture, they bought it for her sweet sixteen. Iris hated to obsess over price tags, but the bag had cost six times as much as her sweet sixteen present, an iPod mini. All of Jasmine's gifts dwarfed Iris's: a smartphone to Iris's flip phone, horseback riding camp to Iris's ballet lessons, and a posse of Polly Pockets when Iris was given one at a time. (For Rose's sweet sixteen, she had gotten a tour of five Christian colleges within driving distance, when she had explicitly stated that she wanted to study engineering in Florida.)

"Were you a middle child?" she asked.

"I was the younger of two. The youngest usually becomes the artist."

Of the three Hagarty sisters, Jasmine was definitely the most like an artist. A performance artist, maybe. "Tell me about your art." When she had googled him, not a single piece of his work appeared in the image results. Had she not seen his name listed among artists represented by a gallery in Milan, she would have assumed his dating profile was a lie. If you weren't on the internet, you didn't exist.

He tapped at his phone and handed it to her. "It's my gallery's secure website," he said. "I don't keep photos on my phone."

A black sticker covered both the front and back cameras. It was odd that a photographer wouldn't use the camera or store photos on his phone. She flipped through the images. He photographed naked and brooding women without a hint of self-consciousness, just like him. They were striking, more like Renaissance paintings than photographs. When she told him this, he smiled.

"Would you like to pose for me?" he asked.

These women were goddesses. Giving birth to Mason had loosened every flap and sinew of Iris's body. Also, the thought of Mason growing up and seeing her nude photos made her die a little. And if her naked body was strewn across the internet . . . !

"Maybe with my clothes on?" she suggested. "Or from the neck up? Or my hands? I like my hands."

He leaned closer as if to tell her a secret, and every cell in her body responded to his gravity. "I only photograph nudes. But you will be happy with the results. When we create your portrait, you will see yourself as I see you."

She wasn't used to men being so earnest; it gave her the willies. But she believed he found her attractive; she believed he would make her look good. "I need to think about it some more," she said, "but it's very kind of you to offer."

The server returned with a stone teapot and two small cups, and a tray of perfect cookies in a rainbow of colors. Iris hadn't eaten lunch; she wished she'd asked him to order her a sandwich.

Christof poured a cup for her, then him, and inhaled the aroma. It was green tea, mild and sort of savory. She usually added a Splenda to every-thing but liked this better unsweetened. "This is really good," she said.

"The tea is mixed with toasted rice. It makes it a little nutty."

"Yeah, nutty. I like it." She selected a green shortbread cookie; it was buttery and not too sweet, with the pleasant fishy flavor of green tea. "Why do you have stickers on your cameras?"

"Because I'm not the only person who can turn them on."

"Really?"

"Have you ever read the terms of use and privacy policies that you have to accept every time you update your apps or your operating system?" he asked, flicking his wrist as if shooing a fly.

"Sometimes." Occasionally she'd run across a clause that gave her an idea for her work, but she rarely had the patience for more than a skim.

"I read them," he said. "And I can tell you, if any of these companies or the government wanted to turn your camera on and record you, they would."

"I heard that they don't hold up in court, because it's assumed that nobody reads them." Or was it the opposite? Like so much of what she read on the internet, she remembered the article but not the takeaway. Anyway, there were laws protecting people's privacy. If a company was found to be recording people without their consent, the fines and lawsuits would be staggering. "Are you really doing things that you wouldn't want other people to see?"

"Taken out of context, any action could look incriminating."

He seemed paranoid. Not for covering up his cameras—even Jeremy had a sliding plastic cover on his webcam—but for believing that he could be a target of some evil regime.

"We're constantly being asked to agree to things like their turning on our microphones and cameras without our knowledge," he said. "We think we don't have a choice, but we do. We can always say no. Our phones aren't life. Our apps aren't life."

"Amen," she said. She didn't like being schooled by his lessons. She had to learn to push back—with everyone but especially men. But mirroring men was the best way to get them to like her. Most men wanted their girlfriends to hang on their every word, to learn from them and be amazed by their intelligence.

"I need to get back to work in a minute," she said. It wasn't really true: her to-do list was overwhelming, as usual, but Jeremy was at the beach, and Barbara was at her desk in case anyone walked in. She'd forwarded her office extension to her cell, though in 2018, if you called instead of emailed when something wasn't urgent, you were basically a monster.

He studied her. "You think I'm crazy."

"I think . . ." Letting herself be caressed by his gaze, her thoughts scattered. An eternity passed before she said, "I think you don't trust the system."

"You're right, I don't. My sister tells me I am too cautious."

"Or maybe I'm too trusting," she said.

"Perhaps we can learn from each other." He took her hands in his; the unexpected intimacy made her breath catch with anticipation. The strangeness between them had passed.

Christof asked her about her family, and she told him about Rose's inscrutable life in Florida and Jasmine's wedding. She mentioned the

Bridesmaids Union, too. He asked to read her writing, but she demurred. He'd think wedding drama was frivolous.

She didn't tell him about Mason. Her dating profile didn't include mention of a son: she didn't want a record of him online until he was older. Maybe she didn't trust the system, either. She usually told guys about Mason if the first date went well, but she didn't see this going past sex—and maybe some photos.

He paid the bill plus a ten-dollar tip and thanked the server, again in Japanese. As a rule she preferred to split the check, but she was glad he'd paid. Her life was filled with people who needed something from her. Christof seemed to enjoy letting her receive.

She faced him on the sidewalk, expectantly.

"I hope I'll see you again," he said, touching her forearm. A sensuous heat curled in her belly.

"I'd like that."

He leaned toward her, and she accepted a kiss. His lips were softer than she had expected. Neither of them was in a hurry to let go.

# Chapter Six

**Electra Collins**

September 17, 2018, 10:08 A.M.

Hi folks, Electra here, Eye Fay's friend and co-bridesmaid for J's wedding. (Hi Eye Fay! So great meeting you, and thanks for inviting me to this amazing Facebook party!)

J and I were former roommates. We met through Craigslist (in those five minutes before Craigslist became dubious) and connected instantly. I've been honored to be a bridesmaid twice before, for my stepsister and my dearest friend from high school. Neither occasion was traumatic. My best friend's wedding did exceed my budget (it took place in Hawaii), but I completely and totally understood.

I find J highly amusing, and when she's mean to people, she's so oblivious about it, it doesn't ruffle my feathers. Take the maid of honor drama. She arranged a competition among her friends to see who was the most knowledgeable about her. Extremely self-centered, right? And kind of nasty, when you think about it. I just think she's so insecure about people liking her that she makes everyone prove it to her, again and again.

XX

Electra

👍 8                                                    3 comments

**Eye Fay**
Thanks for posting! Great to have a different point of view on my
beauteous sis.
💬 1
**Electra Collins**
😋
💬 1
**Jaclyn Arias**
Welcome to the group!

---

Iris had been camping out for fifteen minutes at an artisanal coffeehouse
near Penn Station, attempting not to finish the most delicious chocolate-
chip cookie of her adult life by taking smaller and smaller bites, when
Jasmine appeared at the door in baggy overalls with extravagant tears up
and down the legs, chunky silver heels, oversized sunglasses, and a shiny
windbreaker embroidered, in cursive, with the words "Thirst Trap." She
carried a small silver duffel under her arm.

"So sorry I'm late," Jasmine said, pushing her sunglasses to the top of
her head and hugging Iris with one arm. "I tried like thirty parking garages
before I found one with space for an SUV." She dragged an extra chair
to their table as a pedestal for her bag, which, to be fair, probably had a
higher net worth than Iris. Jasmine unzipped it and, to Iris's surprise, Elsa's
head popped up.

"I don't think you're supposed to have dogs in here," Iris said.

"She's my emotional support animal—I have all the paperwork and
everything." Jasmine scratched behind Elsa's ears.

"I thought only service dogs were allowed in restaurants."

Jasmine rolled her eyes. "Live a little, Iris. You can't follow every dumb
rule in this world."

In truth, Elsa didn't seem like a public health risk. She had nestled back down in the duffel, invisible to onlookers. Still, Iris was annoyed that her sister could break the law without consequence.

"Can I get you something?" Jasmine asked. "Their ginger turmeric coconut lattes are basically liquid crack, and they're so, so beneficial for your digestion and immunity."

"Um, sure, that sounds nice."

The lattes were eight dollars each, but the smitten barista gave them to Jasmine for free. The flavor was pleasant, if a little spicy for Iris's taste.

"This cookie is delicious," Iris said, gesturing to the glorified crumb marooned on the waxed paper bag. "Do you want to try it?"

"That is so nice of you, but I'm trying to lose a few pounds for the wedding," Jasmine said. "I blame it on David—as soon as I fell in love, I ballooned. I have literal rolls of fat."

Iris did not see how her sister could lose even one pound without amputating a breast or a leg. If anyone might benefit from shedding for the wedding, it was Iris, who had long been trying to accept her size-eight figure, despite the barrage of unsolicited diet tips from Connie Hagarty, a permanent size two. "You look great already. I probably shouldn't be eating this cookie."

"Sigh," Jasmine said with a sigh. "Sugar is such a drug. They should make it illegal."

Iris popped the remainder of her cookie into her mouth to get rid of the evidence. "So how are you? We didn't get a chance to talk at the party." Once Iris was awarded maid of honor, Electra offered her a ride to the New Jersey Transit station, and Jasmine had to do social media upkeep, so Iris accepted. She spent the short ride thanking Electra for handing her the maid-of-honor crown. That's when it came out that Electra wasn't the biggest fan of Brittany, either. Iris sent her an invite to the Bridesmaids Union that night. It violated her policy of not inviting anyone she knew, but Electra promised to keep it a secret.

"I'm in such a good place," Jasmine said with a dreamy smile. "It's like I've reached this moment in my life when literally everything is going exactly as I want. Do you vision?"

Was "vision" a verb? "Should I?"

"You write down how you see yourself in five years, like down to the color of your future husband's eyes," Jasmine said. "When I met David, I literally laughed, because he was exactly how I described him in my vision statement."

It was remarkable that Jasmine hadn't visioned a Hemsworth brother. "He's so . . . different from your past boyfriends," was the closest Iris could come to saying this.

"Yeah," Jasmine said, dragging out the syllable with luxuriant vocal fry. "Most of the guys I dated, it was so much about the instant physical attraction that I never paid attention to whether I was in love. And you know what else? I never liked the way my other boyfriends smelled—my nose is so sensitive, it's a total handicap. David smells like home."

"I can't wait to smell him."

Jasmine laughed. "He's so excited to meet you. I've shown him pictures, and he thinks you're super adorbs. Like, I would have been nervous if I weren't so sure of his love for me."

"I will be sure not to steal him," Iris said.

Jasmine pointed a finger menacingly. "If you do, I'll kill you."

Iris laughed, though she wasn't sure it was a joke. "It's really good to be here with you. I was worried that we might never be close again."

"Wait—why?"

"Because, you know, the election."

"What are you discussing, girl? Water under the bridge."

Iris was relieved for the détente, but had Jasmine noticed her silence? She was still appalled at her sister's decision to abstain. It would have been easier to forgive Jasmine if she wanted to be forgiven. But confronting her would only divide them further. Maybe Iris could let it go. "OK, water under the bridge," Iris repeated. "I can't wait to be your maid of honor."

"Me. Too. This could not have worked out better."

Iris was tempted to ask why Jasmine had invited her so last-minute if she'd wanted her to be maid of honor from the beginning, but it seemed ungrateful. "So it's just Electra, Brittany, and I? Is Rose going to be a bridesmaid?"

"Mom and Dad are *making* her do it," Jasmine groaned. "I don't want negative energy in my wedding party, but whatever."

"It'll be nice for us both to be supporting you," Iris said.

"I don't think she knows what support is."

That wasn't fair, but it wasn't completely untrue. Rose permitted no drama in her life or her conversations, which made it impossible to extract sympathy from her. "What would be your perfect bridal shower?"

Jasmine's chest emitted a squawk, and she pulled her phone from her bra. Elsa went on high alert. "Sorry, one sec."

Iris sipped her coconut latte, feeling erased.

Jasmine returned the phone to her bra. "I've been taking some risks on Instagram to boost conversion, because engagement wasn't translating to paw wear sales," she explained, "so I need to be monitoring my ad buys super closely right now."

Iris was impressed, despite her irritation. "Where did you learn all that stuff?"

Jasmine tossed her fingers into the air. "Oh, you know, here and there. I soak up a lot of passive mentorship. Anyway, where were we?"

"Your bridal shower. What if I hosted everyone at my apartment? I could make quiche and bellinis."

"That's really sweet." Jasmine smiled apologetically.

"You hate that idea," Iris said.

"No, no, it's just, I don't want you to go to all that trouble. Maybe we could just do it at a restaurant or something. Thanks to David, I'm entering this beautiful phase of my life that's all about simplicity. I'm realizing that I've always complicated things, and that was a choice I didn't know I was making."

An alarm went off inside Iris. Jasmine had never been easygoing. But maybe she really had changed.

"OK, so for the bachelorette party, do you have a destination in mind?" Iris asked.

"You know what would be fun?" Jasmine leaned in close. "What if you didn't tell me a single thing about it, and then just, like, kidnapped me that morning and took me to the airport?"

"Sure, totally," Iris said, thinking that was a terrible idea. "But are you OK with something within driving distance?"

Jasmine's phone alert sounded again, and she looked at her screen. "Sorry, I get like a hundred requests a day for photo collabs—it's like swatting away flies. Every dude with a camera wants to take pictures of me, and it's like, OK, settle down now."

As Jasmine rejected her latest suitor, Iris decided she would pose for Christof. This opportunity wasn't going to come around again.

Jasmine looked up. "So sorry. Now I'm all yours, for real. Where were we? The bachelorette party? I trust your taste completely."

"Tell me more about your wedding," Iris said, shifting her tack. "I can incorporate some details into the parties."

Jasmine held her hand to her heart. "It's going to be this very rustic, very DIY feeling. Burlap tablecloths, mason jars with punch and whiskey, and those old-school hang tags for the table cards. Dinner is going to be family-style. The string quartet is this adorable group of Princeton students with this down-home kinda vibe. It'll be like barefoot elegance, but, like, with shoes on."

"That sounds beautiful. I guess I thought David would want, you know, something more elaborate."

"David?" She pulled a face. "He lives like a total pauper. If it were up to him, we'd do potluck in our backyard with, like, box wine. Did you know he drives a 2009 Honda Civic? It literally pains him to spend money on himself."

So the Range Rover must have been Jasmine's. And that nine-million-dollar house probably wasn't David's choice. Exhibit A: Jasmine had always wanted to move to Alpine. But who could blame her? She was living the American dream.

"Have you decided on wedding colors?" Iris asked.

"Yeah, pink and white, just like Mom and Dad's."

"So the bridesmaid dresses are going to be . . ."

"Well, they're not going to be white."

Iris hated pink. Every shade of it, from dusty rose to extra-strength Pepto-Bismol, made her face look splotchy. Redheaded Brittany was going to look like a neon sign. At least Mason looked good in everything. "Mason has a pink clip-on tie—it's really cute."

At the mention of Iris's son, Jasmine's eyes snapped into focus. "I'm so sorry, I must have forgotten to tell you. The wedding is adults only."

"I thought you might want him as a ring bearer or something?" She hadn't realized her sentence would be a question until she reached the end and saw Jasmine shaking her head. Her sister wasn't going to make an exception for her only nephew? The threat of tears took Iris by surprise.

"You know I love Mason, and I totally wish he could come, but if he's invited, then it's going to be hard to say no to all the other parents, and we're trying to keep it under a hundred guests." She squinched up her face as if expecting Iris to strike her. "Do you hate me? Am I the absolute worst?"

"Of course not," Iris said. It seemed cruel not to invite your nephew to your wedding, but it was Jasmine's day, and Iris didn't want to start a fight. She'd box up her disappointment and focus on helping her sister be the happiest bride possible.

Jasmine clasped Iris's hands across the table. "You are too good to me. I don't deserve you."

# Chapter Seven

**Kyle Kyle**

September 19, 2018, 10:17 A.M.

Hey girlfriends! Thank you soooo much for letting me join your group. I'm going through a literal shitstorm and I needed to dish.

Bear with me, because this is kind of epic. A couple years ago, I met this guy Baxter, a smoking-hot personal trainer, on Grindr. Usually with Grindr hookups, you pretend you're going to be a regular thing, and then it's ghost city, but we had such a good connection, we actually met up again. And again. And again. Ladies, you have no idea how rare this is. He was like my hookup soul mate.

So we had this perfect thing going: once or twice a week, we'd hang out, watch a dumb show, get our needs taken care of, and go on our merry way. The few times we went out clubbing, we always ended the night in bed together. Our chemistry was that good. Every so often we'd do a feelings check, and it was always like, nope, not interested in a relationship, just loving this no-strings sitch.

After like ten months of this, he goes out of town for two weeks to do some short-term personal training for a famous actor I can't name (but who is like AAA list), who needs to bulk up for a role. And I'm lying in bed, missing Baxter and smiling like a doofus. And I'm like, "Duh, Kyle, you're in love with him."

The next time we get together, I test the waters, like, "Is this friends-with-benefits thing still working for us? Or do you think we should try upgrading?" And he's like, "We have fun. The sex is great. We love going out together. Let's not ruin it with relationship drama." So I held my tongue. We did have a great friendship and great sex. What did it matter what we called it?

Fast-forward to last Sunday, more than three years since we met. We're smoking weed after some pornstar-level banging, and he's like, "I've got big news. I'm getting married."

I'm like, "I didn't realize you were seeing anyone."

And he's like, "I thought you didn't want to know about my life. I thought that's what kept your dick hard."

It's all I can do not to tell him I love him right then and there. He met this finance bro, Frederick, on OkCupid, and they fell in love.

And here's the best part—Baxter said we had to stop sleeping together. Apparently, he and Frederick are going to be monogamous. All I can say is, good luck with that.

Then Baxter's like, "I want you to be one of my groomsmen." And I laugh, because our friendship has nothing to do with all the other people he's friends with. We're in this special bubble, un-touchable by the rest of the world—so when I show up at the bach-elor party or whatever, people are going to be like, who the hell are you?

And he's like, "You're my best friend. I love you. I'm just not in love with you."

Dagger in my heart.

Well, ladies, I said yes. What was my other option? To never see him again? This guy who I am head over heels in love with and who I thought was in love with me?

I know Baxter's making a mistake, picking this rando just because they met on a "legit" dating site instead of a hookup app. I mean, how long have they known each other? A few months? A year? Love like ours comes along once in a lifetime. I just can't believe he would throw it away.

 58                                    14 comments

**Jaclyn Arias**

Your story breaks my heart! Stay strong, Kyle Kyle.
○ 1

**Evelyn Huang**

Not sure if you want advice, but I think you should tell Baxter these things. Maybe it's too late, but if it's not, you'll be kicking yourself if you don't at least try.
○ 2

**Eye Fay**

My heart goes out to you, Kyle Kyle! I agree—tell him how you feel! If he's smart, he'll choose you.
○ 1

**Kyle Kyle**

♥
○ 1

"Can I take tomorrow afternoon off?" Iris asked Jeremy in their morning one-on-one inside his office. "I need to scout locations for my sister's bridal shower. These places get booked way in advance."

He winced. "I would love to say yes, you know that, right? But I'm going hiking that day." Iris's time off wasn't allowed to overlap with Jeremy's— though she couldn't imagine anyone needing their response urgently. "You know how it is. I lost twelve vacation days from the time bank rollover. I need to practice using my vacation days all year, not just during the summer." Jeremy and Barbara received eight weeks of vacation per year. The administration had since curbed this absurd bounty, and Iris, brought on in 2016, received three weeks. It was more than her friends got, but still.

"Can I take Friday afternoon, then?" she asked.

"Sorry, skin cancer screening." He might not have to worry as much about skin cancer if he hadn't spent all summer roasting on the beach. She breathed deeply and tucked away her frustration.

He opened a plastic container of hard-boiled eggs and ate one, squeezing his eyes shut as he swallowed. Sulfur perfumed the air. He cracked a Red Bull and gulped it to get the yolk down. "Can I ask you something? I need a woman's perspective."

Iris hoped her wince made it clear that he could not. She was too tired to deal with his flirting.

"Do you think it's fair to demand that your husband get a vasectomy?"

"Oh," Iris said, trying to project professional disinterest.

"She's been getting some nasty side effects from the pill, so she threw the ball in my court. It's just so emasculating, and what if we want children down the road?"

"I'm sure you'll work it out with her," Iris said with a discomfited smile. She flipped open her notebook, praying he'd take the hint.

He performed a mischievous squint. "You're funny, do you know that?"

"Literally no one tells me that except you."

"Well, you are. And you know what I was thinking just this morning? That in this soul-sucking hellhole of a hospital, the one thing that makes me excited to go to work is seeing you."

Iris couldn't ignore his heartfelt confession—assuming Jeremy was capable of heartfelt anything—but she didn't want to encourage him. She wished she could have one conversation with him that wasn't on a tightrope, because although he had no filter, he was fragile, and if she insulted him, she didn't doubt that he would fire her. "That's very kind," she said with a weak smile.

Irony of ironies, that week's to-do list included revising the sexual harassment policy, which, as Jeremy liked to say, "is the unsexiest writing about sex you'll ever read." Thanks to the Me Too movement, both the state and city had passed new laws requiring annual workplace trainings for all employees, and the hospital was implementing a zero-tolerance approach. Iris doubted this would lead to mass firings of sleazeballs and leches, much less a toning down of Jeremy's horndog banter, known in compliance jargon as a "hostile work environment." All those trainings did was teach people like Jeremy how much they could flirt without getting in trouble.

She finished her redeye—a coffee spiked with espresso—and felt just as bleary and dizzy as she had pre-caffeine. The night before, Mason had refused to go to bed. She ordered him to stop playing Minecraft at 9:00 P.M., and when she took the iPad, he screamed. At first this infuriated Iris. Then, once his brain-piercing shriek forced her mind from her body, leaving her with a cold, dead objectivity, his vocal power began to impress her. He flamed out twenty minutes later but stayed up another half hour crying from the kind of bone-deep grief that children aren't supposed to know, and she held him until consciousness released him into a whimpering sleep. This had been his worst tantrum yet. It felt as if all the quiet time his iPad gave her was ripped from her at bedtime. And then he was bouncing on her bed at 5:00 A.M., ready for breakfast.

She visited Barbara's cubicle, updating her on Jeremy's latest comments under her breath while keeping an eye on his office door. "I should report him, right?" Iris said.

Barbara sighed. "There will be an investigation. It will last until everyone has forgotten there's an investigation, but he will never forget," Barbara said. "If they give him a slap on the wrist, he will make your life hell until you quit. If they fire him, I guarantee whoever replaces him is going to be worse. They'll probably give it to Hitler over there"—she nodded at Chase's office—"and then we'll all have to pledge allegiance to the Republican Party."

"I don't have the bandwidth to look for a job right now," Iris said. Maybe it was her exhaustion talking, but the thought of sending out résumés made her want to cry.

"Can you ignore him? So he says some disgusting things. He's a man. I've worked with much worse than him. My first boss used to brush by me in the hallway. When I asked him to stop, he told me to take it as a compliment."

"It just doesn't seem fair that I have to keep my mouth shut when he's in the wrong. I mean, what's the Me Too movement for if not this?"

"How charmingly naïve," Barbara said. "Maybe you should stop encouraging him."

"What are you talking about?"

"I see you with him, giggling and smiling and making little jokes—"

"Because I'm squirming."

"From here it looks like flirting. Just saying."

It sounded like a classic game of Blame the Victim. She was surprised and a little hurt that Barbara played it, too.

So maybe it was out of resentment that, instead of working on documents that Jeremy probably wouldn't read for a month or three, Iris researched potential venues for Jasmine's bridal shower online. On a wedding website, she searched for Manhattan party rooms that held about twenty, and came up with a surprising number of contenders. She called one that looked nice—a rooftop in Midtown—and was flabbergasted to learn that it would cost three hundred dollars per person. A loft in the Meatpacking District started at one eighty per person. The bridal showers she'd planned before, in Miami and Virginia Beach, could not have prepared her for these prices.

Because of her search, she was getting banner ads for something called Gourmet Restaurant Group, with a photo of four women toasting with Champagne. She clicked on the ad and was taken to a breakdown of the event capacities of eight restaurants in the tristate area. One was the Morning Glory Bakery Café, an upscale brunch spot on the Upper West Side that served the best muffins in America, according to the Travel Channel. She called the number on the page and reached an events manager who laid out the pricing tiers, starting at seventy dollars per person, which included two hours of mimosas. If they could do without lobster salad and hard liquor, the price wouldn't go up. Iris picked a weekend in February after the events manager reassured her that the date could be changed. To pay the five-hundred-dollar deposit, she recited the numbers of her credit card from memory, finding it amusing, not for the first time, that she knew her credit card number by heart but didn't know a single phone number besides her own.

With the same pained, apologetic tone that Jeremy had just used, the events manager informed her that her credit card had been declined. Seized with dread, Iris told her she'd sort it out and call right back.

She logged into her credit card account and scanned her balance activity. She recognized all the charges, and none exceeded two hundred dollars, except for the fourteen hundred for the hotel in Cabo San Lucas for Sophia's bachelorette party. There was a pre-rehearsal dinner for Sophia's bridesmaids and a hair appointment before the wedding, cat food and litter, groceries and wine, an unplanned excursion to Payless when her heel snapped in a subway grate, a present for Rafael's birthday, and of course, cell phone, internet, and electricity payments. She'd managed to avoid going out for lunch by cooking at home, which had resulted in massive grocery bills. And she'd bought a bajillion lattes, because without a steady caffeine drip, she couldn't have survived each interminable day in the basement of City General. Somehow, the pages and pages of purchases added up to four thousand dollars, which was all her existing balance, insatiable with interest, would permit.

Her checking account balance was pitiful, and her next paycheck wasn't due for four more days. How did anyone in New York make ends meet?

In the past, when she'd hit her credit card limit, she'd called the company to ask them to increase it, then doubled down on her scrimping lifestyle— until the next wedding came along. With Jasmine's on the horizon, though, she couldn't fool herself into thinking she'd pay this off. She could open a new card and toss this one in a drawer, but it would haunt her like Rochester's demented wife in *Jane Eyre*, waiting to burn the whole place down.

Online, the advice from actual finance experts (as opposed to the self-promoting bozos on Quora or Yahoo Answers) was to transfer all her balances to a new card with a higher limit and a 0 percent introductory APR, then work with that company to pay off the debt. She filled out an online application for a card that came recommended. After entering her information into the forms, she was directed to call the customer service number to complete the transfer. With the same irritating note of apology Iris had heard twice that morning, the Midwestern rep informed her that her credit wasn't good enough to qualify for the offer. Why did the best deals go to people who didn't need them?

The agent looked up other offers and came back on the line to announce, with a veneer of fake joy, that Iris qualified for a ten-thousand-dollar limit with a 22 percent APR, worse than her current card. Iris begged her to look again. While the woman waited for her supervisor, who was finishing up on a different call, Iris was placed on indefinite hold.

She couldn't concentrate on the sexual harassment policy while awaiting her financial fate. She cleared her mind by checking Facebook, a site she visited so often that merely typing an "f" into the URL bar was enough for the autofill to take over. Her feed populated with the usual potpourri: a couple buying a house in Maplewood, the deadliest wildfire in California history, a dire economic prediction regarding Trump's fiscal policy, a friend's baby turning one, and a vegan influencer's kale power bowl. One friend put her cat down; another got a new puppy. And apparently, flossing could prevent dementia. Visiting Facebook was like opening the fridge: if she'd had a reason for logging on, the bewildering array of random updates made her forget it. But where else could she learn so much so fast about what her friends and distant acquaintances did and thought and cared about? Without it, she would have lost touch with everyone.

In the Bridesmaids Union, a guy named Kyle who had emailed a membership request the night before introduced himself in a humdinger of a post. She read through the supportive comments and posted her hope that Baxter return to him. Then she reconsidered. Maybe Frederick really was better for Baxter. Maybe Kyle, like Forrest, was terrified of intimacy and didn't realize it. She considered editing the comment, but a green dot told her that Kyle was online, and she didn't want to hurt his feelings by cutting out the nicest part. A few seconds later, a heart appeared next to her comment: Kyle had "loved" it. Then he replied to her comment with a heart emoji. It would be overkill for her to "love" his heart, but after a moment of inexplicable panic, she did it anyway.

She clicked through to Kyle's profile, which contained a few pictures of an attractive Asian man and not much else. When she'd accepted him into the group, his eighteen friends had been an asset, as it meant he didn't know anyone she knew, but now it seemed suspect. A reverse image search of his profile pic matched with a photo of a K-pop star.

He wasn't a bot, as his Bridesmaids Union post couldn't have been written by an algorithm, but his fake profile unsettled her.

She wrote him on Messenger:

> Thanks for joining the BMU!
>
> That's industry for Bridesmaids Union

Thanks 4 letting me in!

I love ur stories

Those brides b so cray!

His tone was more enthusiastic than she'd expected.

> Thanks!!! You seem to be in a real predicament! So you're going to confront Baxter?

She cringed at all the exclamation points, but without them, she'd seem stern, even psychotic. A period in a text message could be a mic drop.

LOL, this weekend

Iris wasn't sure how his situation called for a "laugh out loud," but maybe he was trying to be a good sport.

> All you can do is tell him how you feel

> Hey, random question, but are you
> new to FB? I noticed you haven't
> posted much.

I have another account—Kyle Style

Don't tell—I'm on the DL LOL

Kyle's link brought her to a business page with thirty thousand followers. The posts featured an even more attractive Asian man, a cross between the waifish angularity of a model and the musclebound grit of a gym nut. A few posts linked to articles about him. One article described Kyle Style as a "wardrobe stylist-cum-influencer extraordinaire."

> This is you???

Yup

Gotta keep my dirty laundry out of the public
eye LOL

As proof, he sent a five-second video of him saying, "Hi Eye Fay! It's your new friend Kyle Style."

> Your secret is safe with me.

She followed a link on Kyle's Facebook page to his Instagram and was seized by euphoric alarm: he had 1.1 million followers.

In each photo, Kyle wore a different ensemble, each piece of clothing tagged with the name of a designer or department store. She didn't have to follow the links to know that some of these outfits cost in the thousands. The most recent photos were geolocated to New York's Meatpacking District, one taken in a doorway, one on the cobblestoned street, one in front of a gleaming luxury car, and one with Kyle's artisanally shod foot perched atop a Siamese standpipe. A ways down the page was a long series set in the Maldives. In these lushly backgrounded shots, he wore crisp linen shirts, unbuttoned to reveal his clawlike abs, or no shirt at all. His Speedos and square-cut briefs left bare his smooth, meaty thighs.

She glanced behind her to make sure Jeremy wasn't watching. His office was empty.

Clothed Kyle bought spices in a crowded market, riotous with pattern and color; swimsuited Kyle lounged in a thatched-roof villa hovering above an ocean so beautiful it was painful not to be able to dip her feet in. It was also painful to gaze upon his tan, sculpted body and smoldering eyes. Even if he wasn't attracted to women at all, it didn't diminish her yearning.

A recorded male voice interrupted the twangy hold music for the fourth time to reassure her that her call was important to them and request that she continue to hold.

Iris kept scrolling, drugged by a fascination she couldn't explain. Part of it was her connection to Kyle: this minor celebrity had joined her tiny Facebook group, so although they weren't friends, even by the watered-down social media definition, he mattered to her. Knowing about his relationship drama made her curious about his life, and every new row of photos held the possibility of revealing more.

Or maybe what kept her scrolling was simply that he was beautiful.

Finally, she found what she hadn't realized she was looking for: a photo of his lover, alliteratively captioned, "Beside Baxter, my best bud, before a benefit." They stood in tuxedos on one of the rehabbed Hudson piers. According to the photo tags, Kyle wore Armani, and Baxter was in Zegna. Kyle was possibly Filipino and Baxter, Thai?—Iris wouldn't have bet money on either guess. Baxter had dark, piercing eyes, pronounced cheekbones, and a sprinkling of mustache. Beneath the zillion-dollar tux, his body was probably just as chiseled as Kyle's.

Her next goal was to see Baxter's fiancé, Frederick—and, if she was lucky, a shirtless Baxter to solve the incidental mystery of his body; she just had to find Baxter's Facebook or Instagram page. Easier said than done. Kyle Style's Facebook profile was mostly private, so she couldn't search his friends to find Baxter. And every Google search she could think of—"KyleStyle Baxter," "Baxter personal trainer NYC," or "Baxter Frederick wedding," for example—led nowhere. He didn't pop up when she searched Facebook for profiles that included "Baxter," either.

According to her computer clock, she had been on hold for twenty-eight minutes. The plodding, three-chord hold music would be stuck in her head for days. She probably should have hung up, but where did that leave her? Still without a way to pay the deposit for Jasmine's shower—and if this company rejected her, others would, too.

She wrote to Kyle again.

> How does one become an influencer?

Good question—no idea! LOL

> I guess it helps that you look like a model

🖤 I like u! LOL

Anyone else tossing off LOLs as a conversational twitch would have come off as ridiculous. But Kyle seemed lighthearted and funny.

> The feeling's mutual!

What do u do?

> I'm an assistant compliance officer

> Which sounds as thrilling as it is.

ur funny

> And now I've been on hold for half an hour with the credit card company.

Evil fckrs. What's going on?

My card is maxed out

Too many bachelorette parties. 😈

She wondered if he could relate to such a plebeian problem as debt—until he admitted that he was in debt, too.

You have credit card debt???

She immediately felt guilty about the extra question marks.

I mean, I assumed you were
fabulously wealthy.

I shop when I'm sad

I'm sad a lot, LOL

She wrote, I'm sorry to hear that, then deleted it.

We are THE SAME.

Though she imagined that the things she bought to lift her spirits—a bottle of nail polish, a gel pen, a latte—were cheaper than his. It was strange to see a smudge in Kyle's sheen so quickly after meeting him; it made her like him more. She now understood that his "LOL" did not signify humor but rather embarrassment.

The credit cards will screw u if u let them

They screw small businesses and they
screw the American people, all to make their
investors rich

Don't be ashamed to demand a 0% APR

Apparently, her credit card woes had triggered a different side of him, one that his 1.1 million followers weren't shown.

> I asked for it, and they told me they could give me 22 percent, and I was like, kill me first.

What bank?

> MasterCard

That's not a bank, girlfriend

What bank is issuing the card?

It should say in the fine print

She found the name of the bank and told him.

R u on Twitter?

To Iris, Twitter seemed pointless, an echo chamber that inspired countless news stories about this or that celebrity's one-sentence opinion, which was never as eloquent or inflammatory as the world pretended. She gave him her Twitter handle, first confirming that her real name wasn't in her profile. She was embarrassed that her last tweet was a murky shot of her birthday cake in 2016.

The man's voice again interrupted the hold music to remind her that her call was important to them. Now that she had a moment to collect herself and shake off the enchantment of chatting with an internet celebrity, she realized that she had just given Kyle a lot of personal information. Not a password or her Social Security number, but he knew her Twitter handle, what credit card she was applying for, and her job title—which meant he could probably find her name.

**What are you doing?**

He didn't respond.

**What do you think I should do
about the credit card?**

Again, no response. Now she was scared. She hung up the phone and closed her browser window, shut off the monitor just to be safe. The office was silent except for the hum of a purpling fluorescent. She refilled her bottle at the water cooler, trying to shake the feeling that she'd put herself in danger. She'd recently written a policy about information security; had she been taken in by a phishing scheme? She'd been candid with him but hadn't given him the tools to steal from her. Still, she felt violated.

**Please respond.**

The concrete walls seemed to be closing in on her. She needed air. She hurried down the narrow hallway; she could almost feel radiation spewing through the door to the cyclotron. Struggling to breathe, she bounded up the stairs and burst out the door to the sidewalk, where half a dozen nurses were complaining in a cloud of cigarette smoke. She jogged to the corner and gasped for breath. An ambulance wailed past. She tried to think.

Her cell phone buzzed, alerting her to another Facebook message from Kyle. It looked like a link to a Twitter thread. Then:

**All fixed**

Her information security policy had said never to click on a link from a person you don't trust. Instead, Iris opened her neglected Twitter app and saw that Kyle had tagged her in a tweet thread. He'd called out the bank for cheating her out of the promised rate and then keeping her on hold "for hours." He pushed for a boycott of the bank—which seemed extreme, but a dozen of Kyle's followers had already retweeted him, adding their own complaints and expletives. At the end of the thread, to Iris's astonishment, the bank apologized. They offered her a 0 percent rate on her entire balance for two years and five thousand dollars of credit on top of that. On the phone, she'd been told that her credit history prevented her from getting a decent offer, and that no exceptions could be made. But here was the bank, breaking its rule in an extravagant way because someone important had shamed them. In those two years, she could pay off a significant portion of the balance, instead of spending every extra penny on interest. As she walked back to her office, she found herself giggling—she'd never had such a powerful friend!

After direct-messaging her email address to the bank executive who had made her the offer, she opened up Facebook on her computer once more and wrote to Kyle.

> You're an angel—you saved me!

She sent him a friend request, hoping it wasn't presumptuous.

A minute passed without a response. He must have moved on to his next heroic feat. She attacked the sexual harassment policy with new focus.

Kyle accepted her friend request.

> That's what friends are for

She replied with a heart emoji, then, worrying that one wasn't enough to express her gratitude, fired off five more.

# Chapter Eight

**Eye Fay**

September 22, 2018, 7:15 A.M.

Good morning, friends! Today is my sister's engagement party. I get to meet her fiancé! Of course I googled him into a pulp, so I'll try not to let on that I know more about him than his mother does.

Speaking of mothers, I'm dreading seeing mine. Like a women's magazine, she literally cannot stop giving me advice on how to lose weight and attract men. When my fiancé vanished from my life, so did her filter. And now that J found a husband, our mom can focus on her final project in life: marrying me off.

I don't really want advice on dealing with her—but I WILL take a relevant and/or adorable GIF. Bonus points if it's got kitties!

 14                                                    12 comments

**Jaclyn Arias**

**Willa Ho**

**Electra Collins**

I've met David. He's crazy nice. Great hugger—like, he should charge for it.

👍 1

**Eye Fay**

Electra Collins thanks! Good to know! Just a reminder, we're only using first letters of names here. You know, privacy and stuff.

👍 1

**Electra Collins**

Doh! My bad!

👍 1

---

From the front row of the bus to Tenafly, en route to Jasmine and David's engagement party, Iris watched in stunned silence as a compact car pin-balled against the walls of the Lincoln Tunnel. Miraculously, no one was hurt. While waiting for the tow truck, Iris whispered a prayer of thanks to her father for the iPad: absorbed in Minecraft, Mason barely noticed the wreckage.

A Hey you message from Kyle gave her a much-needed lift. She responded with a photo of the wreck, and he shot back a line of surprised emoji.

How's the new credit card?

It feels like a great weight has been taken off me

Is there anything I can do to repay you?

LOL don't worry about it

Yr mom sounds 😂

> She tries. I just wish she wouldn't try quite as hard.

> What are your parents like? Are they proud of your success?

LOL no. I haven't talked 2 them in 6 yrs

> Oh no!

> How come?

They live in Malaysia

My dad broke a liquor bottle over my head when I came out 2 him

Said he wished I was dead

I also got stabbed in a bar

I had enough $$$ from styling 2 get a lawyer who got me asylum in the U.S.

$$$ saved my life LOL

She stared at her phone in disbelief. Kyle's Instagram life was so glamorous, his features so exquisite, she would never have guessed he'd suffered, much less fled his home country and his parents.

I'm so sorry—I can't imagine how
hard that must have been

Now I feel dumb for complaining
about my mom

LOL don't

She sounds bad 2

⁓

By the time Iris and Mason arrived at the Hagarty homestead, the guests were already tipsy. Spike and Connie mingled in the backyard with a handful of relatives and neighbors under a single-use tent made of white shrink-wrap plastic. Spike, in mid-length shorts that showed off his weirdly shiny legs, gesticulated with a Heineken bottle, and Connie, sipping a pamplemousse La Croix, marched in place to get her steps in. The afternoon mosquitos geared up for a feast.

"Who's this big man?" Spike asked, giving Mason a growly hug. "He looks like my grandson, but he's grown so fast it can't be the same guy."

"I'm still me." Mason grinned bashfully.

"Handsome devil. Takes after his grandfather."

"You made it," Connie said without a break in her march.

"There was a crazy accident in the Lincoln Tunnel," Iris said, by way of apology.

"That's why I always leave extra time."

"We have been traveling for *two and a half hours*," Iris said.

"We offered to buy you a car," Connie reminded her.

Iris had declined their offer because she could neither afford the insurance, parking, gas, and tolls, nor tolerate the inevitable strong-arming to do their bidding. Before Mason was born, she had accepted an ergonomic jogging stroller from them, because she'd thought, rightly, that it would entice her to exercise daily. After that, whenever Iris was too busy to see them, her father would half joke, "So you only want us around when we can buy you something?"

Iris asked for a beer and a Sprite from a "bartender," a mop-haired high school student who fished drinks from a cooler. As soda was reserved for special occasions, Mason beheld the can like a holy grail.

"Have you met David?" Spike asked, accepting a chicken satay from another student carrying a tray of them.

"Not yet," said Iris, taking a skewer for Mason and plucking off the meat. As usual, not a ton of vegetarian options at a Hagarty party. Iris wasn't one to police what others ate—and she fed her son and cats plenty of meat—but couldn't bear eating an animal herself, and she wished her parents would honor that. They saw eating animals as a noble and holy act, and vegetarianism as a left-wing political statement. "How long ago did they meet? I guess I was kind of surprised when I got Jasmine's call."

"I believe last November," said Connie. "We met him on Memorial Day."

"Isn't it a little . . ."

"Fast?" Spike said. "Seems that way. But Jazzy's got a good head on her shoulders. She knew as soon as she met him that she wanted to marry him."

"Did you know a guy named Tucker, who used to date Jasmine?"

"The name doesn't ring a bell," Connie said. She stopped her march to nowhere. "Why?"

"No reason," Iris said, relieved that Jasmine had also kept their parents out of her love life. "Did Jasmine tell you why she didn't invite Jillian and Emily to be bridesmaids?"

"She had a falling-out with Jillian over a boy," Connie said matter-of-factly, "and Emily moved to San Francisco."

Living in San Francisco didn't sound like an insurmountable hurdle. "What about Kaitlyn from the youth group?"

"What's with the interrogation?" Spike asked. "You know Jasmine isn't one to cling to the past."

It was one thing for Jasmine not to cling to the past, and another to scrub her life of everyone she loved. But Spike's expression had hardened at the whiff of sibling rivalry, ending this line of questioning. Iris wondered if Spike ever felt protective of her, too, or if his paternal instinct was reserved for Jasmine alone.

Iris asked, "Was she . . . was she not going to ask me to be a bridesmaid?"

"Why would you . . . ?" Connie glanced around, as if to ensure no one could overhear. "She didn't think you and Rose would want to be part of it. I told her to let you two make that decision."

That wasn't how Jasmine had described it playing out with Rose.

"And I thought it would help smooth things over with your aunt Mary if Cousin Lorelei could participate," Connie added.

"Cousin Lorelei is going to be a bridesmaid?" Iris asked. "I thought she didn't leave the house."

Like Iris, Aunt Mary had also stopped speaking with Connie and Spike after the 2016 election. Unlike Iris, she was still estranged. Apparently, Jasmine's wedding would be a diplomatic summit. Mary's daughter, Cousin Lorelei, was objectively the weirdest person Iris had ever known, an opinion she could never voice, because the girl had suffered a nervous breakdown when she was eighteen, three years earlier. The family story was that it had been a religious crisis. When Cousin Lorelei was a teen, Aunt Mary divorced her Catholic husband, married a secular humanist, and became an atheist. A few years later, her daughter was slaying demons in the living room with a tinfoil sword.

"Sarcasm doesn't become you." The "doesn't become you" brand of criticisms was part of Connie's lifelong campaign to implant a "girls are better seen and not heard" ethos in her daughters.

"I wasn't being sarcastic," Iris said. "I thought she had agoraphobia or something."

"She's a fine young woman." That sounded like a threat. "Mary thinks the camaraderie will be good for her."

"I'm gonna go congratulate Jasmine," Iris said. She took Mason's hand and headed inside.

"Watch the slouching," Connie called after her. "You're going to give yourself a bad back."

With only four bedrooms and two bathrooms, Iris's childhood home was famous for its modesty in a neighborhood that was famous for its excess. The split-level ranch was built in 1952, and when the Hagartys threw parties, guests dropped backhanded compliments ("It's amazing how the five of you squeezed into this itty-bitty house!"). When Iris was in high school, her parents had considered tearing it down and building something more modern in its place, going as far as drawing up plans with an architect. But Spike, always the iconoclast, took pride in its age and shepherded a collective nostalgia from raising his daughters there. In the end, they left it standing, which provoked great irritation in Jasmine, who was ashamed to invite her friends over and could not tolerate sharing a bathroom with her sisters. Iris was relieved that the house would live on, and Rose didn't care either way. To her, a house was a utilitarian object that wasn't worth getting attached to, like a toaster or a family.

The far wall of the great room was tiled with casement windows that looked out onto the strip of backyard and the patchy woods beyond, as well as the hot tub Spike had bought himself for his fiftieth birthday. A mosaic of photos told a fairy tale of family unity. Forrest appeared three times in the array, as though Spike and Connie had not accepted that he wasn't part of the family. In one photo, taken at Busch Gardens in Tampa, Jasmine had taped over him with a cutout of Nick Jonas. Iris felt both annoyed and grateful.

Jasmine was holding Elsa and sipping a vodka soda by the kitchen, where guests picked at an antipasto tray. "Hey, sis," she said, leaning forward for a kiss on the cheek. She wore a royal blue minidress over sparkly black tights and a pair of stilettos that could put an eye out. Not the best choice for an outdoor party, Iris noted, unless she was planning on aerating the soil. In heels, Jasmine stood an inch taller than David, who was nursing a bottle of summer ale. He looked just as he had online, and once again Iris had the resounding impression of his modesty. He had a teddy bear body, his button-down shirt puffed at the waist, and his curly hair was mussed. He did have a handsome bone structure and kind eyes, but you couldn't deny that he was a strange choice: in high school, Jasmine had dumped a boyfriend for being too short.

"You must be Iris," David said. "And you must be Master Mason."

"It's great to meet you," Iris said, reaching for his hand and changing course when he went in for a surprisingly warm hug. His body reminded her of a pillow-top mattress. And Jasmine was right: he smelled great, clean and piney. "Mason, this is your uncle David."

"What's a uncle?" Mason asked, gazing curiously at this new being in his universe. As far as extended family went, all he knew so far were aunties and grandparents.

"It's your mommy's brother." She left out the "in-law" for simplicity.

David knelt down and took Mason's hand in both of his. "I take being an uncle very seriously. It involves lots of hugs and *lots* of presents." He glanced at Iris. "If that's OK with you, Mom." She wasn't sure he was a good person—especially if he had gained his millions through trickery—but it was hard to dislike someone who was kind to her son.

"Both hugs and presents are definitely welcome, Uncle David."

"He has good inner beauty," Mason said to Iris.

"Thanks, Mason!" David replied.

"My mommy said you didn't."

Iris felt a slap of panic. Mason was a little too keen on honesty for Iris's taste. "I'm sure I didn't say that."

"You did, Mommy."

"I'll have to be on my best behavior," David said, meeting her eyes, "if I'm going to improve my inner beauty score."

She looked away, unused to interpreting men's gazes as anything but invitation. But his look wasn't desirous, she realized; he just wasn't shy about eye contact. Now Iris understood what Jasmine saw in him. He was attentive and charming, and his sibilant, almost lispy voice gave her an ASMR tingle.

"You're doing great," she said. "A-plus."

"I suspect there's been some grade inflation," he said with a throaty laugh.

"How did you meet?"

"On the apps," Jasmine said. "It was, like, love at first text."

"We met for coffee, and coffee turned into lunch, and lunch turned into dinner," David said. "Our date didn't end until the next day, when I had to get on a plane."

"I wasn't sure I wanted to get married at all until I met David," said Jasmine. "And then I was absolutely certain on day one."

"I thought you played hard to get," he said with a flirty smile.

"Just because I have my techniques doesn't mean I hadn't made up my mind."

"Which app did you use?" Iris asked. "I've been having some luck with Bumble." She thought of Christof and buzzed with anticipation. He'd rushed to Milan unexpectedly, postponing their photo shoot, but they still texted every few days. She imagined he'd be a confident lover.

"I need an ice cube," Jasmine said, swirling her drink. "Anyone want anything?"

"Which app did you meet on?" Iris asked again. It wasn't like it had to be a secret.

"JSwipe," David said.

"Isn't that for Jewish people?" Iris asked.

"And for bagel chasers," David said with a fulsome grin.

"I am not a bagel chaser!" Jasmine said, slapping him playfully. "I just didn't want to limit myself. I don't believe in categories." This would have been well and good, had their parents not been evangelical Christians who decried interfaith marriage. They'd even warned their daughters against marrying a mainline Protestant—though by this point, if Iris or Rose brought home anything with a penis, they'd probably give their blessing. Iris suspected that Rose had never seen one in the flesh.

"So Mom and Dad are cool with it?" Iris asked.

"They're gonna have to be," Jasmine said. "If they disown me, they won't get to see their grandbabies."

"If they were going to disown anyone, they would have disowned me for getting pregnant with this one," Iris said under her breath, with a subtle nod toward Mason, who was racing back and forth from the leather sofa to Iris's leg. "And all they did was never forgive me." A few weeks after Forrest had abandoned her, when Iris admitted to her parents that she was pregnant with his son, they begged her to give up the baby for adoption rather than become an unwed mother. That's when Connie's advice machine cranked up to eleven, and now Iris couldn't enter her presence without a helpful comment flung her way.

Brittany swooped in from outside and hugged Jasmine; Elsa did not seem to mind being squished. "Hey, baby!"

"You made it!" Jasmine squealed.

"Your parents do *not* know how to throw a party. You can't just leave food out and hope for the best."

"Ugh, I know, right? And it's a total oven in here. I begged Mom and Dad to buy, like, a working air conditioner before inviting half of New Jersey."

"Someday they'll learn to listen to you," Brittany said.

"At least Iris is in charge of the rest of the pre-wedding shindiggery. She'll do it up right."

"I'll do my best," Iris said, hoping her best would be enough.

"I'm sure you will," Brittany said to Iris with blistering side-eye.

# Chapter Nine

**Kyle Kyle**

September 30, 2018, 5:35 P.M.

Sooooo . . . I got up the courage to invite Baxter over "just to talk," thinking I'd profess my love and we'd have sweet makeup sex, and he was like, why don't all three of us meet up instead? You guys are going to love each other. And I was like, grrr.

Long story short, we all had brunch.

Frederick is a friendly bearish Black dude. He's the CFO of a software company, very smart, definitely a catch, blah, blah. All through brunch, he was giving Baxter pecks on the cheek and squeezes on the leg and whatnot. Baxter accepted these touches but didn't return them. I think Frederick was marking his territory. I don't blame him—he knew who I was, what Baxter and I were.

Frederick gets up to pee, and Baxter and I are alone for the first time. And he's like, isn't Frederick amazing? He likes you soooooo much. I'm about to tell Baxter I love him and he's making a mistake and marry me instead, but then he's like, I love the way our friendship evolved. Like, past tense. And, "evolved," as in better than it was before.

I'm about to say it anyway, but then this total Becky walks by and is like, "You guys make such a cute couple."

And Baxter laughs and tells her his fiancé is in the bathroom. And to the white girl I'm like, we do make a cute couple, don't we? And Baxter is like, there's more to a couple than cute. And I'm like, maybe she's seeing something deeper. And Baxter's like, I think she's seeing two Asian guys with good haircuts and thinking that's cute.

By this point the Becky is scared out of her shit. She backs away, and when Frederick sits down, he's like, what'd I miss? And Baxter's like, Kyle was just saying how much he likes you.

So that was that. I've decided not to see Baxter until the engagement party. I'll get drunk and tell him then. If he rejects me, I'll have no choice but to give him up forever. No wedding, no happy ending. Gurl, bye.

EDIT: Baxter informed me that he has now deleted all the nudes of me on his phone. He basically told me to do the same, and hell if I'm gonna do that. DM me if you want to see them. Side note: he has a killer phoenix tattoo around his belly button. Anyone curious??? LOL

👍😍😮  52                                          21 comments

**Anna Banana**
Send 'em my way! I promise I won't post all of them on Twitter.
                                                          👍 1

**Arden Woodbine**
I can see how hurt you are by Baxter's actions, and forgive me for speaking out of turn, but I don't think it's right to send nude photos of someone without their consent. Sorry if that's not in the spirit of this group—I just had to say something.

**Kyle Kyle**
LOL kidding! I was partaking in some epic day drinking and I got a little cray. His pix are safe and sound on my phone. Where I can stare at them all day and cry.
                                👍❤ 3

**Arden Woodbine**

Sorry if I seemed pushy.

 1

**Kyle Kyle:**

 1

**Electra Collins**

Not sure if you're accepting suggestions, but maybe tell Baxter about your feelings for him when it's \*not\* his engagement party?

 7

**Electra Collins**

Or were you kidding about that part too?

 1

On the day of the rescheduled photo shoot, Iris texted Christof's full name, address, and photo to Sophia, just in case. She trusted her instincts but admitted to herself that said instincts might be clouded by her desire. Sophia responded with a thumbs-up, heart, and fire emoji.

Christof answered the door wearing jeans and a clingy T-shirt and kissed her hello. His studio apartment had just enough space for a bed, a small dining table with two steel chairs, a lipstick-red loveseat, and a few appliances slotted against one wall. Unlike Iris, with her avalanche of unopened mail and unread magazines and Mason's postapocalyptic landscape of mutilated toys, Christof owned nothing extraneous, unless you considered it extraneous for a single man to sleep in a king-size bed in a one-room apartment.

"I made us lunch," he said. "Are you hungry?"

She was, but she wasn't going to eat right before her picture was taken: she was already self-conscious about her pooch. And if they were going to roll around in the bed, she didn't want food jostling inside her. "I'm fine."

"Can I make you a cup of genmaicha?"

"Sure, that sounds nice."

He scooped loose tea into two filter bags, tucked them into mugs that he retrieved from an absurdly narrow dishwasher, and poured in hot water from an electric kettle.

She took in the room. By the bathroom hung a black-and-white portrait of a nude woman at a writing desk, gazing at the camera in resignation. By the front door, a similar portrait of a nude man reading on the red
loveseat. Christof must have shot those, but probably not the photo above
the bed, so blurry she couldn't make it out. She wondered what it would
be like to live with a picture of a naked man, bits and all, hanging in your
apartment, if you were a straight guy. Maybe he was bi.

He said, "Do you mind if I eat? I don't like to shoot on an empty
stomach."

"By all means."

He brought out a metal bowl with salad, a serving plate with two
grilled-cheese sandwiches, and two appetizer plates. "In case you change
your mind."

She took a little salad. That wouldn't inflate her too badly.

He pointed his fork at her. "Bon appétit."

The salad was delicious, with field greens that tasted fresh from the
field and pea shoots as sweet as sugar. His dressing was good, too, oilier
than she was used to (despite forswearing dieting, she did gravitate toward
the "lite" bloc of dressings in the condiments aisle) and with a pleasant balance of acidity and garlic. She liked the genmaicha even more this time.

Christof handed her his model release form. In three dense para-
graphs, it asked her to acknowledge that she was over eighteen and that
he owned any photographs he took of her. It also explained that he could
do anything he wanted with those photos. This took her aback. The contract was a kind of compliment, though: it meant he took her seriously
as a model.

"The language is pretty broad, but I'll only be selecting one photograph, and I'll notify you if I put it up for sale," he reassured her.

She recalled Kyle's joking offer to send naked pictures of Baxter to all
takers. She didn't want one more thing to worry about.

"Can we include that last thing in the contract?" Iris asked Christof.
"That you won't share anything without notifying me? And what if I hate
the image you choose?"

"This is a standard modeling contract," he said. "I can't change it without consulting my attorney. My livelihood depends on these legal protections."

Was this a date or a business transaction? "If you were in my position, would you sign it?"

He thought about this. "I wouldn't want to relinquish control of my likeness. But I can also tell you that no model has ever balked at the consent form, and it impresses me that you're taking it seriously."

"I guess I'd rather not sign it." She gulped her tea, panicking at the thought of scuttling the shoot, and relieved, too.

He examined the release form, then her. "How about I make you a verbal promise? If I decide to sell an image, I'll get your permission. I'm good for my word."

His word was worth squat if they ended on bad terms, but rejecting the promise and refusing to model would be tantamount to telling him she didn't trust him, and where could they go from there, except their separate ways? She had fantasized about being intimate with him and didn't want to screw it up. Then again, for all she knew, he might sell her pictures to a porn site. Was there a market for tired moms who felt ambivalent about being photographed? Well, he didn't know she was a mom.

"I'm sorry," she said to Christof. "Maybe we could just talk?"

"Sure." She was surprised that he wasn't annoyed.

"What was the emergency that brought you to Milan?" she asked, deciding to eat half a grilled cheese after all. Predictably, it was delicious.

"The art gallery that represents me flooded. I had to go assess the damage and decide what could be salvaged."

"That's terrible!" she said. But he seemed calm, maybe resigned. "Can they be reprinted? I mean, they're photographs . . ."

"When I sell a piece, I only make one print, and then I delete the file. That way, I have control over its dissemination. Most photographers, their work is all over the internet, and then it's basically worthless."

"Is that really how it works? I've never heard of photographers doing that."

"Have you ever read Walter Benjamin?"

"That would be a hard no."

"He argued that once you can copy art, as with photography, the aura of the original is diluted. In the age of the internet, with photographs passing before our eyes a thousand times a day, their value is lost completely. I want to create art that can't be copied. The gallery gets a lo-res version to help them sell the piece. But if I find it on the web, my contract states that the gallery must buy the artwork."

"What about after someone else buys it?" she asked. "Can they post it then?"

He squinted, confused. "If they're buying my art, they generally accept my intention with it."

It was hard to believe that none of his photographs had been swallowed up in a medium that touched everyone, sometimes with a caress, sometimes with a slap. But she had searched for them exhaustively and found none. She could give him the benefit of the doubt. She did want to be photographed. And what was the worst that could happen? Even if her half-naked photos ended up all over the internet, literally no one except her parents would be upset. And Mason, once he grew up, but that's what therapy was for. Iris certainly wouldn't be fired: a guy in accounts receivable did gay porn on the weekends and posted stills and behind-the-scenes shots on Instagram, always with a well-placed eggplant emoji.

"You know what? Let's do this." She picked up the form and signed it.

She sat on the red loveseat. Christof played a folk cover of a pop song on his built-in speakers and unsheathed his camera. It was smaller than she'd expected.

"So do I just . . . take off my clothes?" she asked.

He nodded.

But she felt self-conscious. "Can I leave my underwear on?"

Under his blunt gaze, she felt like an amateur and a prude. "We can start there," he said.

She stripped to her bra and panties. As he hovered the lens in front of her face and snapped photos, she became hyperaware of how she looked. She glanced at the camera, then at her crossed arms, then at his enormous bare feet. "Should I look at the camera?"

"There are no rules here. Just be yourself."

It was hard to be herself with a camera in her face. She crossed and uncrossed her legs, peered at the camera through the corner of her eye, then stared out at the middle distance. She smiled and could tell it wasn't right. Years of taking selfies had taught her what every smile looked like, and she only posted photos with the one she liked best. She stared at him, first with intensity, then curiosity, then calm.

He stepped closer and said, "Good, good."

She tried some faces from a TV modeling competition—sexy cat, pouty teenager, surprised corpse—and he kept the shutter busy. She sat back, having run out of ideas. He took a few more shots and stopped.

"Are we good?" she said.

"I have photos of the Iris you think the world wants to see. Now let go of that person, and show me something deeper, less curated. Stop thinking and just be."

She knew what he wanted; she supposed she wanted it, too. She unclasped her bra and held the cups over her breasts, letting one slide to reveal the edge of an areola, then feared it looked porny—or ridiculous, like a girl in her bedroom seducing a Robert Pattinson poster.

"Good, good," he said, coming closer again. "Let me see you."

"I get veto power over these, right?" she asked.

"I'll get your permission for whichever photo I choose," he said. "But I promise you will love it."

She tossed her bra onto the rest of her clothes and leaned against the side of the loveseat with her forearm covering her chest. His encouragement grew stronger, his camera so close she could smell his cologne. It was one of those European eaux de toilette that reminded her of a clean bathroom, which was possibly the most erotic scent in the world. She let her arms fall to her sides. She felt drugged by his attention, his admiration, his power. He reached into his jeans and adjusted himself. He was at full mast—and it was a tall ship. She savored the delicious interplay of knowing and not knowing that he would soon be inside her. She posed with more intensity, letting herself forget that she was topless. She saw that he'd been waiting for her to stop caring who might see her body.

"Beautiful," he said. "Show me everything."

Here was the paradox: she didn't want to take off her briefs, and she did, for exactly the same reason. Freed by the precarious security of Christof's promise, she wanted to be fully seen, fully admired. But then she imagined Mason coming across the photo. Breasts were one thing; crotch was quite another.

"Put the camera down," she whispered. "Please."

He did as she asked. He peeled off her panties, then plucked open the button of his jeans and pushed them to the ground. He wasn't wearing underwear. Her entire body was sensitized; the slightest touch might send her over the edge. He knelt in front of her, admiring her beneath him, as he rolled on a condom. Then he reached his hands around her waist and lifted her body to meet his.

⌒

Afterward, they lay naked in his bed, drinking Moscato. Christof's collection of folk covers of pop songs continued to play on the speakers. It seemed to be a genre unto itself.

"Those two photos are yours—I mean, you shot them, right?" she asked, now that the coil of sexual tension had unraveled in the best possible way, and she had reclaimed the ability to speak.

"Hanging? Yes, those are mine."

"They're very nice," she said, then wished she hadn't employed the most vacuous word in the English language to describe them. "Complicated."

"Thank you."

"Are they people you know, or just models?"

He pointed at the woman. "She was a model—that photo is in MoMA's permanent collection. I had to make an exception of my no-copies rule for that."

"Did you sleep with her too?"

He looked wounded. "I don't generally make love to the models. I was under the impression that we were on a date."

"We are! I was just kidding." She hadn't been kidding, exactly, more like hunting for validation. She was relieved that he didn't have sex with every woman he photographed. She sat on her knees and stroked his bristly chest hairs. "What about him?" she asked, pointing at the naked man.

"He was my mentor in art school."

"Huh," she said, afraid that any question she asked about the circumstances might offend him.

"People ask me what it's like to have a naked man on my wall, and if I'm gay."

A moment passed before she said, "And what's your answer?"

He shrugged. "I'm an artist—I'm not afraid of bodies."

His stance was liberating, Iris supposed. She'd never met a man who didn't have a complex about other naked men, whether from attraction or repulsion. "That's very progressive of you."

"Actually, I'm pretty conservative, at least among New Yorkers. I'm a Hillary Democrat, not a Bernie one."

"At least you're not a Trump supporter."

"I'm not, but I don't hate him. He's a politician—he's just pandering to his base."

She realized it would be dumb to talk politics with him. It would only lead to fighting. "And are you gay?" she asked with a grin.

"No." She felt stung by his refusal to play, though she admired him for it, too. Flirting could be exhausting; Christof was refreshingly direct.

She lay back down, resting her head on Christof's shoulder. The scent of sweat and sex on his skin was intoxicating. He kissed her forehead. "How's your Facebook group going? What was it called?"

"The Bridesmaids Union."

"That's right. I searched for it, but nothing came up."

"It's a secret group—you have to be invited to see it. Wait, you have a Facebook account? I thought you were anti-internet."

"I have the accounts. I just don't give them any permissions, and I don't post anything."

So he was on social media, despite his privacy lectures. It didn't make him a hypocrite, but it was . . . funny.

"Will you show me some of your posts?" he asked.

"I really don't think you'd be interested."

"I want to read your writing. I want to see what this part of your life is like."

"It's just that when I post on there, it's not me. It's this kind of mean-girl type who says whatever's on her mind and doesn't censor herself. I don't want you to think I'm that much of a jerk."

He considered this. "If you say what's on your mind, isn't that the real you? What are you thinking but not saying with me?"

"No, no—that's not what I meant. The real me is considerate and forgiving, and the Bridesmaids Union me has fun dragging people through the mud."

"I don't want you to be nice to me," he said. "I want you to tell me the truth."

How could she explain that she didn't feel the way Eye Fay sounded? She wasn't an angry person. Privately, she could be judgmental, but despite what he promised, he wouldn't like that part of her if he saw it. "The truth is . . . you're really sexy and I'm so, so glad we met."

"A brilliant dodge," he said, and kissed her deeply. He reached for the bottle and tipped the neck toward her, offering a refill, at which point she remembered that she was on her lunch break. According to the wall clock, it had been almost two hours since she left the office. Jeremy wouldn't care, but Chase would toss off a hostile greeting like, "Long lunch, eh?" She retrieved her clothes from the couch and glanced at her phone. She had missed four calls from Mason's school.

"Excuse me," she said to Christof, listening to the messages as she slipped on her jacket and shoes. The principal explained with a tenuous balance of urgency and calm that Mason had bitten a student. Iris was to retrieve him immediately. He would not be allowed into the after-school program that day. She realized she was hyperventilating. Biting? Where had that come from? And what did they do to biters? Suspend them? Put them in a special classroom for problem children? Expel them?

"Is everything OK?" Christof asked. "You can tell me."

She almost said, "My son," but remembered she hadn't told him about Mason. And now she couldn't find the words. "Excuse me," she said again, not looking back as she left the apartment.

# Chapter Ten

**Shanna Menckler**

October 1, 2018 7:52 A.M.

As a wedding photographer, I wouldn't normally post criticism of my clients on the internet, because no one should be held accountable on the highest-pressure day of their lives, and more to the point, discretion is very important to me. But one groom I worked with a few years ago was a legitimate sociopath—and he doesn't deserve anyone's protection.

In our first meeting, he criticized his fiancée for putting the wrong kind of sugar in his coffee (he didn't like the raw sugar because it took too long to stir in), and when she offered to stir it for him, he rolled his eyes at me. He criticized every photo in my portfolio, mostly for things that were either beyond my control (a rabbi's bad toupee) or artistic license (a shallow-focus shot of a ring). Then he asked me to give them a 20 percent discount because I was a "beginner." I've shot more than a hundred weddings. Of course I held firm. To my absolute shock, they hired me anyway.

On the day of the wedding, he was directing the makeup artist, pointing out his fiancée's blemishes and asking to "make her look presentable." Why was he getting married to a woman who, in his mind, didn't look presentable? Then he told me to make sure my whole team knew not to photograph her profile, because from that angle, "she looks like a turkey vulture." Meanwhile, the bride is taking all of this abuse.

The ceremony goes OK, though his vow is three pages long about how great he is, and hers is three sentences, also about how great he is. Afterward, he gets sloppy drunk and hangs out with his groomsmen. During the toasts, when his brother is about to tell an incriminating story about him, he yanks the mic away and describes to everyone how his brother was repeatedly molested by their uncle. When he's done, you could hear a pin drop.

And finally, during the dancing, right before our five-star groom is supposed to be cutting the wedding cake with his new wife, he aggressively hits on a member of my team. Normally this kind of behavior is none of my business, but not when it involves my staff. I told his wife, and she replied that a lot of people mistake his friendliness for flirtation.

A year later, they still hadn't selected the photos to be made into prints. When I reached out to them, I found out he was serving three years in prison for embezzlement. That made my whole week.

👍😮😢 80                                                   22 comments

**Eye Fay**
I do love a happy ending.
👍 7

**Jaclyn Arias**
Scooping my jaw off the floor!
👍1

**Anna Banana**
I'm with him on the turbinado sugar, but that's where it ends. (Who has time for stirring?!)
👎 3

⌒

Mason's school had let out for the day when Iris arrived, out of breath from jogging from the train station. Anna Chung, the smartly dressed principal, greeted her as though welcoming a mourner at a funeral, and led her to an otherwise empty classroom where Mason waited beside a sinewy woman in sweats. Mason jumped up to hug Iris and burst into tears. She patted his back, soothing him.

The woman accompanying Mason introduced herself as Noreen, the special needs tech, and relayed what his teacher had told her. The afternoon had gone in the usual way: snack, story, naptime, art. But as they were lining up to hang up their artworks, he yelled, "Stop it!" then bit down hard on the arm of his friend Rafael. The teacher was able to separate them, but she couldn't calm Mason down. She called Noreen, who restrained him. Iris tried not to imagine this brutality.

"We had quite a day, didn't we?" Noreen said to Mason, for Iris's benefit.

"Yeah," he said, squeezing his fingers contritely.

Iris kneeled and held her son by the shoulders. "Why did you bite Rafa?"

"I hate him," Mason grumbled.

"He's your friend," Iris said.

"I hate him!" he screamed, pounding at Iris's shoulder until she let go. As her child, his rage wasn't supposed to scare her. But this acting out wasn't contiguous with his behavior before he started kindergarten. It had nothing to do with the son she'd known.

"Deep breath, Mason," said Noreen, ready to act. He glanced at her and pouted.

"We can talk about this later," Iris said to Mason.

Principal Chung escorted them to the sidewalk, stopping at his cubby for his jacket and backpack. "We take biting very seriously," she said, quietly enough so that Mason wouldn't think to listen. "At your convenience, I'd like to set up a meeting to ensure it doesn't happen again."

Iris panicked. What was the threat behind the principal's placid request?

"He's always been a well-mannered boy. Is it possible he's being bullied? I mean, do we know what Rafael did to incite him?"

"His teacher said it came out of nowhere. We spoke with both boys, too." Principal Chung softened her tone. "How is everything at home? Have there been any changes recently?"

Mason had done fine in preschool and pre-K. His nighttime tantrums were new, but Iris wasn't ready to incriminate her son before thinking it through.

"Kindergarten can be a big shock for kids," Principal Chung said. "Sometimes we need to give them a little extra attention, to ease their transition."

"You're not suggesting he get put in a special needs classroom, right?" Iris blurted out. "He's a very smart boy."

Mason crouched, inspecting a crack in the sidewalk, unaware that his fate hung in the balance. She couldn't let him be segregated. All her hopes for his brilliant career would dissolve into nothing.

"Let's not get ahead of ourselves," Principal Chung said. "That's a last resort. We will be keeping an eye on him, though."

Iris was afraid to ask what would happen if he bit another kid. "We'll make sure it doesn't happen again. Thank you." She took Mason's hand. "Say goodbye to Principal Chung."

"Goodbye, Principal Chung." Mason gave the principal a hug.

As they walked to the train, Iris was blinded with worry. She didn't have the energy to handle this on top of everything else. And yet her son's development—his future—was far more important than her job, her sister's wedding, or her search for love. How did other people keep their life on track? Would she ever be able to let her guard down? She began to cry.

"I'm sorry, Mommy," Mason said. "I'm sorry I got mad."

"It's OK, sweetheart," she told him. "Everyone gets mad sometimes. We just have to use our words and never bite people."

He nodded as if finding her comment eminently reasonable. "I didn't use my words."

⌒

That evening, Iris served Mason a salad with grilled chicken and a lemon vinaigrette. Other mothers laughed when she told them about her son's weirdly adult dietary preferences, but his zest for cucumbers and green peppers was a source of pride for her. It was an ordinary meal for him: she never punished or rewarded his behavior through food.

After dinner, they sat on the couch. The cats, as if sensing his upset, purred behind his head and groomed each other, their barbed tongues straying to lick his hair. She asked him to tell her what provoked him into biting Rafael. He shrugged. Was it that he didn't remember, or that he didn't understand that what he'd done wasn't OK? She tried a different tack. She asked what activities they'd done that day.

The kids had been asked to draw family pictures: parents, siblings, house, sun. Mason's, of course, only had two people in the picture, so he drew Grandma Connie and Grandpa Spike, as well as Auntie Jasmine and Uncle David. (He could be forgiven for forgetting Auntie Rose.) Rafael looked at his drawing and explained that he'd messed up with all those other relatives. He was supposed to draw his daddy.

"Is that when you bit him?" Iris asked, as gently as she could.

He shrugged.

"He has a daddy, and you don't?"

He knuckled away a tear.

"Did you bring your picture home?" she asked. "Can I see it? I bet you did a beautiful job."

"I teared it up and throwed it in the trash."

She kissed him. "Every family is different, Mason. Adelaide has a mommy and no daddy. And Tania has two mommies. No family is better just because of who's in the picture."

"Rafa said everyone has a daddy, even if some daddies run away or die."

She was stunned. Who was telling Rafa about these adult realities? She didn't want to lie to him; she also didn't want to scar him with a thoughtless response. "You're right, sweetie. Your daddy ran away before you were born. It wasn't because of you. It was something between him and me."

"Can't you find him?"

She felt his yearning to fit in, felt it in the painful throb of her heart. "OK, sweetie, I will try."

"Promise?"

She stroked his cheek. "I promise."

⁓

After Mason went to bed, Iris listened to a news commentary podcast on headphones and opened Facebook on her computer. As usual, the algorithm surfaced Forrest's profile as a suggested friend. The internet forgot nothing.

Forrest had been a server in a Greenwich Village restaurant co-owned by a celebrity and swarming with them. Back in 2010, Sophia had suggested the place for lunch, but all Iris could afford on her meager postgraduate salary was a side of pasta with marinara sauce. Forrest, sensing her discomfort with the prices, snuck her a dinner portion without charging her extra, then struck up a flirtation when he brought the check. They discovered that they were both vegetarians and had the same favorite restaurant, Angelica Kitchen. Also—impossibly—both their fathers were nicknamed Spike. She didn't give him her number, as she was still with her college boyfriend, a relationship that had no future but that she couldn't bring herself to end. He found her on Facebook and chatted her up on Messenger for hours at a time. Her unavailability was his aphrodisiac. Finally, she broke it off with her boyfriend and went out with Forrest.

He rode a skateboard to work, taught yoga in Park Slope, and volunteered as a climbing instructor for underprivileged kids, and all that exercise had articulated every muscle in his body. After Iris introduced him to her family, Connie *congratulated* her and offered advice on how to keep him, having to do with (a) personal hygiene, (b) diet and exercise, and (c) premarital abstinence. Iris had waited all of two weeks to sleep with him.

Throughout their relationship, he chilled at the slightest romantic approach—buying him Yankees tickets, lighting candles for a sensual massage, texting "I love you," even reaching for his hand on the sidewalk. In retrospect, it made sense that the specter of eternal commitment would end them. Even in their last months together, when she sensed his attraction fading, his arousal sprang to life when she was falling asleep, or on her period, or out of town. Which was why she couldn't bring herself to tell him she was pregnant. She feared he would leave her.

He left anyway, two months before the wedding and six weeks into her pregnancy. His note explained nothing except that he couldn't explain. She wished he'd told her that he didn't love her anymore, or that he'd never loved her, or given her any reason at all. Because the most painful thing wasn't that he left, it was not knowing why.

Before she could terminate the embryo, her mother figured it out—she claimed she could smell the hormones—and begged her to carry it to term. Iris was too heartbroken and lonely to risk alienating her parents, so she decided to give the child up for adoption. Everyone warned her not to hold him in the delivery room, but she wanted to say goodbye. The second she brought Mason's warm, sticky body to her chest, she fell in love, and she couldn't give him away. It was the best decision she'd ever made.

But even with her parents' help, those first few months tested Iris's physical and emotional endurance, and her exhaustion deepened when she went back to work. She called Forrest, but he'd changed his number. Her email was met with an auto-reply from his spam blocker, informing her that her message would not be delivered. Messages on Facebook went unreturned. She wasn't about to post to his wall, letting the world know about Mason. She wanted to protect her son from the internet.

Now Iris clicked on Forrest's Facebook profile. He was still single, still working at the overpriced bistro where they'd first met. And still handsome, though she might not be looking at a recent photo. He had been a middling lover, focused on his own satisfaction over hers, but she'd derived so much pleasure in his crystal eyes and lean muscles that it hadn't mattered. In the six years since he'd ruined everything, most of the pain had metabolized, leaving a ghostly nostalgia for his body, for his slender fingers and elven ears and the diamond of hair on his chest as soft as a cat's belly.

She didn't want to contact him, and he didn't want to hear from her. He didn't deserve one second of Mason's company and never had. She didn't think her son needed a father: she bristled at retrograde ideas like this. His wish for a traditional family would probably pass. And how painful would it be for Mason if Forrest ran away again? But she had no doubt that her son's acting out that day resulted from his feeling different from his peers. She couldn't let him be labeled as maladjusted, the kind of label that could stick for life. She had to try to give him what he wanted.

After an eternity of doubt, she sent Forrest a Facebook message.

Hi Forrest, I hope you've been well.
Sorry to reach out like this, but there's
something I need to talk to you about.
Would you call me?

She included her number. Then, because she knew that he would ignore this message just like all the others, lined up unread in the message panel, she wrote a second message, short enough to get the point across in the preview:

YOU HAVE A SON.

# Chapter Eleven

**Eye Fay**

October 8, 2018, 8:28 A.M.

Remember how my friend S's roommate went missing in Cabo and then didn't acknowledge that I spent like half a day searching for her? Well, she totally redeemed herself at S's wedding! She took me aside and gave me such a heartfelt apology, I almost cried. She said that weekend had convinced her to put a pause on her drinking. I completely forgave her.

S's mother, on the other hand, was in top form. That is one truly special woman. For starters, she wore WHITE to her daughter's wedding. Naturally, her toast was about how she'd never thought any man would ever marry her daughter, and how, when S was in sixth grade, the woman paid this other girl to be friends with her. S, to her credit, sat there and smiled like royalty. BTW, just saying, S looks like a model and has amazing taste. So I don't know if her mom is blind, or . . . ?

On an unrelated note, when I went to the bathroom, S's sister and one of the groomsmen came out together, adjusting their clothes. Had I known in that moment that their condom had clogged the toilet, I would not have given them a wink and a thumbs-up.

XOXO

Eye

👍❤️😢 12 9 comments

**Arden Woodbine**

So great that she apologized.

👍❤️ 4

**Eye Fay**

I know—it let me see her humanity. A real apology is a lost art.

❤️ 2

**Anna Banana**

At least they used a condom.

👍 3

Iris had nicknamed it the Biting Summit, to ward off despair. Nine people were present: Iris and Mason, Mr. and Mrs. Floria with Rafael, Mason's kindergarten teacher, the school psychologist, the secretary, and Principal Chung, whose office was too small to fit them. Iris offered to sit in the open doorway with Mason in her lap. So much for confidentiality, though the only people who might overhear were the last dregs of teachers exiting the building and the custodian, polishing the floor with what looked like a space-age lawnmower.

Principal Chung preambled with a five-minute sentence that touched on the importance of (a) open communication, (b) mutual respect, (c) a constructive rather than punitive process, (d) inclusive classrooms, (e) maintaining the school as a safe place, and (f) confidentiality. Iris was surprised to endure such a torrent of verbiage outside of D-CAT; clearly, the ability to blunt emotions with ground rules and disclaimers was not unique to the legal world.

Mrs. Floria pulled up Rafael's sleeve to reveal a gnarly oval bruise in shades of purple, pink, and brown, like a chemical sunset. Iris winced. "He's been having nightmares every night," Mrs. Floria said.

"Not every night," Mr. Floria said, and then, after absorbing a violent glance from his wife, added, "Most nights."

Rafael was doing his best to look forlorn. Mason kept his head down the whole time. The radiator banged, pumping damp heat into the room.

"We don't feel safe keeping Rafa in this school as long as Mason is in his classroom," said Mrs. Floria. "We would like Mason to be moved."

Iris's stomach dropped. "Mason, sweetie, did you want to say something?"

Mason slid off Iris's lap. Staring at his hands, he said, "I'm very, very sorry, and I won't do it again."

"What do you say, Rafael?" their teacher prompted.

"Thank you."

"And maybe 'I forgive you'?"

"I think that's asking a lot," said Mrs. Floria.

"It's a start," said the psychologist. "If everyone is in agreement, I'd like to meet with both boys a few times to talk about strategies for handling frustration. We've found that in cases like this, when it's a discrete event and not part of a larger behavior problem, the issue resolves relatively easily without disrupting classroom continuity."

"I don't think we can be at all certain this is a discrete event," Mrs. Floria said.

"He's never done it before, ever," Iris said. "He says it happened because everyone was drawing their families, and Rafa told Mason that he was supposed to have a daddy."

"My son didn't say that," Mrs. Floria said.

"According to Mason, he did," Iris replied, heating up.

"Let's slow down a bit," said Principal Chung. "We're not talking about cause and effect. That is off the table right now. Kindergarten can be a difficult transition for many children, and biting is very common in the first few months. We'll administer a behavioral intervention, and we will keep a close eye on them. Nine times out of ten, that's the end of it."

"When my son's safety is on the line, your one-in-ten odds aren't very reassuring," Mrs. Floria snapped. Mr. Floria put his hand on hers.

Iris didn't feel reassured by the odds, either. If Mason wanted to bite again, she felt powerless to stop him. Her frustration with Mrs. Floria turned to despair. What would a better mother do in her place?

"We need to take everyone's best interests into account, Mrs. Floria," said Principal Chung.

"Maybe Mr. Floria is my daddy?" Mason asked that evening, while Iris was reading him a bedtime story about a turtle who was afraid of his first day of school.

"I'm sorry, sweetie, but he's not," she said.

"Did you even ask him?"

She couldn't help laughing. "I'll know your dad when I see him. I'm looking for him, I promise."

"Did you tell him it's *extremerestly* important?"

"I will, as soon as I find him." She combed his dirty-blond hair with her fingers. "We can talk more about this in the morning."

After he fell asleep, Iris poured a glass of wine and lay on the sofa with her feet on the armrest. If she were a more present mother, not spending her weekdays at work and her weekends at weddings and bridal events, she was sure Mason wouldn't be biting. In the absence of her becoming independently wealthy, a little help wouldn't hurt.

She reread her messages to Forrest for the millionth time. Was it possible he hadn't seen them? Maybe he'd found a way to turn off his notifications. It looked like he hadn't been on Facebook in months. But how could he have missed her messages for five years?

She couldn't find Forrest's phone number or email address on the internet, but she dug up his physical address from a people search. He'd moved to Red Hook, a block from their wedding venue, as if returning to the scene of the crime.

Which was more aggressive, she wondered, surprising him at work or at home? Neither seemed kind, for different reasons. But Mason needed her to do this. No matter how calmly the school administration was taking Mason's bite, she couldn't afford to wait and see if he'd do it again.

She messaged Kyle.

**Are you free to talk?**

She didn't understand how a famous influencer could respond promptly whenever she messaged him. Surely he had better things to do than text with a fangirl. But their connection, built on anonymity, was in some ways more valuable than that of a sibling or close friend. They could tell each other almost anything.

> I could use a man's perspective

> My son bit his classmate, and the kid's mother is out for blood.

> He says he did it because the other kid shamed him for not having a father in his family picture.

> My son's father ran off before he was born—I don't think he knows he has a son. I don't have contact with his father and he's never responded to my messages.

> Would I be crazy for showing up at his doorstep?

Iris was careful to protect Mason's privacy, but as long as she didn't use his name or send Kyle a photograph, it seemed safe.

I think the dad wld want 2 know

If u tried to get in touch already, he'll understand

> I worry that he'll think I'm needy and clingy or something

Like I'm being the person he had to
get away from.

That was yrs ago

And if he is the dad u cld call the cops on him
4 child support

Kyle was right. Forrest had a legal obligation to help pay for her son's upbringing. She'd always thought the money wasn't worth the pain of seeing him again, even if she needed it more than ever. He'd of course assume it was the reason she was tracking him down.

You're right. Thank you

I get in my head about my ex. It helps
to have your unbiased opinion.

No one ever said I'm unbiased LOL

😄 What's going on in your life?

More Baxter drama

I'll write about it in BMU when I stop crying LOL

She sensed a lifetime of stifled pain underneath his LOLs. He put on a happy face for the world, but he was hurting, just like her. She hoped he would let her help him.

I can't wait to read it

Take care of yourself

As she got ready for bed, she kept her phone with her in case he responded.

# Chapter Twelve

**Kyle Kyle**

October 9, 2018, 2:14 A.M.

NBD, but I saved a life on Saturday.

It was Frederick and Baxter's engagement party. Frederick's dad rented a yacht and invited a hundred of his closest friends, including the whole wedding party and a bunch of relatives on both sides who clearly did not know how to control themselves when presented with an open bar and giant tins of soggy food.

Side note: I figured out why Baxter wanted me in his wedding party. Frederick has, I shit you not, eight(!) groomsmen and six(!) grooms-maids. And Baxter has (drum roll, please . . . ) three groomsmen. If I'd turned him down, he'd have two—or else he'd have to ask his barber.

The boat started on the East River in the thirties and looped around Manhattan. By the time we reached Battery Park, let's just say everyone was having a very good time. It was so loud inside the cabin, my bones were vibrating. So I waited outside, wishing I'd brought a heavier coat. How I suffer for fashion, LOL.

Baxter comes out to keep me company, though it's obvious he wants to go back inside and keep dancing, because "Toxic" just came on. He's like, I know this is no fun for you. You're an important part of my life, and I don't want to lose you. If you don't want to be my groomsman, you don't have to. And I'm like, I want to do this for you. I just miss us the way we were—can we chill just the two of us sometime? And he launches into this epic soliloquy about how he doesn't want to fall back into old habits and how he wants to start over with me, and, oh, Frederick is so excited about you and let's keep hanging out all three of us, and I promise you will love him very soon if you don't already, which maybe you do?

He literally could not stop talking. He was either saying he wanted a threesome or that he knew if we hung out alone we'd hook up. Probably the latter. And I was thinking, if you want to hook up with me, why starve yourself? Isn't monogamy just a tool of the patriarchy, invented by prudish religions afraid of people having any real fun, the same religions that have oppressed gay people for millennia?

I realize I am not preaching to the choir.

I just said, I love you, Baxter. I've loved you for years, and I don't want to lose you.

And he's like, I love you, too. I just needed to find someone who was marriage material.

It felt like he'd socked me in the gut.

He leans in for a kiss, dodging my parted lips and planting one on my cheek, then goes back inside. I'm standing out there for Goddess knows how long, wondering why Frederick is marriage material and I'm not—I honestly can't think of a single reason, except for Frederick's $$$—when one of Frederick's groomsmen, a fratty white dude with a shark tooth necklace and a goatee (I think his name was Joe but he was a total Biff) comes bounding outside shirtless with a beer in each hand, and flips right over the rail and into the drink. I'm the only one outside, and I'm thinking I might have hallucinated it, but nope, there he is, splashing in the river like a duck trying to take flight. I glance around for some kind of ring buoy: nothing. I do find a life jacket in a storage bench and throw it down to him. Thank Goddess we made it to the Hudson, because if we were in the East River, dude would be fish food—those currents are no joke. I run inside to find someone in the crew, but the air is like a tub of hot beer, and if I don't get out of there instantly, I'm definitely going to ralf. "Welcome to the Jungle" is playing so loud, no one can hear me shouting for help. I run around the deck to the front of the boat and wave down the captain like some kind of whack job. The captain cuts the engine and throws down a rope ladder. Biff was laughing the whole time.

Frederick gives me a bear hug and sobs into my shoulder, so drunk but also so scared, and he keeps thanking me and saying he can never repay me, and if there's anything he can ever do for me, anything at all, he'll do it in a heartbeat.

Am I the worst person in the world? Because I could only think of one thing, and he sure as hell wasn't going to give me that.

👍😮  181                                              25 comments

**Anna Banana**
I am RIVETED.
💬 8

⌒

At the office the next morning, Iris called the restaurant where Forrest worked, pretending to be a former regular in town, to ask whether he'd have the lunch shift that day. He had dinner, which meant he would be home at lunchtime, since he finished his workout by 10:00 A.M.—assuming his routine hadn't changed in the past six years.

She rode the 4 train to Brooklyn and switched to the B61 to reach Forrest's apartment in Red Hook. The low-slung, warehousey neighborhood always seemed derelict—and could not have been farther from the subway—but the homes were blessed with quiet and good light.

On the way, she saw Kyle's post in the Bridesmaids Union about Baxter's engagement party. She found it incredible in both senses of the term.

You saved Biff's life!

Whoop dee 💩

Baxter could care less

It seems like he cares about you

She hoped she wasn't overstepping.

He's just trying to make it work with Frederick.

He's lying 2 himself. He loves me

She didn't know how to respond without pushing too hard.

Sometimes love isn't enough

It hadn't been enough with Forrest. But had he been in love with her?

U shld write greeting cards LOL

She sent back an **LOL** because she really did laugh out loud.

She overshot Forrest's block to gaze at their wedding venue, a rehabbed warehouse on a pier with a view of the huddled skyscrapers of Lower Manhattan. Even after six years, memories of her relationship pricked her with loss, no longer about Forrest or their canceled wedding, but how swiftly time had rushed by. She was almost thirty; what could she be proud of besides Mason? Though she loved him more than life itself, he wasn't enough. He wasn't supposed to be enough.

Forrest lived in a handsome four-story brick building with a dark green wooden door. His last name wasn't on the buzzer panel, but that didn't discourage her. Putting his name on the panel would mean committing to living there, and this escape artist was not one for commitment. While he and Iris were dating, he'd turned down a managerial position at the restaurant because he hadn't planned on working there much longer. Now he'd been there twelve years. One could only stave off commitment for so long. After a while, life had a way of forcing decisions.

She held her breath and buzzed his apartment. The door unlocked without him asking who was there. Maybe he was expecting lunch delivery, or the intercom was broken. More likely, he didn't care who came in. That must have been a guy thing.

She climbed to his third-floor apartment and knocked. She stood straight up and smiled mysteriously in case he saw her through the peephole.

The door opened. He looked the same. Same soul patch, same kind, tired eyes. Same gray hoodie and Ramones T-shirt. Same iron physique. New man bun. His lips broadened into a smile. "Well, shit," he said, lingering on the "i" for two syllables.

"You know I wouldn't show up like this if it wasn't important," she said. "I just need to tell you something, and then I'll get out of your hair."

"It's cool—I've been thinking we should talk again."

She followed him inside. He tossed her a lime seltzer, and they sat on opposite sides of a stained granny couch, probably a sidewalk find or a hand-me-down from his actual grandmother. In place of a TV was an aquarium with tropical fish. He apologized for the incense smell; his roommate burned the stuff.

"You live really close to our venue." She wished she hadn't opened with a reference to their aborted wedding.

He laughed. "Red Hook is my happy place. I probably would never have seen it if not for the wedding."

"There is literally no other reason to come out this far," she said, smiling despite herself. Looking at him, the old apparatus of hurt, frustration, and desire cranked. But those corroded feelings couldn't gain traction. She had moved on.

"Hey, how's Jasmine?"

"Oh—she's great. She's getting married."

He stared for a beat too long. "Good for her. Who's the lucky dude?"

"Some rich tech guy," she said. "I mean, he's super nice. Like, porn-for-women nice."

"Good for her," he said again.

"Anyway, I came because . . . I wanted to tell you . . . you have a son." She watched for his reaction through squinted eyes.

"I wondered about that," he said, nodding as if she'd made a good point.

Oddly, she was disappointed that he wasn't surprised.

"Wondered because . . ."

"I thought you might be pregnant at the end there."

"If you wondered, then why didn't you say something?" she asked, filtering the irritation from her voice.

"I figured you didn't want me to know."

She thought back to Mason's first year, when she was averaging four hours of sleep a night taken in one-hour increments, when her nipples burned and bled from breastfeeding, when her back spasmed from lifting him, when she feared she would fall asleep and drop him, or leave the room and he would die. She'd needed help. Of course she'd wanted him to know.

"So you didn't get any of my messages?" she asked.

"I got your drunk dials. After a while, I stopped listening." His voice had an edge.

This was going all wrong, and she didn't know how to pull back. He probably thought she was using her son to trap him.

"I also wrote you on Facebook, too. A lot."

"When?" He unlocked his phone and scrolled through his DMs, then handed her the phone.

He was right: nothing from her. Then she opened up the "message requests" screen—messages from people who weren't Facebook friends. And there she was, first in the queue. Every message she'd ever sent him about Mason.

"Whoa, I didn't realize this existed," he said, his thumb inching up the screen. "So his name is Mason? I guess he's, what, five?"

"Yeah. Recently he's been asking about his dad."

"Huh."

"I've come here today to ask if you would visit him."

"Sure, definitely." Iris could hardly believe someone so afraid of commitment was ready to be a dad without hesitation. Maybe he'd known about Mason, not just guessed. Iris had kept him off social media, and as a minor, he wasn't listed in the same public records she'd used to find Forrest's address, but the internet might have told him anyway. "Does he like the zoo? I could take him to the zoo."

"He loves the zoo."

He smiled at the floor. "This is gonna be awesome."

⌒

And it was. On the day of the first visit, Mason dressed himself in neon green sweatpants, a firefighter jacket from his Halloween costume, and a wizard's hat from the previous Halloween. They tidied the apartment together and baked sugar cookies shaped like stars and moons. When Forrest walked through the door, Mason glanced at Iris with a devious smile, as if she'd pulled a magic trick and given him the best gift of all time. The cookies on the cooling rack sweetened the air, and the oblique autumn light cast a purplish hue, giving her the disorienting sense of looking at a photograph of the moment, years later. Forrest didn't hesitate before he grabbed Mason and lifted him ceilingward.

"Hey little dude," Forrest said, hugging him tight. "It's awesome to meet you."

"You're my daddy," Mason said, as if convincing himself it was true.

# Chapter Thirteen

**Evelyn Huang**

November 4, 2018, 10:22 A.M.

I'm a graphic designer, and the day after I agreed to be my older sister's maid of honor, she told me to design and print 120 invitations by hand. Not asked, told. She assumes my time doesn't matter because I work from home and my husband provides most of our income.

After I spent days doing that, guess what? Now she wants me to design the program, write the place cards, and create a style guide for all the other wedding materials. I have a ton of (actual work) projects on my plate, and I do not have time to be my sister's private designer. I said no as politely as I could, and she broke down crying and said she was under a lot of stress and needed just one person in her court. I said no again and she told me she would remember my cruelty for the rest of her life.

I could really use any kind words or funny pictures you can give me.

 139

**Verena Lightfoot**

You matter, Evelyn Huang. Your work has value. Don't let your sister, or anyone, diminish it.

∞ 8

**Anna Banana**

◔ 2

**Breanna Naglehopf**

I love that you were able to stand up to her! You rock!

◔ 3

**Jaclyn Arias**

◔ 1

**Jaclyn Arias**

I don't want to horn in on your support circle Evelyn Huang, but I could use some too! My cousin is being a total bridezilla. She asked my sister and I to make these fairy ribbon sticks that guests are going to wave at her as she and her husband run off at the end of the night. We spent ten hours making them using dowels I ordered on Amazon, and she said they weren't pretty enough! She wants us to go into the woods and collect a hundred and twenty twigs and tie the ribbons to those. My dad says I can't put my foot down because his sister (my cousin's mom) gave us her old car last year. Now I have to remake them all in less than two days. I'm drowning. Send memes!

◔ 3

**Alex Oberlin**

◔ 3

**Madison Le Claire**

Sending love! ❤️

1

**Willa Ho**

You are all heroes in my book!

2

**Kyle Kyle**

Loving all this love! 👰🍾🤮 #HonoraryBridesmaid LOL

4

“Welcome, welcome, happy day!” said Veronica, the matronly consultant at the bridal salon in the mall, in the burnt-honey voice of a lifelong smoker, as she filled stemless glasses with prosecco for Iris, Jasmine, and Connie. Adult contemporary from the Lilith Fair era flowed from the speakers. Iris wasn’t a huge fan of Veronica’s fashion choices—a matching pink skirt suit, pumps, statement earrings, and ruffled scarf that threatened to drown her—but her Yelp reviews were unimpeachable.

It was a miracle that they were on time for their appointment, as Mason had insisted on getting dressed and making breakfast by himself. Now that he had a whole new parent, he wouldn’t countenance any more help from boring old Mom. Fortunately, he was excited about a day with Grandpa Spike, probably because for Iris’s father, “babysitting” meant a trip to the toy store, the ice-cream parlor, and the candy store. Mason would be bouncing off the walls. She hoped the stimulation wouldn’t incite a bedtime tantrum. Forrest’s presence in his life seemed to have reduced these eruptions, but it hadn’t eliminated them.

“I’ve got some sensational possibilities lined up for you,” Veronica said. “Just try to keep an open mind, and don’t pull the trigger until it’s perfect.”

Veronica led Jasmine into the fitting room, leaving Iris alone with her mother on a white upholstered bench reserved for the peanut gallery.

“Remember when we did this for your wedding?” Connie asked, gazing at the gowns on the mannequins near the front.

“Yep,” Iris said, preparing herself for an emotional assassination. Couldn’t the woman remember the one topic to avoid when Jasmine was trying on wedding dresses? After Forrest had left, Iris had spent an embarrassing number of nights downing Häagen-Dazs by the pint and fondling her gown. She would never wear it but still couldn't bring herself to sell it. She didn't want to erase that part of her history. Maybe she'd kept the dress to punish herself.

"Would you . . . still consider getting married, if you found the right man?" Connie asked.

"Of course."

"Have you met anyone interesting recently?"

Iris could feel her mother's agenda pressing against her. She maintained her composure. "I'd rather not talk about it."

Connie gave a little grunt and stared straight ahead. Boundaries offended her.

Jasmine appeared in a lace mermaid gown with a sweetheart neckline and a frilly train. She climbed onto the platform and nodded. "This is totally what I had in mind. I love that it's simple and classic, just like my wedding is going to be."

Iris thought it looked a little bland.

"How much is this one?" Connie asked.

"Everything I've pulled today is safely in your budget," Veronica assured her. "This one is twenty-eight hundred." Their limit was five thousand dollars.

"Is there a way to cover the shoulders a bit?" Connie asked. "And the decolletage?" She touched her clavicle as if feeling personally exposed.

"I like having my arms free," Jasmine said.

"I don't think it's all that revealing," said Iris.

"You and I were raised to believe in modesty at weddings," Veronica said to Connie with affected camaraderie. "But these days, it's become much more acceptable to show off the shoulders."

Connie nodded uncertainly.

"That said, I've got a similar gown but with a bateau neckline and illusion lace on the bodice," Veronica added. "The silhouette is just as beautiful, but it's more modest."

Jasmine shrugged. "Whatevs."

Veronica led Jasmine into the dressing room, again leaving Iris and Connie alone.

"You don't have to share anything you're not comfortable with," Connie said with extreme caution, "but do you think you might bring a date to the wedding? We're roughing out the guest list."

"I don't think so," Iris said. She certainly wasn't going to bring Christof. So far, their relationship had comprised three more lunchtime hookups, each more exquisite than the next. She needed to use her precious free hours to look for a viable partner, someone she could commune with, someone who could be a stepfather for Mason. Right now, though, their little appointments were giving her life. She could relaunch her search for love after Jasmine got married.

"You know," Connie said, "if you were seeing someone, even casually, he's welcome to attend."

Now Iris understood. Connie would be ashamed if guests thought both of Jasmine's older sisters were single, and hell if Rose was bringing anyone. "I'm afraid both your older daughters are going to look like spinsters," she said with a discomfited laugh.

"I don't know what you're implying. My only concern is that you enjoy yourself."

Even if Connie was telling the truth, Iris sensed she hadn't reached the end of her conversational stratagem. When her mother spoke carefully and revealed her motives reluctantly, Iris always felt manipulated. She checked her email, hoping Connie would take the hint. Christof had sent a link to his gallery's password-protected website. Angling the phone away from her mother, she took in the photograph he had selected. It captured her from the waist up, breasts in full view. She looked as if about to speak. The black-and-white image was moody and rich with chiaroscuro. And he was right: she looked just as good as his other models. Had he used Photoshop? She gazed at the image, reminding herself that the beautiful woman who stared back was her.

⌒

The more modest dress was not modest enough for Connie. "Could we try something that covers the arms?" she asked.

"Mom, no," Jasmine said. "I told you, I want my arms free."

"If you don't like it, I won't pressure you," Connie said.

"Fine. Pick one, and I'll try it on."

Connie and Veronica left to flip through the racks.

"Be honest—what did you think?" Jasmine asked Iris, when they were alone.

"If you love that first one, you should totally go for it," Iris said.

"But?"

"I feel like it could pop a bit more."

Jasmine slumped onto the bench next to Iris. "Yeah, I kinda felt that way, too."

"When you find the right one, you'll know," Iris said.

Jasmine nodded pensively. "That's what they say." She glanced at Iris. "Hey, is this dress stuff OK for you?"

Iris was touched and a little surprised that Jasmine would consider her perspective. "It's fine, as long as you don't pull a Mom and ask when I'm going to get married."

"I wouldn't do that," Jasmine assured her. "We both know it's never going to happen."

Iris punched the part of Jasmine's upper arm not covered in charmeuse, and they snickered. Almost everything Jasmine said was partly a joke, and Iris could laugh it off. But she remained vigilant for her sister's moments of genuine anger or cruelty.

"By the way, how is David not married already?" Iris asked. "He's twenty-four-karat husband material."

"I know, it's crazy," Jasmine said. "Women jerked him around a lot when he was younger. Most people are turned off by *nice*. It took a lot of work on myself to become someone who could fall in love with a truly kind soul."

"Does he have a brother?" Iris asked.

"No dice. But I would definitely recommend adding a prayer for love into your meditation practice."

"I love that you think I meditate."

"I'm just speaking it into existence," Jasmine said with praying hands.

"It's so nice to spend time with you," Iris said. "Thanks again for letting me be your maid of honor."

"Oh my God, of course. Thank you for wanting to."

"Did you think I wouldn't?"

"Maybe?" Jasmine said, flinching.

"And that's why you waited to invite me to be a bridesmaid, and why you made it into a competition? Because you thought I'd say no?"

"I don't know! I thought you were mad at me about that dumb election."

"I was. Maybe I still am. But I always wanted to do this for you. I never didn't want it."

"And I'm so happy you're doing it!"

"Can I ask why you didn't invite Jillian and Emily? I thought they'd be bridesmaids."

Jasmine made a bloated-corpse face. "Emily and I used to always have our birthday parties together. Then one year, she told me she didn't want to have a party, then went behind my back and planned one for herself. When I confronted her about it, she acted like it was no big deal, and I was the monster for caring about our tradition. And Jillian flirted with my ex. I just thought that was tasteless. The funny thing was, she ended up marrying that guy. I totally would have forgiven her at that point. But I'd said some things we couldn't come back from."

"Maybe someday."

Jasmine sighed. "I blame Mom and Dad. I think they taught us to be suspicious of other people's motives. I think they wanted us to trust only them."

"They don't even want us to trust ourselves," Iris said. "They think I can't make decisions for myself."

"Oh, yeah, they're terrible to you. I just ignore their advice. But their, like, worldview is inside me."

Iris wished she were able to block out the constant criticisms. She was too accommodating, too afraid of hurting people's feelings, too afraid of messing up and needing to be rescued. "Can I tell you something you can't tell Mom and Dad, at least not until I tell them?"

"Duh, of course."

"I got in touch with Forrest, and he wants to be part of Mason's life. We all went to the zoo together. Mason is beyond excited."

"Oh," Jasmine said. "Great."

"Do you think it's *not* great?"

"I mean, do you really think it's a good idea to trust him, after what he did to you?"

"I'm not letting Mason out of my sight, if you're worried he's going to kidnap him or something."

"No, I mean, what if Forrest vanishes again? Mason would be destroyed."

"OK," Iris said, puzzled by her sister's lack of enthusiasm, "but you should see how it's already changed Mason. He's never been so happy."

"I'm just trying to protect you. He could hurt you again, that's all."

Iris realized it had been a mistake to tell Jasmine. She'd despised Forrest from the first. She'd gone out of her way to avoid him.

"I'm sorry," Iris said, choosing her words carefully. "This day is about you, not me. It's your dress, and it's your wedding. Bringing up Forrest was really bad timing on my part. I'm probably just jealous that you get to spend the rest of your life with the man you love."

Jasmine rose and stepped toward the triple mirror, her arms dangling at her sides, her expression darkened by a sobering fear. Again, Iris worried she had said the wrong thing. Was Jasmine unsure about marrying David? "Are you . . . are you OK?" Iris asked after a terrible silence.

Jasmine turned toward her and strapped on a fake smile. "Of course! I was just feeling a little lightheaded—I haven't eaten much today, and the wine went straight to my head."

"Can I get you a snack? I could run to the food court. You still like those almond pretzels from Auntie Anne's, right?"

Jasmine gripped Iris's forearms. "I'm fine. Really."

"I think I found the one," Connie said, emerging from the back room. Jasmine rushed off to try it on, as if she couldn't stand to be with Iris any longer.

Iris again found herself on the spectator bench with her mother. She was reeling from her conversation with Jasmine. What had just happened?

"So . . . there's a handsome rheumatologist who recently joined our church," Connie said, and Iris understood this to be the final maneuver in the campaign her mother had been waging since they arrived. Connie had been gauging Iris's availability and willingness to date before trying to set her up with a loser. Her ploy was so obvious, Iris felt embarrassed for her. "He seems very nice."

"Mom," Iris said with finality. Even if by some quirk of statistics her mother had identified a decent guy, Iris wasn't going to risk giving the woman a lifetime pass for self-congratulation. She would rather spend the rest of her days alone.

"How would it hurt to meet him?"

"Let me guess . . . . he's eighty."

"He is a bit older than you, but you can't discount someone because of an age difference."

"And he doesn't have legs?"

"*Iris.*"

"Then what is it?" Iris asked, delivering maximum side-eye. "Polio? Leprosy? He's gay, is that it?" Gay, to her parents, was a slur.

"I don't see why you always need to pick a fight," Connie said.

"My romantic life is literally the one topic I've asked you to avoid, and it's the only thing you ever bring up."

"I'm trying to help, and you attack me."

"Mom, I might not get married. Process that in any way you need to," Iris said, waggling her fingers at Connie as if casting a spell. "But please stop punishing me for making my own choices."

Connie crossed her arms and drew in an exasperated breath. "This isn't God's plan for you. I know this doesn't jibe with your feminism, but women are happier when they share love with a man." Only to Connie did not being married constitute feminism. The appalling irony was, in the late '70s, before marrying Spike, she'd marched in support of the Equal Rights Amendment. After Jasmine was born, she fell into a blinding two-year depression, finally shaking it with the help of a new evangelical church with more angular architecture, more enthusiastic singing, and more repressive values. As a girl, Iris had grappled with the contradiction of so many religions claiming to be the right one, each threatening hell if you picked wrong. But she'd gone to church weekly with her parents until she left for college, at which point she stopped forever. Jasmine had hated church in high school but now attended dutifully.

"You're right, it doesn't," Iris said.

"I didn't want to get married before I met your father—I was all set to become a nun—but marrying him was the best decision I ever made."

"I don't see you gunning for Rose to dash down the aisle," Iris muttered.

She gazed at Iris tenderly. "You could be happy, if you weren't so stubborn."

"Maybe I don't want to be happy." It wasn't true, but Iris would have said anything to get her mother off her back. She hated fighting with her yet could never prevent it. Connie seemed to draw masochistic pleasure from these squabbles.

To avoid further conversation, Iris checked the Bridesmaids Union page. A frequent commenter named Evelyn Huang had posted about being conscripted to do all the graphic design for her sister's wedding, and it struck a chord with dozens of the now three hundred members of the group. Bridesmaids were either piping in with encouragement or asking for it, or both. It was beautiful to see this outpouring of support, the very reason she'd started the Bridesmaids Union.

She added her own plea:

OMG friends, now I need help too! I'm at my sister's wedding dress appointment, and my mother is eating me alive! She's on a crusade to marry me off. She just tried to set me up with some rando from her church who, I guarantee, is not a catch.

"What's so interesting on your phone?" Connie asked, sliding closer.

Iris angled her screen away. "Just responding to messages." She scrolled through Facebook, liking and loving posts. Connie wandered the atelier, and Iris opened the weather app, read the news headlines, and checked her bank account balance. She tried and failed to beat a level of Candy Crush. She flipped back and forth through the pages of apps, looking for something to help her forget where she was.

The next dress, a tornado of tulle, would have been perfect if Jasmine were trying to hide a full-body tattoo. Connie loved it, of course. "When you look back at your wedding photos in fifty years, you'll be glad you chose a modest dress," she said.

Jasmine's face was as white as the dress. "This isn't right. This isn't right at all. I need to get out of this."

"Then let's get you out of it," said Veronica, guiding her into the changing room with a confident hand. "You're going to be OK."

"Breathe, Jasmine," said Connie, following them into the back.

"I'm breathing," Jasmine snapped.

"Let's not crowd her," Veronica said to Iris, so she sat down and listened to her sister panting and grunting as the dress came off. An alert told her she had five replies to her Bridesmaids Union comment. Electra had written, Oh, moms. All I can say is, you're a total catch, and you should be choosy as hell if you have to spend the rest of your life with the guy! Jaclyn Arias, a woman Iris had never met but who was one of the group's top commenters, wrote, You'll find your Prince Charming soon, I just know it. Iris inhaled a cleansing breath. She felt restored.

Kyle private-messaged her.

Sorry 2 hear you're having a shitty time. What's yr
mom saying?

                              Me getting married is God's Plan

                              My parents only bring up God when
                              they want me to do something.

LOL so true. Mine did too

They use God to justify their hate

They pretend they're good Christians

But they are actually very ugly

                          Agreed

                          I mean, my parents are good people,
                          but they are not shy about using
                          religion as a crowbar.

My parents used an actual crowbar LOL j/k

Connie sat on the other end of the bench, crossing both her arms and legs. As much as Iris appreciated the silence, she didn't want her mother to suffer. She sent Kyle three heart emoji and put down her phone. "How's Jasmine?"

"Where did I go wrong?" Connie asked the ceiling. "I have wanted the best for you since day one, and you waste no opportunity to throw it in my face."

"I know you want the best for me," Iris said. "I just wish you'd understand that when you say you want me to be married, it's for your sake, not mine. Of course I'd like to be married. How could I not want to find love? But you can't force it, and all your advice just makes me feel like you don't trust me."

"From where I'm sitting, it doesn't seem like you're trying."

"I am, OK? I just don't want your . . ." She almost said "meddling," but decided on "input."

Connie considered this. "We all need guidance to live our best lives. None of us can do it alone."

"I'm open to guidance, but you make me feel *terrible*."

"I certainly wouldn't want that."

"If that's true, then stop asking me about my dating life, and stop trying to set me up with men."

A long moment passed before Connie said, "OK. I will try."

Iris knew this conversation had not turned off her mother's advice machine, but at least she'd been able to clarify her position.

Jasmine came out in a beaded white mermaid gown with a stringy halter top. The lacy decolletage dipped almost to her navel, and the plunging back revealed every button of her spine. Satin swathed her hips and flared at the knees over a burst of tulle. This dress cost almost five thousand dollars.

"So this is a more confident look," Veronica said, holding the back of the gown to keep it from falling off.

Grimacing, Connie asked, "Jasmine, do you *like* this dress?"

"I love it," she said. "I think it's the one!" She seemed ready to be finished.

"At least it'll be easy to take off," Connie muttered.

"I'm hearing that Mom has some hesitations," Veronica summarized. "Maid of honor?"

Even ignoring the awkward fit of the sample size, Iris thought the dress was just OK. The problem was, Jasmine didn't look like a bride; she looked like someone dressed as a bride. "It's definitely sexy. If you like it, you should get it. To me it doesn't quite feel perfect."

Jasmine groaned.

"You're going to look good in every dress in the store," Veronica said. "We want to find the one that sings."

"This one sings," Jasmine said. "It's singing, 'Don't Rain on My Parade.'"

"Let's try one more melody." Veronica smiled. "I know you're loving the mermaid silhouette, but you might fall in love with the softness and elegance of an A-line. I have a dress by a local designer—it's a smidge out of your original price range, but in my twenty-eight years as a bridal consultant, I've never been more smitten with a gown. There is a caveat." Veronica held up an index finger. "The sample is in ivory. But that's a blessing in disguise, because you really should consider this shade. Every bride wants to walk down that aisle in white. But with your complexion, you're going to look radiant in ivory."

"Really?" Jasmine said. "It's not 'Here comes the bride, all dressed in beige.'"

"Trust me." And they returned to the fitting room.

⟳

When Jasmine appeared in the ivory A-line, Iris gasped. The full skirt flowed over Jasmine's hips and undulated with each step like waves crashing and spuming on the shore. Pearls and tubular beads cascaded down her side in the shape of a budding willow branch, glistening as if coated in ice. The off-the-shoulder look was more romantic than the plunging halter neckline, and despite the copious bust of the sample size and the seam of clips in the back gripping the loose fabric like sutures, the dress hugged Jasmine's body. And the tint made a dramatic difference: whereas the other gowns looked like something Jasmine wore, this one seemed to be a natural extension of her skin. With this dress, Jasmine could claim her power as a bride, graceful and resplendent.

"What?" Jasmine asked Iris. "Is there a stain?"

"No," Iris said, emotion spreading from her chest to her face and the tips of her fingers, a dizzying concoction of love and awe and regret. "I'm just . . . I think I'm going to cry."

"It's stunning," Connie agreed.

"This one's a mega-wow," Veronica said with a satisfied smile. "You are elegance personified."

Jasmine looked herself up and down in the mirror. "I don't know . . ."

"You don't like it?" Connie asked.

Jasmine squeezed the fabric of the skirt as if it were part of the problem. "Doesn't it make me look sort of fat?"

"Not at all," Iris said.

"Then it's not the dress, it's me," she said, crying. "I'm so gross."

Iris could not believe Jasmine could find a single flaw in her body, except maybe that it was too skinny. Her collarbone stood out from her chest like a tiara, and her cheekbones jutted from her face. Even contradicting her would give too much credence to what she'd said. So Iris just shook her head, wide-eyed and mute. She wished she could take back their whole conversation about Forrest and David. She had unwittingly spooked her sister, and now Jasmine was so in her head, she couldn't see reality.

Veronica dabbed Jasmine's eyes with a tissue, then thrust a few more into her hands—a mascara-tinted tear could ruin a wedding dress.

"You do *not* look fat," said Connie, rubbing Jasmine's upper back. "You're perfect in every way."

Iris didn't love the way their mother had phrased that, but the woman had her limitations. Connie's own mother had dropped one-liners like "The best taste is thin"—and had died in the hospital when Iris was fifteen, after her bones had crumbled from a lifetime of malnourishment. Connie was the only one who had cried at the funeral. Grandma Prudence had been nothing but cruel to her daughter, who was neither devout nor abstemious enough for her—and she'd shamed Rose for everything from skipping her junior prom to eating a whole slice of cake on her birthday. Connie was an *extremely* watered-down version of the old biddy, and for that, Iris could only be grateful.

"You look like a goddess," Iris said.

"Really?" Jasmine asked.

"Yes," Iris, Connie, and Veronica said in unison.

Jasmine sighed. "I guess I do like this dress. But won't people judge me if I'm not wearing white?"

"This gown makes you look luminescent," Veronica said. "Ivory is your white."

"It really is perfect," Iris said.

"I don't know," said Jasmine. "I think I liked the last one better. I guess I like both for different reasons?"

"Why don't we buy both?" Connie offered. "It's the most important day of your life. You can decide later."

Iris was flabbergasted at their mother's munificence. Connie had never been this generous with her.

"Oh my God, Mom, really?" Jasmine said. "I thought you hated the mermaid gown."

"If it makes you happy, I'm happy. And we had some money set aside that it looks like we won't need to spend." Connie threw a meaningful glance at Iris.

"You're the best, Mom," Jasmine said.

"This one is seven thousand," Veronica interjected helpfully.

Iris's own gown had cost fifteen hundred, not that anyone was keeping tabs.

# Chapter Fourteen

**Kyle Kyle**

November 22, 2018, 12:20 A.M.

The union of Baxter and Frederick is less than six months away. Lo and behold, the other night at like 2 am, guess who lights up my phone? I'm awake, because depression, LOL. Baxter is either drunk or high or both, and he asks if I want to hang. So he gets to my place and yes, he's definitely on something, maybe E or Special K or a sprinkle of GHB, and he's like, I don't love Frederick, I love you. He kisses me, not a peck on the cheek, either, and it's like, instant boner. But I surprise myself by stepping back. I'm like, you shouldn't do this if you're high. And he proves he's not high by counting backward from a hundred by sevens. I'm not about to pull out any Asian stereotypes or whatnot, but that shit was convincing.

When he kisses me again, I don't stop him. The next thing I know, we're all over each other in bed. Sex with Baxter honestly felt like I was reuniting with a long-lost part of myself. The heat is crazy powerful in my apartment, even with the windows open, and by the time we finish, we're one big sweaty lump, and all my neighbors know we just nutted, LOL. I've never been so happy in my life. I only wish I'd taken some video, because I just know Baxter is going to deny it ever happened.

76                                                    8 comments

**Debbie Jorgenson**

I don't understand all the acronyms, but I'm here for you!

👍👍2

**Electra Collins**

LOL means "laugh out loud" 😈

😮5

**Debbie Jorgenson**

I know that one . . .

👍1

**Anna Banana**

Is this still a bridesmaid support group? I'm getting an erotic confessions vibe.

👍😮4

**Arden Woodbine**

Be careful with your heart, Kyle Kyle.

👍9

When Rose arrived at Iris's building to drive her and Mason to Tenafly for Thanksgiving, Iris was taken aback, not for the first time, by her older sister's rejection of conventional beauty. She wore no makeup, had an igloo-shaped haircut, and seemed to have plumped further since the previous year; she clearly gave zero fucks about this. Head-to-toe stretch jersey draped over her curves, like priestess clothes for a modernist cult. Her boxy driving sunglasses were for people recovering from cataract surgery. She wore spotless white orthopedic sneakers; Iris couldn't imagine her in heels.

"Auntie Rose!" Mason squealed, dashing in for a hug as she got out of her rental car.

"How have you been, Mason?" Rose asked. Iris found it amusing that she addressed him like an adult, as if a five-year-old could integrate the near and distant past and summarize it on command.

"I have a daddy!"

Iris intercepted Rose's questioning glance. "I'll explain later." To Mason, she said, "Remember, sweetie, we're not going to talk about that until Mommy tells everyone at once."

Mason zipped his lips and threw away the key. She strapped him into the car seat, and he watched a video on his iPad of two guys playing Minecraft. The biggest YouTube celebrities on earth just recorded themselves playing video games—reason number forty-seven Iris was too old for the internet.

They drove south on the Saw Mill, a highway so curvy it seemed to have been designed as a prank. Rose set the cruise control to the speed limit and stayed in the right lane, cars whizzing by on the left.

"How was the flight?" Iris asked.

"Can't complain," Rose replied.

"*Never* give up your right to complain."

Rose smiled dully.

"Did you fly business class?" Iris asked.

"First—they didn't have business." Without a child or a New York apartment, Rose had money to blow on frills. She hired a team of maids to clean her home, ordered bottled water at restaurants, and flew business class (generally not first class, as her goal was comfort, not luxury). And she'd probably paid a hundred fifty a day for the rental car, a Camry.

After high school, Rose had gone to the University of Florida and remained in the state for the eleven years since, in Cape Canaveral, where, as far as Iris could tell, she designed satellites for the government to spy on the rest of the world. She had always kept distance from their family, harboring a quiet wisdom she protected from her sisters. She shared neither Iris's frustration with their parents nor Jasmine's adulation. Instead she acted like a niece, and their parents reciprocated her coolness. Sadly, Rose's detachment from the family extended to Iris.

"Are you excited to see the parental units?" she asked Rose, hoping for snark.

Rose shrugged. "Sure."

"Now that Jasmine's getting married, Mom literally cannot stop trying to marry me off. I think there's something wrong with her brain."

"She's very traditional." Maybe Rose didn't want to hear anything negative.

"How's your job?" Iris asked. "Any cool projects you're working on?"

"I'm not sure I can explain it."

"Try me." Desperation tugged at Iris's belly. She could deal with silence, but silence with her sister was unbearable. It meant that, despite growing up together and sharing half their DNA, they were strangers.

"We're developing smaller and smaller satellites, so one challenge is how to control them and communicate with them when they're too small to contain most traditional aerospace components. We're creating nanocomponents that can work together to achieve complex tasks, the way neurons do in the human brain."

"Cool." Iris basically understood, but she didn't know what question would prove this to Rose. She also knew she would retain none of it and repeat the conversation the next time Rose came to town. "Are they going to be used to spy on other countries?"

"They could be used for a variety of applications."

The traffic was condensing as they climbed onto the bridge. For young Iris, the George Washington Bridge had been a portal to the miraculous metropolis, and now it represented the ignominious journey home. On the Hudson, a tugboat pushed a trash barge, leaving moiré ripples in its wake.

"You and Mason should come visit sometime," Rose said. "I could show you around the lab."

Iris died a little when she thought about all the silences she'd have to endure in Rose's condo. Prison sounded more appealing. "Yeah, we should totally do that."

She took out her phone to distract herself from the awkwardness. Kyle had posted a doozy of a story in the Bridesmaids Union about having sex with his ex. He was on a crash course with his heart sitting shotgun. She wanted to tell him that this kind of post didn't belong in the Bridesmaids Union, but despite how close they'd become, it didn't seem her place to criticize him. She knew she was being a coward.

Amazing that Baxter came back to you.

He's still marrying Frederick 🌚

She sent him a GIF from a TV show she didn't recognize, of a woman clinging to a man's leg, shaking her head as he tried to walk away. Little was more satisfying than hitting upon the perfect GIF.

> When is the wedding? My sister's is also in 6 months . . . May 18

No shit!

Theirs is May 18 too!

> Twinsies!

> I guess you can't come to hers

Baxter needs me as a groomsman LOL

Or else he'll have to do a casting call

"I love the Camry," Rose said, startling Iris.

She sent three heart emoji and put her phone away. "It's a good car."

"It was either this or a Nissan Altima, which is also a good car." Rose kept her eyes on the road. "But the Camry has a better safety record."

"The Altima is good too," Iris repeated, lamely.

⁓

Spike answered the door of the Hagarty house, wearing a plush turkey hat and an apron that read "Keep calm and gobble on" over a thread-bare dress shirt and gym shorts. To show his support for men's health, he'd grown a mustache for "Movember," which made him look like an amateur magician, not the highest-ranking sales trainer at the fourth-largest pharmaceutical company on earth. "What's the password?" he asked Mason.

"I don't know!" Mason said.

"I'm sorry, but I can't let just anyone into Turkey Headquarters. For all I know, you could be hackers trying to steal the secret turkey recipe."

"That's not how hacking works," Iris pointed out, hopping to keep warm. "Could we do the password stuff inside?"

"I didn't hear the password." He crossed his arms and grinned, accentuating his dimples.

Rose waited for the idiocy to end.

Connie's voice rang from within the house. "You're letting in all the cold air."

"What sound does a turkey make?" Iris asked her son.

"Gobble gobble!" Mason exclaimed.

"You saved Thanksgiving!" Spike said. With a sweep of his arm, he welcomed them inside. He ruffled his grandson's hair and cuffed Iris and Rose on the shoulder like a coach congratulating his team.

꩜

The Hagarty family performed a codex of Thanksgiving rituals that an outsider like David could not have understood. They ate at 3:00 P.M. sharp; if Connie was a minute late in getting the food on the table, Spike pretended she was delaying them out of spite. He carved the turkey with the electric knife and trumpeted its features as if hosting an infomercial. Connie hoped aloud that there were no complaints about the thickness of the gravy; Jasmine had opined that it was too thin—when she was nine. Spike led the family in a bit about being sleepy because they'd eaten a turkey with extra tryptophan ("The guy at Whole Foods assured us this was a low-tryptophan bird." "He lied to us!" "I demand a refund!"). When Iris was feeling confrontational, she remarked at how few dishes did not contain meat, and her father would say something like, "God created animals to nourish us." There was never a break in conversation, yet no feelings were acknowledged. Iris used to cry soundlessly during Thanksgiving dinner without knowing why.

This year, they had a topic, at least. Jasmine was "infusing" the wedding with "wow moments," because the original plan wasn't feeling worthy of their love. She was keeping the Princeton string quartet for the ceremony and adding a ten-piece pop band alternating with a rock gospel trio for the reception. She would be partnering with a moonshine distillery and a nearby strawberry farm to create a signature punch she was calling "Country Nectar." A local goatherd would set up a table of artisanal chevre. David and Jasmine would ride to and from the ceremony on horses, and a pair of alpacas, dressed as bride and groom, would be available for photo ops. Spherical flower arrangements would hang from the rafters, and three tons of hay bales would provide lounge seating. Guests would leave with a bottle of moonshine and a monogrammed cowboy hat. Oh, and she was adding more bridesmaids, to improve the photos. Iris couldn't help thinking these "wow moments" were connected to Jasmine's panic at the bridal salon. She'd considered pulling her sister aside to help warm her cold feet, but with Jasmine, it seemed better not to say anything than to be wrong. Anyway, Jasmine had been busy analyzing wedding spreadsheets all day.

"We're thinking we can do it for about two hundred thou," Jasmine said, Elsa sleeping in her lap. "But you can't put a price on memories."

"I'd be happy to pitch in," David said.

"Please," said Spike, holding out a warning hand. "The custom is for the bride's parents to pay. As long as it makes our Jasmine happy, we're happy."

They were letting David pay for the honeymoon, though. Originally, the plan had been a week in Hawaii, but as the wedding evolved, so did the vacation. "You only get married once," Jasmine said, "so I thought, 'Go big or stay home.'" Now they were climbing Mount Kilimanjaro. They were advised to wait until June, to avoid the rainy season, but Jasmine wanted to get on the airplane the day after the wedding, so they were killing time with a two-week safari and a week on the beach in Zanzibar. It sounded exhausting.

"So you won't have a ring bearer, or . . . ?" Iris asked, still upset that Mason wasn't invited.

"That's the best part," Jasmine said. "Apparently, there's this trained . . . what's the term?"

"Kid," David said with a smile.

"Yeah, a kid who comes in with the basket of rings in his mouth."

Iris didn't understand. Why would a child need to be trained to bring in the rings, why would he carry them in his mouth, and why couldn't Mason do it?

Mason came to the rescue. "I'm a kid!"

"Not a boy," Jasmine said, "a kid. A baby goat."

Iris gulped. "You're having a goat bring in the rings?"

"It's so adorable, you won't believe it. It's like a cat video times a hundred."

"It *is* cute," David admitted with a snorty laugh.

"Human children are also cute," Iris said.

"But everyone's done real children before," Jasmine said. "Goats are fresh."

"Goats are sexy," Iris deadpanned.

"Bingo," said Jasmine, tapping her nose and pointing at Iris. "It's gonna go viral."

"Are you getting married by a chicken?"

David laughed again. It pleased Iris to observe that he was not a fan of Wedding 2.0, but she felt guilty about allying with him against her sister.

"No, Dad's officiating," Jasmine said, "but the venue has a coop with heritage chickens. I think. Or maybe heritage chicken is on the menu."

"I thought you weren't comfortable performing an interfaith ceremony," Iris said to her father.

"I won't be," Spike replied. "David has agreed to convert."

Spike's stance on intermarriage was no surprise: this was the same man who considered America to be a Christian nation and who thought the white nationalists' worst crime was bad PR. But for David to leave Judaism just to marry Jasmine with their parents' blessing? It was a step too far.

"What happened to Miss 'I don't believe in categories?'" Iris asked Jasmine.

"I don't," Jasmine protested. "Mom and Dad are insisting."

"We're not insisting; we're encouraging," Spike said. "Our church looks down on interfaith pairings. And it can be confusing for kids for their parents to be different religions."

"You're insisting," Jasmine said.

"We're not insisting," Connie said.

"And you're on board with this?" Iris asked David.

"I said I'd consider it," he clarified with a smile that morphed into a grimace.

Iris didn't know what to believe. It all seemed sort of ugly. She glanced at Rose, hoping for some shared exasperation, but Rose wasn't paying attention. Her mind was probably up in space, communicating with her tiny satellites.

"Jasmine, I made the stuffing extra-crispy for you," Connie said, eyeing her plate, empty except for a slab of turkey. Connie often encouraged Jasmine to eat more, but never Iris or Rose. Meanwhile, her own Thanksgiving feast consisted of a few glasses of wine. She claimed she nibbled while she was cooking.

"Sorry, Mom, I'm on this new diet," Jasmine explained. "I can only eat meat and veggies and fat—like, if I don't get enough fat in a day, I literally have to go into the fridge and eat butter with a spoon. And if I eat one carb, the whole diet is ruined. I've already lost three pounds. I need to lose twelve more if I'm going to look presentable in my wedding dresses."

"I wish you'd told me," Connie said. "I would have cooked something different." Iris and Mason were enjoying the stuffing, but there was no point in interfering with Connie's guilt trip.

"I thought you looked amazing in those dresses," Iris said.

"The camera adds ten pounds," said Jasmine. "If I'm not careful, I'll look like a whale in the photos."

"You look beautiful just as you are," David said, tucking a lock of her hair behind her ear.

She grinned at him. "Of course you think so—you love me no matter what."

"Guilty as charged." He kissed her chastely. "Mason, what's up in your world?"

"Mostly kindergarten," Iris laughed. "And he's loving it." Telling her parents about the bite would be suicide.

"What are the other children like?" Connie asked.

"They seem nice. He's making friends."

"My friends are Adelaide and Tania and Antoine and—"

Mason probably would have listed his entire class had Connie not interrupted him. "Do they come from good families?"

"Sure," Iris said. "What do you mean?"

"Good Christian families who are upstanding in their community and believe in the importance of education?" Connie clarified.

Iris couldn't tell if this was a veiled question about race, single parents, or something else entirely. She wished she didn't have to decode everything her mother said. "Do you want me to take a poll?"

"We just want to make sure he can realize his full potential," Spike said, "the way you and your sisters did in the Christian Academy."

Now Iris understood. When she enrolled Mason in kindergarten, her parents had offered to pay for parochial school—which was a hard no for Iris. In her experience, it created closed-minded conservatives who treated women at best like princesses and at worst like chattel. Apparently, that offer was still on the table. In truth, though, private school would be a good solution right now. Mrs. Floria had started a petition among the parents to get Mason transferred into a special needs class. He didn't qualify because he didn't have a learning disability, and the kids, even Rafael, weren't shunning him, but who knew what lengths Mrs. Floria might go to in the name of protecting her child?

Iris smiled. "He's doing great."

After dinner, Rose offered to do the dishes. Iris didn't have the energy to cobble together another one-sided conversation, so she and Mason joined everyone else for a postprandial soak in Spike's hot tub.

In the ten-foot dash between the sliding door and the hot tub, the frigid air bit into Iris's skin, and the icy pavers numbed her toes, which then burned in the water. Spike and Connie slipped their legs over the edge, their drinks sloshing. Connie was plastered. After two glasses of wine, she relaxed; after four, she sang sailor shanties; after six, she became wild and embittered. Jasmine strolled toward the whirlpool in boy shorts and a shred of a bikini top. With her phone held high, she sidled into the velvety bromine soup. As if she could read Iris's mind, she said, "When I learned to stop being afraid of the cold, it held no power over me anymore."

"Thanks, Zen master," Iris said.

David entered last, carrying Mason on his back. Iris took note of her future brother-in-law's body, lit by the patio floodlight. His torso was barrel-shaped, with an hourglass of untamed curly fur from his chest to his waistband. It pleased her that he didn't have a gym body.

He slotted himself in between Jasmine and Connie. "Good evening, neighbor," he said to Connie, with a tip of an imaginary hat.

"Good evening!" Mason screeched. He adored the hot tub, and Spike was thoughtful enough to keep the temperature low enough for his safety.

"It's the Hagarty way," Iris explained to David. "If you can stand squeezing into a hot tub with us, you're family. Or maybe it's the other way around."

"Forgive me if I'm speaking out of turn," David said, "but I guess I assumed devout people, you know . . ."

"Would keep their clothes on?" Iris said, completing his question.

"We're all family here," Spike answered paternally.

"But we keep the swimsuits on, right?" David asked with a wink at Iris. Was he flirting with her? It seemed unlikely, with Jasmine two feet away.

"I think that's up to your bride," Iris said.

Jasmine was making sexy eyes at her phone, with the turn of the head and coy, upward glance that defined the selfie. Without breaking her gaze, she said, "No one's taking off their bathing suit." Satisfied with her photo, she tossed her phone onto her towel and flipped her legs onto David's lap.

Connie had been staring at Rose through the window. "She's letting her weight get out of control," she whispered.

"Some people literally can't hear the voice inside their head that tells them when they're full," Jasmine said. "Fast food actually alters your brain chemistry."

"I don't think she eats so much fast food," Iris said. "Some people gain weight really easily." She didn't know why she was defending her sister, when Rose had no inclination to defend herself. Maybe she was defending everyone's right to make their own choices without being shamed.

"I worry about her," Jasmine said. "I don't even want to think about how many free radicals are in her bloodstream."

"Then don't," Iris said.

"Testy, testy," Jasmine said, sounding impressed.

"It feels like she's doing this on purpose," said Connie. "She's afraid of getting her heart broken, so she makes herself unappealing to men."

"Why would she want a relationship?" Iris asked. "She does important work, and she likes living alone. Men cause more problems than they solve."

Connie turned her forlorn gaze, pregnant with disappointment, toward Iris. "When did you become such a *feminist?*" she asked, her voice wobbling.

"When I learned to think for myself," Iris said, defiant.

"Ah, so she thinks for herself," said Spike.

"At least I don't swallow every lie fed to me by Fox News."

"The lies of the liberal media are much more dangerous," he said. "They would have us tear up the Constitution."

She couldn't believe she was wading into a political discussion, but her parents roiled up an undertow. She didn't want Mason to think she condoned their pernicious beliefs. Ever since Trump had won the election, any mention of him had chafed, yet it felt morally wrong to remain silent. "That's what your president wants you to believe."

"He's your president too, even if you voted for crooked Hillary," said Jasmine.

"The whole idea of 'crooked Hillary' is just sexism," Iris said, stung that Jasmine would join the fray. "She's a woman with ambition, period."

"Obama was terribly divisive, but we accepted him as our president," Connie said. "The liberals don't accept Trump as president. He won the election, fair and square. You have to accept that, or else you can kiss democracy goodbye."

"In the history of the United States," Iris said through gritted teeth, "we have never had a president more damaging to our democracy than the rapist-in-chief you put in office."

"Touché," Jasmine said with a smile.

"Let's dial this down a notch," said Spike.

"We're not idiots," Connie said, barely navigating her syllables. "We obviously don't condone his treatment of women, or believe everything that comes out of his mouth. But he stands for something, which is more than you could say for Hillary."

"I think you don't believe a woman is worth anything unless she's behind a man," Iris said, holding back tears. "News flash: it's not the nineteenth century anymore."

Connie narrowed her eyes. "Who raised you to be so snide? Is that how you talked to Forrest? No wonder . . ." She glanced at Mason and went silent. At least she knew when she was being monstrous.

"Daddy Forrest!" Mason exclaimed. "He took me to the zoo."

Everyone turned toward her, and Iris's heart drummed in her temples. There was no covering this up. Anyway, she'd wanted to tell them, to show them she had reconciled with Forrest and given Mason his father. They might even be proud of her for taking the initiative. She only wished the news could have waited until her mother wasn't piss-drunk.

"That should lighten your load a bit," Connie said without a drop of enthusiasm.

"He finally responded to your messages?" asked Spike.

"It turned out he hadn't seen them," she said, not wanting to tell them she tracked down his address and knocked on his door. "I reached out again, and he's been excited to get involved."

"Is he equally excited to pay child support?" Spike asked.

Iris saw she'd been an idiot to think she could squeeze approval out of them. Why did they always need to manage her? "I haven't broached that subject, but if it keeps going well, we'll get there."

"Is he going to make an honest woman out of you?" Connie asked.

"Neither of us wants that," Iris said.

"Why not? You have a child together. The problem with you is you're too picky. I offered to set you up with a very eligible bachelor, and you rejected him out of hand. You could wait the rest of your life for Prince Charming. Or you could grow up and learn to compromise."

Iris could not digest this insanity. Did Connie believe she might marry a man who had abandoned her? What was a polite synonym for "back the fuck off"?

"He never wanted to marry Iris," Jasmine cut in. "I knew it the second I met him."

"I can't tell if you just said something extremely mean," Iris said.

Jasmine examined her nails. "I'm just being honest. Honesty is never mean."

"That's definitely not true," David said, lifting his index finger as if requesting permission to speak.

"Why now?" Spike asked, leaning forward. "Why did you reach out again?"

What was this, a cross-examination? "When Mason started kindergarten, most of his friends had dads, and he was feeling left out."

"And he didn't feel left out in preschool?"

"I'm not sure I understand what you're getting at," Iris said, wishing she'd never opened her mouth. She wasn't strong enough to manage a war on three fronts: her mother's marriage boosterism, her sister's dismissive cruelty, and her father's suspicion. "Everyone was asked to draw their families, and one of his friends made him feel bad because he didn't have a dad."

"He's not my friend anymore," Mason said. "I don't like him."

"Yes, Rafa was mean to you," Iris said, squeezing Mason's arm in pulses, as if he could take a hint. He knew not to mention the bite, right?

"I was a bad boy," Mason said.

"You weren't a bad boy, sweetie," she said. She could see the disaster rushing toward her but had no way to stop it.

"Why were you a bad boy?" Spike asked.

"Mason yelled at Rafa," Iris interjected, squeezing Mason's arm, praying he would take the hint, "and we had a parent-teacher meeting about it. It's all settled now."

"No, Mommy, I bit him," Mason reminded her.

Spike and Connie shared a bloodless look. Iris felt her stomach fold into quarters.

"What is going on at that school?" Spike asked.

"It was an isolated incident," Iris said. "He had some overwhelming feelings, and he didn't know how to express them. We've talked about it a bunch, and it's all totally under control. He's actually doing great in kinder-garten. He loves school and he's learning a lot. It's really no big deal."

Everyone, even Mason, was staring at her. She willed him not to con-tradict her.

"It sounds like a very big deal," said Connie.

"Excuse me," Iris said. She handed Mason to David, jumped out of the tub, wrapped herself with her towel, and darted inside before the droplets on her skin could turn to ice.

"Dry your feet off at the door," Connie called after her.

The girls' childhood bathroom was, by any objective opinion, hideous. The wall tiles were a creamy shade of pink, which clashed with the pee-colored fake marble countertop (complete with scalloped sink). A row of spherical light bulbs above the vanity recalled a showgirl's dressing room, and for some inexplicable reason, the *VeggieTales* shower curtain, which their mother had bought on sale at TJ Maxx in the mid-'90s, had outlasted all three sisters in that house.

Iris sat on the puffy pink toilet seat and wrote to Kyle.

**Tonight couldn't be going worse.**

No response. Maybe he was with friends. Weirdly, he never mentioned his friends, except Baxter, of course. She texted Christof.

**Happy Thanksgiving! Are you in New York? 🖤**

Nothing. She wrote Thanksgiving greetings to Amber and Sophia, then put the phone on the vanity and blow-dried the ends of her hair, trying to will away the memory of what had just happened.

Someone knocked, and she turned off the hair dryer. She hoped it was Rose, whom she had rushed past on the way to the bathroom. Rose might not offer encouragement, but at least she wouldn't shame her further.

"Are you decent?" her father asked through the door. Better than her mother, but not by much.

"Yeah," she said, opening it a crack against her better judgment.

He leaned against the jamb and gazed at her with kind eyes. "I'm sorry about your mother. We were both pretty shocked about what you told us."

She sighed. "Yeah. I just didn't want you to worry. I didn't want you to think I'm a bad parent."

"You're a very good mother, Iris, and a very capable woman. We're in awe of what you've done, all on your own." He pressed a knuckle against his lips. "Sometimes, though, the hardest thing, the most mature thing, is to know when to ask for help."

"We're doing fine, Dad. Really."

"Your mother and I would like you to move back home. We'll enroll Mason in the Christian Academy. We've never trusted the public school he's in. You can be a full-time mom until you're ready to pursue a career that fulfills you. Consider it a reboot."

Iris couldn't imagine living with her parents again, nor sending Mason to the same school she and her sisters went to, where boys prepared for Bible college and girls prepared for wifehood. In fourth grade, her teacher had "punished" some obstreperous boys with math problems and had "rewarded" the obedient girls with manicure hour. In eighth grade, all the girls were given purity rings and required to sit in a circle once a week and discuss sexual temptation. The boys didn't have it much better: An effeminate boy in the class had been called a butt pirate in front of their teacher, and the boy was suspended for inciting his classmates' ridicule. Turning Mason's life over to her parents would be spiritual homicide.

"We'd also like you and Mason to start coming to church," he replied. "And we want to see you dating. I know your mother is eager to play matchmaker, but as long as you're making an effort to find a good Christian husband, we won't interfere."

"And what if I say no?"

Spike sighed, filling the air with alcohol breath. "We know you have a lot of credit card debt, and you're not going to be able to stay ahead of it forever. If you come back home now, we will pay off that debt. If you wait past the end of the year, I'm afraid you're on your own."

How did they know about her debt? She never talked about her finances with her family. Maybe Jasmine had seen Kyle's post on Twitter and told them.

"This sounds like an ultimatum," Iris said, furious at Jasmine but mostly at him and Connie. They'd been waiting for an excuse to swoop in and control her. Why couldn't they support her without strings attached?

He touched her cheek; she bristled at his attempt to pacify her. "It's an offer," he emphasized. "We only want what's best for you and Mason." Then he shut the door.

She dropped her face into her hands and sobbed. She gave all of herself to Mason, and they didn't trust her with raising him. They didn't trust her at all.

# Chapter Fifteen

**Eye Fay**

November 23, 2018, 8:40 A.M.

Greetings to my bridesmaids-in-arms from New Jersey, where yours truly was reared. I hope everyone's Thanksgivings were tolerable, which is to say, better than mine. At least I get a break from my skeeve-tastic boss.

Apparently, my sister is radically "reimagining" her wedding. As one of MANY "upgrades," she is renting alpacas for guests to pose with. The alpaca rental company (Dear Lord, how is this a thing?) is dressing them up as bride and groom, with a top hat for the male and veil for the female. To me, they look like zombie poodles. I have literally had nightmares where a herd of alpacas tore my flesh from bone.

This new wedding is now going to cost 200 grand. You could buy a house for that! Maybe not in their town, but definitely where I live. Where are people's priorities? A wedding is a PARTY, people. In college, my suitemates and I threw house parties overflowing with booze for like $200—less than the cost of one plate of heritage chicken at my sister's wedding. And we had a FANTASTIC time. If

I'd woken up the morning after one of these ragers and found myself married, sure, I would have gotten it annulled, but I wouldn't have faulted the truly excellent special event.

What's the most over-the-top wedding you've been to? Did the couple hire a trained goat as a ring bearer? Did they drop a cool thou on decorative hay?

 53                                     18 comments

**Penelope Bradford**

I'm an event designer, and I've planned some very extravagant weddings. Once, a professional football player rented out a stadium and hired top-tier entertainment to re-create a halftime show for his guests. That was probably the most expensive, based on the entertainment costs alone. At another big one, we rented a cathedral and hung huge curtains made of white carnations around the guests. The effect was out of this world. But I overheard one guest say, "They couldn't afford roses?"

🗨 5

**Verena Lightfoot**

When millions of people are going hungry every day, these people should be ashamed of themselves.

🗨 1

**Penelope Bradford**

I do think the money often could be better spent. That said, the adage that it's the best day of people's lives is often true, and as a once-in-a-lifetime splurge, it seems less outlandish. Also, it's not like that money is being thrown away. Much of the cost of special events goes to staff, who work hard and need the income. And if the couple spends hundreds of thousands of dollars on carnations, it's going to farms that grow them. And sure, a lot goes to the owners of those farms, who might not need the money, but some trickles down to people who do.

🗨 2

Someone named Kyle Victorious requested Iris's Facebook friendship the morning after Thanksgiving, while she and Mason were eating breakfast with their family. Though the profile photo was a drawing of Batman, this had to be *the* Kyle under a different guise.

Sorry I was MIA last night

I'm in Facebook jail LOL

What's that?

Someone flagged 1 of my posts 4 being offensive

A tasteful nude

No crack or anything

Girl I know lets her tits hang out with the nips blurred

Fckn hypocrisy

Iris was curious about the offending "tasteful nude," not merely to gauge its propriety.

Be careful what you say. Big Brother might get wind of it.

"Are you going to bury your face in your phone all day?" Connie asked. She hadn't apologized for her drunk harangue the night before, only doubled down on her criticism. "Believe it or not, other people at this table might enjoy the pleasure of your company."

"We have a rule," Jasmine said, gesturing toward a groggy David, whose eyes were half-shut and whose hair was sweetly untamed. Since Spike and Connie wouldn't countenance sharing a bed before marriage, he'd slept on the janky pull-out couch. "No electronics at meals. Or else we'd, like, never talk to each other."

"One of us has more trouble putting her phone away than the other," David said, grabbing Jasmine's fingers playfully.

Jasmine swatted him away with irritation that didn't seem feigned.

"I need to handle this," Iris said. She wasn't in the mood to be friendly.

> When do they let you out of jail?

Maybe in a few days

Maybe they delete my account

They can do whatever the hell they want
because there's no alternative to their product

This fckn monopoly shouldn't b legal

Iris thought he could always stop using the site—it wasn't the same as if one company owned all the grocery stores—but she didn't want to provoke him.

I'm surprised they haven't flagged u yet

They delete accounts with fake names

A frightening thought seized Iris.

> If they deleted my account, would
> the Bridesmaids Union go away?

She'd hoped "Eye Fay" counted as a nickname, but Facebook moderators might not think so.

"Anyone want more of the world's best pancakes?" Spike asked, swinging an oily spatula like a conductor's baton.

"I'll take one more," David said.

"One more of what?" Spike asked, one hand cupping his ear.

"The world's best pancakes!" Mason exclaimed.

"That guy is going places," said Spike.

Jasmine tilted her mug to gauge its fullness. "I could use a refill of the world's best coffee," she said, unperturbed by their father's neediness—and too lazy to get up.

"Could you grab me one more of the world's best napkins?" Iris asked, trying to rub maple syrup off her screen. "Maybe dipped in the world's best water?"

"Don't get fresh," Connie warned. She had a sniper's instinct for protecting her husband's ego.

Iris's phone vibrated.

No, but there'd b no way to moderate it

It'd b like if ur spaceship ran out of gas

U keep going forever but u cld never change
course

U don't have another admin? That's risky

The awareness of her negligence disoriented her, as if she'd woken up in a speeding car. She recalled a subsection of the hospital's internet use policy requiring official social media pages to have two admins, in case one quit or was fired. The Bridesmaids Union was obviously not a hospital account; still, it was remarkably hard to connect the content of those policies with her behavior. It was as if she resisted them on purpose.

In fact, the very existence of the Bridesmaids Union, which had grown by a hundred members after the lovefest during Jasmine's dress appointment, was making her nervous. At work she'd recently revised the hospital's notice of privacy practices, the mother of all policies, to address public worry in the wake of a Facebook data breach. These breaches were only going to get worse from here; was she being stupid in not deleting the Bridesmaids Union, her account, her entire digital footprint? But everyone used Facebook. Lawmakers had a stake in ensuring everyone's safety before anything really bad happened. She knew that logic was faulty, and yet for the sake of her sanity, she was forced to believe it. It was like God. No amount of worldwide tragedy could eradicate her belief in a presence that kept her safe.

**Would you be my backup admin?**

She was unsure both how big a favor this entailed and whether it was a good idea to place the security of her group in the hands of someone who was already in Facebook jail. But what was the chance both their accounts would be deleted at the same time?

**I promise I wouldn't ask anything of
you except to step in if my account
were suspended.**

"What is so interesting on there that you can't put it away for one minute?" Connie asked.

"Just a second, Mother," Iris said, peeking at her phone as Kyle's reply came in.

**Sure! Happy 2**

**Thank you so much!!!**

**Just one thing—I need to be careful
not to invite anyone who knows me.**

> Would you mind letting me do all
> the approvals?

👍 1

"Some days I wish those phones had never been invented," Connie muttered.

> Let me know when you're out of jail
> and I'll add you.

> GTG!

It seemed crucial to tell him exactly when she was putting down her phone, so he would never worry that she was ignoring him. Was he as emotionally fragile as her parents, or did she just imagine he was?

⁓

After breakfast, while Iris moderated Bridesmaids Union posts, encouraging new members and defusing arguments, Jasmine knocked on Iris's open bedroom door.

"Can I come in?" Jasmine asked, looking contrite.

"Sure." They sat on the edge of Iris's childhood bed, with its metal *Bedknobs and Broomsticks* frame. Iris had loved the film as a young girl, and her mother had seen the bed at an estate sale and bought it for her. Around that time, her father had painted the parade of all God's creatures around the wainscoting as part of a Bible lesson about Noah's Ark. As terrible as her parents could be, they had given their all to make their daughters happy.

"You know I'm bad at apologies," Jasmine began, "but I'm sorry about how last night went down. I should have sided with you against Mom and Dad. I thought I was just teasing you, and then everything exploded."

"Thanks," said Iris, cringing to remember the hot tub nightmare, which now felt soupy and unreal. Her instinct was to deflect the apology, to say it didn't matter, but Jasmine's words had stung. "What did you mean when you said that Forrest never wanted to marry me?"

Jasmine shook her head as if to recant everything she'd said. "I was just talking out of my butt. I just meant that he seemed like a playboy. I still hoped it would work out between you." Jasmine had never gotten along with Forrest; maybe she'd sensed he would break her heart.

"Why didn't you tell me that? I mean, at the beginning?"

"Come on, Iris. You were in love. Would you really have wanted me to drop a bomb like that?"

Jasmine had a point—her butting in would have felt like a betrayal, and Iris might have blamed her when the relationship foundered. But wasn't there a way for sisters to tell each other hard truths? "I guess that's why you didn't like him."

"Yeah, pretty much." Jasmine stood, almost too abruptly. "Anyway, I have to go teach my yoga class, but again, I'm really sorry."

"Wait—just one more question," Iris said, steeling herself for another political conversation against her better judgment. "I'm still upset that you didn't vote for Hillary Clinton. I know it's not about me. It just feels . . . personal."

"Oh God no!" Jasmine exclaimed. "Not at all. I really thought about it for a long time. I've become more fiscally conservative since I started my business—the income taxes were killing me. I knew Trump would be bad for our country, but I felt like I could relate to him. He kinda just shoots from the hip, you know? And I really got weird vibes from Hillary. She was only running because she wanted to be president. She didn't care about our country."

At Jasmine's admission that she liked Trump's personality, Iris let a wave of revulsion pass through her. She had felt the exact opposite about the two candidates' reasons for running. "OK, but imagine that Hillary was a man and Trump was a woman. You would be fine with Hillary being ambitious, and you would be disgusted with Trump for being . . . horrible. Right?"

Jasmine considered this and shrugged. "I can't really imagine it. Anyway, I didn't vote for him, and it's not like it would have mattered if I did."

Of course it mattered—personally—that Jasmine hadn't voted for Hillary. Still, Iris was glad she'd brought it up. She felt a little less alone.

As the morning progressed, Rose drove to the library to work, Jasmine taught a yoga class in Englewood, Spike made a pilgrimage to the ShopRite, and Connie was cleaning and refused Iris's offer to help, which was a relief, despite the implied insult. Iris invited David on a walk: she had questions that needed answering. He was surprisingly eager to accompany her. She would have thought a future in-law would keep distance from his strange new family with their unfamiliar customs, but David was no ordinary in-law.

She dug out a cheap stroller from the basement, even though Mason was too old for strollers, and he hopped right in. She wasn't leaving Mason with her parents again. They had probably been waiting for an excuse to take over, marry her off so they could stop feeling so much shame, and program Mason with their retrograde beliefs.

Even on Thanksgiving weekend, when the houses of Tenafly were packed with extended families, few could be found outside walking. Iris had never understood this town-wide allergy to fresh air.

"How are you feeling today?" David said. "Your mom was like a rottweiler last night."

"Oh, that," Iris said, ashamed he had witnessed it. "Par for the course. Get a few glasses of wine in that woman and her filter dissolves."

"For the record, it sounds like you're doing a great job with Mason. I'm sorry I didn't say something—I felt like it wasn't my place."

"Thanks. They'd listen to you, though. It's women they don't believe."

"Sounds like you're pretty mad at them."

His understanding consoled her. "You don't know the half of it."

"Jasmine tells me things. She thinks your mom has an undiagnosed anxiety disorder."

"Yeah, probably. And criticizing me is her Klonopin." It felt impolitic to complain so much about David's future mother-in-law, so she changed gears. "Tell me more about Wedding 2.0. I hear it's going to be the event of the decade."

He shook his head in resignation. "I have to admit, I don't understand what's gotten into Jasmine, but it'll be fun."

"I'm guessing the menagerie wasn't your idea."

"You would be correct. Neither was the moonshine. Or the new registry. Apparently, her friends didn't want to give to charity."

The registry now contained nothing less expensive than an eighty-five-dollar set of kitchen utensils, and numerous items in the thousands: a four-thousand-dollar coffee table, a twelve-hundred-dollar set of Egyptian cotton sheets, a fifteen-thousand-dollar silver teapot. Iris couldn't imagine owning something worth fifteen thousand dollars that would dent if you dropped it.

She glanced at him, unsure how to formulate her next question. "I hope this isn't rude to bring up, but you're converting? Because before you do, I think you should watch *Kirk Cameron's Saving Christmas*. And keep in mind that our parents *loved* that movie."

"I'm considering it. Converting, not watching the movie."

"To be honest, converting would be far less painful."

"I just need to think it through." He kicked a pile of crispy leaves.

"Do you have a strong connection to your Jewish faith?"

"Faith? No, I'm an atheist. But I'm ethnically a Jew, and it would be weird not to be one anymore. I'm just not sure."

It seemed crazy to consider it if he didn't actively want to be Christian. She wondered whether he stood up for himself with Jasmine. He was awfully bendy. "I'm not for or against, but if you do go through with it, my parents are going to take complete control of your life. Control is their drug."

"Sounds like you're against," David said.

"Me? I'm impartial." She grinned.

Mason jumped out of the stroller, found a stick, and swung it at tree trunks and leaves. David picked up another stick and followed suit. Iris noted that he was standing between Mason and the road, keeping him safe from the occasional car that whizzed by.

"Since you're marrying my sister, and I clearly get final say, can I grill you a little more?" she asked.

"Sure, why not? Now that I know who makes the decisions around here." He smiled at her.

"Jasmine said you owned this company called Life Harvest?" She didn't want to admit she'd googled him. "What was the deal with that?"

"We developed personality quizzes that ran on Facebook," he said. "People would share their profile information and activity log to play, and we sold it to companies who did micro-targeted advertising."

"What kind of quizzes?"

"I don't know, 'Where should you live?' or 'What's your Patronus?' It's a Harry Potter thing."

"I think I took the Patronus quiz," she said. "I'm pretty sure mine was a groundhog. Or maybe that was my spirit animal."

"There you go. You gave us your data."

Iris considered this. This was the kind of thing Christof would rail against—and it kind of creeped her out—but why would anyone care about the singers she liked and the cat videos she laughed at? So what if she saw ads for upcoming concerts and animal rescue charities? "In your expert opinion, should I be worried that I gave away my data?"

"In theory, no. It helps companies fine-tune their ad campaigns—it's not personally identifying stuff. Or at least it's not supposed to be."

Bored by this conversation, Mason dropped his stick and plopped back down in the stroller.

"Not supposed to be?"

He sighed. "My company was very careful about protecting people's privacy. Not all companies are quite so scrupulous."

They waved at a couple wrangling a Christmas tree into their house, who probably thought she and David were a couple, Mason their child. Oddly, she didn't mind being seen as a wife for once. "Did you have anything to do with the Cambridge Analytica scandal?" she asked. The scandal was that Cambridge Analytica used stolen data, but Iris had always thought the legal part of it—that the Trump campaign had hired them to trick social media influencers to shill for him—was way scarier. Could Kyle have been one of those influencers? Probably not—she'd never seen anything political in his posts, just clothes and abs and the occasional side-butt.

"No," David said with a surprising vehemence, and she feared she'd insulted him. "But when the scandal broke, it woke me up to a truth I hadn't admitted to myself. I went into the business thinking I could confine the data to the world of marketing. What I didn't realize, or didn't believe, was that social media can be weaponized. I believed for too long that people were too smart to be manipulated."

"People are pretty dumb," Iris said.

"I felt stupid for not seeing it from a mile away," David said. "I got out of the business before it could get any worse."

"And your quiz company sold for millions of dollars?"

"It wasn't just the quizzes—it was the technology behind it, and a deep cache of consumer data—but yes. Basically."

"Excuse me for saying this, but that's kind of insane."

He laughed. "You're right. It was insane. And I hated that I had profited from something that could be used for evil—I'd wanted to shut down the company, but that would have screwed my employees. So I started giving the money away."

"Are you going to get your name on a building? The David Leiman Clock Tower? The David Leiman Cafeteria?"

"I did it anonymously. I didn't want anyone to know where the money came from. And Jasmine convinced me to stop."

"She likes nice things," Iris said. She breathed on her fingers to warm them.

"True, but that wasn't why. She pointed out that the only way for me to make penance was to start a new company that did the opposite—protected people's data—and I couldn't do that without capital. She brought me back to life. And my new company is going to help a lot of people."

Iris was glad they were talking. It helped her understand what he saw in Jasmine, and what she saw in him. And if he really gave millions of dollars away anonymously, that was some true heroism right there. She felt much better about becoming his sister-in-law. He seemed decent.

She hadn't planned on asking about his supposed thievery, but now she could hardly believe he was in the wrong. And he'd taken all her questions graciously. It was almost too easy to talk to him. She peeked around to the front of the stroller; Mason was fast asleep. He'd stayed up later than usual the night before. Mercifully, he'd been too tired to throw a tantrum.

"OK, one last thing, and then I'll give you my blessing," she said, treading carefully. "You went to Harvard, right?"

He nodded.

"Did something bad happen there, I mean, with you? I think my dad said you left on bad terms." She wished she could just ask him outright if he'd been kicked out for stealing, but Connie's presence inside her would not let her be direct.

He sighed. "It's complicated. In my sophomore year, I took a class in cybersecurity. For my final project, I hacked into the Crimson Cash server—it was the payment system linked to our IDs. My goal was to expose a fault in its security, and when I turned in my project, I also sent the information to IT so they could fix it. I'd taken one dollar and immediately given it back. When the administration found out, they were outraged. They thought hackers were evil and didn't understand that some of us were actually trying to help. My parents were called in, and I was supposed to write this long apology about how sorry I was for stealing. I was so angry, I quit."

"If I were you," she said, burning with indignation, "I would never forgive them." She felt guilty for suspecting him of being a crook based on an anonymous comment online. Iris considered herself a skeptical person, yet the most unsubstantiated slander had been impossible to dismiss.

"It's funny, I was a different person back then. I was going to cook up a virus that would obliterate their systems. As I was figuring out how to do it, Bush declared war on Iraq, and watching him talk about weapons of mass destruction, I had an epiphany that changed me. I don't know how I knew, but I was absolutely certain there were no WMDs in Iraq, and we were starting a war for our own collective ego, to prove nine-eleven hadn't defeated us. I realized we were the bad guys. And I was doing the same thing, getting revenge in a blanket way that was only going to hurt innocent people. So I had a choice: I could forgive Harvard, or I could attack them, but if I attacked them, I would be doing evil."

"That's beautiful," Iris said.

"So when I say I'm considering converting for Jasmine, you probably think I'm spineless. In our culture, a man who would convert for his wife is unmanly. But I'm considering it because if I don't convert, then Jasmine could lose her connection to her family. And my family isn't thrilled with the idea, but they know I'm not going to be religious whether I'm Jewish or Christian. I don't want to be stiff-necked about this, or anything, ever again."

"And if Jasmine wants a goat at her wedding, you don't want to say no just because you think it's ridiculous."

"Exactly. Although in that case, the stakes are much lower."

"And goats are very cute."

"Extremely," he said with a broad smile. Their eyes met, and she looked away, blushing.

⌒

Iris and Mason had a Black Friday shopping date with Amber, home from Miami for Thanksgiving. The bride who had neglected to thank Iris six months earlier was nowhere to be found in the Amber who picked Iris and Mason up in her sister's black Jetta, helped install the car seat, and asked warmly about each member of the Hagarty family. This Amber had a cold brew with two Splendas and a stupid amount of 2 percent milk waiting for Iris in the passenger-side cup holder, underneath an egg-white flatbread whose cardboard flavor reassured her that it wasn't going to make her fat. Mason received his hot chocolate with reverence.

"How's married life?" Iris asked, after giving Amber a family update consisting mainly of the word "ugh." She didn't mention the Thanksgiving disaster or Forrest's return. In the months following Forrest's disappearance, Amber had supported Iris by hating him, which had relieved Iris of the burden of hating him herself. But there was no recovering from that barrage of censure, and Iris was afraid to ask her friend to be happy for her.

Amber glanced away from the road long enough to give her a juicy eye roll of bliss. "It's the best feeling. I wake up every morning, grateful to be connected to my favorite person of all time. For life." As if remembering who she was talking to, Amber added, almost bored, "In another way, it's exactly the same. He never washes his toothpaste out of the sink, and he never picks his dirty underwear off the bedroom floor. Sometimes I fantasize about having an affair with Mr. Clean."

"I'm pretty sure Mr. Clean is gay."

"Crap," Amber said. "I guess I'll have to have an affair with the Brawny paper towel guy."

Iris grimaced. "He's a Republican. The Koch brothers own Brawny."

⌇

Cars circled the mall parking lot, waiting for someone to leave. Having skipped the Black Friday shop-stravaganza (or was it shop-mageddon?) for a few years, Iris had naïvely thought the newer days of retail Holy Week— Small Business Saturday, Cyber Monday, Giving Tuesday—would have siphoned off some of the competition for a space.

In the Best Buy, Iris pried Mason from a tower of Xboxes: he'd never sleep again. They wandered toward the toys, as Mason wanted a robot best friend, and stood in front of the robots, making no effort to choose. The nice thing about Best Buy, and also the most infuriating, was that the employees could be relied on to ignore you for hours.

Mason analyzed each box using his budding word ID skills and chose a robot they could build together. After Amber picked up a pair of Bluetooth earbuds for JonJon, they got in line behind a pimpled teen who hugged a PlayStation 4 box with an affection he probably didn't show his mother.

Iris supposed Amber's centerpieces were not going to come up unless she brought them up. So she said, "I loved your wedding. It was definitely the most beautiful I've ever been to."

"Thanks! It really was a perfect day. A little muggy, but my hair was basically glued in place."

"So you liked the centerpieces? I wasn't sure."

Amber shot her a puzzled look. "Yeah, they were gorgeous. Why do you ask?"

Now Iris was the confused one. "Sophia and I made them."

"You *made* them? What?"

"You don't remember? The florist you hired went out of business, so we ran to the beach and the craft store and threw them together in, like, an hour."

"How did I not know that?"

"I told you when you were getting your makeup done," Iris said.

"And what did I say?"

"You didn't say much. There was a lot going on." She tried to recall the moment. Why hadn't she arrived at the obvious explanation? "I guess it was pretty dumb to assume that you heard me."

"I remember being really nervous about my makeup—that girl had a heavy hand with the blush."

"And you were fending off your parents."

"But thank you for telling me now! Iris, you saved my wedding. Did you know those centerpieces were featured in a wedding blog?"

"No . . . that's great!"

Amber shook her head slowly, as if sifting through the disbelief. "It barely registered that there weren't flowers. I was so overwhelmed, I lost track of all the ways you were helping. God, you must have thought I was such a bitch! Why didn't you bring this up before?"

"It seemed petty, I guess."

"Is that why you've barely called in the past six months? Were you going to end our friendship without asking me about it?"

"No—I've just been really busy." In truth, she hadn't called because she'd written about the drama online. Calling her would have forced her to confront her betrayal. She was glad she'd deleted her complaints about Amber along with the other Reddit posts.

Amber gripped Iris's wrists like handcuffs and made secure eye contact. "Thank you for everything you've done for me. And I'm sorry. I will not take you for granted again."

# Chapter Sixteen

**Eye Fay**

November 29, 2018, 7:59 A.M.

Hola bridesmaids! I need your help—I know I can rely on you. I'm panicking about my sister's bachelorette party. I wish I could spare no expense on her, but I have so much credit card debt, it's like my own personal raincloud. And there's no way I'm asking our parents for money. They're emotional kidnappers who trample over boundaries with their generosity. I'd basically be handing over the keys to my life.

So how do I give her an amazing bachelorette party on a budget? Not counting our eldest sister, who is most def not participating in ancillary jubilation, we are now seven bridesmaids—the deets are changing as we speak. I'm thinking it should be within driving distance, because that would eliminate plane tickets and car rental. The wedding is going to be farm-themed, and we both love animals, but are there, like, luxury petting zoos?

∞ 31                                                              16 comments

**Breanna Naglehopf**

I feel your pain! My friend had always dreamed of going to London for her bachelorette party—it was high season, and it was going to cost 3K each for a three-night vacation. She had four bridesmaids, and one of us (who makes six figures and has no kids) wanted to spend the money, while the other three knew we couldn't afford it. I got all of us to sit down and talk about it, and my friend agreed to go to Chicago instead. We had an amazing time.

♥3

**Erica Black**

I went with my husband and two daughters to a very cool farm stay in the Poconos this summer. It was really romantic and beautiful there, and you could pet and feed some of the animals. My older daughter milked a cow! The inn itself is top-class—highly, highly recommended!

♥4

**Electra Collins**

Maybe we could do Atlantic City? I went with some friends in college, and it was really fun. Just don't stay in the Trump casino. 🤬

♥2

**Breanna Naglehopf**

Don't mention his name. Worst day of my life when he was elected.

♥5

**Verena Lightfoot**

You must live a very sheltered life if that was your worst day.

♥1

**Breanna Naglehopf**

It was definitely the worst day for our country.

♥3

**Verena Lightfoot**

I would humbly suggest September 11, 2001, was worse.

♥1

**Breanna Naglehopf**

With all due respect Verena Lightfoot, fuck off.

♥5

**Eye Fay**

Thanks all! Just a gentle reminder that this is a politics-free group! Keep those stories coming!

♥2

**Electra Collins**

My bad, Google says the Trump casino went bankrupt. Sorry to stir
up controversy! 👻
⊶ 4

⌒

Paint Party! was an event space in a posh strip mall in Montclair; it hosted
rich kids' birthdays on the weekends and adult painting lessons four nights
a week. Brittany booked the activity for the expanded bridesmaid cohort
to mingle and bond. She didn't run it by Iris first.

When they arrived, Cousin Lorelei was waiting on a bench outside,
seeming odder than ever. She wore her hair in short pigtails, and she
moved stiffly, as though she might crack. She was twenty-one going on
nine.

"Cousin Lorelei, so great to see you!" Iris said, sensing her cousin did
not hug. "I feel like it's been, what, three years?"

"I'm an artist," Cousin Lorelei said in her high-pitched wheeze. "I won
a big national competition."

"That's . . . great!" Iris said, though it didn't seem likely: that was the
kind of detail Spike and Connie would have shared.

"She's such an amazing talent," said Jasmine, grinning at their strange
cousin. She had always adored Cousin Lorelei, for no reason Iris understood. Even before the nervous breakdown, the girl had given off horror
movie vibes.

Two more bridesmaids arrived. Stefanie, Jasmine's fortyish personal trainer, boasted an enviable tan and the sculpted upper arms of a
decathlete—which Iris knew because the woman was wearing a tank top
in freezing weather. Allie, Jasmine's hairstylist, had a bubbly laugh and a
blond buzz cut, a strange choice for someone in the profession—though
Iris's hairdresser was a bald man.

⌒

The venue's vibe was industrial and loftlike, with a polished concrete floor
and an exposed-brick accent wall. In addition to Jasmine's bridal party
were two middle-aged sisters and an attractive gay couple who apparently

had no interest in conversation that didn't involve boisterous complaint. Sky, the tipsy painting instructor, lit tealights and poured wine for everyone but Stefanie and Cousin Lorelei, both non-drinkers.

"Wednesday is our Free Spirit Watercolor Night," Sky said, standing with her feet weirdly far apart, legs bent as if she might pounce. Her gray hair was twisted into long braids; her fingernails were chewed to the quick. "We won't be painting from reference; instead, you'll pour everything you are onto the paper. Use intuition to select your colors, and let Spirit guide your brush."

No one, not even Electra, was snickering, so Iris snuffed her skepticism.

"Tonight, I urge you to toss away your perfectionist impulses, your need to make things look just so," Sky continued, breathing each pronouncement like an incantation. "To facilitate that, I'd like you to paint with your non-dominant hand. If you're right-handed, paint with your left hand tonight."

All the bridesmaids held the paintbrush in their left hands except Jasmine, a proud lefty, who moved Elsa from her right arm to hold the brush. Iris wetted her brush and hovered it over the watercolor palette. She didn't feel any of the colors calling to her. Maybe Spirit was taking the night off. She went with red—it had energy, at least. She tried painting a square, and it came out looking like a blob. She decided it was a fire.

"Brittany, you genius," Jasmine said. "This is exactly the kind of fun I hoped we'd all have together. It's like you read my mind."

"I knew if I didn't do it, it wasn't going to happen," Brittany replied. "I've learned to stop waiting for other people to step up."

Iris couldn't help feeling criticized. "Thanks for organizing this, Brittany. This is fun."

"Iris, I know how busy you are. If you're having trouble planning the other events, I'd be happy to take over."

"Don't worry, the shower is all planned, and I've got some great options for the bachelorette party." In truth, she was struggling to pick the right destination. The Upstate New York yoga retreat she'd found seemed a little too Hindu for Jasmine and her Christian friends, and the nice-looking spas within driving distance were horrendously expensive. She'd considered a four-night cruise up the coast until discovering that ships had spotty Wi-Fi. Jasmine might die from phone withdrawal. Someone from the Bridesmaids Union had suggested a quaint farm stay in Pennsylvania; Iris needed to ensure it was luxurious.

"I'm sure you do," Brittany said with a fake smile that implied an eye roll. "I'm here if you need me."

Iris would rather have asked the devil himself than shown Brittany a crack in her facade.

"I'm majorly vibing on this," Stefanie said, stabbing dark blue sparks onto her paper. "I never let myself be this free."

"That's beautiful," Iris said, mesmerized by Stefanie's painting. "So how long have you known Jasmine?"

"Going on three years. She's my most inspiring success story. She could run a marathon if she wanted."

Iris searched for a way to ask why Jasmine had invited her to be a bridesmaid—and why she'd accepted. "How many weddings have you been in?"

"I did a bunch of them when I was younger." She continued to jab at the canvas. The splotches looked like inverse stars, or black holes—something cosmic. "But it's been a minute."

"When was your last?"

"Ninety-two, I think?"

That was twenty-six years ago. Iris's eyes widened before she realized it might seem unkind.

Stefanie laughed. "I'm older than I look."

"I thought you were, like, late thirties, max."

She pointed the butt end of the brush at Iris. "Try fifty-eight."

"You look *amazing*."

"Thanks. It's all diet and exercise—you could do it, too."

Iris ignored the recruitment pitch. "So did you have to think about being Jasmine's bridesmaid, or were you just like, 'Let's do this.'"

Stefanie glanced toward Jasmine and lowered her voice. "I did think about it, and not just because I'd become the most ancient bridesmaid in history. I knew it'd be an investment, with my girl Jasmine heading things up. But she's like a daughter to me, and I thought this would be a fun way to give back."

Translation: she was doing it to keep Jasmine's business. But maybe Iris was being ungenerous.

"Totally, right?" said Allie, sitting on the other side of Stefanie. "My salon manager was like, 'Why are you so excited about your client's wedding?' And I was like, 'You don't understand how tight we are.' She is such a breath of fresh air. And so wise."

"Right there with you, Baba Looey," said Stefanie, rapid-fire pointing at Allie. "We must be sisters from another mister."

Stefanie washed her brush in her Dixie cup, squeezed it dry with a paper towel, and painted yellow arcs that looked like shooting stars. Allie painted a perfect flower in five pink strokes. Iris outlined her bonfire in black to give it some shape and added a dab of blue to the center to rein in all the red. Every choice she made looked terrible.

"That is some Bob Ross–level perfection," Iris told Allie.

"Yours is super interesting, too," Allie said. "I'm seeing some Richard Prince in there."

A camera flash startled Iris. A muscular photographer, dressed in a black T-shirt and shorts and with wild, sand-colored hair, was snapping photos of the bridesmaids. He traced a wide ellipse around them, strafing them with shots.

Jasmine skipped over to Iris and forced her into a pose, startling her with a sudden manic energy. Elsa, squeezed between them, knew to look at the camera.

The photographer took a few shots, then, staring at his viewfinder, held up a finger. "Could you try to loosen up a bit?" he asked Iris in an Australian accent.

Iris hadn't realized she looked tense.

Jasmine took the camera and flipped through a few images. "Yeah, Iris, so sorry, but you need to pretend Miles isn't here. You look like you're in Madame Tussaud's."

"So you're Miles?" Iris asked him.

"You know Miles," Jasmine told her. "My Instagram boyfriend?"

Meaning he pretended to be her boyfriend in photos, or . . . ? Iris couldn't recall seeing him on her page. "Boyfriend?"

"He's her photographer," Brittany explained as if barely tolerating Iris's idiocy.

Jasmine frowned. "Miles and I are inseparable. You . . . haven't met him?"

"I guess not." Iris waved at Miles. "I'm Iris."

He gave her a thumbs-up.

"I thought you weren't posting so much about the wedding," Iris said to Jasmine without moving her lips, as they toasted to the camera with almost-empty glasses of wine.

"That was months ago," Jasmine replied without breaking her smile. "The trend now is authenticity. If I don't put my wedding on social—when my followers have been waiting for *years* to see me get married—I'm going to look super fake, totally unworthy of my platform."

"Bigger smile, please," said Miles.

Iris smiled hard at the camera, trying to bring her eyes into it. She could feel how crazy she looked, but Miles gave them a thumbs-up.

"What are we channeling over here?" Sky asked, tilting the wine bottle into Iris's glass. Her braids smelled like orange and clove.

"Nothing short of infinite possibility," said Stefanie in a surfer voice.

"I won a major painting competition," Cousin Lorelei piped in. She had yet to dip her brush.

"Beautiful," said Sky, reaching toward Allie's painting, as Miles documented every angle. "Your eye for color is astounding, and your line is devastating. Are you really painting with your nondominant hand?"

"I'm ambidextrous," Allie said. Her peonies, painted from memory, looked professional, whereas Iris's painting resembled a literal dumpster fire.

"You should have told me," Sky said. "I would have blindfolded you."

"I'm actually pretty good at painting blind," Allie said. "I could hold the paintbrush in my teeth if you want."

"I can paint blindfolded, too," said Cousin Lorelei.

"What's holding you back, honey?" the instructor asked Cousin Lorelei. "Who are you trying to please?"

"I don't work well under pressure."

"Toss away that fear!" Sky exclaimed, sinking into a wide-legged squat. "We can burn your painting tonight if you like. Embrace the now. Channel your creative mojo."

"You go, girl!" Brittany said.

"Lo-re-lei! Lo-re-lei!" Stefanie chanted, and they all joined in.

Cousin Lorelei dabbed her brush in black and touched it to the paper as if placing a needle on a record. Everyone watched a dark tear slide down the paper.

"Beautiful!" said Sky.

"Brilliant!" said Allie.

"Slam dunk to the max!" Stefanie exclaimed in announcer voice, pumping her fist until Miles captured it. Iris wanted to know where she came up these hilarious one-liners.

"You're such an inspiration," said Jasmine, giving their cousin a hug that was not reciprocated.

Cousin Lorelei gazed at the wobbly gray line as if awestruck by her talent.

⌒

When time was up, Sky commented on each painting.

"Jasmine, with this painting, you're saying, 'It's all about me.'" Somehow, this didn't sound like an insult. "The abundance of green represents personal growth, and the orange represents your immense potential. Your future looks very bright—as long as you keep the focus on yourself."

"She won't have any trouble with that," Brittany said.

"Hey!" Jasmine laughed.

Stefanie's constellation revealed practicality and joy; Allie's, femininity and creativity. Each interpretation seemed as baseless as a palm reading, but to Sky's credit, she was nailing everyone's personality.

Cousin Lorelei's painting was a row of gray lines. Iris couldn't decide if it was good or not. The erratic journey of each droplet was sort of interesting.

"I'm perplexed and intrigued," Sky said, a hint of a smile on her lips, "but I think that's precisely what you wanted."

Cousin Lorelei nodded, grinning impishly.

"Black is the color of mystery, and your composition is as mysterious as your color choice. You don't let anyone know you, and you like it that way."

When Sky looked at Iris's painting, she nodded for a beat too long. "I've been teaching color psychology for years, and rarely do I see someone so clearly through their painting."

"I hope that's a good thing," Iris said with an anemic laugh. She hated that everyone was staring at what was quite possibly the ugliest image in history.

"Red can represent either passion or anger. Here, it feels like anger."

"Really?" Iris asked.

"Rage burns inside you. But see this black outline? You keep it bottled up. You're afraid of what your anger might destroy."

If Iris were a different kind of person, she'd take offense. Couldn't Sky tell her she was passionate and leave it at that?

"This right here is what gives me hope," Sky continued, pointing to the blue at the center of the fire. "It's your true self, the real you that no one sees. You want to be loved and appreciated for who you are, but you're too afraid of disappointment to let people in."

"Um, that is totally off base," Jasmine said. "You make her sound like some kind of psycho."

"These are not judgments," Sky said. "I'm sharing what I see in the art. If it's not helpful to you, then ignore me."

Iris couldn't pay attention to the rest of Sky's interpretations. Angry? If anything, she was far too nice. She wished she could be angry, so people would stop walking all over her. Sure, she snapped at her mother from time to time, but who didn't have a beef with their parents?

"I think your painting is kickass," said Stefanie, giving Iris a side hug.

# Chapter Seventeen

**Eye Fay**

December 14, 2018, 12:02 P.M.

It's the moment you've all been waiting for: tomorrow we try on bridesmaid dresses. Yay. Can you feel the excitement spilling out of me?

I am packing a literal suitcase for the journey to New Jersey, because J has requested that each of her bridesmaids bring the following: (1) Three choices of nude or pink bras, including one strapless. (2) A plain white pump, its height inversely proportional to the height of the bridesmaid (her wedding party must be equally tall in the photos, and she needs to be two inches taller). (3) The $300 sterling silver jewelry set J required everyone to buy.

I also bought, and am bringing, a new set of shapewear reserved for the wedding, to make certain every part of me will remain in its place for the entire night, particularly throughout any song with the word "jump" in it, including but not limited to: "Jump" (Kris Kross), "Jump" (Van Halen), "Jumpin', Jumpin'" (Destiny's Child), and "Jump Around" (House of Pain). I don't want to be blamed for embarrassing those members of my family who are, shall we say, less than body positive.

Sigh,

Eye

👍 12                                                                3 comments

**Electra Collins**
So pumped for tomorrow's train wreck.
👍 2

⌒

"You are going to *love* the dress I picked out for you guys," Jasmine said once her army of bridesmaids had assembled at the bridal salon for the fitting. "I know every bride says you can wear the bridesmaid dress again, and you can't, but I swear, this is the exception. You're going to want to wear it all the time."

Unless it was black, knee-length, and wrinkle-free, Iris doubted that.

Brittany passed around nondisclosure agreements, which promised not to share images of the dress, or anything about the wedding, before the big day. Iris shared a gleefully puzzled look with Electra. Who cared if people saw the bridesmaid dresses? Iris decided to start drawing up counter-agreements. If Christof wanted control over her nude photos, she could earn a cut of the sale. If Forrest wanted time with Mason, he could pay child support. If Jasmine wanted to keep her bridesmaid dresses a secret, Iris could negotiate Mason a wedding invite.

Veronica, in a baby-blue skirt suit and another statement scarf, distributed prosecco. Because wine wasn't on Jasmine's new diet, Veronica poured her a finger of whiskey. Her assistant, a trim, feminine man named Fernando, retreated into the back room to pull samples of the dress.

Iris met another new bridesmaid, Selena Bermudez. She had saucer eyes, full painted lips, and a chest tattoo of a mythological vixen whose tresses reached up the sides of her neck. She was a YouTube influencer with 166,000 subscribers for her beauty tutorials, makeup tests, and unboxings; Jasmine had met her at a press preview for a CBD-enhanced cold brew. It took Iris a moment to understand why her sister would be invited to a media event, but apparently, nine thousand followers made her a micro-influencer in the wellness industry.

"Your wedding is going to kill on social," Selena told Jasmine while texting. "You'll reach ten thousand followers in no time. And that's a complete game-changer in terms of visibility and customer conversion. I just posted that I'm more excited about your wedding than anything else on my content calendar for 2019."

A moment later, Iris's phone buzzed. Selena had sent an idea for the bachelorette party on the bridesmaids group text thread. Her next message was a hyperlink to a five-star resort near Playa del Carmen. Each room had a private pool, and the spa offered a "rainforest essence massage" and "volcanic mineral experience." Had Brittany asked the new bridesmaids for suggestions? Selena added:

**The publicist offered 20% off rack.**

**J is going to LOVE.**

Iris checked pricing for their tentative dates. With the discount applied to shoulder season rates, it would cost six hundred dollars a night per person, not including meals, drinks, spa treatments, or flights. Iris looked up, shocked, and Selena winked.

⌒

The bridesmaid dress was a column of pale pink silk crepe with a racer top and a ribbon around the waist. Having expected princess-grade bows and flounces, Iris was pleased with its simplicity, not to mention the ninety-five-dollar price tag. Was a zero missing? The sample size was a six, which should have been too tight, but in the fitting room, the dress slid on easily. It accentuated her breasts and hips and glossed over the rest, and by some miracle, her arms looked slender, despite being visible in their entirety. Maybe she didn't hate pink as much as she thought. She put on the necklace and earrings, stepped into her white heels, and was first out of the changing room. Jasmine gaped.

"This was a great choice," Iris said.

"Thanks, babe," Jasmine said. "You look amazing."

"Bridesmaid in the house!" Stefanie shouted into an imaginary megaphone as she swept the curtain aside. Her toned and tanned arms looked fabulous, but the dress draped over her taut frame like a nightgown.

"I would kill for your body," Jasmine said.

"Keep training with me, kiddo, and you'll have it." She clapped Jasmine's shoulder.

"This is going to look beautiful on you once we get it in your size," Veronica said, cinching the loose fabric with clips, though Stefanie did not have the curves to work any size of this dress, unless it came in a bikini version.

The dress suited Allie's hourglass figure. Cousin Lorelei looked, as usual, like a disturbed child.

"This was the perfect choice," Veronica said. "Iris, would you mind if we took some photos of you in the dress for social? We'll embargo them until after the wedding."

"Sure," she said, blushing. The rule of the Hagarty sisters had always been that Jasmine was the pretty one and Iris was the friendly one. (Rose was the smart one, which carried no currency in their household.) Here was the first moment in their lives when Iris felt beautiful next to her sister.

The dress dwarfed Brittany's Lilliputian body and made her freckles look like a sunburn. It flattered Electra but didn't reach past her knees.

"I thought you were going to wear flats," Jasmine said with a forced smile.

"I like heels," Electra replied. "I don't make apologies for my height."

"Don't get me wrong, your self-esteem is super inspiring to me," Jasmine said, "but it's going to look really weird if I'm not the tallest one in the photos."

"You could stand on a stepstool," Electra suggested. Iris admired her defiance.

Selena tapped at her phone, her acrylic nails clicking against the screen. "Just as I thought," she said with a wince. "Unfortunately, this style has already appeared a bunch this year. It's not going to play well on social."

"But you'd still come, right?" Jasmine asked, her panic vibrating in the air.

"Yeah, totally! For you, anything. It's just, I don't think it would make sense to post to social. And I'd request that you not tag me."

"You know, Veronica," Jasmine said, pressing an index finger to her chin, "I think we should try on some other options. I don't want to do something stale, you know what I mean?"

"This dress comes in a few different versions," Veronica offered. "We have one with a sweetheart neckline and an Empire waist, and one with an asymmetrical bodice and more of a trumpet fit. Perhaps those would look different enough from what you're seeing online?"

Selena shook her head, and Jasmine wrinkled her nose. "I take full responsibility for my ignorance of the bridal landscape—it's not my industry. I think we should do a three-sixty."

"You mean a one-eighty," Electra said. "A three-sixty means you're turning all the way around."

"Yeah, a three-sixty. We need to do something a hundred percent fresh."

"No, it's—" Electra began, but Jasmine and Selena were already following Veronica into the back room.

As Fernando snapped iPhone shots of Iris in the dress, she considered buying it anyway. Even if she never wore it outside her apartment, she could spin around her living room and be fortified by its celestial rightness.

The replacement dress that Selena picked had about fifty layers of pink tulle, with a front slit up to the hip and a jumbo tassel hanging from the butt like a horse's tail. On Iris, the pink lace bodice looked like a skin disease, the skirt like a troll doll's bad hair day. Best of all, it cost four hundred and fifty dollars.

Veronica barely concealed a grimace. "What do you think?" she asked.

"It's . . ." Iris began, casting puzzled glances at herself. "Unique?"

"It's so unique," said Jasmine, clasping her hands.

Inexplicably, the dress looked great on Allie: the shock of color popped against her pale skin. It also flattered Cousin Lorelei, giving her demented-doll aesthetic a punk-rock twist, and Selena looked red-carpet ready. But the dress was a tutu on Electra, and it was so foreign to Stefanie's gym/beach aesthetic, it reminded Iris of a bad Halloween costume. The Calamine pink made Brittany look even more like a burn victim, and the mounds of fabric swallowed her alive.

The bridesmaids stood in a semicircle, silently daring each other to complain.

"Is this a trendy shade of pink?" Iris asked.

"I've never worn something so edgy," Stefanie said.

"If I twirl, you can see my special parts," Electra said.

Allie asked, "Could we try something with a little less tulle?"

"Jasmine wasn't asking for feedback," said Brittany.

"It's magical," Selena said. "I've never seen anything like it before. This is going to break the internet."

"It's revolutionary," Jasmine said, grinning and clapping silently.

"I think it's revolutionary, too," echoed Cousin Lorelei.

"I knew you had good taste, cuz," Jasmine said with a wink and a snap.

"Is Rose going to wear this?" Iris asked.

"Why wouldn't she?"

"Our older sister is a bit . . . full-figured," Iris explained to Veronica.

"You can just say 'fat,'" Jasmine corrected. "It's not a dirty word."

"We do carry the dress in up to a size twenty-six," Veronica said, wearing her professionalism like armor amid the rumblings of mutiny.

"I feel like something more modest might look better on her," Iris said.

"I'm sure she'll wear it for me," Jasmine said. "It's the one day my whole life I get things the way I want them."

Iris was not as confident in Rose's willingness to please her sister.

"Maybe we could try something satiny," Allie said.

"Ew, no," said Jasmine. "Not in the barn. Matte textures only."

"How about jersey?" Veronica suggested. "It looks good on everyone, and we're seeing it a lot more on formal occasions."

"How about everyone comes to my wedding in pajamas?" Jasmine asked. "This is a really chic dress, if you all could be a little open-minded."

This was Iris's last chance to avert fashion armageddon. But if she didn't go along with Jasmine's growing list of demands, she feared her sister might demote her from maid of honor and possibly never speak to her again. Iris couldn't let herself fail at sisterhood.

"I'm sorry, but I can't wear this," Allie said. "Can we please try another one?"

Everyone's head whipped toward her.

With the self-conscious poise of a reality show bachelorette, Jasmine said, "I so appreciate your honesty, Allie. But I have made my final decision. My wedding will not be design by committee."

Right, Iris thought, she wanted it designed by her nine thousand followers.

"I love you to death, and I am so, so flattered and grateful that you invited me to be in your wedding party," Allie said. "But I'm literally going to break out in hives if I have to wear this." Of everyone in the room, Allie looked the best in the dress. It seemed unfair for her to complain—but Iris was glad she did.

Jasmine pressed her temples as if attempting telepathy. "Allie, the spirit of my brand is fresh wellness. Everything not fresh jeopardizes my career. The dress I initially chose will bore my followers. If all I have to do is pick a more stylish dress, that is a literal no-brainer."

"I have to take this off," Allie said. She returned to the fitting room and yanked the curtain closed.

"Wait, so you're going to throw a tantrum because you don't like a dress I'm asking you to wear for literally one day?" Jasmine called through the curtain.

"So immature," Brittany said.

"*Very* immature," said Cousin Lorelei.

"I don't even understand her hesitation," Selena said. "The dress is so editorial, so runway. So much better than your typical princess Barbie shit."

"Not everyone has our taste level," Jasmine agreed.

Iris wished she were strong enough to stand up to her sister. She was a coward, she saw. She had been raised to believe it wasn't her place to speak up, and now she didn't know how.

"Allie, what the heck?" Jasmine called into the fitting room. "You know you can't be a bridesmaid if you don't wear the dress."

Allie swept the curtain aside and stuffed the pink tumbleweed into Jasmine's arms. "Perfect. I quit." She swung her bag over her shoulder and strode out.

"If you think you're going to keep me as a client after this, think again," Jasmine called after her. "Everyone tells me to get a new hairstylist. I only kept seeing you because I don't bail on my friends, unlike some people I know."

"If you'll join me at the register," said Veronica, letting the second half of her sentence go elegantly unspoken.

All raised eyebrows returned to their resting positions, and within moments, everyone could pretend the fight had never happened. Iris felt sick at her complicity.

She glanced at the tag and googled the brand name. A used dress website was selling it for fifty dollars. Against all logic, it appeared to be a popular style, which confirmed that bridesmaid dresses were nothing more than a weapon wielded by heartless brides. She bookmarked the page. On the bus back to New York that afternoon, she called the bridal salon and canceled her order. Through the phone, she thought she could hear Veronica grinning.

# Chapter Eighteen

**Eye Fay**

December 17, 2018, 9:25 A.M.

This just in: my sister is now the sheriff of crazytown. Here's just a taste of what I've been privy to since I last posted:

1.     First of all, the bridesmaid uniforms have been chosen, and they are, to put it kindly, an affront to all that is decent in this world. Our sister R has politely declined to wear it (which, side note, is the sanest choice anyone has made in months). Our mother wouldn't let J kick R out of the wedding party, so now J doesn't want R in any photos with the other bridesmaids. She says it will "unbalance the composition." I guess I get it . . . ? I mean, it would look weird to have R be the only one wearing something different, but to cut her out of ALL the bridesmaid photos? I don't see the point, except revenge.

2.     J wants to serve natural, unfiltered wine at the wedding—she says it's much healthier and better for the environment than conventionally produced wine. Our father took one sip and spat it out. It's J's wedding (and technically her fiancé's, though even he doesn't really believe that), but our parents are paying for it. Also, J doesn't drink wine—it has too much sugar for her diet. She called me in tears to ask my opinion—since Thanksgiving, all her emotions have been

on overdrive. I suggested she serve both kinds. This had occurred to no one.

3.    According to an email dispatch from my mother, J had a category five meltdown over . . . wait for it . . . TABLECLOTH SEAMS. Apparently, she wants this tablecloth that looks like burlap (but is made of raw silk . . . go figure), and it has a seam! She called the manufacturer to find out (a) why it had the temerity to contain a seam and (b) whether they could make a seamless version just for her. After two hours on the phone, the manufacturer's public relations person basically told her to curl up and die. When D tried to walk her back from the ledge, J threatened him with a KNIFE (OK, so it was a butter knife) and made him wait in the car until she was ready to see him again. How my mother collected this intel, I will never know.

Yours in solidarity—
Maid of Dishonor

👍😆   95                                        18 comments

**Alexandria Canas**
Hahaha Eye Fay you are so much spunkier than I could have guessed from our brief time together as bridesmaids. Where was this firecracker hiding IRL? You keep a tight lid on it.
♾️4

**Verena Lightfoot**
Your sister has gone too far. These things are not OK, especially #1. You need to be straight with her.
👍1

**Eye Fay**
Honesty with my sister is not a skill currently in my repertoire—but get back to me in twenty years.
👍3

**Evelyn Huang**
Tablecloth seams are truly evil.
😆2

**Alexandria Canas**

I feel like I should explain how insane that bridesmaid dress was, but I'll leave that to Eye Fay. What I will say is you don't really see someone's true colors until you try on the bridesmaid dress they picked out for you.

👍 2

**Eye Fay**

I know we signed an NDA (which, I can't even), but I'm tempted to post a picture of the dress—it's like what Cyndi Lauper would wear to a Brony convention.

👍 2

**Electra Collins**

If you went to prison for violating the NDA, at least you wouldn't have to wear that pile of rags ever again.

👍 2

**Eye Fay**

It's like a prom dress for a sex doll.

👍 2

**Eye Fay**

And it has a tail, because . . . ?!

👍 2

**Anna Banana**

I feel very excluded from all this fun you're having.

👍 1

The *Dick Clark's New Year's Rockin' Eve* hosts were manufacturing bland, cheerful banter on Jasmine and David's eighty-six-inch TV at their sparsely attended party. Iris was working on her third Christmas ale, and Jasmine, rhinestones cascading down the side of her face (apparently facial bedazzling was a trend), stirred a hot toddy with a cinnamon stick. Elsa the wheaten furball napped in front of the fire with her paws over her eyes. The TV was on for the countdown clock, as well as the occasional commercial, during which Jasmine would unmute, and everyone would pause their conversation to watch. At some point in the past few years, a kind of singularity had occurred, when commercials on high-profile telecasts became more engaging than the shows themselves. Iris was mostly drawn in by ads for electronics, for their sweet portrayal of family. When the actor in one ad summoned Alexa, the disembodied voice inside the Amazon Echo, Jasmine and David's own Echo quieted the TV, anticipating instructions, which resulted in a volume-button tug-of-war with the machine.

At Christmas at their parents' house, Jasmine had announced her New Year's Eve party. Trouble was, Electra and Selena already had plans, Rose was not leaving Florida, and Cousin Lorelei wasn't allowed to stay up past ten for health reasons, so the entire guest list comprised Iris, Stefanie, Brittany, and Brittany's boyfriend, Hakim. Mason was technically in attendance—for days he'd been shouting, "Ball drop!" in frantic anticipation—but he'd conked out at eight thirty and now occupied one of Jasmine and David's ten thousand guest rooms with Beepbop, his new robot best friend.

Iris had almost skipped Christmas to avoid seeing her parents, but she didn't want to deprive Mason of family, so she simply refrained from asking anything of them, even to pass the salt. Her rejection of their proposal was implicit, and their implicit response was a war of attrition they all knew she would lose. It might take years, but when she needed their money, she'd have to move back home. She already felt like a failure.

She dipped a blue corn chip in a mango sriracha salsa David had made. He was talking about football with Hakim, a bartender and amateur sports podcaster with cavernous dimples and a bottomless well of masculine friendliness. Hakim was the perfect boyfriend, according to Brittany, except for the not insignificant problem that they had been together eight years and he hadn't proposed. (His Muslim parents weren't thrilled about the prospect of a Methodist daughter-in-law.) As bossy as Brittany could be, she reverted to Rapunzel in a tower when it came to marriage traditions.

At least Brittany had someone to love. Iris was a thirty-year-old woman with a fuck buddy. Yep, she'd hit the big three-oh a week earlier. She'd refused Sophia's offer to throw her a party, seeing nothing about her life to celebrate except for her son, so she'd taken him to a trampoline park. After he went to bed that night, she drank three glasses of box wine and read her Facebook birthday greetings, which cheered her up, even if most of them came from near strangers.

"Hey, can we talk?" Brittany asked Iris.

They stepped into an adjacent room, one of three living rooms where no living took place. "What's up?" Iris asked.

"I have some concerns about the bachelorette party," she said. "This farm thing? It seems like an interesting place and all, but I don't think it's very *Jasmine*. What did you think about the Mexico resort?"

Iris knew Jasmine would prefer the spa in Playa del Carmen, especially for the Instagram cred, but if Iris spent that money, she'd have no hope of being free from her parents, even with the breathing room from her new credit card. So she'd booked the Pennsylvania farm stay. They'd all sleep in the adorable inn, and during the day they'd milk goats and collect eggs from the henhouse. "She loves animals," Iris said. "When we were kids, our favorite activity was going to petting zoos."

"If you don't want to do Mexico, I would look into Vegas," Brittany said. "There are some good deals to be had even at name casinos."

Casinos and nightclubs were the opposite of the barn wedding—and Vegas too would shatter her budget, especially if they wanted to see Cirque du Soleil or eat at a celebrity chef's restaurant. Jasmine was already going on a twenty-thousand-dollar honeymoon; couldn't the bachelorette getaway be human-scale? Did Jasmine need everyone to go broke to feel supported?

"She's going to have animals at her wedding," Iris said. "The farm stay fits the theme perfectly."

"Her wedding is farm-*inspired*, not farm-themed," said Brittany.

"Animals perform really well on Instagram."

"Infinity pools and smoothies is her brand," Brittany countered. "Rocking chairs and pig shit is not."

They stared each other down.

"OK, fine," Iris said. "I can't afford the spa. I can't afford Vegas. Stefanie and Electra said they were on a tight budget, too. As much as Jasmine would love going to Mexico, I know she'd rather have all her bridesmaids with her. The farm stay might not be as glamorous, but I think we're really going to bond."

"Don't say I didn't warn you." Brittany flashed a pinched smile and walked away.

Iris grabbed another beer to calm down. This fucking wedding. Why did Jasmine get to live in a nine-million-dollar Barbie Dreamhouse and marry a kind and decent man with a stupidly lavish wedding, when Iris was pissing away her best years in a crappy rental with no real prospects? Why did Jasmine win their parents' love when all Iris got was their censure?

"What's your favorite football team?" David asked her, startling her.

"I like the one where the players aren't dying from traumatic brain injury, and where no one is fired for protesting institutional racism," she replied. "Sorry—I'm in sort of a bad mood."

"That's cool—you don't have to be in a good mood for me. I'm family." He smiled. "What's got you down?"

Hakim trickled the dregs of his beer into his mouth and said, "Nature calls." He fist-bumped David and headed for the bathroom.

"I'm just feeling sorry for myself. You and Jasmine are so happy, and you live like royalty, and nothing in my life has turned out the way I imagined. I know it's because of choices I made, but it's hard not to blame my parents for their favoritism. It feels like everything bad in my life sprang from that."

"Who's your parents' favorite?" David asked, leaning in closer on the wraparound sofa.

"If you don't know, then you shouldn't be marrying my sister. But I'll give you a hint: it's her. By far."

"You're good at hints," David said with a smirk.

"I'm kind of famous for them," said Iris.

David held his beer a few inches from his lips, as if the bottle wanted to kiss him and was waiting for a sign. "So how do you know they love Jasmine more?"

Iris glanced at Jasmine. Stefanie was showing her and Brittany the proper form for an overhead triceps extension, using a Voss water bottle as a dumbbell. "You can't let your elbow splay out," Stefanie said to Jasmine with outsized insistence.

"They treat her like an intelligent and capable human being, whereas they treat me like a moron, and when we were kids, they gave her every-thing she asked for—there was no effort to be equitable," Iris said. "And I didn't even get the shortest end of the stick. They treated Rose like literal garbage. But at least that gave her the freedom to cut ties. I still want their approval, and I'm continually surprised when they don't give it to me." Iris couldn't believe she was trash-talking her family with Jasmine's fiancé. One of the cardinal rules of in-law diplomacy was painting the whole family in a good light. But in the wake of her parents' ultimatum and Jasmine's bridesmaid dress freak-out, Iris didn't feel like being diplomatic. And David's eyes were like truth serum.

She leaned in to make sure Jasmine wouldn't hear. "When I was nine, our mom took me to Toys 'R' Us to pick out some Polly Pockets to give to Jasmine for her seventh birthday. I picked out two—which was a respect-able gift. Each one comes with its own little dollhouse. Our mom accused me of being stingy, and she bought like five more. I'd been collecting Polly Pockets for three years—I didn't ask for any other gifts so I could have a whole city of them. But now Jasmine was going to have almost as many as I had in one fell swoop."

"Yikes," David said.

Hakim came back from the bathroom, wiping his hands on his jeans. He weighed both conversations—Iris and David's tête-à-tête and Stefanie's weightlifting demo—then dropped a log on the dying fire, showering the hearth with sparks, and poked at it until flames spilled out of the embers. Elsa woke, looked around until she found Jasmine, then tucked her head beneath her paw and fell back asleep.

"So that night," Iris continued, "I snuck into our parents' room and took everything meant for Jasmine except the two dolls I'd picked out. I mixed them in with my collection and threw all the packaging in the neighbors' trash—somehow I believed if our parents didn't see the pack-aging, they wouldn't realize what I'd done."

"Iris Hagarty, criminal mastermind."

She laughed. She loved hearing him speak her name. "In the morning, our dad spanked me so hard and for so long, I vowed never to spank my future children."

"And did you keep that vow?"

"To this day."

"Impressive," he said.

"Is it, though? My mother would always say, 'Just wait, when you have kids, you'll understand the need to spank them,' but Mason is the most precious, innocent little boy, and she thinks I would hit him? My own flesh and blood?"

He touched the mouth of his beer to his lips pensively. "Well put."

"Anyway, my parents calculated how much the stolen dolls had cost, and they made me use my allowance over the next eight months to buy them. They took Jasmine on a shopping spree for her birthday, and she got a huge plush pony and a play kitchen. I put all my Polly Pockets into a box and never looked at them again."

"You're still upset about it," David observed.

She nodded. Weren't people supposed to forgive their parents by the time they turned thirty?

"That was a shitty thing they did," he said.

Instinctively she looked away. She wasn't used to men being so attentive and supportive, and she had to remind herself he didn't desire her. Or did he? She wished men would hand out courtesy cards declaring their intentions.

"What are you two lovebirds talking about?" asked Jasmine, pressing two water bottles over her head.

Iris slid away from David on the sofa, feeling her cheeks burn.

"Your parents," David said.

"Don't listen to that one," Jasmine said. "She despises them for reasons no one understands." She kneeled on the couch next to David and put her head on his shoulder. He wrapped his arm around her. Iris felt as if she'd been pushed out of their car.

On the show, a woman with a pleather bra and an absurd volume of hair belted out a song Iris didn't recognize. They watched the countdown clock tick past the one-hour mark, just as the Hagarty girls used to stare at the odometer on long car trips, excited when 999 rotated to 1,000. Waiting was anachronistic, maybe nostalgic. Boredom had been the signal mood of her childhood, and technology had rendered it obsolete.

Everyone picked up their phones; Jasmine held one in each hand. Kyle had written Iris:

I always get depressed at New Years. And
my #s r down 😫

Messaging with Kyle over the past few months, she'd learned how anxious the life of a social media celebrity could be. He monitored his engagement constantly; if an Instagram post racked up fewer than ten thousand likes in forty-eight hours, he deleted it. Of course, the shirtless photos got the most likes, so he showed as much skin as the censors would let him—the side of a hip or the north end of a butt crack—then felt miserable because his love of classic tailoring had won him his fan base, and now he couldn't show clothes without losing followers. If he dipped below a million, the most lucrative sponsorships would flee.

> The numbers always come back up,
> right?

Saw a 4head wrinkle this morning

Iris wasn't going to tell him he sounded a little dramatic, especially because he still looked like a god.

> Don't they have a filter for that?

Filters only do so much.

> Then rebrand as a "gentleman," and
> the wrinkles will make you rich.

I'm Asian—it's twink or I don't exist.

> You're very attractive to me.

FWIW

Thx. If only u had a penis. I'm desperate for
some bois to slide into those DMs

Trying to 4get Baxter with sex therapy LOL

Forgetting Baxter sounded wise, but it seemed condescending to say so.

Can't you go on the apps?

I don't use those anymore

2 many assholes r like No Asians.

There must be thousands of guys who
would kill to sleep with you.

No better way 2 feel empty inside than fckn a
starfckr

What about looking for a boyfriend
who wants commitment?

She was nervous that he might sense her irritation, but regardless of what she told him, he was going to do what he wanted. Maybe he was on his way to a New Year's party. Weren't influencers paid to attend parties?

"Oh, shoot," Jasmine said, staring at one of her phones. "This can't be happening. Of all the times . . ."

"What's wrong, love?" David asked with a kiss on her temple.

"My production manager is saying the factory overbooked, and they can't produce my order in January."

"It's a small run—can't they do it in February?"

"The factories close for Chinese New Year for like a month," Jasmine said. "It's going to be March by the time they get to it. Who in the frig is buying paw wear in March?"

"Winter might last a few extra months this year," Iris offered. "The weather has been pretty random."

"He emailed me on New Year's Eve on purpose," Jasmine said. "He thinks I'll be too drunk to care. I'm calling him."

"Now?" David asked. "You can't do it tomorrow morning?"

"He's in *China*." She pronounced it the way Trump did, with a "J." "I can only call him at night. And tomorrow night, it might be too late. Honestly, if you're not frigging Walmart, those factories could give a rat's patootie." It was funny and sweet to hear Jasmine cling to the wholesome approximations of dirty words they had to use when they were kids.

David wrapped her in a bear hug and kissed the top of her head. "Give 'em hell, kid."

Stefanie slapped Jasmine's shoulder and kneaded the muscle with her fingers. "I'm gonna jettison, Baba Looey. Kickin' par-tay. Thanks for including me."

"You're leaving?" Jasmine asked. "We were going to toast at midnight. We made up guest rooms for everyone."

"I really wish I could stay." It wasn't much of an excuse, Iris thought.

As Stefanie left, Brittany raised her hand, making a false show of timidity. "I'm so sorry—Hakim has to get up early tomorrow for work."

"Isn't he a bartender?" Jasmine asked.

"People start drinking early on holidays," Hakim said. "The tips are really good."

"You guys can stay the night, though. We'll have breakfast together. That was, like, the reason we bought a big house: so we could have tons of guests."

"He needs to get to sleep," Brittany said. Though Jasmine's lack of close friends was absolutely her fault, Iris felt sorry for her.

Jasmine left the room, Elsa trotting after her. And then Iris and David were alone with the silent TV and the hissing fire. Jasmine promised she'd just be a minute, but David assured Iris that between sorting out the shipment and wading through her inventory spreadsheets, this would take hours. Iris knew she should go home. Two guests made a gathering; one was a third wheel. But it would be painful to leave David's presence. He wasn't as handsome as Christof and obviously not available, but he was the answer to a question she hadn't known to ask. He was nourishment when she hadn't known she was hungry. Everyone she'd dated assumed she was what they wanted, because she never told them who she was. David paid attention. He treated her with empathy and respect. This feeling of openness and trust and connection, this was love. She hadn't felt it before. She met his gaze, hoping he couldn't see what was now obvious to her.

"Too bad Mason hit the hay," David said. "I like that kid."

"Thanks for liking him," she said. "He likes you, too."

"How's he doing in school?"

"Pretty well, but every time my phone rings, I worry it's the principal, telling me he's bitten someone else."

"That sounds hard."

"I'm trying to give him the best life he can have. It's just hard because he's a kid, so he needs a lot of attention, and I'm trying to balance parenting with work and all the shopping and bill-paying and phone calls you have to do just to keep life from blowing up."

"I was never good at those things," David said. "I hire people to do everything for me. For us," he corrected.

"I thought Jasmine was super organized."

"She's great. But she has her business and her online presence and her yoga classes, and whenever she has a minute to herself, she works on the wedding. I beg her to slow down, but she's under so much pressure from your parents to be this golden child . . . she feels like if she isn't, she'll destroy them."

Iris hadn't thought about the pressure Jasmine, as the favorite daughter, might feel. It surely wasn't as bad as coming in second place. "She told me you're the one who works all the time."

"Me? Sure, it takes a lot of work to launch a new venture, but she's on her phone every waking moment. The amount of energy she puts into her platform and her business—it's a little scary. I made her agree not to look at her phone when we're eating; otherwise I can barely catch her eye." Jasmine had presented this as a mutual decision, but she believed David's version. Iris knew she shouldn't enjoy hearing about their relationship problems.

"It's like me with Mason," Iris said, "though I usually give in to the iPad. He loves his game more than life itself, so it feels mean not to let him have it. And I really need the free time." She didn't mention his tantrums.

"What if Jasmine and I came to visit sometimes?" he offered. "You know, so Mason had more family in his life."

His proposal shouldn't have excited her so much. It would be beyond terrible to fall in love with her sister's fiancé—she could still pull back and prevent disaster. Why wasn't she willing to do it? On the other hand, she couldn't tell them not to visit her. Maybe it would be healthy to spend time with both of them together, rather than engaging in these private conversations that made her fizz with hormones. "I bet he'd love that."

"I'd love that, too."

They fell into an electric silence. A halo of fire swirled around the last log. Iris uncapped her fourth beer of the night, not yet enough to quiet her nerves. She could hear her sister on the other side of the house, arguing on the phone. Jasmine seemed good at this. Her line of dog booties might have been frivolous, but manufacturing them was not. Nor was the social media marketing engine she'd built to promote them. She certainly had more passion for her work than did Iris, trapped at a meaningless desk job. Yet another thing Iris envied her for. The list was getting embarrassingly long.

Outside the studio in Times Square, the ponchoed throng looked desperate and crazed. Iris wished she could put her head in David's lap. She wished she didn't want to.

"So tell me what you love about Jasmine," Iris said, hoping to defuse the tension. "I mean, besides the fact that her looks are completely unfair."

He chortled. "That's definitely part of it. She's the most beautiful woman who's ever shown an interest in me. She's very smart, and always surprising, and she has an incredible business sense. I think she's hilarious, and she thinks I am too—or at least she's a very good liar. I love that we never get bored of each other. And this is a kind of weird thing to love about someone, but I was blown away by how direct she was. I've never met another woman who says what she thinks so unapologetically. My last girlfriend never expressed the slightest dissatisfaction with me, until I caught her cheating. With Jasmine, I know where I stand."

"That does describe her," said Iris, disappointed that he had such a great answer. "Hey, have you decided what you're going to do about becoming one with Christ, et cetera?"

He stared at the room's entrance, where Jasmine might reappear at any minute. "I don't know. I told Jasmine I'd do it if she could convince me it really was important to her. It seems like she wants me to convert so people don't judge us, and I don't know if I can go along with that."

"And what did she say?"

"She said your dad wasn't going to marry us unless I converted. Which, again, is not a valid reason in my book."

"For what it's worth, if my dad won't marry you, there are zillions of people who'll do it," Iris said. "Heck, I'll marry you." When she realized what she'd said, she hastily added, "I mean, I'd perform the rite of marriage with you and Jasmine. Not . . ."

He smiled his intoxicating smile. "You can't take it back now. You've promised yourself to me."

"It's always good to have a backup wife," Iris said, feeling this crossed a line. David must have felt the same way too, because he didn't respond. This was the moment they would have kissed, if he'd been single. How could she have so little respect for her sister that she'd consider kissing her fiancé?

They watched TV, but Iris couldn't concentrate on it, so strong was her wish to touch David. It would be insane to slide closer when they had plenty of room to spread out. In fact, she should probably have scooted away, but he wasn't moving, either. She decided to lie perpendicular to him on the sofa, her toes making contact with his thigh. If Jasmine walked in, it wouldn't read as intimate touch.

As Iris got into position, she felt she should explain her move, so she said, "Gotta take advantage of all this couch space," which was possibly the most ridiculous statement ever uttered.

"Wise use of resources," he responded, giving her foot a squeeze and leaving his meaty hand there.

Her heart thudded at the risk they were taking. This was the life she wanted. If only she, not Jasmine, belonged in this domestic tableau.

At five minutes to midnight, David said, "I should probably check on her."

They looked at each other for a long time.

"She probably knows what time it is," Iris said.

"I should do it," he said, and left the room, which made Iris feel despicable. She lifted the Champagne out of the ice bucket, dried the bottom with a tea towel, peeled off the foil, and untwisted the wire loop to release the cork's cage.

David shuffled back into the room, gliding in his socks on the hardwood floor. "She shooed me away." He seemed relieved—or was she imagining it?

"I guess you're stuck with the backup wife," said Iris.

"I knew it was a good idea to have two."

Soon, the ten-second countdown began. When midnight struck and the soaked Times Square crowd went wild, Iris popped the Champagne cork and filled two flutes, and they wished each other a happy New Year, clinked glasses, and took a sip. Everyone was kissing on TV. David's lips glistened.

"You know, there's all this talk about the ball dropping, but it's more of a slide," David said. "The word 'drop' implies gravity, don't you think?"

She grabbed him and kissed him hard on the mouth.

He didn't kiss back.

"Sorry, sorry," Iris said, stumbling around the living room and staring at the floor as if she'd lost an earring. She downed her Champagne and burped. "I'm drunk. That was really stupid."

"It's OK," he said, reaching tentatively for her.

She felt sick. She had to get out of there. Her phone vibrated. It was a text from Amber:

**Happy New Year, babe!** ✎ 🗡

"I missed it, didn't I?" Jasmine asked, bounding into the room. "Shoot!"

David poured her a glass and said, "Happy New Year, my love." He kissed his fiancée deeply, as if to draw a boundary.

Iris couldn't look Jasmine in the eye, lest her sister realize what happened. "I have to go home," she said.

"Really?" Jasmine asked. The rhinestones on her cheek glinted like tears in the waning firelight. "Do I smell or something?"

"Pickles is sick—my neighbor said he's peeing blood. I have to take him to the animal hospital."

"You don't have to leave, really," David said. "We'd love it if you stayed."

"Why would you say that?" Jasmine asked David. "She just said her cat is *peeing blood.*"

Iris wished Jasmine would act more selfishly about this; then she might not feel as terrible for betraying her.

# Chapter Nineteen

**Kyle Kyle**

January 30, 2019, 3:19 P.M.

I'm in a dark place, hoping to reach the light soon.

Baxter swung by this morning for a quickie while Frederick was at work. This time I said no. I guess my conscience kicked in. If he's promising monogamy to Frederick, he shouldn't be sleeping with me or anyone else (he's on all the apps). And he went off PrEP, since he's supposedly not hooking up anymore. I'm not gonna risk getting HIV for a roll in the sack.

He doesn't love Frederick. He says Frederick is bad in bed and boring as hell, and after a long day at the office, he gets pissy if Baxter has any feelings about anything. I'm like, why are you marrying him if you don't love him? And Baxter's like, he's rich, and he loves me, and I know he won't cheat on me. That is some fucked-up shit.

He's also stealing from Frederick to buy drugs. Every pocket has a different high: weed, coke, crystal, E, G . . . if the cops caught him, they'd think he was dealing.

Before he leaves, I get up the courage to say, if you ever want to hook up with me again, you have to break if off with him. Not for my sake but for yours. And he's like, you're just jealous. OK, maybe I am, but I'm also a good person, and I thought he was one, too.

 88                                          39 comments

**Jaclyn Arias**

We're here for you, friend. Your number one priority is taking care of yourself. Maybe some distance from Baxter will put you in a better mind state.

◯5

**Alex Oberlin**

Stay strong, Kyle Kyle!

◯◯1

**Shanna Menckler**

This seems to go beyond this group's mission. Eye Fay could you step in?

◯2

**Eye Fay**

Yes, let's stick to weddings everyone! I'll reach out to Kyle.

◯1

**Electra Collins**

Maybe it's time to bow out of this wedding and say goodbye to your friend Baxter.

◯4

On the Sunday in February when Jasmine and David were coming to Yonkers, Iris was juddered awake at dawn by Mason bouncing on her bed, chanting, "Uncle David!" They bundled up and walked to the ShopRite to pick up lunch ingredients and snacks that fit Jasmine's diet. Scaly patches of ice floated on the Hudson, and the Palisades looked flinty and ragged in the wan morning light. No one was outside except cops waiting in police cruisers by the train station, as if expecting a crime.

She'd thrown up every roadblock she could think of to delay Jasmine and David's visit, using Mason as an excuse: he had plans with friends, he was sick, he was grounded. Ninety-nine percent of people, when deflected so consistently, would have taken the hint. But David wouldn't let it drop, so said Jasmine. He was president of the Mason Hagarty fan club. Even if David was ready to forgive Iris for her kiss, she wasn't ready to be forgiven.

A few days after New Year's, she'd gone out with another guy on Bumble, the twenty-nine-year-old Libertarian Democrat real estate broker she'd matched with the same night as Christof. If she was building a relationship with someone instead of just hooking up, she might not be kissing other people's fiancés.

Their date had started out well. He loved cats, hiking, and lazy Sundays with the crossword puzzle. He'd grown up evangelical like her, but he belonged to a progressive church and was pro-choice and accepting of LGBT people. She mentioned Mason when the entrees came. In the span of three minutes, he wolfed down his steak, dropped a fan of twenties on the table, and tripped over his chair in a break for freedom. That was the first time she'd gotten *that* reaction to the motherhood disclosure. She knew it was an anomaly, but it still stung, and she hadn't had the courage to open up a dating app since.

⁓

Jasmine and David arrived a few minutes after one with a low-carb Riesling and a pack of Minecraft-themed Legos, which sent Mason rocketing around the room like a deflating balloon. Jasmine wore an oversized red neoprene coat over a form-fitting zip-up hoodie, black tights, and red leg warmers. Elsa wore a shearling coat and matching boots—both presumably vegan. Jasmine's eyelids shimmered; when Iris asked about them, Jasmine handed her a tube of Unicorn Snot, which appeared to be glitter suspended in gel. "It's all yours," she said. "I have like four more in my bag."

Seeing David again felt like running into an ex-boyfriend Iris had dumped via text message: her desire was muddled by guilt and embarrassment. She weathered a kiss on the cheek and stepped back a beat too fast.

"Looks like he's feeling better," David said.

Iris remembered she'd used Mason's illness as an excuse twice since New Year's. "Yeah, his school is a petri dish. Thank God for vaccines."

"Did you know kids get forty-nine doses of vaccines by age six?" Jasmine asked. "That's a lot of mercury."

Iris glared at her. "Don't tell me you're an anti-vaxxer now."

"I'm a critical thinker," she said, as if talking to an idiot. "I don't automatically accept everything the government tells us."

Iris didn't have the energy to debate the merits of scientific consensus. "Are you a 'critical thinker' too?" she asked David.

"No, but I'm open to discussing the vaccine thing, when we have kids." His adaptability was astonishing. No wonder they got along.

Iris served the wine they'd brought with cheese and low-carb crackers— Jasmine ate the cheese without the crackers. Mason dismantled the packaging from his gift and, with the "help" of Beepbop, his robot best friend, assembled structures on the carpet.

"How's your kitty cat?" David asked.

"So much better. He had a bad case of crystals," she lied. "Thanks for asking."

"Seems like you've had a rough go of it," David said.

Jasmine smiled patiently; she must have known Iris had been lying.

As if summoned, the cats emerged from the kitchen, where they frittered away their lives waiting for kibble, and rubbed their gums on David's shin, claiming him with their scent. Elsa barked a few times from the crook of Jasmine's arm, then quieted. The cats barely noticed the tiny beast in their midst.

"There was like, no traffic at all," Jasmine said. "I was worried there'd been a zombie apocalypse and no one told us."

"We took the new Tappan Zee," David said. "That is one beautiful bridge. Did you know the piles don't go all the way down into bedrock? They're just floating in mud."

"That's kind of unsettling," Iris said.

"Have you seen the video of the old bridge getting demolished?"

Iris shook her head.

"I'll show you—it's really cool." He patted the pockets of his jeans and sucked through his teeth. "Jazz, would you get my phone from the car?" It seemed like a dick move to ask her to run his errand, and it surprised Iris that Jasmine was willing to do it. Maybe she was looking for excuses to get away from him. A few months earlier, they'd been a PDA machine; now they guarded their personal space like coworkers.

Jeremy could have taken a cue from them. He had come back from two weeks off over the holidays to tell Iris that he and his wife were going into couples counseling. Not five minutes later, he said her skirt flattered her figure as his gaze lingered on her curves. She almost went to HR. Almost. After Jasmine's wedding, when her life had room for a job search, she would report him.

"It's OK," Iris said. "I can watch it later."

"Actually," he said to Iris, "I was hoping to have a moment to talk to you about the wedding—wink, wink."

The bottom dropped out of Iris's stomach. There was no escape from this reckoning. She supposed it would be healthy to process New Year's with him, even if she would have jumped out the window to avoid it.

Jasmine smiled wryly. "I'll go the long way."

Once she was gone, David asked, "Could we talk in the other room?" with a meaningful nod toward Mason.

Iris led him into her bedroom and closed the door behind her. They stood facing each other at the foot of her bed. It was just a conversation, she told herself. A conversation wouldn't kill her.

"I didn't follow up about what happened on New Year's," he said. "OK, 'follow up' sounds like a work email. What I wanted to say is, you took me by surprise, and Jasmine was in the other room, and everything happened so fast."

"I'm really sorry," she blurted out. "I was drunk, and I got caught up in the whole New Year's kissing tradition. It was beyond inappropriate of me, and I promise it will never happen again."

"Ah, OK." He considered the black-and-white photo above her bed, of a couple making out in a rainstorm. Iris had loved that image since she was a child. Now it made the conversation feel doubly awkward. "That simplifies things."

She was about to say, "Are we good?" when he met her gaze, vulnerable and hungry, and the connection they'd felt on New Year's again pulled taut. Desire hummed in her, and she couldn't let the conversation end without knowing more. "You sound sort of disappointed," she said, her body trembling from the force of her heartbeat.

He looked down again, and she noticed beads of sweat caught in his mustache. "No, not disappointed. Relieved. I think I misjudged what was going on. Anyway, I'm glad we're clearing the air." When their eyes met again, she felt paralyzed with want. "If you really regretted kissing me."

"What did *you* think was going on?" she asked. "Because I also felt something going on, and I think it might have prompted me to, you know."

An agonizing moment passed before David plopped on the bed and groaned, "I'm really excited to marry Jasmine."

Iris was dumbstruck. She wanted this, had wanted it since Thanksgiving and possibly before, but it wasn't supposed to happen. It couldn't happen.

"I love her so much." David wiped his face with a handkerchief. Iris had never known anyone who used a handkerchief, and the gallantry made her want him more. "She's brought out a side of me I didn't know I had, and I'm excited to marry her, I really am. It's just, I have this weird connection with you. Being near you has this mystical quality, like we're old friends from childhood or a past life."

Iris found it strange that he was attracted to both of them—she got creepy sister-wife vibes from the idea. But she believed he felt it honestly: he saw the best in everyone and seemed to adapt to whomever he was with. He would be an ideal man to make a life with. For Jasmine, not for her.

"Would you like to get lunch sometime, just us, outside of this whole . . . wedding? You know, make our own little friendship bubble?"

Seeing him privately would be a sure path to sex. If he wasn't going to protect himself from adultery, she had to, for the sake of her sister. She pinched the bridge of her nose. "I think maybe it'd be better if we didn't talk like this again."

"I understand. I didn't mean to put you in an awkward position."

"You didn't," she lied. "We are completely on the same wavelength. I just think the optics would be kind of terrible if we started hanging out."

He was silent a moment. "I needed to hear this. It's just that I'm afraid I'm making the wrong choice."

Again, she was gutted by desire. She wished she could go back to New Year's Eve and give her lips a stern talking-to before they latched onto his. No, this conversation would have come sooner or later. Better to nip it in the bud before they got married. "If anything happened between us, Jasmine would never speak to me again, OK? My parents would never speak to me again. My relationship with my sister is already on thin ice. I can't risk losing her for good."

He sighed. "I understand. You're a good person, Iris."

"Based on my behavior up to this point with my sister's fiancé, I would beg to differ."

He laughed.

"So we're done here?" she asked. "You and Jasmine are going to live happily ever after, and we're not going to mention this again?"

"I don't know if I can trust my self-control," he said. "Maybe we shouldn't talk at all."

She couldn't trust her self-control, either, though it killed her to make this pact. "That sounds wise." Jasmine would probably never notice the distance. Plenty of in-laws never spoke. Exhibit A: Jasmine had said almost nothing to Forrest while he and Iris were dating. It had been uncomfortable for Iris but not anything to be annoyed about.

David slapped his thighs and stood. "I guess this is goodbye. My soul bids yours adieu."

"And mine yours. Adieu." They had never dated, so why did it feel like a breakup? Their bodies would interact as in-laws had to, but their souls would remain separate. This was what Kyle should have done with Baxter. A clean break. A permanent adieu. Now she felt in her heart how painful it was. She was about to say, "I'll miss you," but even that small acknowledgment would make it harder to end things.

David said it anyway. "I'll miss you."

She nodded, keeping her lips pinched, afraid she might cry.

⁓

Jasmine returned a few minutes later, ecstatic. "The light here is ridoncu-lous," she said, handing David his phone and putting Elsa on the floor. "I got the most amazing selfies along the water."

When she and David kissed, Iris looked away, sodden with anguish for losing David and guilt for wanting him in the first place.

Jasmine's forehead wrinkled. "What? Were you not done planning your surprise?"

"No, we're done," Iris said. "David was saying you need to get going pretty soon."

"What are you discussing, girlfriend? We literally just got here."

"I just meant we have some errands to run before it gets too late," David said with an apologetic glance at Iris. "We have some time." He sat cross-legged next to Mason and picked up a Lego character holding a pickaxe. "Who's this guy?"

"It's Alex," Mason explained. "He's the hero." He showed David proper pickaxe technique.

"Question," Iris said to Jasmine, loud enough for David to hear but quiet enough so Mason wouldn't think to listen. "Mom said it would be OK if I brought a plus-one? I'm seeing someone, and it's getting pretty serious . . . is it OK if I invite him?"

David cocked his head. He would know why she was inviting Christof.

"I insist that he come," Jasmine said. "Tell me everything—what's his name? How did you meet? What's his sign? Can I see photos?"

Iris offered the basics about Christof, which stirred Jasmine into a froth, especially the German accent. She didn't have a photo of him, though—he didn't like to be photographed, and he'd taken his Bumble profile down. She tried not to dwell on the implications of this. He was probably satisfied with the sex with Iris and didn't want to add a relationship to it. Or he, like Baxter, was getting serious with someone else while enjoying his side piece. Either way, he would probably come with her to the wedding, if he was in the country. He always pressed for more about her life, and here was the perfect opportunity to learn all the sordid details. She'd introduce him to Mason as a friend.

"He sounds great," David said, fiddling gamely with Mason's Legos.

"He really is."

"Attack! Attack!" Mason shouted, thrusting a Lego action figure toward the zombie David was holding.

"I've been hit!" David shouted. "I'm dying!"

"That'll teach you to mess with Alex!" Mason's lips glistened with saliva as he muscled them around the words.

"It was really nice of you to get him Legos," Iris said to Jasmine. "He's always begging for his video game, and then convincing him to go to bed is like pulling the needle out of the heroin addict." She knew it was dumb to admit any inadequacy to Jasmine, but she was ready for the subject to move away from Christof. She didn't want to reveal that he wasn't, and would never be, her boyfriend.

"That's, like, a totally apt comparison," Jasmine said, examining her nails. "Video games activate the same pleasure centers as drugs, and they completely stunt the developing brain."

"Where did you learn that, Dr. Hagarty?" Iris asked.

"There was a whole Twitter thread about it. I'd *never* give my kid a video game."

As usual, Jasmine paraded her certainty with no expertise. Iris would have let it go, but she didn't want David to think she was a bad mother. Somehow it mattered more than ever what he thought of her. "You try raising a son all by yourself, with a full-time job, and see how long you last without video games."

Jasmine flinched. "Jeez, testy much? I was just saying it's a total fact they rot kids' brains."

"I've played them my whole life," said David. "I turned out fine."

"Debatable," Jasmine sang. "Anyway, they say you're supposed to put kids on a 'technology fast' for, like, a month. It cures all kinds of behavior problems."

Though it sounded like a good idea, Iris couldn't imagine an entire month without screens. The tantrums would undo her.

"Don't feel like you have to keep playing if you don't want to," she said to David. Now that she'd rejected him, his affection for her son might cool. "He's good on his own."

"It's fun," David said with a goofy grin. "I wouldn't mind winning just once—"

"Never!" Mason shouted.

"Inside Voice," Iris warned.

While David and Mason continued to wage war, Jasmine updated Iris on the wedding in the kitchen. Iris had planned on helping more, but Jasmine had hired a team to handle every detail, from sourcing artisanal candies for the gift bags to triaging media requests.

"It sounds really special." Iris plated the lunch she'd prepared, egg salad lettuce wraps and celery sticks with sunflower butter.

"You probably think I'm crazy," Jasmine said, restraining Elsa from eating their lunch.

"I think you're expressing your love for David the way you do best— with beauty."

"I just worry people will look at us and see his money and my looks and think we can't be in love, when our love is *so* deep and strong and, like, indestructible."

"Don't worry what other people think," Iris said. She was afraid to ask if she did love him enough to marry him. Someone needed to ask her, but Iris had too much skin in the game to bring it up.

"I guess I've been feeling kind of insecure. Like, maybe he's obsessed with me but doesn't want to marry me. I keep hearing Mom in my head, saying, 'Why buy the cow when you can get the milk for free?'"

"He definitely wants to marry you." Iris focused on scrubbing a stain on her countertop.

"He's not converting," Jasmine said under her breath.

Iris admired David for setting a boundary, but this would not go over well with the Christian Coalition, aka Spike and Connie.

Jasmine threw up her free hand. "I was like, you can still consider your-self Jewish, you know, like Jews for Jesus, but he thought that was dumb. So we're just telling Mom and Dad he converted privately so his family wouldn't find out. That way, everyone will think it's a secret and no one will say anything."

"You're OK with lying to Mom and Dad?" Iris whispered, in case her honesty-obsessed son could hear. "Dad's going to marry you guys, think-ing David is a Christian."

"Does it matter?" Jasmine asked. "It's all the same God. And that God has bigger fish to fry than my husband's religion."

Iris didn't think God would mind, nor did she care if their parents found out. What irked her was Jasmine could get away with it. She had always used her faith for convenience. When they were teens, Jasmine had slept with a different boyfriend every year, then found her virginity anew at summer faith camp. Iris had denied three boyfriends, one of whom dumped her because she wouldn't go all the way—yet became a pariah when she got pregnant with Mason.

"The truth will come out sooner or later," Iris said.

"Tons of secrets are taken to the grave. That, like, wouldn't be a phrase if it didn't happen all the time."

Iris couldn't help smiling at her sister's logic.

"What?" Jasmine asked.

"You're just funny, that's all."

Jasmine waved her away. "You're funny. Funny looking."

Iris giggled at Jasmine's infantile joke. Then Jasmine giggled, which made Iris laugh harder. They could always make each other laugh by laughing. Moments like this, Iris remembered how deep their bond was. Despite their differences, despite Iris's resentments, despite her feelings for David, their sisterhood would survive.

⁓

Jasmine and David left at sundown. Mason clung to David's thigh and begged him to stay. Iris feared another tantrum, but he remained sweet and obedient for the rest of the evening. They ate a dinner of veggie burgers and salad, then dangled a ribbon in front of Pickles and Meatball and watched their feral instincts emerge. She read him picture books until he fell asleep, at 8:00 P.M. on the dot. This was the Mason she remembered, before he'd started kindergarten. Was the stress of school making him more volatile, or was it the iPad? Iris was afraid of how he might react if she took it away. All his friends played video games, some more violent than his.

She drank a glass of wine on the couch, trying to let go of her guilt, envy, and regret over David. Meatball sauntered onto her chest and purred, his front paws crossed under his chin and his hind legs tucked at his sides like a trussed chicken. She scratched behind his ears. She'd done the mature thing, yet her heart told her she'd made an irreversible mistake.

She drafted a text to Christof, inviting him to Jasmine's wedding, then deleted it. She couldn't decide whether she wanted him there. Even if her mother OKed her bringing someone Iris wasn't serious about, she didn't want to confuse the rest of her friends and relatives. Nor did she want to give Christof the wrong idea. She would revisit the question in a few months, and if he was busy, so be it.

To distract herself from the mess of feelings, she opened Facebook. Kyle had written a disturbing Bridesmaids Union post. She felt for him, yet she wished he wouldn't post about the sex he had and drugs he took in the bridesmaids' support group. Was he trying to get Baxter arrested?

Here was Iris's theory: Baxter was in love with both Kyle and Frederick, but he was trying to commit to Frederick, the stable and reliable choice. Kyle's persistence was confusing Baxter, harming him, even, and he turned to drugs and sex to blunt his feelings. What did it say about her friendship with Kyle—and about her—that she couldn't tell him this? She'd been thinking about what that quack art instructor at the painting night had said, about her bottling up her anger, in the context of what Christof told her, that the real Iris was the one without a filter. She did censor herself a lot, but it seemed better to keep quiet than to butt in and hurt people with her unsolicited opinions. Not all relationships were strong enough to withstand honesty.

She messaged Kyle:

> Hey friend, are you OK? I saw your post.

I miss B

I need him

> I know

> I can feel how hard it is for you.

I feel so alone

I look around and all I see is darkness

It's so dark it's hard to breathe

Are you open to some advice?

Yeah

I think Baxter is hurting too, and you
both might be in less pain if you bow
out of being a groomsman.

I think you will be happier if you can
let him go.

Meatball rolled onto his side and spread his hind legs, and she rubbed her knuckles on his belly fur to calm herself.

I don't think I can

He still loves me

If you love Baxter, the kindest thing
you can do is step away.

He didn't respond. Maybe she had offended him. She decided not to apologize or retract, because she knew she was right. It was cruel to seduce a man who so clearly needed boundaries. He needed to accept Baxter's decision. That was what responsible adults did: they made sacrifices. They gave up on a selfish love out of decency and respect.

# Chapter Twenty

**Eye Fay**

February 4, 2019, 8:25 A.M.

Hi everyone. I'll keep this short. I want to apologize for the gleeful, mean-spirited tone of some of my earlier posts. I think I was writing from a place of frustration, and I crossed a line. I don't want to get pleasure from tearing my sister down.

For some reason Facebook isn't letting me edit my previous posts, and it feels against the spirit of this group to delete them, so I'm going to leave everything up. But going forward, I'm making a commitment to kindness, and I hope you all will, too. This group is about building people up, not tearing them down.

Sending love to everyone—
XOXO
Eye

 35

**Madison Le Claire**
Not sure what posts you're referring to, but I haven't seen anything outright mean.

3

**Anna Banana**

Agreed. Everyone mentioned deserves the shade.

◉2

**Electra Collins**

If your sister ever sees what you wrote, I think she'll have a good laugh.

◉2

**Eye Fay**

Really? I'll take your word for it . . .

◉1

ᔐ

The Morning Glory Bakery Café was more upscale than its homey name suggested, and though the private room in the back received no natural light, it was appealingly designed with mirrored walls and steel girders crisscrossing the ceiling. In short, an ideal venue for Jasmine's bridal shower. If only Iris could enjoy it.

Electra arrived an hour early to help Iris set up. The rest of the bridesmaids were MIA; Iris wondered if Brittany had warned them not to help. She longed for the day when she never again had to see that Fabergé egg of nastiness.

"Are you OK?" Electra asked her. "I know no one likes to be told they look tired . . ."

"I didn't have the greatest night's sleep," Iris admitted.

The night before, she'd lain awake for hours, burning with anxiety. When she finally drifted off, she dreamed that David was her husband and Jasmine was attacking her with a wedding bouquet. She was awakened at 4:00 A.M. by a gloomy message from Kyle. After coaxing him out of his "dark place," she couldn't fall back asleep.

Kyle's messages had been waking her almost every night. She would have put her phone in "do not disturb" mode, but the one time she ignored a message and fell back asleep, he kept sending texts, each more desperate than the last. Yes, it was annoying, and yes, he was acting immature about Baxter, but she reminded herself that he was suffering. He'd been generous with her; she could offer pure support now. She thought of herself as on call for a close friend in crisis. Because he *was* a close friend, even if they had never spoken on the phone, much less met in "meatspace," as the internet geeks called it. Even if they didn't know each other's real names.

Also, caring for Kyle through his breakup made it easier to tolerate her own. She'd heard nothing from David since they agreed to stop speaking, and though she had been tempted to text a hello or a waving emoji, just to maintain contact, she knew better. Even thinking about him, wondering how he was doing, felt like a betrayal of her sister. She was surprised to feel heartbroken from losing a relationship that had never existed. But in a way, that made it worse, because it had been pure potential. It had never burned her. And she could tell no one. She was afraid to admit it even to Kyle.

The sleep deprivation made a bleary soup of her workdays and corroded her reserves, so that Mason's bedtime tantrums became unbearable. She was counting down the days until May eighteenth. After the two weddings, she and Kyle could move on. She hoped.

"Once you get some muffins in you, you'll rally," said Electra.

"So this place is good?" Iris asked. "It has some serious die-hards on Yelp."

"I came here all the time in college. You just have to commit in advance to how many muffins you're going to eat."

"I'm not known for my restraint with carbs."

Electra laughed. "If you were, I would hate you."

Iris had bought a cluster of pink and white helium balloons to match the wedding colors, and she tied them individually to burlap ballast using jute twine while Electra sprinkled dried lavender and silver glitter stars on the long table. (The salesman at Michaels had warned her against using traditional glitter, "the herpes of crafting supplies.") Iris had also bought battery-operated tealights embedded in tree slices; these she placed at regular intervals. Together they festooned pink streamers from the walls and decorated Jasmine's "throne" with string lights and the remaining balloons. Lost in a whirlwind of decorating, Iris could forget her troubles.

The shower was to start at noon. At eleven forty, Brittany strode in, inspected the glassware, and reamed out the server for all the smudges, which Iris was pretty sure she herself had made. Ten minutes to twelve, Connie showed up and commented anxiously that the balloons might impede sight lines. Most of the twenty-four guests were in their seats on time, the gift table piled high with neatly wrapped boxes.

Jasmine burst into the restaurant at twelve fifteen, wearing a clear plastic raincoat over a pink spandex catsuit and gripping a shimmery handbag studded with spikes, which conveyed Elsa in a pink party dress, gazing lovingly at her doggie mom. In a frenzy, Jasmine embraced everyone and thanked them for coming, then plopped into her seat at the head of the table, leaving the raincoat on, and placed the bag with Elsa on a chair Iris provided. Jasmine downed the glass of whiskey that had been waiting for her and ordered another. Her intensity made Iris nervous, as if all the people and furniture in the room were floating a foot off the ground, ready to drop at any second.

Pink menu cards at each place setting included the hashtags #weddingofthecentury and #jasmineanddavidforever—these had come from Jasmine's media consultant. Each guest would receive unlimited muffins, a choice between a vegetable napoleon and no-carb chicken parmesan (fried meat under a slab of cheese seemed perfect for Jasmine's fat-forward diet), and a sugar-free yogurt parfait for dessert. Only Iris and Electra ordered the vegetarian entree. Electra probably ordered it out of solidarity.

The muffins came in steel baskets, swaddled in cloth napkins and smelling heavenly, and the server enumerated that day's flavors (five berry, peach cobbler, rum raisin, powdered doughnut, salted caramel, peppermint latte, and corn) and butters (honey, lemon, and cinnamon). Nothing pleased Iris more than choosing among butters to moisten warm baked goods. Jasmine received a separate basket with three almond-flour hockey pucks.

"Let's cut them into quarters," suggested Electra, the self-appointed muffin doula. "That way everyone can try everything."

The guests tucked in with lowered eyelids and moans of pleasure. Iris felt pride in having chosen a restaurant everyone liked. But she was afraid to look at Jasmine, who poked at her gluten-free, sugar-free muffins with the butt end of her fork.

"Yum," Stefanie said, stretching the word over three syllables.

Iris arranged a few muffin quarters on her plate. She was trying to limit her calories so as not to look like a hippo in the bridesmaid tutu, but a slather of honey butter elevated every warm, fluffy bite into a torrid romance. The powdered doughnut muffin tasted doughnutty, the peppermint latte imparted a rich coffee flavor, and the corn . . . ! It was possibly the best thing she had eaten in her life.

"Jesus Christ, Iris," Jasmine muttered. "Have an orgasm, why don't you."

"Sorry." She took another bite in silence. It didn't taste as good.

"You know I can't eat carbs." Jasmine's voice quavered. "Why did you hold this at a *muffin* restaurant?"

"Everything else is Keto."

"*Girls*," Connie said.

Jasmine pressed her temples with her index fingers. "I can't. I just can't."

Iris cringed at her failure. But when she'd put down the deposit, Jasmine was still eating carbs. What was Iris supposed to do after her diet changed, take the best muffins in America off the menu? It was a well-planned party, and she didn't have to feel bad because her sister was upset. She couldn't wait for the wedding to be over, so she wouldn't have to feel guilty every minute of every day.

After staring down the muffin, Connie forked a crumb into her mouth. She said, "Very nice," with a neat smile.

As they polished off the first round of muffins, more baskets arrived. Iris took her sixth quarter: powdered doughnut again. She decided it would be her last. Then she took a corn muffin wedge and decided that would be her last.

꘎

Cousin Lorelei and her mother, Mary—Connie's sister—arrived an hour late with two gifts but no apology. Mary wore a rust-colored linen shirt and overlapping turquoise bead necklaces, and Cousin Lorelei wore a faded black jumper over a white button-down shirt. Mary asked what kind of muffins there were, and Iris delivered the roll call under her breath, out of respect to Jasmine, who was eating a prepackaged protein bar that she'd brought.

"What's the best?" Cousin Lorelei asked.

"You're not going to believe this, but . . . corn?" Iris said.

"You are so right," Brittany said. "One bite and I knew I had been living wrong."

Iris felt her dislike of Brittany soften.

"The rum raisin is the unsung hero," Electra said. "It's sort of like a rum cake."

"It's making me tipsy," Selena said with a giggle. "Oh, wait, I had three mimosas."

"I'll try this one," said Aunt Mary, grabbing a corn muffin with her hand and splitting it with her thumbs. She gave half to her daughter and took a big bite. "Marvelous!"

Cousin Lorelei wolfed down her half, wiped her face with her hand, and rooted in the basket for another. She tossed a peach cobbler muffin quarter into her mouth as if to keep it from running away. "Holy cats," she said, biting into a powdered doughnut muffin like an apple. Crumbs were lodged in her hair.

"Tell us about your wedding dress, hon," Aunt Mary said to Jasmine.

"I actually have two," Jasmine said. "One is this daring mermaid silhouette with a sexy ice queen narrative. The other one is this romantic and sumptuous Cinderella ball gown fantasy Iris picked. I haven't decided which one I'm going to wear."

"You should wear the one you're more comfortable in," Iris said, not wanting to be responsible for a wedding day meltdown.

"I won't be comfortable either way, so I might as well look hot!" Jasmine said with an unnerving manufactured laugh.

"I hope that's not true," Aunt Mary said with genuine concern.

⟁

"Presents, mofos," Jasmine said, when the desserts came. The parfait was delicious: dense and tart, balanced with a sugar-free strawberry coulis and toasted coconut chips. Iris was disappointed that Jasmine didn't try it, as she'd selected it just for her. But now was not the time to suggest what Jasmine should or should not eat.

Iris heard the clicking of a shutter: Miles the Instagram boyfriend had arrived. She sat up straighter, stopped eating, and applied her most photogenic expression, which looked as if she had just spotted a friend from across the room. Jasmine shifted, too, hiding her anxiety behind a picture-perfect smile.

Connie's gift was a photo album half-full of family pictures, from as far back as Jasmine's infancy—the second half was reserved for Jasmine and David's life together. Brittany gave her an alarm clock that would begin rolling away as soon as it went off, "to make sure you wake up in time on your wedding day," she said with a passive-aggressive cackle. Cousin Lorelei presented the masterpiece she'd created at Paint Party!, signed in the lower-right corner. "I bet it'll be valuable someday," Jasmine said, "though of course I'll never sell it." Connie nearly blew a gasket when her liberal atheist sister gave Jasmine a pink "massage wand." Whether from politeness or ignorance, Jasmine went on about the benefits of frequent massage. "I'm gonna use it like a hundred times a day, Aunt Mary. And it's so convenient! I'll be on the subway and I'll be like, 'OK, let's whip out this bad boy and melt away some of that tension.'"

"That's enough, Jasmine," said Connie.

"She can use it *with* David," Aunt Mary said, as if confused why her sister would be upset. "It's like insurance for your marriage."

"I didn't realize you were the expert on keeping marriages together," Connie sniped.

Mary folded her hands on her lap. Iris could feel the effort it took for her not to respond. It was refreshing to see her mother brandish her teeth at someone other than Iris, especially because that someone was her own sister.

When Jasmine came upon Stefanie's contribution, a pair of high-tech wool socks, she turned them over, as if the real gift might be taped to the other side.

"They're for Mount Kilimanjaro," Stefanie explained. "They're super-duper warm and moisture-wicking. It's crucial to keep your feet dry on a long climb."

"They're so . . . practical!" Jasmine exclaimed.

"You're gonna be so psyched you have them," Stefanie said.

Jasmine took Stefanie's hand in both of hers. "I'm just so appreciative of your friendship. Bring it in." Stefanie submitted to the pity hug, then sat back down and flicked her spoon.

Jasmine opened Iris's gift last. It was a set of two interlocking silver bangles, with a mini ruby set into one and a mini blue zircon in the other. Jasmine understood what this meant: she was born in July, and ruby was her birthstone; Iris was born in December, and her birthstone was the blue zircon. Iris had agonized over whether to include Rose, but ultimately, aesthetics decided for her: Rose's garnet would look too similar to the ruby.

Jasmine began to cry, and Iris could feel her sister's anxiety fall away—or maybe it was her own. "This is so, so perfect," she said, embracing Iris as Miles came in for a close-up. "I'm going to wear it every day."

"I love you, Jazzy," said Iris, woozy with relief. She might have messed up with the muffins, but at least Jasmine liked her gift.

"I love you the most," said Jasmine.

✧

A few weeks before the bridal shower, Iris had bought a bag of clothespins for the traditional "don't say it" hoarding game, in which a guest could take another's clothespin if she caught her saying a predetermined forbidden word, like "dress" or "cake." Then Jasmine called to request-slash-demand the "not-yet-newlywed game," which wouldn't have been a problem had Iris interviewed David about his likes and dislikes before agreeing never to contact him again.

"What's David's favorite movie?" Iris now asked Jasmine, as the guests looked on. A server had come around with orange juice and Champagne to refill glasses—the mimosas remained bottomless for another half hour—but only Electra and Connie were still drinking. The acid soup of orange juice and muffins in Iris's stomach bubbled into her throat.

Jasmine, wearing Iris's masterpiece of a bridal crown, corkscrew ribbons bouncing in front of her face, considered this. "Is it weird I don't know? Let me think . . . you know what? I think I know. Is it *Eternal Sunshine of the Spotless Mind?*"

"It is!" Iris said. "Another point for Team Jasmine and David! Next question: What's his favorite color?"

"I'm pretty sure it's blue," Jasmine said.

"And the answer is . . . blue! You're cleaning up—I should have asked harder questions."

Jasmine shrugged. "I mean, we *are* getting married. I should know him at least a little bit."

"You guys really are simpatico," Iris said, covering up her guilt with the titanium smile of a game show host. She felt good about her sacrifice. Jasmine deserved happiness. Iris would find another man to love, someone who was free to marry her. Or she might remain single, and she and Mason would be just fine.

"OK, how many kids does David want?" Iris asked.

"Fifty!" she exclaimed.

"Is that your final answer?" Iris asked.

"LOL, no. I want five, but I think he wants four."

"Close," Iris said. "He said he knew you wanted five, so that's what he wants now, too." She needed to rein in her lies—she didn't want to be responsible for a future fight. But this was the first time all day when Jasmine seemed relaxed. It would be heartless to take that from her.

"He's a keeper!" Brittany shouted.

"Don't you steal him!" said Jasmine. "I'll kill you."

Laughter warmed the room.

"OK, that's nine correct for Jasmine and none wrong," Iris said. "Last question: What does David love most about you?"

"Can I get multiple choice?" Jasmine asked, to more laughter. "Just kidding, let me think . . . . I think he loves my stick-to-itiveness, that I never give up on my dreams."

"That was one of the things he said. Do you want to guess the others?"

"Nah, I'm gonna sound like a psycho if I'm wrong."

"Well, first of all, he loves how beautiful you are—you're the most beautiful woman he's ever known," Iris said, wiping away a tear as she pretended to read from her phone. She could still hear what he'd said about Jasmine on New Year's Eve. His voice lived in her mind. "He loves your sense of humor, and he loves that you think he's funny."

"That's what he thinks," Jasmine said, for a laugh.

"He loves your business sense," Iris continued, her voice cracking. "He loves that you two never get bored of each other. And he loves that you say what you mean. He knows where he stands with you." Her wobbling voice jumped into a higher register as she gave in to her tears. "I think that was the biggest thing, your honesty. He thought it was too rare in this world."

Now Jasmine was misty-eyed, and Iris sobbed, from joy or grief, guilt or despair, she had no idea. In their most potent expression, all emotions felt the same, blind and raw and wild.

"Well, this was no fun," Jasmine said, addressing the crowd with a broad smile and fanning her face as if to evaporate the tears before they fell. "David and I are too much on the same wavelength. Sorry, guys. You'll have to get your schadenfreude elsewhere."

"Your love is beautiful and holy," Connie said. "God has blessed your union."

"I know," said Jasmine, tugging on the ribbons in her crown. "I'm grateful for it every minute of every day."

# Chapter Twenty-one

**Electra Collins**

March 4, 2019, 5:16 P.M.

I apologize in advance, because most of you will not understand what the heck this post is about. But I experienced a revelation this weekend: if I ever get married, my wedding is going to be muffin-themed. In other news, I gained four pounds this weekend.

Also, what is the point of a bridal shower except to force people to give you more gifts? And why is it only women who are expected to buy them? Yet another reason why wedding traditions were obviously invented by men. That said, the entire day became truly exceptional when J's aunt gifted her a vibrator. Eye, please invite your family to all future events involving sex toys and/or muffins.

👍😂 6                                                    3 comments

**Eye Fay**
OMG Electra Collins, I am so glad you're part of this group.
❤1

**Electra Collins**
Feeling's mutual!
❤1

**Eye Fay**

BTW I probably shouldn't admit this, but was it obvious that I didn't interview D for the newlywed game? I just told J she was right about every question.

👁 1

**Electra Collins**

Whaaa??? IT MAKES SO MUCH SENSE NOW.

👍 1

**Alexandria Canas**

You're an evil genius, Eye Fay.

❤2

**Eye Fay**

I wish you had been there, bridesmaid emerita.

❤2

⁓

Through her living room windows, Iris watched snow fall in downy clumps as she sipped a mug of coffee and considered opening the bills on her lap. Despite having lived her entire life in the tristate area, known for its capricious, indefatigable winters, she felt personally wronged when it snowed in March. Before she became pregnant with Mason, she and a few friends would fly to Florida or the Caribbean this time of year for a turbo boost of warmth to survive winter's death rattle. Now she toyed with taking Rose up on her invitation to visit her in Florida.

Mason was with Forrest for the afternoon at the Legoland Discovery Center, a theme park–cum–shopping wonderland in a nearby outdoor mall, and Iris had not crossed a single item off her to-do list, though she had indulged in a sumptuous nap, her first in what felt like decades. Mason and his dad had been enjoying occasional unsupervised afternoons since late January. Forrest's visits hadn't cured Mason's bedtime freak-outs, but the school psychologist didn't think he would bite again. He and Rafael had reconciled; now they played Minecraft together.

She put her coffee down and opened her credit card bill, bracing herself for her monthly reckoning. Her recent charges amounted to three thousand dollars, including the bridal shower, which the other bridesmaids would chip in for. She could pay this, but she wouldn't have anything left to put toward her still-overwhelming balance, emergency savings, or Mason's college fund. She envied Jasmine, who would never have to worry about money again, thanks to David's wealth.

David. She couldn't go an hour without thinking of him. Maybe after the wedding it would hurt less. But she didn't want it to hurt less, because the pain reminded her of how much he wanted her. She felt guilty for enjoying that feeling, which made her hurt in a different way.

Kyle messaged her:

**Hey, did u get my present?**

She realized with a start that she had forgotten to open it. Kyle had asked for her address earlier that week—he said he wanted to send her a "thank u." After careful consideration, she gave him her work address. She wasn't supposed to receive personal mail at the hospital, but the guys in the mailroom didn't care. None of the rules she or anyone else wrote mattered in the slightest. The institution was ruled by a collective set of behaviors that could never be codified.

She hadn't opened the box when it came, wanting to protect it from Jeremy's prying eyes. At home, she hadn't wanted to open it in front of Mason. But now she was alone.

She peeled off the tape and poured the packing peanuts into the trash. Inside were a dozen bottles and tubes of expensive-looking spa products for her hair, face, and body. She popped the cap on the body wash and sniffed. It smelled like lavender and mint, two of her favorite scents.

A card was tucked at the bottom:

*To my clear-seeing Eye,*
*Thank you for supporting me through my dark days. You are a true friend, and I will try to be a better one.*
*XO*
*Kyle*

She was touched. Not only were these products going to enliven her mornings, they would save her a chunk of change. She messaged Kyle an enthusiastic thank you.

Ur very welcome!

I hope you didn't spend too much on these . . .

LOL no. I get sent a lot of product

If u saw my bathroom u wld know u were doing me a favor

I picked them out just 4 u tho

The Eye Fay Collection LOL

Thank you.

This means a lot to me.

And it did. Just because he didn't pay for the gift didn't mean it wasn't thoughtful.

Thank u 4 being such a loyal friend!

I know I'm not easy

My emotions hold me hostage

He wasn't lying—it had been challenging to support him through his dark nights. But he would have done the same for her. When she'd first messaged with him, he was a star and she was a new admirer. Now they were equals—she didn't care about his million followers anymore. She knew a different Kyle than the one in the photos, one who had suffered, who doubted himself, and who offered a sympathetic ear when she was struggling. His gift grounded their connection in something real. His stubbornness about Baxter could be frustrating, but she believed he would grow. She was seeing him through to safety.

She glanced at the address on the box, written in tidy block letters. Eye Fay. They'd known each other almost six months, and she hadn't told him her name. At first the caution had been sensible, but now the wall could come down. His address, on West Forty-Third Street in Manhattan, was on the return label, but not his name. She liked knowing his address; she took a picture of it with her phone.

> I'd like to share my name with you

> Is that OK?

Her heart drum-rolled as she prepared to expose herself in this small but important way.

> Yes! I didn't think it was Eye!

> LOL

> It's Iris Hagarty.

> Thank u Iris Hagarty

> My name is Kyle Goh

> Thank you, Kyle Goh.

She moisturized her hands with a tube of almond-scented cream, held her palms to her face, and breathed in. She felt as if he were in the room with her.

Mason burst through the door later that afternoon, recounting every high-light of the day simultaneously. Forrest, laden with Lego kits, followed him in, deciphering his boisterous pronouncements.

"We made race cars together, and Mason's won," Forrest said. "It was killer. He was way younger than the other kids, and his car flew past theirs."

"That's incredible!" Iris said, giving Mason a high five. She offered to split the cost of the Legos, but Forrest wanted to pay. He had also bought annual passes. Maybe he wasn't as impoverished as she'd thought.

"He needs to grow a teensy bit to go on the rides, and we'll do the virtual reality stuff when he gets older," Forrest explained, and this inti-mation of a long-term commitment pleased Iris. "He loved the model of New York City."

"It was awesome," Mason said, using his father's hang-ten intonation.

Once Mason could be persuaded to sit down with Beepbop and eat a bowl of SpaghettiOs, Iris and Forrest convened on the couch. "Can we talk about something for a second?" she asked.

"Sure." He seemed tense.

"What's most important is you're back in Mason's life. That's invalu-able, and I'm so grateful you guys have this bond. But the truth is, we're having a tough time making ends meet . . ." Iris hated how hedgy she was being. The law stated he had to pay; why couldn't she just tell him?

"Do you need money? Are we talking about child support?"

She let out a breath she didn't know she was holding. "A little extra income would make a huge difference in our lives. I could put money toward Mason's college fund. And we could travel. Nothing extravagant, but he's never been on a plane."

"Sure. And we could make this dad thing official?"

She dispensed with the rest of her arguments—apparently he didn't need convincing. "Yes, with paternity rights and everything. Thank you."

"Awesome." He eyed her skeptically. "How long have you been waiting to bring this up?"

Sensing criticism, she went on the defensive. "I wasn't sure how you'd respond if I started making demands. I was so glad you and Mason were hitting it off, I didn't want to jinx it."

He kept starting to say something. Finally, he did. "I'm telling you this because we're going to be seeing each other a lot, and I don't want to fall back into our old patterns. I spent a few years in therapy after . . . us, to figure myself out, to figure out why I left the way I left, and this is one thing I realized."

"What is it?" The longer he went on, the worse she feared his revelation would be.

"You waited a long time to talk about child support, and when you did, the way you were presenting it, it felt like you were expecting me to say no. But if you had just brought it up when you thought of it, like, casually, it would have been fine. It's like you assume I'm going to fail you without giving me the chance to be better. You've set it up so you get to be disappointed in me."

She wasn't going to be blamed for him abandoning her. "I don't think I'm crazy to expect you to disappoint me."

"Of course, I get that," he said, holding his palms out as if she were threatening him. "I left you in the worst way. I still feel shitty about it, and I'm sorry. I'm not asking you to forgive me."

"I don't think I can," she said, watching Mason line up bits of pasta on his spoon. "But I've moved past it."

"Good. I mean, thank you. I mean . . . you know what I mean."

If Forrest wanted directness, she could give him that. "And just to settle this thing you've discovered about me? When we were together, every time I told you what I wanted, you shut down. You taught me to tiptoe around you, to hide my real self at all costs, and then you left, so the lesson I learned was that all my tiptoeing hadn't been enough. So yes, maybe I do expect you to disappoint me. And the fact is, you could have brought up child support, too. You didn't have to wait for me to say something."

He pursed his lips. "I'm sorry—it didn't seem my place to suggest something more permanent with Mason. And for the record, I wasn't aware that dynamic was happening, and that's not why I left. But I've grown a lot since then. I'm just asking you to be direct with me going forward."

"So why did you leave?" She blurted it out, this question she'd agonized over for years. Her heart knocked her about, making her breaths shallow.

He pierced her with his gaze. "I wish I could tell you. But I can't."

Her disappointment turned to irritation. "You see how that went."

"I'm sorry. But trust me, you don't want to know."

# Chapter Twenty-two

**Kyle Kyle**

April 21, 2019, 10:56 P.M.

I just got home from you-know-who's bachelor party. #notcute. Both grooms and all seventeen members of the wedding party flew down to New Orleans for the weekend and stayed in some bougie-ass digs on Frederick's dime.

On Friday, they rented out a private room in a restaurant in a dusty old bank building. Frederick's friends all went to Ivy League schools, and dinner was a three-hour pissing contest. "Have you read the latest Knausgaard interview in The New Yorker? Oh, you didn't know it's pronounced with a hard K?" "Oh, these? They're not macadamia nuts, they're Marcona almonds. Aren't they divine?" "No need to wash your hands after a tinkle, fellow scholar. Urine is sterile."

Anyone still awake at midnight was treated to a round of sambuca. Frederick geared up for a long-winded toast about his love for the man I love, so I went to my room. I half expected Baxter to knock on my door, begging for some action. Next thing I knew, it was ten in the morning and I'd slept through breakfast.

That day, the two sides split for bachelor time. Frederick and fourteen of his closest friends did a Garden District tour and went to a Pelicans game (I thought it was some kind of cockfighting thing, but it's basketball, LOL), and Baxter and his three amigos (including me) drove way the hell out of town for a swamp tour. Baxter's brother, Barton, is a nice guy, but note to self: don't trust a horticulturist to plan any of my future vacations. The swamp tour was basically two hours in a puttery boat on a gray pond, and we saw a grand total of one random bird and a gross rodent called a nutria. Not a single alligator. And it was muggy as fuck. At this point I was like, does the Louisiana Purchase have a return policy?

After dinner, while we're walking down Bourbon Street, drinking hurricanes, this crazy mofo offers us a shoeshine. We were all wearing sneakers, but dude would not give up. Hell if I was going to let him touch my McQueen sneakers with his nasty rag. Finally, Baxter lets him wipe down his Nikes. As the guy is working on the foxing, he's like, that'll be forty dollars, sir. And Baxter steps back and is like, no effing way! And the dude is like, you pay for the line, not the shine. We're all like WTF?, and he repeats his weird-ass rhyme. Then Baxter pulls out two twenties and gives them to him! I could not believe what shit was going down. Barton and Tomas, Baxter's college friend, keep their mouths shut. After we walk away, Baxter reaches into his shoe and pulls out a baggie of cocaine. You pay for the line, he says. Good one.

At the casino, Baxter blew six hundred bucks on blackjack. Later I heard him snorting the coke off the toilet seat in the handicap stall with some twink. I'm like, you can't go around pretending you want to be monogamous and then hook up with every piece of ass in the lower 48. And he's like, Frederick can afford to take care of me, and what he doesn't know can't hurt him.

On a hunch, I looked at a few escort sites, and lo and behold, Baxter is hustling under the name Will Typhoon. He charges three hundred an hour. Who isn't marriage material now? Now I'm thinking

Frederick can have him and all his freaky STIs. I'm staying the hell away.

  108                                    22 comments

**Gloria Abernathy**
It's so hard to give up a toxic love. I think you both would benefit from a Sex and Love Addicts Anonymous meeting.
2

**Evelyn Huang**
Kyle Kyle, have you considered telling Frederick about Baxter's secret life? His behavior is very concerning, and Frederick has a right to know.
7

**Anna Banana**
I guess this is relevant to the Bridesmaids Union because . . . ?
9

**Madison Le Claire**
This group is straying far from what it used to be. It's not my place to judge anyone, but I'm realizing it's not for me anymore.
1

**Eye Fay**
Please DM me, Kyle Kyle. We need to talk.

All the bridesmaids were waiting when Iris's Uber pulled up at David and Jasmine's mansion for the bachelorette party. After a fifteen-minute photo shoot for Jasmine's Instagram story, Jasmine, Iris, Brittany, and Electra climbed into Jasmine's Range Rover, and Cousin Lorelei, Stefanie, and Selena took the Civic. Thanks to Brittany's logistical genius, all their luggage fit, too.

Iris had been too anxious to eat breakfast. She had told Jasmine they'd be staying on a working farm, but Jasmine, wanting to preserve the surprise, had resisted details. Iris had suggested she not bring heels, but Jasmine packed two pairs "just in case." Something wasn't computing.

To Iris's great relief, David was visiting a friend in San Francisco. Jasmine muttered something about David "needing space" when they were "two seconds away from walking down the aisle." Iris guessed this was not a superficial spat. She would never forgive herself if she poisoned her sister's marriage, and yet it seemed she already had.

On the ride, the group sang along to a satellite radio station playing classic pop from the boy band era, though after a few minutes, Jasmine asked Electra not to sing, which improved the timbre but soured the mood. Iris had spent nearly an hour researching restaurants along the route and found a Keto-friendly, dog-friendly café. Jasmine ordered a salad with a double portion of steak. When Stefanie critiqued her diet for being unsustainable, both nutritionally and environmentally, Jasmine sulked to the bathroom, gripping Elsa like a security blanket. You didn't need a master's in diplomacy to know not to challenge her so close to the wedding. Iris could feel a fight in the offing, the way people with metal implants could sense a storm coming.

༄

The tension among bridesmaids wasn't the only storm on the horizon. That Monday, when Iris had read Kyle's post about the bachelor party, she was surprised by a flare of resentment: Baxter was sinking deeper, and not only did Kyle show up to the bachelor party, he treated Baxter's addictions with derision and contempt. She'd been supportive and understanding for months, and he ignored her advice and seemed incapable of learning from his mistakes. The intimacy that blossomed after his gift of the spa products worsened her irritation: it felt as if he'd purchased her complicity.

She'd seethed with frustration. After tamping down her anger, she voiced her concerns and asked if he'd check in on Baxter. He didn't respond. She suggested they meet in person, as relying on his reports made the whole thing surreal. He apologized and said he was getting on a flight to Paris. She sent five messages over the next few days and heard nothing. Maybe he didn't have cell service overseas.

She had to stop worrying about a lover's tiff that didn't affect her. Baxter's dissolution was none of her business, and there was nothing she could do short of reaching out to him, which would be insane. But twenty members had left the Bridesmaids Union since Kyle began posting about sex and drugs, some after writing pointed comments. He was poisoning the group. Maybe it was time to kick him out. But she didn't want to give up on their friendship. She wasn't in close contact with any of her other friends, and when she wanted to message someone, she thought only of him.

Everything was going to be OK. Everything would settle down. If only her nerves would do the same.

～

Jasmine and her bridesmaids pulled into the farm at two. The white clapboard farmhouse inn had pastel yellow shutters and a robin's-egg-blue door. A massive oak tree shaded the house; further down the driveway, cows flapped their ropy tails in a field beside a weathered gray barn with a big rusted star above the doorway. It was picturesque yet modern, authentic yet manicured, humble yet dignified.

Iris's shoes sank into the soft, damp earth. Electra stretched her arms above her head, and Stefanie pressed against Jasmine's SUV and did a figure-four with her legs. A light scent of manure wafted past on a chilly spring breeze. Finally, Iris began to relax.

"This place is . . . quaint," Jasmine said, placing Elsa on the ground to do her business. "What is this I'm smelling?"

Brittany laughed viciously. "It's animal shit. It's a farm."

"OK, but where's the hotel?"

"This is the hotel," Iris said, ironing the irritation out of her voice. "I told you it was a farm stay. That means it's a working farm."

"I guess I thought it'd be, like, a farmhouse spa."

"Your suite has a Jacuzzi, and they offer in-room massage. And I made up mani/pedi kits for everyone."

Jasmine looked from the inn to the barn and back at Iris. Her smile dissolved into a pout. "OK, we can do this," she said as if giving herself permission.

"I told her you would hate it," Brittany said to Jasmine. "She wouldn't listen to me. She doesn't listen to anyone."

That wasn't fair—Iris had listened to everyone and realized they had no chance of coming to consensus. But she was too focused on Jasmine to be sidetracked by Brittany's sniping.

"Can we ride horses?" asked Cousin Lorelei, staring at the cows.

Jasmine wiped tears from her eyes. "I'm sorry, I know this is super ungrateful of me, but this isn't how I pictured my bachelorette getaway. And what keeps running through my head is we're sisters, but you don't know me at all."

A pit had lodged in Iris's stomach. She didn't know whether to talk up the vacation or apologize, so she chose both options. "The photos on the website made it look amazing. It's a million Instagrams waiting to happen."

"How can you not see that the colors are all wrong?" Jasmine wailed, gesturing at the inn. "My brand palette is pink and teal, not blue and yellow."

"It's really not you," said Selena with a sympathetic nod.

"This is unacceptable," said Brittany, suppressing a smirk. She took out her phone and jabbed at the screen with both thumbs.

"It's like a petting zoo for adults," Iris said, feeling all her hopes for the weekend collapsing. She'd sensed from the start that this was a bad idea; why hadn't she given in and planned the Vegas trip? What was wrong with her brain? "We used to love petting zoos." She heard how out of touch that sounded.

"I think it looks kind of luxurious," Electra said, looking at the website on her phone. "They offer turndown service and cookies made with goat butter."

"I can't eat cookies," Jasmine whimpered.

"We should find someplace else," Selena said.

"Let's take a deep breath and shake off those negative thoughts," Stefanie said, placing her hand on Jasmine's upper back. "Iris worked super hard to plan a killer weekend for you. Attitude of gratitude, m'kay? The Jasmine I know is a strong woman who can push through any challenge, no matter how hard, to meet her goals. Let's find that Jasmine now."

"This smell is making me feel really nauseous," Jasmine said in a high-pitched voice that broke into sobs. "It's all wrong. I can't go through with it. I can't go through with it." She crouched above the muddy soil, cradling her face in her hands.

"You can't go through with the bachelorette party, or . . . ?" Iris asked, afraid of what lay on the other end of that sentence.

"This can be a fun weekend of bonding," Stefanie said to Jasmine, "or we can go home and you can sulk in your bed. Your choice."

Brittany blocked her microphone with her fingers and said, "I've got a four-star hotel in Philadelphia on the line. They can offer us seven rooms at a rate of one ninety-nine a night, they welcome dogs, and they'll up-grade you to a suite. It's a fun city—great nightlife. Should I book it?"

"Um . . ." Jasmine began.

"The rooms aren't refundable," Iris said, gazing at the inn as if at a photograph from her distant past. She was numb with regret.

"So you don't care that Iris planned this sweet-ass vacay," Stefanie said. "You don't care that she thought out every single detail to show you how much she loves you."

"Why are you being so mean to me, Stefanie?" Jasmine asked, her sad-ness extinguished by indignation. "This is my bachelorette party. I only get one chance to do this right. This is not right. Brittany is making it right." She turned to Brittany. "Yes, please book the hotel. Thank you, friend."

"Ten-four," Brittany said, then stepped away to complete the reserva-tion.

"I used to admire how confident you were, how willing you were to speak your mind and love yourself without reservations," Stefanie said. "Now I see that it's because you're so self-centered, you don't even realize other people have feelings."

"You don't have to do this," Iris said, feeling the wrongness of Stefanie's approach like sandpaper on her bones.

"Yes, I do," Stefanie said, without taking her eyes off Jasmine. "If you could consider anyone besides yourself for one second of your life, you'd learn how to be grateful for what you have and to stop finding fault with others' good intentions."

"You know what, Stefanie?" Jasmine's voice was cold and sharp. "It sounds like you don't want to be my bridesmaid. Which is fine with me, because I don't want you to be my bridesmaid, either. I think it's time you went home."

"I think I will," Stefanie said. She rotated her jaw.

"And you're fired as my trainer," Jasmine added with Trumpian petulance.

"Fan-fucking-tastic. Best news I've heard all year."

Jasmine hopped into the SUV, placed Elsa in her lap, and stared straight ahead.

"Make that six rooms," Brittany said into the phone.

Iris stepped inside the farmhouse and scraped her shoes against the welcome mat. The great room was painfully charming, painted in pastels and decorated with antique furniture. In the sitting area, upholstered armchairs huddled around a massive fireplace with a pyramid of birch logs in the andirons, aching to be lit. An elderly woman, reading a yellowed hardbound book on a rocking chair, greeted Iris and ushered her toward the reception desk.

"I'm really sorry, but my sister doesn't want to stay here," Iris said. "Is there any way you could give us a partial refund?"

"I'm afraid we have a strict cancellation policy," the woman said. "No refunds within seven days."

Seven rooms for three nights had come to almost five thousand dollars. Iris didn't see how she could ask the other bridesmaids to pitch in; they had warned her against this place. Why hadn't she listened?

"I'll tell you what," the innkeeper continued. "If we resell any of the rooms for this weekend, I'll reimburse you that amount. I heard what happened out there. You deserve a place in heaven for putting up with that woman."

～⌒

By the time Iris dropped Jasmine and the other bridesmaids off at the hotel in Philadelphia, drove Stefanie to her apartment in Weehawken in rush-hour traffic, and returned to Philadelphia, it was almost 9:00 P.M., and she was too tired to feel any more guilt. The others were out to dinner at a glitzy fusion restaurant, so Iris fused with the hotel bed and ordered room service. She'd missed Mason's bedtime phone call. With Marilyn's help, he'd left a sweet message on her voicemail; Iris listened to it again and again, wallowing in her sadness. Stefanie was the lucky one. Stefanie had been spared. She wished she could stand up to Jasmine the way Stefanie had. She had always been a pushover, and she hated herself for it. She often blamed her mother for criticizing her constantly, teaching her that her voice was unwanted. But Jasmine and Rose had the same mother, and they weren't afraid of being themselves. How did they do it?

Once she'd eaten, she felt less brittle. She squeezed into a little black dress and touched up her makeup. She could have carried groceries in the bags under her eyes, so she sifted through her purse detritus, found the glitter gel Jasmine had given her, and dabbed some on. Not perfect, but better.

She joined the rest of the group in the hotel bar. A handful of drunk conventioneers in ill-fitting suits bopped to a jazz guitarist off to one side, but otherwise, Jasmine and the bridesmaids—minus Cousin Lorelei, with her 10:00 P.M. bedtime—had the place to themselves.

Iris waved at her group, feeling sheepish about having screwed things up, but no one seemed to blame or judge her, and Jasmine, pickled with booze, didn't let on that anything had gone awry.

Iris ordered a Chardonnay from the exceptionally cute bartender and sat with Electra at a highboy.

"As soon as this wedding is over, I'm never speaking with her again," Electra said. "If I'd been in your shoes, I would have gone home and let the rest of us take the train."

Electra's anger took the pressure off Iris to cling to her resentment.

"I considered it," Iris lied.

"You know Brittany's maid of honor now, right?"

"What?"

"Yeah, Jasmine gave it to her."

Iris was stunned. She'd spent dozens of hours researching and booking venues, hammering out logistics, communicating with the other bridesmaids and the shower guests, talking Jasmine down from panic attacks, choreographing the bridesmaid dance, and planning the bachelorette party within an inch of its life. She'd spent thousands she didn't have and wouldn't get back. She'd tiptoed around Jasmine, acquiescing to every demand and apologizing for every misstep, in hopes of winning back the sisterly relationship she deserved. She had swallowed her opinions, utterly doormatted herself, to rekindle her relationship with a sister who was incapable of being a friend. All for nothing. After the wedding, she would probably be discarded with the decorative bales of hay.

"She was unhinged at dinner," Electra said, glancing over her shoulder at Jasmine, who was laughing at a joke Brittany had made. "Want to know my theory?"

Iris nodded.

"She's getting cold feet, but she's too chicken to call it off. And all of this"—Electra made a big circle with jazz hands—"is because she's freaking the fuck out."

Iris shrugged. Electra's guess wasn't far from her own. But she believed Jasmine and David would be happy together, whether or not they were in love. Maybe she had to believe it. "I'm not sure marriage is about love."

"Excuse me while I go slit my wrists," Electra said.

"I don't mean it in a bad way. I just think following your heart usually blows up in your face. Love is great and all, but it's better to pick someone you can live with." Iris wondered when she'd begun to believe that. "And David seems really easy to live with—he almost never stands up for himself, like, on principle. He just goes with the flow."

"I'm going to wait until I'm in love," Electra said. "If I end up as a spinster, so be it."

"Here's to being spinsters," said Iris.

"To spinsterhood!" They clinked glasses.

"When all this is over, you should come over for dinner or something," Iris said.

"That'd be cool," Electra said. "Or we could go to a farm stay. I hear there's a nice one nearby."

Iris grimaced. "I don't think I can ever show my face in there again."

"You know those farm people live for drama."

&#10086;

After Electra called it a night, Iris migrated toward her shitfaced sister, who was trying to convince Selena to sleep with the bartender.

"She should totally go for it, right?" Jasmine slurred as Iris maneuvered her butt onto a velvet-cushioned stool. Iris could smell her sister's alcohol breath from three feet away.

"You wouldn't be upset if she ditched you on your bachelorette weekend?" Iris asked.

"At least one of us would be getting some. David's penis is *so small*, Iris." She held up two fingers a centimeter apart. "I can't even feel it in me. Usually I just fake a headache. And Brittany and Hakim are like an old married couple. They're down to like, once a month."

"Hey!" Brittany said, flicking Jasmine's arm.

"Don't hate me for speaking truth."

"David seems like he'd be a generous lover," Iris said, hoping she wasn't exposing her desire.

Jasmine stuck out her tongue and blew a raspberry. "I'm just kidding. Can't you take a joke? Anyway, I'm probably going to leave him after we have kids." Jasmine ran a finger along the edge of her martini glass. "Did you know Stefanie's present to me—like, her *wedding* present—was a pair of eight-pound dumbbells? I looked them up—they cost thirty bucks. That cheap old biscuit was going to be my bridesmaid. Selena, are you going to talk to him or what?"

Selena adjusted her cleavage, approached the bartender, and asked with a feline smile if he'd make her his favorite drink.

"You're planning on . . . leaving him?" Iris asked Jasmine. She was having trouble putting breath behind the words. Her vision bleached, and her face flushed with a prickly chill.

"Not right away," Jasmine said. "But he's, like, a five-year husband.

We'll have a bunch of kids—they'll be geniuses like him—and then I'll take my half of his assets to raise them and grow my business. He is totally aware of this plan. At least he would be if he were half as smart as he thinks he is."

So Jasmine didn't love David. Iris had suspected this for months and refused to believe it, but here was proof. She should tell her sister not to marry him, not to promise herself forever while planning on breaking his heart. She was probably the only person in Jasmine's life who could tell her this. But she had kissed David, maybe loved him, which made dissuading Jasmine an act of selfishness. Anger burned inside her, and her arms shook as if bound by handcuffs.

"What?" Jasmine said with pursed lips and slitted eyes. "You hate David."

"I don't."

"Then why do you never want to see him or talk to him or talk about him? Every time we want to come over, someone's mysteriously sick. The one time you deigned to let us visit, you tried to kick us out after like five minutes."

Iris couldn't refute this, couldn't look at Jasmine, couldn't keep her head up, so she put it on the metal table. The cold radiated into her skull.

"You OK?" Brittany asked.

"Just tired," Iris said, propping up her head with the tented fingers of one hand. "I need to go to bed."

"You should have worn sunglasses for driving," Jasmine said. "You'd be a lot less tired now if you'd blocked out some of the glare. UV rays are super damaging to the eyes."

"Next time," Iris said.

In the elevator, Iris checked her phone. Finally, a Facebook message from Kyle:

How's the trip?

She was so desperate for a sympathetic ear, she forgave him for ignoring her.

It couldn't be worse.

Jasmine hated the beautiful inn I picked, so we're in a dumb hotel and I'm out five thousand bucks.

And she told me she's planning on leaving David after they have kids.

Inside her room, she peeled off her dress and shapewear, threw on an XL men's T-shirt, and collapsed on the bed. Her body vibrated with gratitude.

Ur surprised?

I actually was. I mean, she makes me crazy, but she's my sister.

I want to believe there's a human being under all that lip gloss.

I feel like I'm partly to blame for her entitlement. I never stand up to her.

She needs 2 learn that her actions have consequences

She was grateful for the support. He could be a good friend when he wasn't plotting to destroy Baxter.

Ugh, I don't think I can do it. I guess I'm a coward. Not everyone can be brave.

Maybe I can help

Thank you

She was too tired to ask what kind of help he was offering.

Let's talk in the morning.

She wrote a short and vicious Bridesmaids Union post about her sister's monstrous plans. She needed witnesses. She recalled the version of herself who vowed to be more positive in her posts, but she was too angry to listen to that naïve stranger. Jasmine deserved all the shame in the world. Iris wanted to shove it down her throat.

She fell asleep without turning off the bedside lamp.

# Chapter Twenty-three

**Heather Fried**

April 26, 2019, 10:04 A.M.

Eye Fay would you get in touch with me? I'm doing a story on the Bridesmaids Union for the New York Times, and I'd love to get your response to everything that's been going on. Cheers!

👁 229

⁓

An unholy banging yanked Iris out of a bewildering dream. Sunlight burned along the edges of the blackout curtains. Her head was throbbing, her saliva tacky. She hadn't drunk that much—could you get a hangover from a bad day? She extracted herself from the layers of damp hotel sheets, surprised by a sheen of glitter on her pillow, and pushed herself out of bed, her brain sloshing inside her skull. She spread the curtains wide, wincing at the light, then guzzled the overpriced water on the desk and fumbled her way to the door.

"Coming!" she shouted.

Through the peephole, she saw Jasmine pacing in the hall, wearing fuzzy blue pajamas that made her look like the Cookie Monster. Iris flipped open the swing bar lock and pulled the door open.

"I'll kill you." Jasmine lunged at Iris's neck. Iris's head thudded on the carpet, light flashing into her vision. Jasmine squeezed her windpipe, making Iris gag. "I should rip your frigging throat out."

Blinded by Jasmine's hair in her face and dizzy from sleep, Iris couldn't push her off. Jasmine's long, sharp fingernails cut into her neck, and she could only suck in sips of air. She feared her sister would actually kill her.

"Please," Iris begged.

Jasmine loosened her grip and glared at her with unrecognizable fury. "You ruined my wedding! You ruined my life!" She stood and kicked Iris.

"I honestly don't know what you're talking about." Gasping for breath, she scooted away and pushed herself up to sitting. Fear made it impossible to think.

"If you hated me so much, why didn't you say it to my face?"

Now Iris understood what happened. A moment later, she understood how. She'd destroyed her sister's reputation with the righteous mockery of a victim. She'd sensed something off about Kyle: his inability to let go of Baxter, his dramatic vows that were forgotten as soon as they were made. Why had she trusted him with the keys to her privacy? "I'm sorry," she said, an apology so inadequate it almost sounded like a joke. This was the moment when she should explain why she set up the Bridesmaids Union page and complained about Jasmine online, but she had no excuse. She couldn't remember why she'd done it. "They weren't lies," she said.

"So you really are a heartless jerk." Jasmine walked out, then grabbed the door before it closed. "Don't talk to me again. I'm serious. If I ever see your ugly face, I really will kill you—and I will *enjoy* it."

The door clicked shut, and Iris was alone.

With an immense physical and emotional effort, she hoisted herself to standing and examined her throat in the bathroom mirror. Jasmine hadn't broken the skin, though surely a bruise was on its way. Overnight, the glitter makeup had spread all over her face. Even after scrubbing with cleanser, the metallic flecks seemed glued in place. She wondered if Jasmine had given her the Unicorn Snot as a prank. Herpes, indeed.

She checked her phone, charging on the nightstand. The lock screen was inundated with hundreds of tweets, sixty-eight emails, twenty-one text messages, and twelve missed calls from Jasmine, Jeremy, and various friends. She didn't know where to begin surveying the damage. Her Facebook account had been suspended. Five of her Bridesmaids Union posts had been flagged as inappropriate. She burned with shame.

What had Kyle done when he was in Facebook jail? Put up a new profile to let his close friends know what happened. Friends! What kind of friend exposed all your secrets to the world in the name of revenge?

She created an account with the name Eye Eye Mate and searched for the Bridesmaids Union Facebook group. Indeed, its status was "public," and all the posts were visible. The group had four thousand members, up from seven hundred—anyone could join without approval. A *Times* reporter had posted, asking Iris to get in touch with her. First, she needed to figure out whom she'd offended and by how much.

Her posts usually garnered a handful of supportive comments. Now each had more than a hundred. Some members were appalled at the excesses Iris had described, but most were horrified at her for sharing personal information about Jasmine and sabotaging her wedding. Her eyes caught on "monster," "bitch," and worse. She threw her phone on the bed as if it had bitten her.

But she didn't have the luxury of leaving it there. She friend-requested Kyle to keep her messages out of the nefarious "message requests" folder, then sent him one without waiting for him to approve the friendship.

THIS IS EYE/IRIS. MY ACCOUNT WAS
DEACTIVATED. PLEASE MAKE THE
BRIDESMAIDS UNION SECRET AGAIN.
PLEASE ADD ME ON FOR ADMIN
PRIVILEGES.

No response. Of all the times he'd be away from his phone. Or maybe he was getting his abs spray-tanned, oblivious to her pain.

It was terrifying not to be able to hide any of her posts that exposed her family and friends and called out Jasmine for her selfish and petty demands. Worse yet, everyone else's posts were now public, and someone had reposted Iris's original complaints from Reddit, which she thought she'd deleted.

If she tried to defend herself in the comments of the Bridesmaids Union, it would only start a flame war, so she moved on to her email app, which was packed with messages from people she didn't know. She held her breath and read one from Amber:

Seriously, Iris, WTF? I thought we were best friends. I can't think of a single reason why you would have smeared me on the internet. I thought it was weird you waited six months to ask me about those centerpieces, and now I see why: you had already dragged me through the mud online.

You seemed totally happy with every aspect of being my maid of honor. JonJon thought I shouldn't let you take on as much as you did, but you didn't complain once. I just assumed you had this weird masochistic obsession with bridesmaid shit.

I find it ironic that you wouldn't understand how the pressures of a wedding could fuck with a bride's head and make her momentarily lose sight of what's going on around her. When your wedding was called off, you were so self-pitying, I couldn't get a word in for months. No wonder you had to go find lonely online strangers to be your friends. All your real friends were sick of you.

And *I'm* the self-centered one who's oblivious to the needs of others? Did it not once occur to you that someone might read the shitty things you wrote about them?

Iris deserved every word of Amber's rebuke. She couldn't bear to read Sophia's.

On Twitter, she waded through the vitriol of the strangers who had tagged her: a wedding influencer had tweeted out her meanest lines, and those tweets had been shared thousands of times. Whereas the Facebook haters targeted Iris, the Twitter critics mainly attacked Jasmine for the trappings of her wedding.

"She should be ashamed of herself, spending so much on frivolous junk when people are starving."

"Tablecloth seams? This whack job needs to get real and get a life."

"#animalabuse"

Iris felt defensive on her sister's behalf. Yes, she'd ridiculed the wedding in the Bridesmaids Union, but she'd never doubted Jasmine's right to celebrate in her own way.

Everyone had an opinion. Some linked the wedding's excesses to the corruption of traditional marriage, the downfall of America, and a laundry list of other ills, from social inequity to global warming. Some called Iris fat and ugly; others called Jasmine a whore.

She tweeted, "Dear everyone, I am a HUMAN BEING. Words matter." Immediately it started collecting likes and both supportive and dismissive comments. Then a string of nauseating tweets appeared: "I know what to do with sluts like u." "I'll be waiting for u when you get home." "I bet u like big cock." She told herself to stop reading them, but fear kept her from closing the app. The last tweet in the series hit her like a truck: it was her real name and home address.

She thought of Mason and gasped. She called Marilyn. While the phone rang, she paced the narrow path between the foot of the bed and the desk, trying to make a plan. She needed to go to the police. But first she had to protect her son. What then? Wait for a monster from Twitter to hunt her down?

"Iris!" came Marilyn's wry, sleepy voice through the phone. "How's the party?"

"Mason" was the only word that came out of her mouth. Then she managed, "Tell me he's OK."

"He's fine. What's going on?"

"I need to talk to him."

"OK, you're on speaker," said Marilyn. "Mason, say hello to your mother."

His giggles calmed her. "Mommy!"

"Oh, my sweetheart, it's so, so good to hear your voice."

"When are you coming home to meeee?"

"Soon, sweetie, so soon," she said. "I'll be there in a few hours."

"How long is that?"

"It's very, very soon."

"We thought you weren't coming back until Sunday," Marilyn said.

"Something very bad happened. I'll explain later. But please don't let him near the windows, and don't bring him outside."

After hanging up, she again tried to make a plan. First, Mason. Next, the police. But beyond that, what kind of damage control did she need to do? Pester Kyle to hide the Bridesmaids Union again? Compose an official apology? Her thoughts slipped away before she could commit them to memory.

After a breakneck shower, she threw on jeans and a sweatshirt, jammed her rolling bag shut, and downed a four-shot latte and morning glory muffin at the coffee bar in the lobby. Fortified by caffeine and empty carbs, she got in line to check out—behind Brittany, gripping the handle of her jumbo hard-shell suitcase.

"Look who decided to show her ugly face," Brittany said with a withering side-eye. "You know, Jasmine only invited you to be a bridesmaid because your mom made her. I don't understand why you didn't just say no."

Crushed beneath the pileup of disasters, Iris didn't have the energy to flay herself for Brittany. "You don't care that she doesn't love David and wants to leave him in a few years?"

"She does love him," Brittany said. "She jokes about leaving him because she thinks that's what you want to hear."

"Why would I want to hear that?"

"Because guilt, genius!" Brittany approached the front desk clerk, a wiry young man wearing glasses with heavy black frames. "We need to check out. All six rooms booked under Brittany Thompson."

The clerk clicked his mouse and typed, then clicked again. "You're leaving us early? Was there an issue with your stay?" he asked in a buttery voice.

"Yes, but it's not your fault. Iris here ruined my best friend's marriage,"

Brittany said, pointing to Iris. "Have you ever heard of the Bridesmaids Union?"

The clerk pursed his lips apologetically. "I can't say I have."

"Count yourself lucky." Then, "She'll pay for her room. I'll pay for the rest."

"Thanks," Iris said, because it seemed more than fair. She handed over her credit card. "Why would she feel guilty toward me?"

"She blamed herself when Forrest left you," Brittany said.

"I'm sorry, what?"

Brittany spoke slowly, as if dealing with someone very stupid. "Forrest and Jasmine were in love. She wouldn't act on it because she actually considers other people's feelings."

Iris's memories of Forrest rearranged. Had he cheated on her with Jasmine? Had he stayed with Iris because Jasmine wouldn't return his advances, or was that why he left? Now Jasmine's distance, beginning when Iris met Forrest, made sense. As did her panic at the bridal appointment— her doubts about David must have multiplied when Iris told her Forrest was back. Now Iris understood how Jasmine could be certain Forrest had never loved her.

In truth, she never would have forgiven Jasmine if she'd dated Forrest, exactly as Jasmine should never forgive her if she spoke to David again. Not that she would. She wanted to get as far as possible from the mess she'd made.

She said to Brittany, "I've never known her to spare my feelings."

Brittany stuffed her receipt into her leather backpack and zipped it closed. "Then you've never known her."

Amid all the bewildering hurt whizzing around cyberspace, it surprised Iris how much Brittany's judgment stung. She would have thought the relentless internet shaming would have numbed her, but instead she felt more thin-skinned than ever before. She had a breathtaking capacity for pain.

"Now give me the key," Brittany said.

"I'm sorry?"

"The key to Jasmine's car. Give it to me."

She'd forgotten she had it. She handed it over, and Brittany wheeled her suitcase away, her heels clicking on the polished concrete floor. Like Jasmine, she'd brought heels for the farm stay.

⌒

Public transportation home would take forever—even after getting to Thirtieth Street Station and hopping a bus or train to New York, she'd have to dogleg on the subway to Grand Central and wait up to an hour for the commuter train to Yonkers—so Iris priced out a one-way car rental. Its exorbitant cost was the least of her worries.

Before she could confirm the rental, Electra texted:

**Wait out front. I'll drive you home.**

Electra pulled into the porte cochere a minute later in David's old Civic, and Iris hopped into the passenger seat. Janelle Monáe thumped through the speakers. "I'm on Jasmine's blacklist for associating myself with the Bridesmaids Union," Electra said. "But she said I could take this car home, as long as I promised not to give you a ride."

"I can rent a car. I don't want you to get in trouble with her."

"Don't worry about it. This is the only way I can live with myself."

"Thanks," Iris said. "You're a good friend."

"I can't take you all the way to Yonkers, though. Jasmine is going to get suspicious if I drop off her car too late. OK if I leave you at your parents'?"

Iris groaned. She hadn't spoken with either of them since the bridal shower. "Can you drop me in downtown Tenafly? I'll Uber from there."

On the drive, Iris responded to as many messages as she could without getting carsick, apologizing where appropriate and reassuring her few remaining friends that she was OK, though she wasn't. Stefanie thanked her for exposing Jasmine, and Allie sent a variety of heart-based emoji. Forrest asked if she needed anything, but Christof remained silent. They'd been hooking up for months. Wouldn't he come to her defense? Then again, he probably hadn't looked at Facebook in weeks.

All those brides, and especially Jasmine, had every right to hate her, she knew. She'd betrayed their confidence, exposing them with flippant cruelty. But hadn't they deserved the callouts? They had been awful, Jasmine worst of all. Brides had every reason to expect others to help them realize their wedding fantasies, and Iris was on board for the organizing and the crafting, even the ugly dresses. It was the lack of gratitude and the constant fault-finding that irked her.

Then again, Jasmine's and Amber's chastising gave her pause. Instead of communicating her irritation to them, she'd posted about it. Why had she held it in? What would have been so catastrophic about getting angry? Worst-case scenario, Jasmine would have disinvited her to the wedding. That scenario had come to pass.

〜

Kyle messaged her Eye Eye Mate account as they passed New Brunswick.

**OK, BMU is closed**

**And I made u admin**

                                        **Thank you.**

In the arcana of Facebook groups, closed wasn't as private as secret—utterly undiscoverable—but as long as the general public couldn't read the posts, it wasn't worth fighting over. After all, there was no keeping the Bridesmaids Union secret anymore.

**Crazy shit going down, yeah?**

**Epic coming out day 4 everyone!**

Was it possible his followers hadn't known he was gay? He'd strewn both their secrets to the winds.

                                        **Why did you do this???**

U wanted 2 teach her a lesson

I wanted 2 teach Baxter a lesson too

> I'm getting death threats, Kyle.
> Someone literally said he is going to
> rape me.

I get that stuff all the time

It's not real

She was too angry to hear him. He had destroyed her life.

> Unless it is.

Lay low 4 a day, and it'll all blow over

Don't respond

Everyone will forget about u

> You think my sister is going to forgive
> me in a day?

U hate her

U will be happier without her in ur life

Did she hate Jasmine? Sometimes, but she loved her, too. Or maybe she loved a version of Jasmine that hadn't existed for a long time. Maybe that version of Iris no longer existed, either. The thought saddened her.

> I would have liked to make that
> choice.

He didn't respond, and for the first time, she didn't care if she had offended him.

"For what it's worth," Electra said, turning the stereo down, "I think the Bridesmaids Union was revolutionary."

Iris looked out the window. "Too bad most revolutionaries don't make it out alive."

⌒〇

Tenafly's town center was anchored by a train station with no train: residents had recently voted against reinstating service to keep out the poor—which, unfortunately, included Iris. She requested an Uber and watched with mounting rage as the six-minute wait time crept up to twelve. The car was fleeing. Did she have a one-star passenger rating? Lyft showed no cars available. Ride-hailing apps had eviscerated local cab outfits, and now, when she called the nearest one, the raspy-voiced dispatcher said someone could pick her up in two hours.

Panicking, Iris called her father's cell.

"I don't recognize this number," Spike said. "I think it used to be our daughter's, but she hasn't called in months."

"Dad, could you not joke right now? I need your help."

"Should I be surprised that you only call when you want something from us?" he asked. "A family isn't a buffet—"

"I'm in the center of town, and I have to get home right now," she cut in. "I'll explain on the way."

"You can save your breath," he said, the humor drained from his voice. "Jasmine just got here. I've never seen her so upset."

So it was too late to plead her case. She pinched her nose to keep from crying. "I have to get to Mason. You don't know what people are saying online."

He sighed. "Maybe you'll learn that your behavior has an effect on other people."

She couldn't believe his coldness. Of course he'd feel protective of Jasmine, but he was acting like a spurned lover. "Please. You know I wouldn't be calling you unless I really needed help."

"That's exactly the problem." He sighed. "But Christ teaches us to forgive. Give me five minutes."

Five minutes later, Spike's orange Corvette pulled up to the café at the defunct train station. At least he'd rushed.

They drove toward the George Washington Bridge in silence. Though Spike was going seventy in a forty-five-mile-an-hour zone, cars weaved around them. Were the drivers in those cars more skilled or just reckless? Did they not know a crash at that speed would kill them, or did they not realize they were vulnerable?

"I'm sorry," she said, "for what I wrote about Jasmine."

"It's one thing to be cruel to your sister when you're at home," he said. "Your mother and I have learned to stop blaming ourselves for this never-ending fight. But it's quite another to go into a public forum and speak ill of her. In the future, we would appreciate it if you didn't broadcast your grievances to the world."

"I really thought it was private."

"We raised you to be smarter than that!" He slammed the steering wheel, and the car swerved into the shoulder, rumbling on the grooved pavement.

"I didn't mean to cause anyone harm," she said, crying, and she could feel her father softening toward her. "I accept now that I was angry, but I thought it was a safe outlet for that. It felt like the only way I could keep being nice to her when she was living this perfect life and I was fighting just to keep going."

"You don't always have to be nice," Spike said. "You should be yourself."

"That's not the message I've been getting from you and Mom. You criticize me constantly. It makes me feel like there's something wrong with me. Like you want me to be someone I'm not."

Spike sighed. "It's hard for us to see you stumbling, especially when you don't want our help. What you hear as disappointment is just us saying, 'Come back. It's safe here. We love you.'"

It seemed typical of her father to be disappointed that he couldn't control her forever—but maybe Iris's failures really were painful for him.

As he navigated the concrete warren of ramps and exits on the lower level of the bridge, he said, "When Forrest left you, your mother and I were heartbroken—obviously not in the same way you were, but our pain was real, because you were hurting and there was nothing we could do. You needed to grieve alone, and we understood, but we felt shut out. And so we haven't been able to move on the way you have. When you decided not to raise Mason in the church, that was painful for us too; it was a tear in our bond with you. And now this, with Jasmine . . . it's between you two, but it also feels like an attack on the wholeness of our family and on the lessons we instilled in you."

"I'm sorry, but if I'm going to learn how to be in this world, I have to make my own decisions—I have to make my own mistakes," Iris said. "But any time I try to take space, you treat me like I've just told you I don't love you. When that's the furthest thing from the truth."

Spike put his hand on Iris's forearm. The touch was soothing. "When we asked you to move back home, it was because we thought it would help you and Mason. But we don't want to push you away, and we weren't trying to cause you pain."

"Thank you," Iris said. "Will you tell Jasmine I'm sorry? I really was trying to be a good sister."

He looked at her pensively. "You should tell her. But give it time. It might take months or years, but I believe she will forgive you."

⟡

Two TV news vans were parked outside her apartment building, with raised satellite dishes. Two improbably skinny blond women in stilettos waited in front of cameras, their logoed microphones at the ready.

"Looks like you've got a welcoming committee," Spike said. "You want me to drive you and Mason home?" In other words, back to Tenafly.

"I don't think I can face Jasmine."

"We could give you the basement."

She weighed Jasmine's threat to kill her against the death threats online. At least in her apartment, she could lock everyone out. "I'll be fine here." She steeled herself with a deep breath and opened the car door. As she reached for her luggage in the trunk, one of the reporters marched toward her. "Iris! Why did you start the Bridesmaids Union?"

Reporter number two, not to be scooped, asked, "What was Jasmine's reaction when she found out?"

The cameras were trained on Iris, their recording indicators lit, and she had enough presence of mind not to flip them the bird. She offered an expression that was neither smile nor frown, one her mother had told teenage Iris to practice in the mirror, that wouldn't be off-putting to men but wouldn't encourage them, either. She gave Connie a silent thank-you for this nugget of misguided advice. "I'd rather not talk about it," Iris said, dropping her suitcase on the sidewalk and shutting the trunk.

"Was all of it true?" asked reporter number one.

Iris beelined for the front door of the apartment building, lugging her rolling bag and a tote full of board games and mani/pedi kits. Her keys bit into her palm.

"Are you coming from Jasmine's bachelorette party?" reporter number two asked.

"Do you hate your sister?" asked reporter number one.

Iris shimmied her key into the lock and opened the door. As both reporters reached for it, she pulled it shut behind her without letting her expression harden into anger or soften into fear.

✎

She knocked on Marilyn's door before opening her own. When Marilyn appeared, Iris fell into her arms.

"What's going on?" asked Marilyn, rubbing Iris's back.

"I've been canceled."

"I'm not sure what that means," Marilyn said.

"Mommy!" Mason shouted. He dropped a handful of Kix onto the dining table and latched onto Iris's waist.

"I missed you so, so, so much," she said. She kissed his face and breathed in his milky scent. He was safe—that was all that mattered. For the moment, she could breathe.

She told her neighbor everything.

"I can't say I fully understand," Marilyn began, "but it sounds like you'll be happier if you stay off the internet for a while."

"I wish it were that easy," Iris moaned.

⌒

When Iris opened her apartment door, Mason in tow, something streaked across her vision, and she froze. But it was only Meatball making a bid for freedom. She barked at Mason to get inside and lunged for her cat, pinning him by the hindquarters to the hallway floor. Once all cats and humans were safe inside the apartment, she locked the deadbolt and secured the chain. She drew the curtains and investigated every room and closet to make sure no one lurked in ambush. She looked under Mason's bed, thinking she would never again tease him for worrying about monsters. She crouched on the floor, sucking in breaths.

"Pull it together, Iris," she whispered to herself. She didn't want to scare her son.

Heading to the police station wasn't an option with the reporters outside, so she called the non-emergency number for the local precinct. She was put on hold; in place of hold music was nothing but dead air. She kept glancing at her phone screen to make sure she was still connected.

After bracing herself for the rude condescension she associated with cops, Iris was surprised by the gentle voice of Officer Camille Rogers. "How can I help you?" the officer asked.

Iris gave her name, explained that people on Twitter had threatened to rape and murder her and asked if she could file a police report over the phone.

"You'd need to come into the station to file," Officer Rogers said. "Do you know your harasser?"

"No, but one of them tweeted my address."

"How did he get your address?"

"I don't know," Iris said. In the moment of seeing the tweet, she had assumed he'd been stalking her, and she'd felt exposed, as if she were being recorded. But of course he'd found her on a people-search website, the way she'd found Forrest. She should have known how vulnerable she was to a

Twitter fiend posting her address. She should have tested her privacy by turning her investigative skills on herself. She couldn't believe she'd been so lax.

"Do you know anything about him?"

Iris searched for the tweets on her phone. When she saw them, she again felt sick and disoriented. She tapped the username, FreeDumb1977. His profile picture was the Confederate battle flag; his "about me" section was a fire-and-brimstone verse from the book of Revelation. His tweets to Iris had been his first and last. He might be a bot. That didn't reassure her.

Officer Rogers asked, "Did he tell you when he was planning on doing it?"

"No," Iris said.

"Did he write it in response to something you posted, or did he target you randomly?"

Iris was too tired to explain. "I wrote some mean things about my sister that got out. A lot of people on Twitter got angry, and then more people showed up just to write nasty things to me."

"Wait a second . . . Iris Hagarty . . . your sister wanted a goat at her wedding?"

Iris beheld her phone for a surreal moment. "How did you hear about that?"

"I saw an article about it on Twitter. It's none of my business, but that girl deserved every word you wrote." She chuckled. "You're a hero, in my book."

If there was one article about her, there were probably more. With cold fear seeping into her belly, she realized a lot of strangers knew her name. She had been naïve to think her first-letter-only policy offered privacy. "Thanks . . . ? So is it OK if I wait until morning to file the police report? It's been a long day."

"I bet it has. I'm supposed to encourage you to file right away, but to be honest, we see this kind of threat all the time, and I've never heard of a stranger making good on it. If he was an ex-boyfriend or someone you'd been corresponding with, that'd be a different story. And it's really hard for us to prosecute cybercrimes: multiple jurisdictions, and you've got your free speech protections. But because of the high-profile nature of the situation, I'd say definitely come file a report."

Iris sat on the couch behind Mason, cross-legged on the floor, glued to his iPad. She was still confused about what to do. Officer Rogers had told her to file a report, but what good would it do if there was no chance of it leading to an arrest? Maybe Kyle was right, and she should ignore the threat. That hateful thread had received no comments, likes, or retweets; if the algorithm was doing its job, no one else would see it. But the TV crews had seen it—or found her address on their own. The thought of going outside frightened her. Staying in the apartment wasn't much better. Even if Twitter responded to her complaint and took down the post, she couldn't feel safe there again.

Emails, Facebook alerts, and tweets spewed onto her lock screen, and the *New York Times* reporter who had posted on the Bridesmaids Union had found her number and left a message, asking her to call. A Twitter alert led her to a story trending on BuzzFeed, recounting twenty-three of "Iris Hagarty's best Bridesmaids Union posts." Somehow, she was already a household name. Each quote was illustrated with a GIF of an extravagantly gesticulating drag queen. She'd meant to be funny, but now it sickened her that people were laughing.

She had to stop looking at her phone. She set it to vibrate and put it in a drawer. She cooked a tofu stir-fry for dinner, bracing herself to defend against any of the thousands of Twitter haters who might break down the door at any second. She divided the stir-fry onto two plates but could only force a few bites down. Mason wasn't hungry, either, and after a few minutes, she let him return to his video game. Thank God for that iPad, she thought. She scraped the food into a Rubbermaid container, washed the dishes, and wiped down the counters, keeping one eye on the door.

When she peeked through the curtains, the reporters were gone. It relieved her to know that her story wasn't worth camping out overnight. A flood of office workers streamed from the train station, untucked and slouching, settling into the weekend. A homeless woman pushed a shopping cart of coats and ratty paperbacks up the hill. Iris watched the sun setting behind the shadowy Palisades, illuminating a scrim of clouds in pink and bluish gray. She let herself be calmed by the ancient solidity of the cliffs and the boundless sky. Online, people wanted to rape and kill her. Outside, the world seemed indifferent. Was it?

She tore off a piece of masking tape from a roll in her junk drawer, ripped it in half, and stuck the pieces to the front and back cameras. She did the same with the iPad, eliciting a wordless protest from Mason, and, just in case, taped over what looked like a camera on her television. It seemed as paranoid as it had sounded when Christof recommended it, yet it calmed her by a nontrivial amount.

Compulsively, she checked her phone again. On Facebook, someone had lifted a photo from Jasmine's Instagram—of Iris at Paint Party!, holding her glass of wine and grinning maniacally for the camera—and added quotes from the Bridesmaids Union. It became an instant meme. "This just in: my sister is now the sheriff of crazytown." "There have been DEVELOPMENTS." "Yay. Can you feel the excitement spilling out of me?" Someone had juxtaposed the photo with a shot of Jasmine from her bridal shower, captioned "I'm getting married!" Drunk Iris responded, "Hold my beer."

She knew she should stop, but she had to know what people were saying about her. She told herself that if she could just find every article and post about her, every photo and GIF and snarky tweet, she could relax, and yet she knew nothing would let her relax.

As she scrolled through more Twitter notifications, a photo caught her eye: it was an image of her, copied from her Facebook profile and Photoshopped to look as if she were lying in a pool of blood, her neck and wrists slashed. The caption was "Die roastie bitch!!! #incel"

Her apartment dissolved around her, and she thought she might faint. How could someone create that unspeakable picture?

Mason shouldn't see her like this. She had to maintain composure until he was asleep. She breathed deeply until her breath stopped rattling.

"Wrap up your game, Mason," she said. "It's time for bed."

"No, please," he said.

"It's past your bedtime." She didn't soften her voice as she usually did when addressing him. "Time's up."

"No, please," he repeated without looking at her.

"I said it's time to *stop*. Give me the iPad."

He didn't stop.

She yanked the iPad from his fingers, and he lunged at her and hammered her thigh. Tears splashed onto his cheeks.

She had no patience left. Her reserves were dry. "We don't hit people," she snapped. "Brush your teeth and get in bed."

Screeching, he slapped and kicked the floor.

"You want to lose iPad privileges for tomorrow? Is that what you want? Because if that's your goal, you're doing a bang-up job." She counted down from five. "OK, no video games tomorrow. How about Sunday? Want to lose them for Sunday?" Again, she counted down from five. He screamed louder; Marilyn probably thought she'd stabbed him. "OK, no video games all weekend," she said. She couldn't punish him further: the iPad gave her a break from parenting, and if she was to keep her sanity, she would need that break in the coming days. He certainly wasn't going to school on Monday. His cries persisted. "Do you want to lose them for next week?"

He grabbed her hand and bit down. Pain flashed through her body, and she shrieked—she didn't recognize the ugly, tortured sound coming from her. Mason stared at her, frightened, as if she were a stranger. She dashed into the bathroom and slammed the door, rinsed her hand, splashed her face and drank a cup of cold water, then another. She had to get out of the apartment—her fear was eating her alive.

Underneath the tumbler, she noticed the coaster Jasmine had given her bridesmaids, the one that read,

*I'm getting hitched!*
*Won't you be my b!#/h?*

With another shriek, she flung it against the wall. It dented the plaster and clattered on the tile floor, unbroken.

⟳

They checked into an extended-stay hotel amidst a labyrinth of office parks in northwest Yonkers, where suites cost a hundred sixty dollars a night. If the front desk clerk recognized her face or name, she didn't admit it.

The suite came with a king bed, a sitting room with a pull-out sofa, and a kitchenette with dining table. Surrounded by the sterile veneers of anonymous furniture, Iris felt less anxious. She got Mason into his pajamas and put him to bed without making him brush his teeth. He hadn't said a word since she'd screamed, just stared at her as if she'd kidnapped him. She said, "I'm sorry I scared you, sweetie. You just cannot bite people ever again. You have to use your words." He nodded timidly. When she kissed him on the forehead, he shrank back, and she felt a rush of hot, acid guilt.

She changed into a nightshirt and fell into bed. Her body sang an aria as it greeted the mattress; the crisp sheets welcomed her into their folds. She couldn't afford this hotel. She couldn't spend another night in her apartment. She couldn't move home, either, not while Jasmine lived there. But when she considered the effort it would take to break her lease, rent a new place, and move, her anxiety spiked.

She couldn't imagine falling asleep, and she couldn't imagine getting out of bed.

This had definitely been the worst day of her life, unseating the previous champion, when Forrest left. There was relief in knowing her worst day had been caused by her own actions, rather than Forrest's; it gave her a shred of control amid the utter absence of it. Then she considered what Brittany had said, that Forrest and Jasmine had been in love. Iris had thought they'd hated each other. Maybe that was how they'd hidden their attraction. She couldn't believe Jasmine had given him up for her. Well, it would be easy to give David up. She'd probably never see him again anyway.

A few minutes later, or maybe an hour, her phone buzzed. Caller ID guessed it was the *New York Times*. At 10:34 P.M., no less! It would be madness to talk to that reporter . . . wouldn't it? At present, she didn't see how things could get any worse. Telling the world her side of the story might sway part of the Twitter mob. A heartfelt apology went a long way. She unplugged her phone from the charger, crept into the bathroom and, without turning on the light, picked up.

The woman identified herself as Heather Fried, the reporter who'd posted on the Bridesmaids Union page, and apologized for calling so late. She explained she was on deadline for an article about the Bridesmaids Union and asked if Iris had a moment to talk. It was strange for the *Times* to write about a Facebook group. Weren't there more important things to report on, like climate change and the end of democracy? But it was certainly important to this reporter: she'd been trying to reach Iris all day. Heather Fried did not give up!

"Sure," Iris said, sitting on the toilet seat.

"How does it feel to break the internet?" Heather asked slyly. Was that a real question?

"The internet seems to be working just fine."

Heather laughed. "That it is. What's been going on for you?"

Iris considered what she wanted the world to know. Definitely not her brawl with Jasmine in her hotel room. Had it really happened that morning? It felt like weeks ago. "Well, Jasmine's not talking to me, and I'm not going to her wedding."

"I'm sorry to hear that," Heather said.

"It's OK. If I were her, I wouldn't want to see me again, either. I was pretty mean, and if you could just tell your readers I'm really sorry—"

"Your stories are very funny."

"Thanks," she said, surprised a reporter would offer her opinion. "It was a good outlet for a lot of anger I wasn't really aware of. And I didn't stop to consider how any of the brides might feel. I really believed they'd never see any of it." It was nice to be listened to. She felt good about this conversation and her ability to steer it toward her apology. She'd heard somewhere that reporters always asked the hardest question last, and she reminded herself she didn't have to answer anything she didn't want.

"Have you heard from any of the other brides?"

Iris rubbed her toe in the grout of the floor. "I got emails from some of them. They're understandably very upset."

"Did you lose friends over this?"

"I think so, yeah."

"How did you hear about the trend of bride shaming?" This question made Iris nervous: "bride shaming" seemed loaded.

"This is the first I'm hearing of it."

"Surprise—it's a trend!" Heather laughed, and Iris joined her to be polite. "Bridesmaids, mothers-in-law, and other friends and relatives go online to vent about the bride."

"It was never about trying to shame anyone. It was a support group, since it was hard, being a bridesmaid so often."

"Tell me more."

"I'm all for brides getting their perfect day, and I love helping out. I just wasn't feeling a lot of gratitude . . ." She heard herself slipping into complaint. This was not the forum for that. "You know what? I've already hurt them enough. Please don't put this part into your story."

"I think those brides deserved it. Your posts connected with thousands of women. This went viral for a reason."

"Then you should quote some of them about this. I'd rather not have any more meanness attributed to me."

"Fair enough," Heather said. "Tell me about Kyle Style. How did you meet him?"

"I've actually never met him, believe it or not. He joined the Bridesmaids Union a few months ago, when he found out his friend with benefits was getting married."

"That's a sign of the times, right? That you've never met one of your closest friends in person."

How did Heather know Kyle had been a close friend? Had she talked to him? It didn't matter now. "We're not friends," she said.

"Well, you co-moderated a popular group. It's pretty remarkable, I think."

"I don't know."

"Last question, and then I'll let you go," Heather said. "How did that photo get leaked onto the internet? Did an ex-boyfriend post it?"

"I'm sorry, what photo are we talking about?"

Heather paused. "The beautiful portrait of you? It's black-and-white?"

"I don't know if I've seen it," Iris said.

"The one where you're stripped down and unapologetic?"

Now she knew what photo Heather was referring to. Christof said he'd been meticulous about keeping her pictures off the internet. She couldn't believe she'd trusted him. And she'd thought the day couldn't get any worse.

"Right, that photo," Iris said.

"I wondered if it might be an act of revenge," said Heather.

Christof didn't seem like the type to take revenge, but it was a documented fact that Iris had terrible insight into men.

"I can't comment," Iris said. "But could you please not run it in your newspaper? I'm going to try to get it taken down."

"It's not my decision, but I can certainly communicate your wishes to the photo editor. Do you know who took it? It's beautiful."

She closed her eyes and tried to center herself. She'd have to search for it eventually. "Just a sec."

With Heather on the line, she image-searched "Iris Hagarty nude," and thumbnails of Christof's photo filled the results page. She remembered again how sexy she'd felt as he'd trained his camera on her, peppering her with blandishments, and now she felt not only angry at his betrayal but also ashamed of her lapse. Her nude body was on the internet forever. He was a scumbag, but she could have prevented this.

"I honestly don't remember his name," Iris said.

"You're sure? If you want to look through your email, I can wait."

"Sorry, I don't remember."

"Sure you don't," Heather said. "Good luck getting it taken down. From what I hear, it's basically impossible once a photo has been shared."

"Fuck you very much," Iris said after she hung up.

She scrolled through the pages of notifications she'd gotten during her interview with Heather, resisting the urge to respond. She wished whoever had dreamed up Twitter had never been born, or at least that she could choose how he died.

She texted Christof:

> Your photo of me is a big hit on the internet.

He replied instantly. He'd never responded so quickly to a text.

> I know. You destroyed my career.

# Chapter Twenty-four

**Kyle Kyle**

April 27, 2019, 4:47 A.M.

Dear members of the Bridesmaids Union,

It was me. I was the one who opened the group up to the public. I am sorry I violated your trust. I was selfish and stupid, and I regret it from the bottom of my heart. I am also truly sorry I lied. Baxter did not hook up with me again after he told me he was marrying Frederick. He did not use any substances, either. I wrote those lies because I thought, once they became public, Frederick would break up with Baxter. All I accomplished was losing my best friend.

I deleted all my posts, and I am leaving the Bridesmaids Union. I am in a very dark place now, but I hold on to the hope that I will find my light again.

👍😮😠 878                                    290 comments

**Alex Oberlin**

Don't go! We forgive you. Or at least I do.

 18

**Alex Oberlin**

I've been a fan of Kyle Style for years. I'm actually a little starstruck that it was you all along. You are an inspiration to so many.

                                       👀 5

**Electra Collins**

Whaaa??? I don't know what to believe.

                    👍 1

**Anna Banana**

Holy. Shitballs.

       👍 1

**Verena Lightfoot**

Kyle Kyle, I have held my tongue for months, but you have gone too far. You have corrupted the spirit of this group with your salacious stories, and now we learn that you have betrayed our trust. I hope you can find a way to make amends to those you have hurt.

**Alex Oberlin**

Jeez, go easy on him. He made a mistake. He apologized. Can't you see he's had a really hard time?

                👍 3

**Verena Lightfoot**

It seems "going easy" has not worked. Life is not easy. Now he must journey down the hard road of repentance.

**Verena Lightfoot**

I see no one has "liked" my comments. This does not bother me in the slightest.

〜〇

"My sister figured out what happened," Christof said on the phone the next morning, as Iris and Mason ate Cheerios from little boxes at the dining table in the hotel suite.

Iris could barely pay attention. A double dose of Tylenol PM the night before had not put her to sleep, only made it agonizing to lie awake as her mind resisted the sedative. When she finally fell asleep, she dreamed she was targeted by a sniper; she woke when the bullet entered her brain. Now she had a pounding headache.

"The gallery's server was compromised last fall," Christof continued, "and the hackers posted all my female nudes to a pornographic website. When your page went viral, someone must have recognized you on that site and shared your photo." He was more charitable than he'd been the night before, though she heard a hard edge of blame in his voice—and resented it. Her unwanted fame was not responsible for his photos being leaked. She didn't agree that the photos had lost value by being shared. And his life hadn't been threatened on Twitter, nor had he fled his home. But he was convinced she had destroyed him.

Christof had been right about one thing: her privacy had been an illusion all along. The internet rendered consent meaningless.

"So all your art is on the internet now?" she asked.

"The pictures of the women are. I can still sell the men."

"Everyone will think you're gay," she said, indifferent that this did not amuse him.

"My attorney has contacted the webmaster of the pornographic site, and the photos should be taken down today. We've also asked the major search engines to remove my work from their listings."

"That's a start."

Mason was trying to open a second cereal box. She reached over to help, but he jerked away. Since their clash the previous night, he had treated her with mistrust.

"Unfortunately, some of the nudes were copied to Tumblr and reposted thousands of times," Christof said. "Tumblr recently started deleting adult content on its site, so most of those should be cleaned up soon, if not already. But the damage has been done. The photos could resurface at any time, anywhere, like cockroaches. I can't sell any of them. My name has been tarnished permanently."

"I don't see why they wouldn't sell," Iris said, ignoring his egotistical dramatics. It satisfied her to know he wouldn't survive her exposure unscathed. "Every other photographer sells work that's online."

"But my purpose was reclaiming the singular value of a photograph. That's over now. I've failed. The internet won."

"I hope you can find a way to continue your art," she said, not bothering to muffle her sarcasm. She hung up. She never wanted to speak with him again.

Mason wrenched the cereal bag open, and Cheerios exploded into the air, covering the table and floor. Wordlessly, Iris went back to bed.

⁓

A stampede of news and commentary sites had run stories about the Bridesmaids Union and Jasmine's wedding. Most of them roasted Jasmine the "bridezilla" for the offensive extravagance of her wedding. This was not vindicating to read. She emailed every address she could find—writer, editor, webmaster—demanding they take the articles and images down.

At least none of the stories published the topless photo, though it was mentioned here and there as implied evidence of Iris's poor judgment. According to one site, an ex-boyfriend had shared it as revenge. According to another, Iris had posted it in a bid for attention.

Twitter had removed the tweets threatening violence against her, including the one with her address. She scanned through the hundreds of notifications and flagged a few more sickening threats. Her direct messages were rife with vile criticism, plus a marriage proposal that included a murky snapshot of the aspiring groom's genitalia. She was called a litany of disgusting names. There was no end of synonyms for a woman who dared voice her opinion.

Facebook had set her free from jail. An apology would have been nice. She checked the Bridesmaids Union to make sure its privacy was still set to "closed" and found a post from Kyle, admitting he had lied about Baxter's behavior.

Kyle wasn't the type to come clean. Iris trained her internet research skills on him and pieced together what had happened. Baxter's brother had come across the BuzzFeed article recapping highlights from the Bridesmaids Union—including some of Kyle's lies—and forwarded it to Baxter, who denied all of it in a Bridesmaids Union post that was amplified on Twitter. The internet haters, especially virtue signalers and religious conservatives, flooded Kyle's Instagram page with condemnation for trying to seduce Baxter after his engagement to Frederick, hanging Baxter out to dry when he was suffering, and lying about all of it. The *New York Post* had held it up as a cautionary tale about the perils of idolizing influencers, when many of them were morally rotten. The article urged people to unfollow Kyle. To prevent an exodus, Kyle adopted the script for men who behaved badly: apologize, hide, come back unscathed. It was rich, asking for pity in the same breath.

Overall, though, the army of internet sheeple hadn't funneled as much bile toward him. She wondered if he'd been let off because he was a man, or because doing hard drugs, trying to steal someone's fiancé, and lying about it wasn't as interesting as bridesmaids sniping at brides.

The first rule of the internet was not to believe everything you read; somewhere along the way, Iris had become lazy and gullible. When she'd believed Baxter was sleeping around, sick with ambivalence, at least she could empathize with Kyle's tortured desire. Now that she knew the truth—or what felt true—he seemed mentally ill, an enfant terrible with no moral compass. Somehow, the world had decided this enfant terrible would be an influencer. And she had been influenced.

Thinking back, she'd been skeptical of his stories from the beginning. Yet she'd gotten caught up in that seductive Instagram feed and those 1.1 million followers—1.3 million, she now saw when she checked his page: the publicity had brought more than enough to replace those who fled. She had been bewitched by Kyle's glamorous life and these beautiful photographs. All lies. She would be glad to be done with him forever. He could find his own way out of his "dark place." Maybe he'd been lying about that, too.

⌁

By the afternoon, Mason had come down with a raging case of cabin fever. He begged to call a friend and bristled at the suggestion that he play with Mommy. She knew his grudge was temporary, but it stung nonetheless.

The sunny Saturday beckoned, and she couldn't think of any other damage-control tactics except to wait for the internet to lose its shit over something else. She prayed for the release of Trump's tax returns, though one of his gaslighting tweets would probably do.

At the door, she stopped. Even though she had told no one of her whereabouts, she felt vulnerable. For all she knew, someone could have hacked into her phone and posted her location on the dark web. She tied her hair up in a bun and put on sunglasses. A paltry disguise but better than nothing. Gingerly she stepped out of the hotel room with Mason. No one was in the corridor.

In the hotel's canteen, she bought a bottle of regular Coke and a bag of full-fat salt-and-pepper potato chips, because she was no longer trying to lose weight for Jasmine's wedding. A man nodded hello, and fear shot up her spine. Did he recognize her, or was she being paranoid?

Across North Broadway lay a parcel of forest crisscrossed with paths that sloped toward the Hudson. When she considered leaving the safety of the hotel, the threats of the Twitter trolls flashed in her mind, and her heart raced, making her dizzy. This was how agoraphobia began, she thought. She couldn't give in to the impulse to barricade herself from the world, not just for her sake but for Mason's, too. But she wasn't going to risk being alone in the woods, not now.

She sat on a bench in front of the hotel, in view of the woman at the front desk, while Mason lunged about, wielding an imaginary sword. She tore open the potato chips and began her new diet with gusto. The Coke was cold and sharp and sweeter than anything needed to be. It was quiet here, and she could almost relax. But anxiety raged behind every thought. Every pleasant sensation was shot through with terror. It would be stupid to look at her phone, but she couldn't stand not knowing what was being said about her. It seemed that if she was aware of every insult and death threat, she could protect herself better. She knew this was untrue but couldn't resist.

In a People.com exclusive, Iris learned that David and Jasmine had broken up. The article quoted Brittany, who said that Iris's damaging comments in the Bridesmaids Union, exacerbated by the media attention, had sent David running the other way. Iris didn't know how to feel. On the one hand, Jasmine and David were not meant for each other. Everyone could see it, including them. But Iris still felt responsible for their split. And her desire for him, still simmering in the rubble, made her heartsick and forlorn.

She followed a Facebook link to yet another story about her and was sideswiped with unutterable panic. The article included a recent photo of her with Mason, and the caption used both of their names. She didn't remember the photo, didn't know how this random site had found it, and a reverse image search didn't pull anything up.

She had been careful about keeping Mason off the internet. She hadn't posted a single photo of him, had never used his name, had checked to make sure he didn't show up in any directories. She'd done everything to protect him until he was old enough to make his own decisions. And he'd been found anyway. How could she let him out of her sight now? How could she ever return to the world, knowing he could be a target?

"Come over here!" she barked at him.

He stared at her, confused, and she jumped up and grabbed him.

"Stop it," he cried. "Get away."

"No. You have to stay really close to me. This is important. Let's go inside."

He cried, and his body went limp. She was scaring him, confusing him—she had to calm down. Too tired to lift him, she let him slide to the pavement and knelt beside him, whispering apologies. A pair of business-women slowed as they passed. Iris didn't care that she was making a scene.

# Chapter Twenty-five

**Kyle Kyle**

May 2, 2019, 3:20 A.M.

I have no one left in my life. The days are endless; the nights are longer. I am afraid of what I might do to myself.

 1,288                                         458 comments

**Arden Woodbine**

You are loved, Kyle Kyle. If you need help, go to an emergency room.

♡ 4

**Alexandria Canas**

Hugs 🖤

♡ 1

**Alex Oberlin**

Stay strong, Kyle Kyle. We are here for you.

♡ 12

**Jaclyn Arias**

♡ 1

**Verena Lightfoot**

When I reached my lowest point, Christ redeemed me. If you repent with a pure heart, He will redeem you, too.

♡ 1

**Gloria Abernathy**

I struggled with depression for years. I attempted to take my life four times and almost died twice. I couldn't bear to live, and when I thought about all the people I'd be letting down by dying, I felt worse. From someone who has been at the edge of death and returned, please believe me when I say you have so much to live for. Hold on. It will get better.

∞3

**Breanna Naglehopf**

You are in my prayers.

◯1

Iris called in sick for three days. She wasn't ready to ride the train or walk down a New York City street or sit eight hours in an office where everyone knew what she had done. And she absolutely wasn't going to drop Mason off at school, where she couldn't protect him. They stayed mostly in the hotel suite, and she let Mason play video games all day while she doomscrolled through her notifications, flagging death threats. She still wasn't sleeping.

She couldn't avoid work a fourth day without a doctor's note, and she couldn't bring Mason with her. Though she trusted Marilyn to watch him, she didn't want him anywhere near her apartment. Anyway, relying on her neighbor, to whom she was already hopelessly indebted, was not a solution.

So on Thursday, Connie picked them up from the hotel and gave Iris a ride to the Metro-North station. She promised to take Mason home to Tenafly and keep him inside until it was time to drop him back off at the hotel. Iris didn't want him around Jasmine, but Connie assured her that Jasmine had no beef with Mason, and besides, she probably wouldn't get out of bed.

The atmosphere inside the car was cordial but distant. Iris hated that it had come to this. Still, she was grateful for her parents. After everything, they were there for her.

When Iris trudged into work, Jeremy was leaning back in her chair with one black wing tip pressed against the lip of her desk. "I thought you might make a miraculous recovery today," he said, grinning.

She was too tired to respond.

"We have a date with destiny," Jeremy said. "But not in a good way. We have a nine-thirty with Mika in HR."

Barbara periscoped above her cubicle wall to deliver a supportive wince. Chase, rubbernecking from outside his office door, mouthed, "Sorry," without bothering to wipe off his smirk. Iris was wearing the only remaining clean outfit she had at the hotel, stretch jeans and an oversized sweater, not ideal for meeting with a VP. At least the sweater sleeves were long enough to cover the bruise from Mason's bite. She didn't leave her purse in her cubicle. She sensed she might be gone a while.

The administrative offices were on the highest floor, the sixteenth. Most hospitals reserved the top floor for patients, the theory being that a dramatic view can aid healing, but City General was built this way and had never changed, except to add more offices as the administration swelled.

Jeremy filled her in while they journeyed to the original wing of the hospital, passing through low-ceilinged basement corridors, microclimates suffused with bitter and savory odors, and rode the ancient, rickety elevator to the top. As the story of the Bridesmaids Union had snowballed, the hospital was implicated, because Iris had listed her job in her LinkedIn profile. During an emergency summit, the vice president of communications formed a Triple C—a Crisis Communications Committee—which recommended an investigation into Iris's social media use.

"Am I going to be fired?" she asked. She didn't have the energy to look for a job right now.

"I doubt it," Jeremy said. "No one here has ever been terminated for their social media activity—we've never enforced the policy. Just tell them you didn't write any of those Facebook posts on company time. That's true, right?"

"Yeah," she said, relieved she'd drawn that one boundary.

"You're a willful woman, Iris. But in HR, you have to bow and scrape and fall on your sword. Say you've learned your lesson and you'll never do it again. They have to go through this process to cover their butts, but none of their threats have teeth. The investigation will last forever, and then, when everyone's forgotten about it, they'll quietly let you stay. They'd rather keep you on than risk a lawsuit."

"Got it." Despite Jeremy's assurances, it sounded like she was going to be fired. Everyone dragged on the internet got fired. She would go bankrupt, and the death threats would continue, and no one would ever be kind to her again. She knew she was catastrophizing, but how could she not in the middle of a catastrophe?

"If Mika asks about your photo, tell her a jealous ex posted it," Jeremy said. "Don't make her think you put that out there on purpose."

It took her a moment to realize he was referring to the topless photo. "I didn't," she said, though she didn't see how the on-purpose/accidental distinction mattered. After all, there was the porn star in accounts receivable.

"Beautiful image, by the way—you look stunning. Who shot it?"

She flashed him a bulletproof smile. "A jealous ex."

⁓

Inside the HR suite, brightly lit and smelling of printer toner, an assistant ushered them into the office of Mika Yamamoto, vice president of Human Resources. A cheerless union representative, Manuel Rojas, sat in the corner, recording the meeting on his phone.

"Welcome, welcome," said Mika, a woman in her fifties with lustrous black hair and cheekbones you could rappel from. She pressed herself up from her desk and motioned for them to sit in upholstered chairs around a small conference table by the window, which looked out on the Empire State Building. "Have a candy. They're from Switzerland."

Iris took one with an illustration of a raspberry on the wrapper. She crunched down and reached a cough syrup–like substance that made her cough.

"We're going to talk about some serious things," Mika said as she sat across from Iris. "This is purely a fact-finding exercise. It is one step in the process of a thorough investigation into any alleged or perceived breaches of your contract with City General. At the conclusion of the investigation,

I will meet with the president of the hospital and the president of the union to make a decision."

Manuel nodded, confirming this protocol.

Mika opened a manila folder on her desk and paraphrased the top document. "Since last Friday, we've been dealing with a communications crisis, based on Facebook posts you made over the past year. There was some concern your continued employment would damage the reputation of this institution. Then there was a photo that circulated widely, showing you inebriated, and again, we received queries from certain parties about how that might reflect on us, especially considering 'wellness' is at the core of our brand DNA."

From the same manila folder, Mika produced screenshots of Iris's social media profiles, a thick printout of the entire text of the Bridesmaids Union, and the photo of her drinking at Paint Party! that had become a meme. Iris looked like she'd escaped from an insane asylum, but it didn't seem uncommon or incriminating to drink a glass of wine. After everything that had been written about her and to her, she couldn't believe she had to defend this dumb photo. At least Mika wasn't showing her Christof's tour de force.

"Did you post any of the offensive material in question during work hours or on equipment owned by City General?" Mika asked Iris.

"I'm sorry, but what's wrong with holding a glass of wine?" Iris asked.

Jeremy banged his knee against hers.

"Ms. Hagarty," Mika said, "the materials were deemed offensive by multiple parties at City General, including multiple members of the board of trustees. That is not up for debate. Did you post any of it during work hours or on City General equipment?"

"No, ma'am," Iris said, chastened. "None of it."

"Did you really feel that Facebook was the best place to air your criticisms?"

Of course the answer was no. It had been a huge blind spot. Was it better to admit that and risk Mika thinking she wasn't qualified for her job, or to try to make a case for why her sister and (former) friends deserved it, and look like a terrible person?

Jeremy had said to fall on her sword.

"From this vantage, definitely not," Iris said. "I regret very much what I did, and if I damaged the hospital's reputation in any way, I am very, very sorry."

Mika nodded: Iris seemed to have chosen right. "What were the circumstances surrounding this photo?"

"It's from a party with my sister's bridesmaids. My sister posted it without telling me."

Mika spoke calmly but not kindly. "Ms. Hagarty, everything you say or do on the internet, and every picture of you, represents you. You need to practice immaculate social media hygiene, especially considering your position in D-CAT. You must be an exemplar of ethical conduct."

Iris swallowed. She knew now that she should never have created the Bridesmaids Union. On the other hand, she doubted that anyone's social media footprint could withstand such meticulous examination without turning up at least one embarrassing photo or stupidly worded comment. "I hear you, loud and clear. I am going to be much more vigilant from here on out."

"We are also concerned about something you wrote on November twenty-third of last year," Mika said, riffling through the Bridesmaids Union transcript and stopping on the post in question. "You referred to Mr. McDonnell as your 'skeeve-tastic boss.' What did you mean by that?"

Jeremy asked the same question with his eyebrows. Iris remembered writing that phrase, but she'd been so sure of the Bridesmaids Union's security, it hadn't occurred to her that he might see the insult. "I'm sorry to have offended you. I can see how hurtful that was."

He looked out the window, chagrined.

"You can be honest," said Mika, leaning toward Iris. "What did Mr. McDonnell do that made you uncomfortable? If he's been inappropriate with you, we need to address that."

Despite Mika's assurances, Iris knew she could not be honest without repercussions. But she had been bullied and abused online all week. She was afraid to go out in public and even more terrified of what strangers might do to Mason. She had barely slept or eaten. The part of her that feared offending Jeremy, or anyone, was broken. She didn't want to lose her job, but she refused to protect him any longer. He deserved to be fired, and maybe she could make it happen, even if she burned up in the flames.

"He flirts with me constantly," she said. "It makes me dread going in every morning."

Silence thickened the air.

"Say more," Mika said.

"He's always telling me how beautiful I am and staring at my body, and he invites me out for drinks when his wife is away. He told me he was getting a vasectomy, I guess because he thought it would help convince me to sleep with him. He showed me naked photos that he's used to masturbate."

"These are some serious allegations. Mr. McDonnell, is this true?"

"I have never been inappropriate with her or anyone," he said, staring at Iris.

She couldn't believe the audacity of his lie. It came down to her word against his—and of course Mika would believe him. Despite the promises of Me Too, women's accusations were still received with skepticism. After sixty(!) women had come out against Bill Cosby, Connie had responded, "Those women knew what they wanted when they approached him." Spike had added, "They're just looking for a payday."

"Why would I lie about this?" Iris asked, though she knew the answer: because her job was threatened, and she wanted to bring her boss down, too. "It's been going on since I started working here."

"This is news to me," said Jeremy.

"Did you ask him to stop?" Mika asked her.

"I did."

"I have no idea what you're talking about," Jeremy said, sounding monstrously reasonable.

"You needed to report it," Mika said to Iris. "Why didn't you report it?"

"Because he's the one who fields these complaints!" she said.

"You should have come to me," Mika said. "Did you tell anyone?"

Iris tried to remember whom she'd told what. She'd confided in Barbara, and her coworker had blamed her. She hadn't told her parents, because she didn't want them to blame her, too. She'd been too embarrassed to tell her sisters; she was already losing at the game of life. She remembered talking about Jeremy with Amber and Sophia, but she couldn't call them, not now or ever again. She'd mentioned him to Christof but hadn't gone into detail, not wanting to sound negative or shrill. She hadn't thought Kyle would want to know. She'd censored herself, believing no one wanted to hear her complain. Now her feelings and experiences might as well never have existed. "I told Barbara."

"And she didn't tell you to report it?"

"She told me not to. She said it would only make things worse."

"She was obligated to report it herself," said Mika.

Barbara would deny it happened rather than admit to ignoring Iris's complaints. Jeremy would not be fired, Iris realized amid a suffocating despair.

"I see we'll need to conduct another investigation," Mika said. "Mr. Rojas, do you have anything to add?"

"Not at this time," Manuel said, his face expressionless, bloodless.

"What in fucking fuck just happened?" Jeremy asked as the elevator doors closed.

"You've been harassing me for *years*."

"You come to work with everything hanging out, always making sexual innuendo, always touching your hair, always crossing and uncrossing your legs. I assumed I was some kind of conquest for you."

She could feel her anger making her wild. She didn't try to hold it in. She couldn't if she'd tried. "I was not flirting with you. I was bracing myself for the next hideous thing you'd say to me. If I couldn't sit still, it was because being in the same room with you made me sick."

"You have an awfully interesting way of 'not flirting.'"

He hadn't been able to hear her refusals, she saw. Or she'd been so afraid of hurting his feelings, she hadn't been clear. That didn't mean he wasn't a sleaze. "Well, your idea of professional conduct is revolting."

"I was on your side," he muttered through a clenched jaw.

For two years, Iris had sacrificed her comfort and safety to spare his feelings. For two years, she'd delayed her dreams in the name of stability. She'd bitten her tongue until it had practically fallen out of her mouth. She'd founded the Bridesmaids Union instead of confronting her friends and family. And where had all that politeness gotten her? Jeremy hated her. Her friends hated her. Her family hated her. The entire fucking internet hated her. She would not silence herself again.

"You know what?" she spat. "You're a disgusting pile of garbage, and I hope your poor wife finally wakes up and dumps you. I quit."

The elevator doors opened onto the basement. Iris strode up the stairs and outside. She was shaking with an exhilarating rage. For the first time in years, she felt powerful enough to change her future.

⌒

At Grand Central Terminal, Iris took a window seat on the Metro-North train. Her mom wouldn't drop Mason off for another seven hours, and she was looking forward to getting some sleep. A man stared as he walked by, and for the first time, Iris didn't care if he recognized her.

She opened the Bridesmaids Union page. Now that she didn't have to "practice immaculate social media hygiene," she felt like telling all the haters to fuck off. Kyle had written an upsetting message in the middle of the night. It was a cry for help, but why would he put it in a forum where no one could help him? And hadn't he said he was leaving the group? She wasn't surprised he had alienated all his friends. She was sick of his histrionics. She was done.

The barrage of well-meaning comments on his post seemed like cold comfort if he was considering taking his life. She was tempted to ignore it, wipe the Bridesmaids Union off Facebook and let him float away on his raft of lies. But he was a human being, in danger of harming himself. She was a human being, too, though battered and bone-tired and ready to explode.

**Do you need help?**

**I'll be fine**

**No one cares if I die**

She squinched her eyes and groaned.

**I'll be there in fifteen minutes.**

**Don't do anything stupid.**

She heaved herself up and, battling an attack of wooziness, stumbled off the train.

⁓

Kyle lived in a walk-up above a strip club on Eighth Avenue and Forty-Third Street, the last bastion of seedy, pre-Giuliani Times Square. He opened the door and flung his arms around her. "You came," he said into her neck. He smelled like coconut lotion, and his cheek was as soft as a baby's. It was surreal to be touching him, to be hearing his lightly accented voice. It was hard to believe he was the real Kyle and not an impostor.

"Of course," she said, patting him on the shoulder blade.

He wore well-fitting joggers and a tank top. He looked like the Kyle from his Instagram page, just less . . . perfect. She couldn't put her finger on why. Maybe because his skin didn't look as sumptuous and flawless without a filter, or that without the fattening effects of the camera, he looked emaciated.

She'd expected him to be tearstained and miserable, his place a mess of crumpled tissues and dirty clothes. Instead, he gave her a spirited tour of the narrow apartment, a railroad layout with yellowish wooden floors and very few places to sit. Plastic barrels of protein powder and an alphabet of supplements were lined up on the kitchen counter. Half the bedroom was taken up with portable closets crammed with designer clothes. In the bathroom, a shelving unit across from the medicine cabinet held a farrago of lotions, gels, tonics, and sprays, product samples sent by publicists hoping he would tag one in a social media snap. The curation he had mastered in his virtual life was absent in his real one.

He gave her an "enhanced water" from his fridge, packed with a gourmet market's assortment of drinks—yet more product samples—then reclined on his flimsy Ikea couch and rested his feet on the coffee table, cluttered with books with uncracked spines, as well as a mirror and a rolled-up dollar bill. Even she knew what that was for. She sat on a plywood workout box away from the window. Though she and Kyle had chatted for months and confided in each other, she didn't feel comfortable sitting closer to him. She'd understood from the moment she saw him that their friendship was over. They had been friends, and now they were not.

"Seems like your mood has improved," she said.

"I'm doing better. Thanks for coming. I couldn't be alone anymore."

"You said you didn't have anyone in your life . . . you don't have other friends who could support you?"

He shrugged. "I have a hard time trusting people. You can see what happened with Baxter."

What happened with Baxter, as far as Iris could tell, was he had wanted to stay friends, and Kyle had spread lies about him until Baxter cut him out of his life.

Automatically she began to formulate an anodyne consolation for Kyle, about being careful with his heart. Then she caught herself: she was censoring her feelings, exactly as she'd done with Jasmine and Jeremy and everyone else. Jeremy had seen it as coy, Forrest had seen it as passive-aggressive, and Christof had seen it as presenting a fake version of herself. With Jasmine and the other brides, Iris's silence had held back a volcano of anger. Why was she so afraid of telling people what she thought? Why did she believe her feelings could destroy?

"You were kind of shitty to him," she said.

"Yeah, maybe," Kyle said. "I guess so."

"You lied about him. You lied to my group. You lied to me."

He shrugged. "He *was* cheating on Frederick, just not with me."

"But all the stuff about him being desperate wasn't true, was it?"

He shrugged again.

"Was he escorting?"

"He used to, when he first moved here. Not anymore."

"Did he tell you he didn't love Frederick?"

Kyle shook his head.

"Was he doing all those drugs?"

He massaged his rotator cuff with two fingers. "Nah, he's straight edge."

"So you just made all that up?" She glanced again at the mirror on the coffee table and understood. His post from Baxter's bachelor party had been true, except for one crucial detail. Kyle had bought the cocaine. Kyle had snorted it in the casino bathroom with the twink. She'd wondered how he had known what Baxter was doing behind closed doors. Now it made sense.

"Was any of it true?" she asked. "All those times we chatted, were you lying to me?"

"No, never! And I told the truth in my posts. Baxter and I really did have an amazing connection. I really did save that guy's life on the boat. I joined the group to have a private place to tell the truth. But after Baxter's engagement party, I realized he would never care how much pain I was in. That's when I knew what I had to do. He left me no choice."

"So you lied about Baxter, tricked me into making you an admin, made the Bridesmaids Union public, and then somehow thought this would break Frederick and Baxter up?"

"Not like that. I wanted to start rumors, but I wasn't trying to trick you. And I didn't think exposing them would break them up—Frederick knows it's not true. But their friends and family don't. Most people believe what they read, especially if it's in the news. They postponed the wedding—and the world thinks Baxter's a whore and a druggie. I wanted to make them suffer, and it worked."

Iris stared at him, aghast. Kyle had dragged Baxter through the mud while believing in his own victimhood. And Iris had been a loyal sidekick. She felt used.

"I can't believe I was stupid enough to think we were friends," she said, staring at the cocaine mirror.

"We *are* friends!" he protested. "You're my closest friend. And you're here, aren't you? No one else came to check on me."

She studied him. What kind of person could consider someone their close friend and purposely ruin their life? But hadn't she done the same to her friends and Jasmine? On the deepest level, she had wished they could read what she'd written about them. One difference was that Iris hadn't written lies. And she never would have pulled the trigger. She never would have released the Bridesmaids Union to the world.

"You know," she said, "I was under investigation at work because of this. I quit today."

"Oh, shit. Sorry." He covered his mouth—was he grinning?

"I take full responsibility for what I wrote, and I'm sure if you hadn't made it public, those stories would have gotten out eventually."

He finished his water, screwed the cap back on, and chucked it across the room into a blue recycling bin by the front door. "That's nice of you to say."

"I'm still pissed at you for doing it. Everyone hates me, and I'm afraid to be in my home."

"I get it," he said, suddenly angry. "I said I was sorry."

She flinched. It was hard to let him be angry with her; at the same time, it made her feel strong. "I wasn't rubbing it in. I just want you to understand that you betrayed my trust. You violated my privacy, and you lied to me multiple times. You can't go around being shitty to people and then feel sorry for yourself because they're mad at you. OK?" It was invigorating to give him a piece of her mind. She could get used to this.

"Jeez Louise," he mumbled. "This isn't rubbing it in?"

She stood. "I'm gonna go. I'm glad you're feeling better. Just a suggestion: you might want to consider therapy."

As if by a snap of the fingers, his expression became plaintive. "Can't you stay a little longer? I'm all alone here. I have no one."

His reversal gave her emotional whiplash.

"Do you want to pose with me for my Instagram?" he asked. "I can help you get followers. You're a celebrity now—you might as well milk it."

Against her better judgment, she considered this—she did need an income. With enough social media presence, could she live off sponsorships, as Kyle did, instead of applying for another soul-sucking job? She let the fantasy flutter through her and die. Only then did she know what she had to do. "That's nice of you. But I've decided to shut down all my accounts."

⁓

On her way back to the hotel, when the Metro-North train emerged from the tunnel in East Harlem, she got a text from . . . David?

**Did you see this?**

**Yikes.**

He sent a link, which opened Heather Fried's *New York Times* article, "Why Do We Love Shaming Brides?" It was a reported opinion piece, exploring and interrogating the trend of wedding shaming. It lumped the Bridesmaids Union with wedding horror story threads on Reddit and brides who had been bullied online for wearing a too-revealing dress or for being demanding. One bride had gotten death threats after charging her guests a thousand-dollar admission to her wedding; another had been verbally abused because her dress looked snug. Fried suggested Iris and all the other wedding shamers were acting from a sexist impulse handed to them by the patriarchy. Iris was quoted in support of this theory, saying, "It was a good outlet for a lot of anger I wasn't really aware of." Nowhere did it mention the Bridesmaids Union was a support group. Iris sounded like a monster who scorned women for being assertive.

She should have known not to speak to that reporter. She'd thought she was being careful, and now everyone would think she was a misogynist. It hadn't felt that way, but who knew? If a man had put his foot down and declared he needed a goat as a ring bearer, or his bachelor party was ruined because it was on a real farm as opposed to a fake one, would she have found him unreasonable? She thought so. But she couldn't imagine any man she knew acting like Jasmine. Men had much more destructive ways of being terrible.

The story already had hundreds of comments, none of which Iris had the stamina to read. Apparently, it was the *Times*'s most popular article.

She slid into a deep slouch and rubbed her eyes. Her fifteen minutes of shame were not over.

Thanks, but also ugh.

How are you holding up?

I've seen some of the stories about you. It's awful, what they're saying.

Honestly? Not well

But I'm learning a lot, too. Growing.

My mom would say everything happens for a reason, and while that is objectively a terrible thing to say to anyone, I think I'm finding my inner warrior.

That's beautiful.

The worst part is that the trolls know everything about me

I have to move, and even then I feel like they could find me at any time.

That sounds really scary.

She drank in his compassion. She was glad to be communicating with him, relieved that he wasn't mad. Besides Electra, who had sent a few supportive texts over the weekend, Iris had no one on her side.

I just don't know when it's going to end

If it's going to end

Do you want to try out my new company's
privacy software? It takes a few weeks for all
the requests to process and the directories to
update, but after that, your data won't be on
the internet anymore.

She was moved by his generosity. She'd exposed his marriage to the
world, amplifying Jasmine's nasty comments about him. And here he was,
tossing her a buoy. It felt good to have a friend.

That would be amazing

That's really kind of you

Believe me when I say it's my pleasure.

Thank you

How are you doing? I saw that you
guys broke up.

Yeah.

I dodged a bullet there. I owe you one.

So he was grateful to her. She felt a little less terrible.

Thanks. That's nice of you to say to
the lady who blew up your marriage.

I don't think I would have gone through with it
anyway.

You just helped me see that more clearly.

Also, I need to tell you something:

She saw that he was typing and waited for his next message. It took a
long time to arrive.

I know it's a crazy time for you right
now, and I'd understand if you didn't
want to see me again. And please don't
feel pressured to give me an answer—
you don't even have to respond to this
message. But I want you to know that
those things I said when we last talked,
about having feelings for you, are still true.
When I think about you, I feel a tug in my
soul. I didn't feel that with Jasmine, and
that's why I left. I don't want to freak you
out, but I love you, Iris.

As she read and reread the message, a hardness inside her softened,
and she teared up. She didn't love him, but she could. She felt that same
tug in her soul. Was the possibility of love worth betraying Jasmine a second time? At least when Jasmine had scuttled Iris's engagement, she'd had
the decency to cut Forrest out of her life.

I want to see you again. I just need
time to think.

Take all the time you need.

# Chapter Twenty-six

**Eye Fay**

May 2, 2019, 3:51 P.M.

Dear friends,

You have been a powerful source of validation and entertainment in the year since I founded this group. Each time I posted about my bridesmaid drama, I felt your love, because you've been through this, too. Each time you posted about yours, our community—our union—grew stronger. Together we built an island of sanity in the sea of wedding madness.

Now it has to end. What we saw as a supportive haven for expressing our frustrations has been misconstrued as a group of nasty wedding shamers, and it's been overrun by trolls. The funny thing is, I know why those trolls feel free to terrorize us. Unknowingly, I was one of them. I used the anonymity of the internet to take potshots at brides, one of whom was my sister. I wrote mean things about her because I believed it wasn't my right to tell her how I felt. I am truly sorry for the mistakes I have made, and I'm trying to become a better person.

But I did not deserve the insults and slurs and death threats. You have no idea how it feels to be doxxed, to have unspeakable threats tweeted at you, to feel that no place is safe. So I will tell you all first: I am shutting down the Bridesmaids Union and leaving social media. I am wiping my footprint off the internet. I hope the cretins who made my life hell will wake up and realize what terrible people they are, but at this point I could honestly give a flying fuck.

Apparently, Facebook groups can't be destroyed as long as one member is present. The only way to end it is for everyone to leave. I'm going to keep the page up for one more week, to give my fellow bridesmaids the chance to save their posts and any others they found inspiring—because I know there was good in all this. Then I'll disinvite everyone before closing my account and saying goodbye forever to the cesspool that is social media.

To my friends, and only to my friends: thank you so much for this journey we've taken together. I will cherish our union forever.

Love,
Iris Hagarty

👍😮😢  1,804                                          435 comments

**Anna Banana**
No!!!
👍 3

**Shanna Menckler**
So sad to see this end. Reading these posts was always the highlight of my day. I hope we hear from you again soon, Eye Fay.
👍 10

**Arden Woodbine**
I am mourning the Bridesmaids Union with you, Eye Fay!
👍 2

**Alex Oberlin**
This just sucks. 😭
👍 1

**Erica Black**
I've read all the stories about what happened to you, Eye Fay, and I think

you were wronged. You were never mean, just honest. People can't stand honesty, and so everyone lies to each other. It's depressing.

👍 17

**Ang Fitch**

I've come to the party just as it's ending! Dammit!

👍 1

**Breanna Naglehopf**

Worst day ever.

👍 6

**Verena Lightfoot**

An overstatement, to be sure. That said, I will miss this curious corner of the internet!

👍 1

Rose could be relied on to call every few months, then let the phone go silent while Iris scrambled to gin up conversation. She called the next morning as Iris and Mason ate a breakfast she couldn't afford in the hotel room she couldn't afford. In breaking the internet, Iris had been broken by it. Now she treated her phone like a land mine. Even after reading her sister's name on the screen, she picked up warily.

Rose had a topic at the ready: "I saw you in the *Times* this morning. I didn't realize you were blogging about Jasmine's wedding."

Of course Rose wouldn't understand the difference between a Facebook group and a blog. She had never used social media. She didn't even have a personal email address; in the rare instance when she sent Iris an email, she used her work account.

"You know it's off, right?" Iris asked.

"Yeah, Mom called."

"Jasmine and I are celebrities. I'm unemployed. And Mason and I are living in a hotel. Every time I think about going back home, I practically have a panic attack." Marilyn was feeding Pickles and Meatball. Iris could never reciprocate her generosity, nor could she afford to pay her. Her neighbor insisted she was happy to help.

"What did you write about her?" Rose asked with the faintest whiff of blame.

"It wasn't about what I wrote, more like . . . you didn't see any of this? We're the story of the week. And a week on the internet is like what a decade used to be. I'm basically as famous as Betsy Ross."

"I didn't see anything except the *Times* article," Rose said.

That gave Iris hope. For those rare souls not addicted to the infinite scroll, what had happened to Iris didn't matter. She hoped she could be one of those people. She'd closed every account but Facebook and turned off all her notifications, and it was hard to make it through the day without the constant stream of news and updates. She didn't know what to do with her attention. Every few minutes, she picked up her phone, only to put it down when her mind caught on to what her body was doing.

"Are you looking for a new job?" Rose asked.

"I quit literally yesterday. I have to figure out what I'm going to do."

"You could visit. I have two spare bedrooms with a private bathroom— Mason could have his own room."

The idea lifted Iris like a feather in a warm breeze. She had forgotten about Rose's invitation. What better time to travel than when she was cut off from her friends, her job, and her home? In Florida, a thousand miles from where the haters would look for her, she might get some sleep. "Actually, that would be amazing. When could we come?"

"How about today?" Rose asked. "My neighbor can give you a buddy pass—she's a flight attendant. Just show up at the airport and get on the standby list."

❧

Iris enlisted Marilyn to accompany her into her apartment while she packed a suitcase and hugged and kissed her poor neglected kitties, who meowed in protest over her long absence. Though it was tolerable to be in her apartment, she knew it would never bring her the comfort of home again. She'd already gotten permission from her landlord to break her lease.

As Iris knelt on her suitcase to compress it into shape, Marilyn held Pickles and ventriloquized in a high-pitched voice, "We miss you,

Mommy." Mason wheeled his own suitcase of toys around the living room, overjoyed by the prospect of a vacation.

"I'm sorry," Iris said to Marilyn. "Thank you for being so good to me. I don't deserve you."

"I've always sensed you needed someone to take care of you," Marilyn replied in her own voice. "That you needed more than you got. Well, I have enough to go around. You don't need to feel guilty about this."

Iris got up and hugged her. It mattered that Marilyn acknowledged the unevenness of their relationship and forgave her.

⟳

Having never been on an airplane, Mason was delighted by every moment of the flight: the jet bridge, the tiny television in the seat back, the force of takeoff, the earth turned miniature as the plane climbed into the sky, his mid-flight cup of Sprite, the strange pressure of descent, and the miracle of finding himself in hot, damp weather when they emerged from the plane into the Orlando Melbourne International Airport.

Iris wasn't exactly excited—after a week of fight-or-flight, the respite was causing her body to shut down—but she was grateful to Rose and curious about her life in Florida. None of their family had visited in almost ten years, and she'd assumed Rose's occasional invitations were purely to be polite.

Rose met them at the baggage claim, her body draped in breathable gray jersey, her head crowned with her cataract-surgery sunglasses, and drove them up the coast in her Subaru Legacy to her townhouse, two blocks off the beach.

On the way, while Mason exclaimed, "Mommy, look!" at every new treasure he saw (A palm tree! A lady on a bike! The ocean! McDonald's!), Iris told Rose about the Bridesmaids Union and the implosion of Jasmine's wedding. Rose didn't think Iris was to blame.

"When I met David, I was sure it wasn't going to happen," Rose said. "I didn't buy the bridesmaid dress."

Iris grinned. "Am I detecting snark from Rose Matilda Hagarty?"

"Not at all. It was obvious to me they weren't in love."

The interior of Rose's townhouse was practical and convenient to the tiniest detail. Her living room set was upholstered in sturdy, stainproof brown microsuede. Her enormous pantry was stuffed with bulk foods. A drawer in each accent table contained a tube of hand cream, single-serving bags of almonds and gummy bears, and a cell phone charger. The air-conditioning was powerful enough to keep peas frozen. Her television—impossibly—needed just one remote.

While Mason napped, Rose and Iris sipped wine on the balcony, gazing out at the peach and turquoise houses on the other side of the street—Rose was not the type to spend an extra hundred thousand dollars on a condo with an ocean view. Iris told her about David, Christof, Forrest, Jeremy, and all the bridesmaids, leaving out the embarrassing details, which was most of them. Predictably, Rose didn't spill about her love life. Iris and Jasmine guessed she was a lesbian—possibly married to a woman—since she had not once mentioned attraction to a man. Spike and Connie were offended by this suggestion, as if it were an insult. But if Rose knew romantic love, she left no evidence. In her condo, she displayed no photos of anyone outside their nuclear family. Even coded signs of affiliation were murky. Subaru was the unofficial car of lesbians, but not the Legacy, Iris was pretty sure. Eileen Fisher, Rose's clothing brand of choice, was lesbian-friendly, but straight women wore it, too. In college, a friend had told Iris the secret to her gaydar: she looked for women with their hands in their pockets. Most of Rose's wardrobe had pockets, but she didn't use them.

Iris knew she was being an idiot.

The days flew by. They climbed the exploration tower in Port Canaveral, where Mason learned about Florida wildlife and the space industry; on an observation deck, he gasped at the hulking cruise ships spewing swarms of tiny passengers. They strolled through the manatee sanctuary and, though no sea cows deigned to appear, Mason derived manic glee from feeding the ducks and turtles. They visited Rose's office and lab, where she showed them a satellite she'd helped design, and the Kennedy Space Center, which excited Mason, though less than Iris had anticipated. They spent a day at Disney World, which Iris hadn't seen since a family trip two decades earlier, and which Rose, who'd lived within driving distance for fifteen years, had only visited once more, on a company retreat. Iris found peace in the long stretches of silence.

In Florida, the juggling act of her life seemed manageable. Yes, her stomach still churned when she thought about the Bridesmaids Union; she felt guilty about letting the group's members down, and she shuddered to recall those threatening tweets. But the sting had dulled, and she could compartmentalize it while enjoying the vacation. A few times, she left her phone at the condo. The freedom felt glorious.

Mason too had separated from technology. Iris brought the iPad everywhere, but he hadn't felt like using it. He left Beepbop, his electronic friend and protector, on the other twin bed in his room, with a granola bar in case he got hungry. Mason didn't want to watch TV, either. In the evenings, when he would normally play Minecraft, he begged to trawl the beach for pretty shells, which he lined up on the coffee table, then told stories in the voices of the creatures that had lived in them. Rose bought him a picture book about local flora and fauna and, with Iris's help, he memorized it. They did paint-by-number watercolors of undersea life, and with a red crayon, Mason copied the names from the book to the paintings.

Without screens, Mason became the compliant, gentle, inquisitive son Iris remembered from before he'd gotten the iPad. He went to bed without a fight and woke up smiling. She hated to admit the idea of a "technology fast" had come from Jasmine. But now that she'd seen its benefits, she couldn't justify giving him video games again.

⌒⊃

On Monday night, they ate out with Rose's friends, five effusively positive women who dined and vacationed together and shared an encyclopedia of references. Two of her friends were married and one was divorced; no one mentioned Rose's relationship status. The only differences Iris could detect between these friends and everyone else she knew were that Rose's posse showed up ten minutes before the reservation, ate enough garlic to kill a vampire, and didn't complain once.

Around her friends, Rose became more animated than Iris had ever seen her. Apparently, she liked baseball and birdwatching and had read all of Jane Austen. Iris felt honored to witness this side of her sister, though it hurt to know that Rose had hidden it until now.

⁓

Christof called on Tuesday to say his attorney had been successful at removing Iris's nude photo from the internet. He advised her to google her name every few weeks and alert him if someone had reposted it. She didn't think the onus should be on her for a security lapse by his gallery; then again, she couldn't trust him to be vigilant. To him, the image was worthless. Maybe David's software could protect her.

Strengthened by a few nights of sound sleep and a few days of Florida sun, she didn't feel as angry at Christof. Nor did she care as much about her topless photo being on the internet. It was beautiful; so what if everyone she knew had seen it?

"I've been thinking since we last talked," he said, while she paced Rose's living room, where Mason was setting up armies of cockles and scallops and conches to do battle. "I stand by Walter Benjamin's theory of art, but I now accept that the internet makes it impossible to uphold."

"So what are you going to do?" she asked, digging a toe into the sisal rug. "Macramé?"

He ignored her joke. "Since the *Times* article came out, my gallery has received dozens of queries about purchasing your photo. I'm thinking about changing my business model. Instead of creating one image and destroying the rest, as if it were a painting, I could move in the opposite direction, creating iconic portraits of internet celebrities known for their selfies."

"I think that's called photography."

"I see that I haven't explained it well enough," he said.

"Does this mean you're going to sell my photo to thousands of people?"

"Essentially, yes."

"Can I say no to this?"

"You signed a release."

"And you said you wouldn't use anything without my permission."

"You gave me your permission."

She lay back on Rose's quick-drying sofa. She imagined her breasts hanging in bachelor pads and man caves the world over. Iris, who had always envied Jasmine for her beauty, had become the sex symbol. It was validating and sort of funny. "Do I get a cut?"

"That's not how it's done."

"I'm a celebrity," Iris said, taking a note from Kyle's playbook. "I could raise a big stink about this on Twitter." He didn't have to know she'd deleted her account.

He sighed. "Fine, you can have ten percent."

"Twenty."

"Fifteen. You're lucky I'm in a good mood."

"Pleasure doing business with you."

Iris was about to hang up when Christof said, "I miss you."

She wasn't sure she'd heard him right. "I thought you hated me."

"No, never. I care about you a great deal. I had hoped you might be the one."

Iris was moved by his sincerity, when he must have known she had never seen him as a viable boyfriend. His presence commanded her admiration, and he piloted her body with finesse. He was intelligent and considerate and unfairly gorgeous, and his attention was a drug. But he didn't need her, or anyone, except to reflect his brilliance. When they were together, she either admired him or mocked him but couldn't commune with him, and so their attraction for each other felt more like flattery than love. And though he pressed to know her, she never felt seen. So she behaved with him as she'd behaved with Forrest, trying to mold herself to him instead of telling him who she was.

She said, "I had a really good time with you. You're an incredible man. And you deserve someone who can love you."

On Wednesday, while slathering sunscreen on Mason for the beach, Iris got a text from David and felt a tickle of excitement.

> Hey there. I was just thinking about
> you and smiling. I know this—us—is
> complicated for you, but I miss you.

She badly wanted to pick up the phone to hear his sibilant voice. But she needed to think about it more. Her mind traveled the same tired rut it had all week: her heart wanted to see him, and her conscience didn't. She "loved" his message but didn't write a response.

Rose packed beach chairs, an umbrella, towels, a backpack cooler filled with bottled water amid ice packs, a plastic bucket and shovel for Mason, and sunscreen and books in a waterproof tote. They drove five blocks to a quiet stretch of beach and unloaded the car; miraculously, they managed to carry everything in one trip. Again, Iris marveled at Rose's life, engineered for comfort and ease.

Mason didn't know how to swim, so Iris held his hand as he danced in the foamy surf. Then she showed him how to dig for crabs and stood with Rose on the dark, wet sand, wavelets lapping their feet. Iris wore a two-piece swimsuit, and Rose wore a quick-drying wrap dress.

"Can I ask you something that might reveal I'm a terrible person?" Iris asked.

"Of course," Rose replied. A pelican, flapping over the ocean, dived for its lunch; when it ascended, the imprint of a fish was visible in its beak sac.

"So . . . it turns out David left Jasmine because he's in love with me."

If Iris had been expecting Rose to widen her eyes and press her hands to her cheeks, she would have been disappointed. "Huh," Rose said.

"Would I be the worst person in the world if I went out with him?"

"Not the worst person in the world, no. But that wouldn't be very considerate of Jasmine. Why wouldn't you look for someone else?"

She had been sure Rose would tell her to go for it. Iris had believed the "plenty of fish in the sea" hypothesis, that if marrying one man was unwise, she could fall in love with any number of others. With David, that didn't seem to apply. They had a special connection, and it pained her to consider losing him. If he was her soul mate, wouldn't it be morally acceptable to choose him over the slim chance of finding forgiveness in her sister? Jasmine had already said she'd never speak to Iris again. "I might be in love with him, too."

"Do you think it's because he was Jasmine's?" Rose asked.

"You think that's a plus? No. Ew. He's going to need reparative therapy just to, like, purge his mind of her."

"I don't think that's what you mean," Rose said. "That's how they try to turn gay people straight."

Iris considered whether Rose's matter-of-factness about such an awful thing suggested anything about her own sexuality. "Well, he'll need some kind of therapy that hasn't been invented yet."

Mason stomped into the water to fill up his bucket; Iris warned him to be careful, watching in case she had to rescue him.

Rose looked up the beach toward where she'd parked, probably to confirm the car hadn't been stolen. "Do you think you planned a bachelorette party she wouldn't like on purpose?" she asked.

"No!" Iris protested, though she could see Rose's point. Iris had sensed all along Jasmine would hate it. Was it possible she'd wanted that? No, she'd planned a party for the sister she'd wished she still had. She hadn't been malicious, just willfully blind.

"You've always resented her for getting more than you," Rose observed.

"I wouldn't say *always*."

"Remember when you quit *Romeo and Juliet* because she was Juliet?"

Jasmine had won the lead as a freshman; Iris, a junior, would be Juliet's nurse. It wasn't a bad role, but Iris had found it demeaning to serve her little sister. "That was about preserving my dignity."

"What about when you stole her birthday presents?"

"Maybe if Mom and Dad had made the slightest effort to treat us equitably, I wouldn't have done it," Iris said, remembering the Polly Pocket debacle with the usual toxic stew of shame and anger. "They bought her almost every Polly Pocket in the store. On my birthdays, I'd get one or two at a time. And sometimes my birthday was just folded into Christmas, as if I wouldn't notice."

"Wasn't that the year her appendix burst?" Rose asked. "Her birthday party was canceled. I think they were trying to make up for it."

Their parents had assumed Jasmine was faking a stomachache to get out of school, and then she'd almost died. Iris had a vague memory of the canceled birthday party, too . . . had all that been the same year as the Polly Pocket birthday? Sadness washed over her, at having held a grudge long after forgetting the circumstances. She must have taken the presents while Jasmine was recovering from surgery. No wonder their father had spanked her. What was wrong with her?

"I understand why you stole her presents," Rose said. "You were a kid, and you thought your feelings of deprivation justified the theft. What I don't understand is why you still think you were right. And why you would see David, when you'd be doing the same thing again."

Iris felt the truth in Rose's words. Her desire for David probably did spring from competition—and on an unconscious level, she justified taking him, like the Polly Pockets, because she had less than Jasmine. Not until David had anyone looked at the two younger Hagarty sisters side by side and chosen Iris. Come to think of it, how could he be a match for both sisters, opposite in every way? He was a beautiful chameleon, humble and flexible, an enlightened citizen of the world. And even if her desire was rooted in competition, it felt real. That couldn't be the same as stealing Jasmine's presents. Maybe lust could grow from jealousy, but not love . . . right?

But was a chance at love really worth giving Jasmine another reason to hate her forever?

"I made you a mud pancake," Mason said, holding out a clump of wet sand, as if he'd sensed she needed cheering up.

"That looks delicious," she said, accepting the sand and pretending to scarf it up. "You are the best chef." She dropped the imaginary pancake and hugged his sticky sliver of a body. He wriggled out of her embrace and scampered off.

"You never resented the way they treated Jasmine?" Iris asked Rose. "And me? I felt like you always got the short end of the stick."

"I was the eldest," Rose said, as if that explained it.

"Come on. You must have hated them a little bit, or you wouldn't have Mayflowered yourself down to Florida the second you turned eighteen."

"My industry is down here."

"And you almost never spend time with them because . . . ?"

Rose tightened the cloth belt on her dress. "I understood a long time ago that I couldn't live the way they wanted me to. They also have very specific ideas about their God, and the presence I believe in isn't so particular about how people should live. I knew we'd all be happier if I kept my distance."

"I think they resent you for not needing them."

"I see the way they look at me when I visit. Not everyone gets the parents they need."

"I'm kind of inspired by your strength," Iris said. She wished they'd talked about this a long time ago. She'd felt like an island in her family, assuming she was the only one with feelings. Maybe her sisters too had felt like islands. Why had none of them thought to build a raft and seek out another shore? As important as sibling loyalty was to their parents, their family didn't discuss emotions, and doing so seemed like betrayal.

"You might be happier, too, with some distance from them," Rose said.

"I tried to take distance, and Dad accused me of being selfish."

"I mean emotional distance. They only get to you because you let them."

That didn't seem fair—Spike and Connie were objectively intrusive. And maybe detaching worked for Rose, but Iris wasn't built that way. She needed parents.

"Are you seeing anyone?" Iris asked.

Rose looked confused at the change of subject. "No."

"Are you looking?"

"Not really."

"Is it rude for me to ask why not?"

Rose shook her head. "Not rude. I just like being single."

Iris persisted. "Have you been in a lot of relationships?"

"Some."

"With men or women, or . . . ?" This question was probably rude, too, but Rose didn't seem to mind.

"Mostly men."

That answered that. With no mention of relationships, Spike and Connie assumed she was straight, Jasmine and Iris assumed she was gay, and none of them were right. "And you don't feel lonely?"

Rose shrugged. "Sometimes. But I keep busy, and I like having my place to myself. I like myself, and everyone I've dated has tried to change me."

Iris stared at her sister, amazed. It must have been freeing not to waste her time choosing and chasing lovers, swerving between heartsickness and heartbreak, hogtied by desire. It must have been isolating, too, opting out of partnership in a world that demanded it.

Mason hurtled toward them, his hands cupped together. "Mommy! Mommy! I found a hermit crab!"

"That's wonderful!" Iris said, bending to meet him.

Mason opened his hands, and a little crab in a burgled white shell skittered through his fingers and onto the sand, despite his fumbling attempt to contain it. It burrowed into the sand, and he dug into the little hole it left.

"Why don't you let it go, sweetie?" Iris suggested. "It wants to be free."

"OK, Mommy." He ran off, scattering seagulls from their watchful formation.

꩜

When they returned to Rose's condo, Iris texted Forrest. His day with Mason was coming up, and she hadn't told him they were on vacation. He took it well, though he asked for more notice in the future, since he now had paternity rights.

How are you doing? I've been worried
about you.

Better now, thanks

I don't think Jasmine is OK though.
David left her, not sure you knew that

I didn't

She's not talking to me

I think she could use a friend right
now, if you wanted to send her a note

I know you were in love with her

All week, Iris had tried to recall if she'd ever noticed intimacy between Forrest and Jasmine, and she couldn't. She hadn't. All she'd noticed was their chilly remove. Had Jasmine and Forrest been subtle traitors, or had Iris been oblivious? She had a fine-tuned sense for hostility and a botched sense for love.

The in-progress ellipsis appeared, then vanished.

Whatever happened between you
two, I forgive you.

I would have done the same thing.

To Iris's surprise, a series of text messages ticked upward:

Thanks

We kissed once, that was it

Jasmine begged me to propose to you

In the end I couldn't go through with it

**She made me promise never to speak to her again**

**Sorry I couldn't tell you this before**

She stared at her phone, smudged with sunscreen, until it went black. The old hurt and shame and heartache flooded in but also the peace truth brings. No wonder Jasmine had kept her distance from her all those years. She'd had to break her own heart.

**Thank you for telling me.**

**I don't know if you still love her, but if you do, I don't want to stand in your way again.**

She had taken everything from Jasmine, the coup de grâce in a lifelong war she didn't know she was waging. Even if Jasmine never forgave her, at least Iris could give her this.

**Thank you.**

Sun-scorched and drowsy, Iris, Mason, and Rose ate a dinner of cold pasta with garlic on Rose's balcony as dusk crept between them. Perhaps it was the three glasses of wine, but Iris was feeling nostalgic for the Bridesmaids Union. It had been a good idea that the internet had enabled and destroyed. She would shut it down in the morning, having given its members a week to salvage their favorite posts. She'd stopped looking at the page once she'd come to Florida, as it would remind her of everything she had lost because of it and everything she would lose by deleting it. She wondered how many invitation requests were in the queue—probably thousands. So many frustrated bridesmaids and lovers of gossip. Most probably wouldn't notice it was gone.

Iris and Mason's vacation was another good thing that had to end. Friday would make a week of leaning on Rose's hospitality, and since Rose hadn't hinted that they should limit their time in paradise, it was up to Iris to leave. She didn't want to. She adored the ocean breezes and the hegemony of the sun, the long, carefree days, and the hermetic darkness of the nights. She'd treasured her languid conversations with Rose, and Mason had never been so engaged with the physical world. Iris's life had been hard for a long time. Here, it was easy.

But she missed her cats, and she couldn't ignore the mounting anxiety over her lack of a job when her rent and credit card debt had to be paid. She also had to move, either to a cheaper apartment or back home, and hope her father would honor his promise not to colonize her life.

"Mason and I should get going in a day or two," Iris said.

"We're leaving?" Mason asked. "Nooooo!!!!"

"Inside Voice," she said. Rose's neighbors couldn't have wanted to hear shouting at 8:00 P.M.

He looked around. "But we're outside."

"He has a point," Rose said with a sip of wine. "Why don't you move down here? I could find you a temporary position in my company while you figure out what you want to do. You could stay with me until you find a place. We'll get Mason into school in the fall." She made it sound simple.

"Ooh, can we?" Mason begged, his hands clasped in prayer. "Can we, pretty please with sugar on top? And chocolate and vanilla and the biggest cherry in the whole world?"

It had never occurred to Iris that she could leave the tristate area. Now her fantasies took flight. She could escape the crowds, cold, and cruelty of the city. She could live more cheaply and afford to take a job in criminal defense, even go to law school. Her relationship with her parents would probably improve with the distance, and she could fly back every month or two to give Mason time with them and Forrest. Though Forrest would want to keep Mason nearby, she couldn't imagine him fighting it. Mason could start over in a new school. And if she decided to try for a relationship with David—and that was a big if—he could come to her. He could certainly afford it.

"That is so generous," Iris said to Rose.

"It's nothing."

"Please, Mom? Please? Cinderella please? Dancey pants please?" Mason asked, twirling with excitement.

"You wouldn't miss Rafa and Adelaide and Tania?" she asked him. "You wouldn't miss Daddy Forrest?"

"I! Don't! Care! Can we? Can we?" What else was there anchoring her to the New York area? If their attraction to the radiator was any indication, her cats would love the hot weather. Her few remaining friends would understand.

"OK, let's do it." She laughed at the idea that she could change her life in an instant.

"Yay!" Mason shouted, raising his hands to the sky. "Yippee yay yay!" This time, Iris didn't shush him.

# Chapter Twenty-seven

**Jaclyn Arias**

May 3, 2019, 2:23 P.M.

Eye Fay! Your last message is literally killing me! Please don't shut this group down! Let me take it over instead! It helped me survive my cousin's wedding. While I was slaving away, tying ribbons on sticks and coordinating the staff because she fired her event planner, the Bridesmaids Union helped me see I wasn't alone. This is a forum to support each other in the face of mean-ass brides, and it is utterly necessary.

3,167                                                                915 comments

**Willa Ho**

Yes yes! Keep the Bridesmaids Union going! Your strength inspired me to stand up to my hateful mother-in-law and plan the wedding I want.

 1

**Tamika Johnston**

Hi Eye!!! Thanks to you, I said no to being a bridesmaid for a friend who I just knew would drag me into her drama. Don't take this page down! There is serious wisdom here.

2

**Ellen Wagner**

Eye Fay I'm an agent with Quill Literary, and I'd like to sit down together and brainstorm book ideas. There is a lot of interest in celebrity memoir these days. DM me, and we'll talk.

OO♥ 115

～

Friday morning, while Iris was in the planning stages of leaving Rose's outrageously comfortable guest bed, Jasmine's name on her phone screen made her instantly alert. What would impel Jasmine to call two weeks after promising never to speak to her again? If Iris remembered right, she had threatened murder, maybe attempted it.

"Hey," Iris said, her voice logier than she'd expected.

"Guess what?" Jasmine asked.

"I literally have no idea."

"I'm marrying Forrest!"

It was too early in the morning to make sense of this madness. "Um . . ."

"He saw all the news stories about us, and he called me to be, like, a shoulder to cry on."

As long as Iris lived, she would never get used to her sister's reversals. One minute their relationship was dead; the next, they were best friends. One minute she was marrying David, the next, she was marrying For-rest. "That's wonderful."

"We realized what we should have known back when he was engaged to you," Jasmine continued. "Which is that we're perfect for each other! We're so grateful to you for bringing us together. You're like, our fairy god-mother. And P.S.: I owe you one for saving me from David. I can't believe I almost pledged my life to a total jerkface."

"Um, anytime."

"Have you checked out my Insta recently? Guess who has a hundred and eighty-four thousand followers? This gal!"

"Amazing!" No wonder Jasmine wasn't angry anymore: Iris had not only paved the way for her to marry her true love, she had made her a star. "I'm sorry about all the haters."

"Whatevs—they moved on after, like, ten minutes." It didn't sound like forgiveness, but Iris was relieved that Jasmine was no longer mad. "Did you get TV cameras? I was on the news. I sold out of my paw wear that night."

Iris imagined her sister shilling her dog booties while a befuddled reporter asked about her wedding. "Even the kitten heels?"

"Those were the first to go. Who doesn't love getting dressed up?"

Iris stifled a laugh.

"So . . . not a lot of notice," Jasmine said, "but would you still be my bridesmaid? I wanted you as my maid of honor, but Brittany would be devastated. She puts up a good front, but she's super fragile."

Iris couldn't imagine planning another bridal shower or spending money she didn't have on another exhausting bachelorette vacation, for Jasmine or anyone. "That's so sweet of you. I'm really happy for you. It's just . . . I don't know if I can go through all that again. I'm sorry. Can I support you in a different way?"

"No, dummy. The wedding is still next Saturday. The venue hadn't rebooked, and Mom and Dad were going to have to pay for most of it anyway, so we uncanceled everything! We're even doing the same honeymoon. Forrest has wanted to climb Mount Kilimanjaro his entire life."

"That's . . . great! So you're doing all of it? The baby goat and the goat cheese and the alpacas?"

"All of it. I mean, if I were starting over, it wouldn't be so complicated. I know I went a little overboard in my panic about David. But I was just looking over the plans, and OMG Iris, this wedding is so *me*. It's going to be stupid fun. And marrying someone I really and truly love at the same time? I can't even."

After judging Jasmine's wedding online for months—and being tarred and feathered for it—Iris was surprised to feel excited that her sister was going forward with the whole shebang. "Count me in. Doesn't most of his family live in California, though? This might be kind of short notice for them."

"People make last-minute arrangements all the time for funerals," Jasmine said, "and a wedding is a much happier occasion, so they'll be way more motivated to get here."

"Can Mason come to this one?"

"Sorry."

Iris again felt burned by her sister's breezy cruelty. But after a week of pure relaxation, she felt equipped to riposte. "How about Forrest's son? Can he come?"

"Forrest doesn't have a . . . hey, aren't you the trickster! Fine, whatever, just make sure he doesn't hog all the attention."

Iris laughed. "We wouldn't want to take any away from you."

"Bingo."

"Wait, one thing," Iris said, interrupting the beat of silence that paved the way for goodbyes. "Brittany told me you broke it off with Forrest the first time because you didn't want to steal him from me. Is that true?"

"I would have been a crap sister if I'd married him while you were in love with him," Jasmine said. "This time, it was just different."

Jasmine's reasoning made a kind of sense. Seven years earlier, Forrest was Iris's fiancé. Now he was just a single skater dude who loved Jasmine—and happened to be the father of her nephew. Iris couldn't help wondering how many years she would have to wait before David was fair game. Or did the statute of limitations end once Jasmine was married? Maybe seeing David would help Iris forgive Jasmine for taking Forrest. Something about this logic seemed crazy.

"Well, thanks for waiting," Iris said. "For what it's worth."

"I always got your back," Jasmine said. Maybe, in Jasmine's incomprehensible ethos, she was telling the truth.

◦

Once Iris had showered and eaten breakfast with Mason and Rose, it was time to end the Bridesmaids Union. It would be too risky to let it live on, untended. Then she could be done with social media forever.

When she opened Facebook, an alert told her a new post on the page had gotten almost a thousand comments. She braced herself for what new disaster was unfolding. As she scrolled, she was confused, then surprised, then touched. The members of the Bridesmaids Union were begging her to keep it alive. Women told her how it made them feel not alone in their bridesmaid hell, convinced them to set boundaries when signing on for the role, and taught brides and bridesmaids alike to be kinder to each other. It gave some the courage to stand up to tyrannical brides. For others, it sparked laughter amid the tension and sniping. These comments felt like an enormous group hug.

She didn't know how much time had passed when she reached the end of the comments. She put down her phone and wiped her eyes. To her family, she'd been selfish in telling her stories; to her friends, she'd been heartless; to the media, she'd been sexist; but to these women and probably more, the Bridesmaids Union had been a gift.

She opened her laptop and composed her response. Then she messaged the literary agent who had reached out. A book deal might let her survive until she found another job. Without trying, she had become a celebrity, and she'd suffered for it. Now she could reap its rewards.

# Chapter Twenty-eight

**Iris Hagarty**

May 11, 2019, 10:43 A.M.

Dear bridesmaids, groomsmen, allies, and sundry voyeurs,

I've read your comments, all of them, and halfway through, I was crying. I'm touched by your love of this amazing group, and because of you, I've decided not to shut it down.

I do think we need some revised ground rules—or at least I do! No names, not even initials. No potshots: just the facts and how you feel, no putting anyone down. No comments on appearance, though that goes without saying. And most importantly, DON'T POST ANYTHING YOU WOULDN'T WANT TURNED INTO A MEME. Because here's the big thing: in three weeks (aka as soon as Facebook lets me change the privacy settings again), this group will be PUBLIC. At that time, we'll be joined by the HUNDRED THOUSAND people who have requested membership. It's gonna be Pantsuit Nation up in here.

If I might suggest one more rule (and it's one I promise to follow from here on out): before you post to this group, talk with the bride (or groom) and tell her, with kindness, how you feel. Sometimes all it takes is a conversation to help her understand what you're going through. And then you can get back to the fun of celebrating her marriage in style.

Here's to a beautiful friendship!

XOXO

Iris

  3,873                              512 comments

**Jaclyn Arias**

We did it!

👍👍 21

**Anna Banana**

Woot woot!

👍 1

**Electra Collins**

Beyond pumped for you, Iris Hagarty.

👍 2

**Brittany Thompson**

And so proud of your BOOK DEAL!

👍 26

**Stefanie Kalinsky**

Couldn't have happened to a better person.

👍👍 10

**Selena Bermudez**

Let me know if I can help with your social reach. 💄🦚🔥

👍👍 8

**Lorelei Gell**

I can design the cover.

👍 3

**Iris Hagarty:**

Thanks all! But FYI I don't have a book deal yet—I just signed with an agent.

**Alexandria Canas**

We'll always be here for you.

👍 4

**Jazz Hagarty**

My posse rules! Friends 4eva!

👍👍 10

For all her (many) faults, Brittany was a standout maid of honor. The morning of the wedding, she stood outside Jasmine's dressing room and blocked everyone—Connie, the florist, the first violinist, Forrest's best man, and Iris—from entering. She might have looked like a tween playing dress-up, but she could make people afraid.

Iris mingled with the other bridesmaids, surprised at how much she'd grown to like them. Their trials had bonded them, and none of them gave her a hard time about the Bridesmaids Union. She already had plans to get together with Electra before flying back to Florida. She'd never been so excited about a new friend.

She also hoped to meet up with Amber in Miami. After three weeks of silence, her best friend had texted to say that she was still hurt but was willing to talk it out. **Friends give each other the benefit of the doubt,** she had written. Iris was moved by Amber's maturity and loyalty.

She'd been pleased to see Allie that morning, styling Jasmine's hair. Stefanie had been switched out for Jasmine's acupuncturist, a woman with a similar build and an astonishing density of tattoos. Rose was not in the wedding party and must have been thrilled about the demotion, though she gave no indication either way.

Brittany cleared the grand staircase, and three photographers, including Miles the Instagram boyfriend, took their positions like snipers. The bride emerged, bathed in sunlight from the window at the top of the stairs, delighted by her beauty, like Cinderella watching herself transform. Her hair was a sculptural masterpiece, crowned with wildflowers, and she had chosen the ivory A-line gown Iris had loved.

Jasmine descended the stairs with measured grace, proffering a precise nod to each of the women who had gathered in the foyer. When she reached Iris, she took her hand. She was wearing the birthstone bangles Iris had given her at her bridal shower. Iris's breath caught at the perfection of the moment. As the photographers converged, she understood why

Jasmine invested so much into documenting her life and sharing it with her followers. It was the same reason the artist slaved over a canvas, the drive to create and preserve beauty.

The bridal party migrated to the pond for group shots. When they lined up, Jasmine frowned, studying her bridesmaids. "Iris, what the heck? Your dress is a different color."

To Iris, her dress was the same medicinal pink as everyone else's. "I didn't wash it or anything."

"I bet it's from a different dye lot," Jasmine said. "I'm going to kill that bridal consultant."

Just weeks earlier, Iris would have cowered at her sister's outburst—and lied to calm her. That instinct had quieted in her. "I bought it used," she admitted. "I couldn't afford it new."

"Why didn't you just ask me for the money?"

"No one can tell the difference."

Jasmine silenced her with her index finger. "If I can tell the difference, other people can tell the difference. The pictures will be ruined."

"Can you tell the difference?" Iris asked the photographers.

"It's subtle," Miles said. "I can fix it in post."

Jasmine crossed her arms.

"I don't have to be a bridesmaid," Iris said, enjoying the rush of anger. It felt good not to be ashamed of it anymore. "I have another dress at the hotel. One that doesn't make me look like a psychotic toddler." She wondered if she was taking this honesty thing too far. Tact was important, too.

Electra stifled a giggle.

"If you're not a bridesmaid," said Jasmine, "how will you talk smack about me online?" Before Iris could respond, Jasmine said, "Whatever. I'm not going to fight on my wedding day. Stress gives you wrinkles."

As she watched Jasmine resume her merriment for the photographers, Iris understood something so essential to her sister's personality, it was kind of nuts she hadn't noticed it before. Jasmine didn't hold grudges. She expressed herself without any filter, then moved on. Iris had been a historian of her relationships, cataloging slights and fights, monitoring an algorithm for each family member and friend, deciding how much was owed to her and how much guilt she should feel. Jasmine didn't waste her intelligence on being nice. She had her scruples—after all, she'd stayed away from Forrest for seven years—but didn't worry, moment to moment, about being considerate and innocuous. It seemed like a relaxing way to live. Maybe, when you devoted your life to the electrical storm that was the internet, with the ever-present threat of brutal public censure, it was the only way to survive.

But moving past a fight was different than forgiveness. Had Jasmine had already forgiven her for the Bridesmaids Union, or would she move on without doing so? Iris hadn't really forgiven Jasmine for her bachelorette party meltdown, either, just diluted her anger with guilt.

"How much?" Electra mouthed, gesturing toward Iris's dress.

"Fifty," Iris whispered.

Electra widened her eyes with feigned outrage.

⸎

The ceremony took place at the edge of the pond. Elsa, carried on a pillow by Aunt Mary, was the flower girl. Forrest had shattered his wrist falling off a horse as a kid, so the horseback procession was nixed; instead, the wedding party paced up the aisle to a sweeping violin arrangement of "November Rain." Weeks earlier, Iris had pointed out that a song about a relationship broken by suicide wasn't the best choice for a wedding, but Jasmine swatted her away. It was her favorite song.

Everyone rose as Jasmine and Spike emerged from the farmhouse and approached the altar, dripping with wisteria. Jasmine handed her wedding bouquet of iris, jasmine, and rose to Brittany, and Spike took his position as officiant. When Forrest lifted Jasmine's veil, tears speckled his cheeks. Iris had never seen him cry.

Spike delivered a stand-up routine about Jasmine's "husband switcheroo," asking Jasmine to triple-check that this was the guy she wanted to marry, because no returns or exchanges were allowed. He segued into the importance and power of marriage, and entreated Jasmine to love and support Forrest and make him a better man. Iris noted, with irritation but not surprise, that Forrest was not asked to make Jasmine a better woman.

"In the beginning, we were star-crossed lovers, and I was afraid we would never meet again," Forrest said in his vow. Iris was relieved he didn't mention the reason their stars were crossed. "I missed you every day of our separation. I thought about you every morning and night. I believed you were finished with me forever. When Iris told me your wedding was canceled, I took a chance, because I couldn't have lived with myself if I gave you up a second time. From the moment I saw you again, I knew I wanted you by my side forever. Jasmine, here is my vow: I will treat you as my queen. You will never want for anything while we are together. I will be faithful, always. I will love you for eternity, in this life and the next."

"Dear, dear Forrest," Jasmine said, "when I gave you up, I made the biggest mistake of my life. I have never felt so cherished by anyone else. I love that you see how smart and driven I am, that you respect me and want me to flourish. I love how strong and sure you are, and I'm inspired by your care for your body and your reverence for nature. I am so blessed and grateful and proud and excited that we're getting married!"

Holding the last syllable with Oprah-like gusto, she turned to the congregation and raised her arms, eliciting claps, whistles, and photographs.

"Here is my vow," she continued. "I promise to be my best self with you, the most loyal and loving wife you can imagine. I promise to be honest about my feelings and never take you for granted. I promise to give all of myself to you always, because I love you with all of my heart and all of my soul."

Iris felt tears forming. She'd heard these sentiments in a dozen weddings before, yet they always moved her. This was love, beautiful, fragile, and inspiring. She wanted it desperately.

The baby goat marched up the aisle, the basket of rings in its mouth. It kept peeking back at its trainer for guidance, which was adorably human and seriously YouTube-worthy. Iris tried to be present for the sweetness of the scene without thinking about how it might look to millions of faceless internet consumers. She didn't want to consume this moment; she wanted to experience it. Fortunately, Allie was recording it with her phone.

The goat came close enough so that Jasmine and Forrest could take the rings, then scampered back to its trainer, who lifted it into her arms and nuzzled its snout. Iris's heart melted into a puddle.

⌒

After the ceremony, Jasmine changed into gown number two, the plunging mermaid, which took the team of bridesmaids half an hour and a roll of double-sided tape to secure against a wardrobe malfunction. The bridesmaid dance Iris choreographed was a hit, especially because Cousin Lorelei could not dance in heels and resorted to the Macarena atop wobbly ankles. When the song ended, Jasmine led the crowd in a chant of "Lor-e-lei," and Cousin Lorelei bowed to thunderous applause.

Once the reception was underway, Iris took in the sumptuous details she'd mocked online. The barn was decorated with gilded wreaths and strategically positioned hay bales. Undulating sheets of fabric draped from the rafters, and three magnificent crystal chandeliers somehow did not look out of place in a building designed for animals. The tables, draped in sensuous silk burlap—with no seams!—were set with glazed terra-cotta chargers and mason jars. The centerpieces were sprays of black-eyed Susans and purple coneflowers nestled amid birch logs, under giant flower orbs suspended from the ceiling. A five-tier wedding cake decorated with a cascade of rose petals stood sentry at the far end of the barn. The servers, dressed like farmhands in denim overalls and straw hats, passed hors d'oeuvres in wicker baskets and on butcher-block cutting boards.

How had Iris not known this rustic pastiche would feel so romantic? How had she not anticipated it would also feel so lonely?

She took Mason outside, where guests circled the small pond and sat on benches that faced the weeping willow, brushing the water with its fronds. Ducks floated in formation, scanning for croutons, and three iridescent chickens motored in and out of a coop. Mason wanted to meet the alpacas, so they got in line, even though Iris hated the alien beasts with a burning passion. The sacrifices she made for her son!

Iris had worried he wouldn't understand why his father was marrying his aunt, how his father could also be his uncle, but he had no questions, only enthusiasm. When he grew up, this would be a topic for therapy, along with her topless photo and a thousand other mistakes she'd made. Or not. She would continue to try to improve as a parent, but she was learning not to stew over things she couldn't control.

Spike and Connie approached, each cradling a glass of wine, their complexions gilded by the setting sun. "If it were a little quieter in there, people could actually enjoy the music," Connie said, making a visor of her free hand.

"That bridesmaid dress has got to be the ugliest thing I've ever seen," Spike said. "Did our Jasmine pick it out?"

"Ten bucks says it'll be a meme," Iris said.

"It's not going in your blog, is it?" Connie asked.

"No more 'blogging' for me," Iris replied. Though she might be turning the Bridesmaids Union into a book. Ellen Wagner, the literary agent, was putting together a proposal. If a publisher took the bait—and Ellen had already gotten a "nibble"—Iris would work with a writing coach to pen a memoir-slash-advice manual about her life as a serial bridesmaid and accidental celebrity. Iris considered it hilarious that anyone would take advice from her. When Iris had asked how much money they were talking, Ellen had replied that it might be a lot, but added, "Don't quit your day job," at which point Iris had burst out laughing.

She probably would have cried instead had Rose not already found her an administrative position in her lab. Rose promised her it was the kind of gig that would allow her to take night classes toward her law degree, so that she could finally pursue a career as a defense attorney. In New York it had been impossible, but in Florida, with its cheaper cost of living and easier way of life, it seemed realistic. Every time Iris thanked Rose for her superhuman generosity, her sister shrugged and said Iris would have done the same thing for her. Someday she would find a way to return the favor.

"We thought we'd taught you not to speak ill of other people," Spike said. "It's no good when siblings meddle in each other's affairs."

They always had to teach her something. But absorbing the blistering hate of the Twitterverse had strengthened her, and she could ignore their criticisms, which they had dispensed since she was a child and would not stop until they died. Maybe this is what Rose had meant by taking emotional distance from them: instead of letting their barbs sting, she could try to hear them as love. She couldn't see her parents as enemies any longer. Even their adoration of the president wasn't worth her indignation. Someday he would be gone, but they would still be her parents.

"Are you registering an official complaint?" Iris asked. "Because the complaints department opens on Monday at nine. And there is a *very* long line."

"Aren't you funny," Connie observed. "Most men don't want funny, you know. They only want women to laugh at their jokes."

"Were you funny before you met Dad?" It made her sad to think about her mother changing to be palatable to her father.

"I was an astute observer of the male species," she replied.

"She's still funny," Spike said. "Like, 'what's that funny smell?'"

Connie slugged him on the upper arm.

"Hashtag me too!" Spike said, pretending to cower. "Me too!"

Mason glanced from his grandparents to Iris, unsure whether to be concerned.

"Rose said you were moving to Florida?" Connie asked, ignoring Spike's act.

"Just for the summer, till I figure out our next move." She planned on living there forever; it just seemed unkind to break this to her parents the day they gave a daughter away. She privately admitted it was easier to love a place where she'd only vacationed, but she owed it to herself to try. Forrest and Jasmine were already planning visits. Mason wandered in a daze, too giddy to speak. As for David . . . she wasn't sure how he would fit into her new life. When she thought about marrying him, the symmetry of two sisters, each with her sister's ex, gave her the willies. She alone could prevent that. But was that reason enough to walk away from happiness? As she stirred herself into a froth for the zillionth time, Iris sensed that she was asking the wrong question, that her decision shouldn't be about David or Jasmine but about herself.

"You're still welcome to live with us," said Spike.

"You'd have to share a bathroom with the newlyweds," Connie said.

"They're going to live with you?" Iris's amazement turned into laughter.

"Until they buy a place, yes," said Spike.

"Not in Alpine, I hope," Iris said.

"They're looking in Jersey City," said Connie. "Apparently, it's very trendy."

It was their turn to pose with the alpacas. The male wore a top hat, the female, a veil on its head and a wreath around its neck. Their smushed faces and dumb stares made them look like zombie stuffed animals. The photographer arranged the Hagartys beside the stinking beasts and aimed his camera. The male alpaca sniffed her hair; she shuddered at his damp animal breath on her neck. When it pressed its nose against her ear, moist and mushy like a cold sponge, Iris leaped away with a screech.

‿⊙

Spike gave the first toast. "Forrest was my favorite of my daughters' boyfriends," he said, gesticulating with a bottle of beer. "He gave me skateboarding lessons in our driveway. That last boyfriend—what was his name again?—Connie and I didn't trust him. Too sensitive. I wouldn't be surprised if he had one of those pussy hats in his closet. Or if he was hiding something else in that closet." He rambled for fifteen minutes, forgetting the difference between a toast and a roast, then raised his beer and handed the mic to Forrest's mother, who spoke inaudibly for two minutes, wept, and returned to her seat without raising her glass. Forrest's best man, a bartender at the restaurant where he worked, talked about how Forrest used to live in a van because he was afraid of settling down, and how Jasmine had finally caught the "runaway groom." Iris didn't love being implicated in this.

Brittany's toast focused on the paw couture and how it revealed Jasmine's strengths: business acumen, design savvy, and compassion. She talked about how Jasmine had promised her the maid of honor role as soon as she got engaged, making it sound as if Iris didn't exist. Iris was disappointed not to give a toast, but she also couldn't think of anything to say that wasn't either self-deprecating or mean. She'd been mean enough online.

The sound of her name pulled her from her thoughts. "Iris," Brittany said again. "Did you want to say a few words?"

It was gracious to consider the fallen maid of honor, but Iris waved her off, not wanting to delay dessert, which, in addition to the five-tier, five-flavor cake, included a variety of puddings in miniature mason jars, three kinds of cobbler, and a chocolate fountain with all the fixings. Brittany persisted, and the audience clapped in encouragement. Iris had no choice. She couldn't tell whether Jasmine's dull stare indicated interest, irritation, boredom, or fatigue. She decided not to look at her.

She held the microphone to her lips and said the first thing that came to her. "As I'm sure you all know, I used to be engaged to that one over there. I now realize I was giving him a test drive for my sister." The audience laughed, and she wondered if "test drive" was lewd. "Jasmine discovered the secret to getting him to commit: an extremely short engagement. She didn't give him time to change his mind." More laughter. But jokes were empty fun, and this was her chance to say something meaningful to her sister, to prove her love after the damage she'd done. She considered what she admired about Jasmine, filtering out the ways in which she could be self-absorbed or cruel. Someday Iris would level with her about their monstrous behavior during the past six months, but a wedding toast wasn't the place for the unvarnished truth.

"As you all know, Jasmine is the baby in the family. But even when we were young girls, I looked up to her. She knew who she was from the day she was born, and she wasn't afraid to speak her mind. When we were kids, our mom took us to auditions—I think she wanted us to be movie stars. I remember this commercial we landed, for a dollhouse. I was older, so I had the speaking part. I had literally one line: 'I love it!' I tried and tried, but the director just didn't believe that I did love it. Jasmine said it once, and they had their commercial.

"And Jasmine has always been able to ask for what she wanted. She never held herself back to be more ladylike, more palatable to men. In high school, we both auditioned for *Romeo and Juliet*. I went out for the role of Juliet's nurse, because I thought that's what I deserved. Jasmine was a freshman, and she auditioned to be Juliet. I was clinging to a strict hierarchy of having to start at the bottom and work your way up, and the belief that it was inappropriate for a woman to ask for more. Well, what do you know, she got the role. All the teachers said she was the best Juliet in our school's history.

"I've never been confident. I've never known how to ask for what I wanted. I've never felt deserving of a voice. And I resented everyone who did, including, it kills me to admit, my sister. I went to the internet to say everything I didn't let myself say in real life. It was the first time I used my voice, and it was incredibly empowering. But I used it to disempower. I shamed people for wanting nice things, for having standards, for speaking up. I took all the disgust I used for silencing myself and flung it at people who didn't. I wrote terrible things. I smeared Jasmine's name in the mud. I hurt her."

The toast was veering off course. Iris took a deep breath and brought the focus back to Jasmine.

"What's so wonderful about my sister is she has this incredible capacity to forgive," she continued. "Or at least not to dwell on the cruel things other people have done to her. She says her piece and moves on. She invited me to her wedding when she had every right to cut me out of her life. She allowed me to speak to all of you when my words were so hurtful. Nothing I say could communicate how deeply sorry I am. I don't know if she can forgive me, but the fact that I'm standing here is a testament to her character."

Iris glanced at her sister, afraid of what she might find.

Jasmine mouthed, "I forgive you."

Iris mouthed, "Thank you."

Letting Jasmine's forgiveness soak in, Iris silently forgave her for all the thoughtlessness and impulsivity that had marked her tenure as a fiancée. It felt good not to be in a fight, for her relationship with Jasmine not to be tinged with resentment or envy or guilt. It felt healthy. Which is how Iris realized that she had to give up David. Sure, if she dated him, Jasmine would have no right to be angry. They would be even, and their sibling rivalry would continue apace. But Iris didn't want to play that childish game anymore. She wanted to break free of the tug-of-war that had always defined their sisterhood. She wanted to admire Jasmine's boldness without feeling trampled on, to root for Jasmine's success without hoping for her downfall. Seeing David right now would be fair, but it wouldn't be kind—to Jasmine or herself. She could start fresh with her sister, building a new relationship that didn't begin with an affront. Maybe one day she and David would find each other again, but not before she sorted out her competitive, destructive impulses and found a way to see him not as stolen goods but as hers alone.

Without breaking eye contact, Iris said, "So here's to my sister, a woman who is unapologetically herself. It took me too long to realize this, but from the beginning, you have modeled how to be a woman in this world. You showed me how to use my voice when I thought I wasn't allowed to speak. You showed me how to be fearless in the face of adversity. I've tiptoed through life, and you leap. You showed me how to leap."

Iris lifted her Champagne flute, and the twinkling sea of glasses rose in affirmation.

# Acknowledgments

This book would not exist had it not been for Stephen Power and Samantha Zukergood, whose creative spark I fanned into a bonfire; Thomas Dunne, who took a chance on it even as a misshapen early draft; and Hannah O'Grady for adopting the manuscript and raising it as one of her own. The physical book represents an incredible amount of design work, and for that, I'm grateful to Rob Grom, who offered me six(!) options for the cover, Devan Norman, who designed the complicated and emoji-rich interior, and Lisa Davis, the careful and thorough production editor. I'm also grateful to Alexis Neuville and Maria Vitale, whose marketing and publicity expertise helped the book find its way into your hands.

I am also in debt to my former agent James Fitzgerald, may he rest in peace.

A special shout-out goes to all the bridesmaids whose travails inspired this book. Having never been a bridesmaid myself, I immersed myself in countless how-to articles and horror stories online and spoke with many women who have smiled through some hurricane-force bullshit, most memorably Lindsay Ford, Katie Godfrey, Molly Simpson, Cara O'Donnell, and Kristina Williamson. Much of what I know about wedding gowns (and barn weddings) comes from a fascinating conversation I had with Eliza DeRocker years ago. *Say Yes to the Dress* helped a lot, too. Sarah Chandler gave me invaluable insight into dating apps. Erika Scott and Nora Simpson both offered parenting notes. For knowledge about evangelical Christianity, I read *Pure* by Linda Kay Klein, listened to the *Good Christian Fun* podcast, and shared a draft with Vanessa Kliest Kensing. Grace Andrews taught me about visioning.

Many writers read part or all of the book. Most of my writing group—Kathleen Crisci, Judith Padow, Cheryl J. Fish, and Carol Bartold—read it twice, and gave me additional insight into parenting. Myra Alperson commented on a portion as well. Christine Reilly offered generous feedback when I wasn't sure if the book worked at all. A group of Vermont Studio Center comrades, Fulla Abdul-Jabbar, Naomi Washer, and Mika Yamamoto, counseled me on the Christof sections. Lacy Phillips gave the book an eleventh-hour authenticity read, which helped enormously with the character of Rose.

I am also grateful to be bolstered by a community of writers, in addition to those mentioned above: Lauren Acampora, Cara Blue Adams, Bethany Ball, Marcia Bradley, Adam Chandler, Jennifer Croft, Melissa Faliveno, Grant Ginder, Christy Harrison, Jay Michaelson, Jerome Ellison Murphy, Denne Michele Norris, Anna Qu, Anne Ray, Emily Saladino, Eric Sasson, Charity Shumway, Cam Terwilliger, Sara Weiss, Amy Beth Wright, and so many more.

Many people helped me choose the cover, but Sally Rinehart and Alex Van Buren were exceptionally insightful and convincing.

I'm grateful to my colleagues at FIT, especially Linda Angrilli, Alex Joseph, Loretta Lawrence Keane, and Carol Leven, for their support and understanding of my writing and teaching obligations outside of work.

I wrote a third of this book at Vermont Studio Center and did a major chunk of editing at the Writers' Colony at Dairy Hollow.

A special thank-you goes to Phil Gates, who provided support, encouragement, knowledge, and a steady stream of bridesmaid news stories and pet videos.

And Morty, husband of the century, has offered spot-on feedback on multiple drafts of this novel and everything I write. You hold me when I'm in crisis and lift me when I doubt myself. You share in my triumphs and tend to my wounds. You sit on the throne of my heart, now and forever.